THE CONDUCT OF THE GAME

THE
CONDUCT
OF THE
GAME

John Hough, Jr.

HARCOURT BRACE JOVANOVICH, PUBLISHERS

SAN DIEGO   NEW YORK   LONDON

Requests for permission to make copies of any part of the work
should be mailed to:
Permissions, Harcourt Brace Jovanovich, Publishers, Orlando,
Florida 32887.

Library of Congress Cataloging in Publication Data

Hough, John T.
    The conduct of the game.
    I. Title.
PS3558.O84C66   1986   813'.54   85-27101
ISBN 0-15-121625-8

Designed by G.B.D. Smith.

Printed in the United States of America

First Edition

A B C D E

I want to express my deepest gratitude to Greg Kannerstein, Marge Merklin, and Roger Lane, who enabled me to write this book. I also want to thank three good umpires: Bob Nelson, Bob Schwartz, and John "Red" Flaherty.

To Kate

PART
1

1

Lucinda Fragosi—even her name was gawky. She was a born victim, a mournful, sparrow-faced little man of a girl who lurched when she walked and hunched when she sat and wiped her nose with the back of her skinny hand. Her dresses were too big. Her socks slid down the sticks of her ankles. Her crow-black hair tussled with her pink barrettes, escaping before the school day even began.

Lucinda lived down the street from us in a pastel-green ranch house. The place was new, the land still scraped bare, with nothing but a couple of sapling trees wriggling up in the front yard, tethered on silver wires. In the first hot weather, azaleas bloomed angry red against the minty sidewall of the house. There was a German shepherd by the name of Sam who went for your leg when you flew by on a bicycle. I never risked it on foot.

The neighborhood kids said that Lucinda's step-mother, a fat, swarthy woman—not old—made Lucinda and her half-brother, Ernie, wash their own clothes in tubs of cold water in the backyard, even in winter. *Especially* in winter. I once asked Ernie about this. Ernie turned very solemn, gazing big-eyed at me as if I'd stumbled onto some tragic secret of his, and nodded slowly that it was true. I still doubted it. What would be the point? But the neighborhood kids said that Ernie and Lucinda spent all their free time scrubbing floors, sweeping, ironing, and washing their clothes in those tubs of cold water, and who knows? You never saw Lucinda around town on the weekends or during school vacation. You never saw her at the movie theater or at a football game. Ernie ran track after school, but Lucinda always lurched straight home.

I wish I knew where Lucinda is now. I wish I knew how the world is treating her. For all I know, she is married to a millionaire or starring in a play on Broadway. But as a kid Lucinda Fragosi was stuck on the bottom rung of the ladder. Skinny Lucinda, dirty Lucinda, gross Lucinda. On the school bus they threw spitballs at her and shot paper clips with rubber bands. They ragged her. "Why do seagulls have wings?" Answer: "To beat Lucinda to the dump." A laugh would go up, mouths honking like trombones. "Lucinda's old man got a new job drivin' the garbage truck. . . . Fifty dollars a week and all he can eat." More laughter. Busloads of laughter. Lucinda this, Lucinda that. Lucinda washes her face in the toilet. Lucinda brushes her teeth with birdshit. Skinny Lucinda, dirty Lucinda, gross Lucinda. Ernie, her half-brother, sat minding his own business. Most of the girls shunned Lucinda, as if her condition might be catching.

Lucinda would sit quietly while they tormented her, her face pushed low to the school bus window. She wore a hard, unforgiving look on her small, pale, bright-as-pearl face, watching the elm trees and houses drift past the window.

Some days they left her alone. They'd forget her for a while, forget she existed. She must have begun each day praying that they would. Please, God, let me ride the school bus in peace. Let me walk the hallways . . . let me eat my sandwich in the cafeteria . . . in peace.

When I was eleven, my brother Joey said, "We don't turn our backs on the Old Man." It was the law in our family—Joey's law. Joey was thirteen at the time. Paul was fourteen. There were the three of us plus the Old Man, Frank.

He was always "Frank," never "Dad" or even "Pop." There wasn't any disrespect in it. It brought us closer in a way; it set aside Frank's age. He was older than other parents, and different. Other parents went zipping around in their new cars and slept late on Sundays. They played golf and went to benefit dances. Frank never went anywhere except to the movies and to work, which was clerking at West's Hardware on Main Street. His body, small to begin with, had dried and shriveled. Crisscross lines slashed the hide-tan skin around his eyes. His thistly hair was squirrel gray. He drank. People figured the drinking had been brought on by the desertion of my mother, who had left for unknown parts when I was two. The Old Man had never heard from her. The world had swallowed her. He'd been a lot older than she was. I don't remember her.

We don't turn our backs on the Old Man. What had happened was that I'd overheard Martha Hollister, who lived down the street, tell her sister, Judy, that Frank had invited her out back and exposed himself, as the saying goes. I'd heard it while hiding in the bed of honeysuckle behind our house. The honeysuckle grew beyond a wooden fence, a miniature jungle, soft and viny. I could disappear inside it. Beyond lay the railroad tracks. There weren't many trains—just the Boston Budd car and an occasional sleepy diesel dragging a few boxcars—and people, especially kids, liked walking the tracks. It seemed private, with the trees and thickets on both sides and the rails zooming away and meeting finally in the empty, glassy distance. It *was* private—except when I was in the honeysuckle. Then it was like tapping the phone system.

Martha and Judy Hollister were teenagers now. They were pretty girls, plumpish, all rounded lines. They had a slow, rolling way of walking. Their skin had a silky shine, as if they took their baths in milk.

Nestling in the honeysuckle one gray spring afternoon, I heard the Hollister girls coming. First Martha's throaty purr notched the silence, growing till I could make out words. Now I could hear the slow scratch of their footsteps on the stones and cinders.

". . . said he had something to show me. I said, 'Like what, for instance?' 'Something you'll like,' he said. I don't know why I went."

"Why did you?" Judy said. "You know he's an alcoholic."

I knew then it was Frank they were talking about. The Old Man had done something terrible, something crazy. I knew it already, and it was like being slapped hard in the face.

"I don't know why," Martha said. "Honest to God. I followed him around the house . . ." The girls were puttering along slow as molasses, almost standing still. It

6

must not have occurred to them that our house was fifty yards away. ". . . He unzips his pants and pulls everything out, balls and all."

Nausea swooped in my belly; I saw old prune balls and a withered pecker. I felt also a distant amazement at hearing Martha Hollister say "balls."

"I don't believe you," Judy said firmly.

"I swear it," Martha said.

"Bullshit," Judy said.

This, too, astonished me.

"I'm *telling* you," Martha insisted.

"All right," Judy said.

"I swear it, Judy."

"All *right*."

They'd gone by, and their voices sank as if the ground was swallowing them.

"I just turned and walked away," Martha said. "I didn't even give him the satisfaction of screaming."

"The whole family's crazy," said Judy's now small voice.

"That Paul's a creep," Martha said.

Another stab of surprise. A creep? Paul? Shy, yes. Lank and bony. Gentle, skilled hands that could build the perfect model airplane and fix a radio. Patient hands, grease-marked from changing the oil in the Old Man's clunker Ford. Quiet, yes, but never a creep.

Judy was saying something I couldn't make out.

Martha purred an answer.

"Jesus," Judy blurted, and laughed.

The voices fell—lower, lower, gone. I waited, then crawled out of my burrow in a kind of daze. Frank didn't look at women. He never made cracks the way Joey did when a sexy actress appeared on TV. On the other hand, how could Martha Hollister produce such a gigantic lie?

Martha was good, wholesome, *perfect*. Her picture had been in the paper: Honor Society, Rainbow Girls, drama club. And how could Martha and Judy cuss like that? I didn't know what to make of it all. That night, naturally, I told Joey.

We were in bed. Joey was lying stomach down, golden arms wrapping his pillow. Our bedroom, Joey's and mine, looked down over the street bending by. A street lamp threw its chalky light in through our bedroom window.

"That *bitch*," Joey said, rolling over and propping his head on his hand. "That fucking *bitch*."

Our door was open. Paul was in his closet of a bedroom down the hall, his light still on. Paulie sat up late, tinkering. The table in his room always was strewn with tubes and wires and the metal guts of radios he'd lugged home from the dump. Paul came down the hall and put his head in our door.

"Who's a bitch?"

"Martha Hollister," Joey said.

"Martha Hollister?" Paul said.

"Tell him, Lee," Joey said.

I did, omitting the part where Martha called Paulie a creep. Paul's mouth dropped open as he listened. He drifted inside our bedroom. The Old Man was asleep in his room at the end of the hall.

"Jesus," Paul said softly.

"What if it's true?" I said.

" 'Course it's not, for Christ sake." Joey spat it at me. "How the hell can you say that, Lee?"

"I just . . ." I couldn't look at Joey then. Warm tears filled my eyes.

"Listen, Lee," Joey said, gently now, "Martha's got sex on the brain. She's at that age. She wants her little twat diddled."

"Maybe," Paul said, "Frank was taking a leak."

"Could be," Joey said.

I felt better then. The Old Man would go out with the dog, usually before turning in for the night, and pee. He would stand on the dirt patch that was our front yard, peeing, while the dog wandered here and there, hitching up his leg. Car headlights scything by didn't faze him. Martha could have seen him, cruising by in her father's sharklike Pontiac. She could have been walking by.

Paul said, "Maybe we ought to say something to Martha."

"*Say* something?" Joey sat up, covers dropping from the muscle of his upper body. "I'm gonna beat the shit out of her," he said.

"Beat up a girl?" I said.

Paulie, too, looked doubtful.

"We don't turn our backs on the Old Man," Joey said.

"Yeah, but a girl," Paul said.

"Girl, boy, I don't care. We don't turn our backs on the Old Man."

Next morning, Joey waited, watching out the window. The girls had to pass our house on the way to the bus stop. Paul and I hovered behind Joey. Frank slouched over his coffee, red-eyed and gloomy. He didn't know or care what was going on. Pretty soon the girls came strolling by, hugging their school books against their wide, soft boobs and smiling their lazy, lovely smiles. Joey yelled good-bye to the Old Man and banged out of the house, with Paul and me scrambling behind.

He overtook the girls in several loping strides. He was only thirteen but built like a man, muscle knotting his shoulders. He could run like a pony, chin himself fifty times, and almost dunk a basketball.

"Hey, Martha," he said.

The girls stopped. They turned. They eyed Joey in a bored sort of way.

Joey said, "What's this lie you been spreadin' about our father?"

Martha's round, creamy cheeks flashed a dark plum red. Blushing, she summoned up an uneasy smirk. She wasn't afraid—yet. Joey was in junior high, a kid.

Judy, meanwhile, was staring at her sister, wondering who else Martha had told that it had reached Joey. The girls must have gone crazy trying to figure it out.

Joey said, "Here, Lee," and handed me his one school book, thrusting it behind him without looking at me. I grabbed it. Joey took a long, gliding step to Martha and yanked both her arms, which held her books against her. The books hit the sidewalk with a *whomp*, like a paper bag exploding. Joey gave the books a terrific kick, sending a loose-leaf binder skidding out into the street. He picked up a book and lobbed it underhand into the long grass on the other side of the road. He was picking up another when Judy dropped her own, threw herself at Joey, and tossed a floating roundhouse punch at his ear. Joey got the book off, scaling it backhand, dodged the punch, and shoved Judy with both hands backward into a viburnum bush, where she collapsed butt down as if she'd been heaved into a pond.

"God*damn* you," she shrieked. "God*damn* you."

Joey's face was stern, firm, all business. Martha had begun to cry. She stood with her arms dangling, helpless, watching Joey through swollen eyes, with makeup swimming down her cheeks. Joey kicked a third book into the street and tried to underhand a fourth up into the crotch of a tree. The book slid over and fell, resting spine up like a tent. Joey stuck out his hand. I gave him back his book. The three of us walked on.

"All right?" Joey said.

"You didn't beat her up," I said.

"She's lucky," Joey said.

"He did enough," Paul said.

"She got the idea," Joey said.

"Yeah," I said, satisfied as if I'd done it myself.

Joey said, "We got to start takin' care of the Old Man. We've reached that age."

"I haven't," I said.

"You will," Joey said.

But I didn't want to. I just wanted to be Joey Malcolm's kid brother.

I began playing baseball when I was nine. No one taught me. It's something you grow to; one day the moment arrives. That spring, a hardball fit in the two hooked fingers of my right hand. I could swing a bat now—not wave it, *swing* it. In March I told Joey I was going out for Little League. "You're old enough," he said and asked the Old Man to bring me home a ball glove from the hardware store, which carried sports equipment. Frank grumped a little. Joey planted himself on the arm of the sofa, the Old Man deep below with his reddened little eyes on the TV, not saying yes, not saying no. Joey had told me to stay out of it. He'd told me to wait. A few nights later the Old Man came home with a glove, a $7 McGregor, bulky with padding, thick fingers radiating out like sunflower petals. Joey oiled it for me, and the next day we biked down the road to the sandlot field.

The ball was from last year. It was stained turtle green and covered with nicks and scratches. Joey backed off about twenty feet and tossed it to me, bringing his arm around slowly, lobbing the ball in a lazy arc like a pitcher beginning his warm-ups. I one-handed it nonchalantly and pegged it back to Joey. It was as if I'd been playing for years. Joey sent it back a little harder, and I gloved it just as neatly. Joey retreated to about sixty feet and let her fly; I plucked the ball off my shoulder and shot it back chest high.

Joey grinned. "You hot shit," he said.

I felt weightless, giddy with pride.

We were Little League teammates that year. I sat on the bench and watched Joey lead the team. He played with joy and abandon, the way he would later play football—as if he'd been shut up for days in some small, dark place and was rediscovering movement and daylight, going wild with having them again. I was never as intense as Joey, never as hungry. I stayed away from football.

Paul had graduated, and now Joey was beginning his junior year. I was in tenth grade, not a kid anymore, thickening in the chest and shoulders, growing in my own quiet way. It was early September, still summery, still bright blue and bottle green. Joey was sitting near the front of the school bus with his arm around Debbie Williams, his new steady. Lucinda Fragosi sat a few seats behind them, staring out her window.

Howie Gladding started it. Who else but Howie? Howie looked as funny as he acted, the oval jaw and head tapering upward, narrowing to a near point at the brush-cut summit. He'd collected a hatful of nicknames: Egg-head, Turniphead, and Pinhead, among others. They should have called him Pearhead, I always thought.

"Hey, Woodpecker," Howie began. Woodpecker was Howie's friend, Otis Peck. Otis was seated across the aisle and down a way from Howie. "Lucinda got a new bra— you hear about that, Woodpecker?"

Already Otis was giggling. The question itself was funny.

"Yeah," Howie brayed, "two Band-Aids and a rubber band."

Laughter exploded in the narrow, crowded school bus. Fat Mr. Hodges, pink-faced with a wire-gray crew cut, drove sleepy-eyed, unhearing. Lucinda stared hard out the window. And Joey stood up.

After all these years, Joey stood up, unhurriedly, hands stuffed in the pockets of his maroon jacket with the big white *L* on front, the *L* littered with little gold footballs, basketballs, and crossed bats. Joey looked around and located Howie Gladding—old Turniphead, the class clown. Joey came down the aisle, balancing neatly with his hands pocketed while the bus wound along throwing its weight this way and that. The light flowed over Joey, morning golden on his lion-gold skin and spun-gold hair.

The laughter died. People turned to watch. I saw Mr. Hodges following it in the rearview mirror. Joey stopped in front of Howie Gladding and stood there with his hands in his pockets.

"You're gonna stop that now," Joey said. "You're gonna cut it the fuck out."

Silence. The bus zoomed along, jouncing. Gears clanked. Gladding blushed darkly. He tried to smile, but the smile curdled.

Otis Peck giggled. Joey turned. He found Otis.

"You think it's funny, Otis?"

Otis only smiled a sick, sour smile like Howie's.

Joey's voice jumped and tightened. "I asked you a *question*, Peck." Joey had reddened, too, the blood whipping through him. You could see the muscle thickening in his neck and jaw.

Otis Peck shook his head no. He didn't think it was funny. The silence held—Joey's power. He was moving again. He was standing above Lucinda, who sat alone with her face to the window.

"Hey. Lucinda."

Lucinda Fragosi unstuck her gaze from the window. Her pearl-bright face was set stubborn as ever. She studied Joey with dark, untrusting eyes.

Joey said, "If they give you any more trouble, you tell me."

"They don't bother me," Lucinda said. Her voice was dry and scratchy, like sandpaper.

"They bother *me*," Joey said. "So help me, Jesus"— he was talking to the whole bus now, to everybody but me—"if there's any more, I don't care *who* it is, I'll break his neck."

Silence. The bus grumbled up a hill, gears grinding. Joey fell into his seat. He draped his arm around Debbie Williams. Gradually, conversation bubbled up but stayed quiet and cautious.

That year Lucinda Fragosi rode the school bus in peace.

The Old Man loved the movies. They were his balm, his joy. The more sentimental, the better. Fred Astaire, Ginger Rogers, Greta Garbo, Nelson Eddy and Jeanette McDonald. The town had one theater in those days, the Empire. It was a friendly, run-down joint in the middle of town, vanilla stucco walls with a jutting marquee you could stand under on a rainy Saturday till the lady opened the slot and began selling tickets, which dangled in a strip off a roll above her head. Inside, the theater was drably lit and smelled richly of popcorn. The wooden seats had petrified wads of chewing gum stuck to their flip-up bottoms. There was a balcony, but they never let anyone up there. I suppose they thought the kids would throw things. I always wondered what the hell they'd built it for if they were never going to use it.

The Old Man would dress up for the movies, in a clean shirt and black shoes instead of the yellow leather work boots he lived in. He would take the three of us to the early show, seven o'clock. We had to behave; if we got to wriggling or whispering, Frank would lean out and shoot us a glare, eyes sharp and bright in the dancing light of the movie screen.

As time went on, Frank watched his movies more and more on TV and less and less at the theater. We were partly to blame. We were getting too busy to go to the movies with him. Joey was going out with girls. A few times Paulie went alone with the Old Man, but it felt empty somehow to both of them. Eventually, Frank never went anywhere except to work.

In those days the TV movies didn't begin until after the eleven o'clock news. Frank would wait. He didn't need much sleep. He would sit in the dark, the dog snoring on the cushions beside him, a glass of gin or whiskey on the floor between his feet. He still wore his boots, which were laced with rawhide up his skinny ankles. The sofa cushions were soaked with his smell, a dark sweetness like peat that clung also to his flannel shirts, even after washing. You could smell dog in the sofa, too, like wet, dead leaves. The room swam with smells: Frank, dog, mildew, the night's fried supper still floating in from the kitchen. After a while would come the sour tang of booze. Sometimes Frank fell asleep before the movie ended. It's all vivid to me because the summer I was seventeen I watched *The Late Show* with Frank every night. That was after Joey was killed on the Shore Road less than a week after he'd graduated.

They said he was speeding. What kid didn't speed

on the Shore Road—so wide, so flat, so open beside the beach? He hit a telephone pole. I'll never understand it. I could see plowing into a dune or even belly-flopping a car into the herring run. But how wide is a telephone pole, a foot and a half? You'd have to *try* to hit a telephone pole on the Shore Road.

Debbie Williams had been in the car. Debbie went to the hospital with her skull broken, and lived. Joey had been driving Debbie's old man's station wagon, which was demolished. Her family was chilly toward us at the funeral—resentful, maybe, that Joey had risked Debbie's life and destroyed their automobile. Frank cried while the minister was reading, the tears hurrying down the hollows of his cheeks. He didn't make a sound; he just stood there leaking fat tears, staring blindly past the young minister. There must have been a hundred kids at the funeral but not many grown-ups. Joey's coaches came, and everyone who worked with Frank at the hardware store. Later, back on the sofa with his eyes fixed on the ice-blue flicker of the TV movie, Frank looked ready to cry again. He didn't. Not all summer.

I was mowing lawns by day and pumping gas nights at Billy Dimmick's Gulf Station. Dimmick's closed at eleven in the summertime, so I would get home just in time for the movie. It was just Frank and me. Paul had his own place. He'd gone to work as a carpenter after graduation. He could frame a house and do the cabinet work as well. He was learning masonry. There wasn't anything those hands couldn't do.

Often the movies were junk. I sat through them to be with Frank, though we hardly spoke to each other, even during the commercials. The Old Man got looped, but it was his right. He would get up early in the morning. He would go to work on time.

When the picture ended, the Old Man would rise stiffly, slowly, a little bit at a time. He would stand wobbly and hesitant in his loose khaki trousers and heavy boots, as if he'd forgotten how to walk and had to piece it together again. Then he would set out either for the stairs or the front door to relieve himself before turning in. I would shut off the TV and wait till he tackled the stairs. I would help him up, my arm around his middle. I wasn't as tall as Joey, but I'd grown broad through the chest and was pretty strong. Anyway, Frank was as light as a child. The dog, a big mutt named Zeke, climbed the stairs behind us, pausing when I would to give Frank a heave. Zeke slept with the Old Man.

The wallpaper upstairs was dust brown. The floors were bare. A bookshelf made of planks and bricks crouched in the hallway, half filled with the Zane Greys Frank had owned as a kid, some Hardy Boys mysteries, *Bill Stern's Favorite Baseball Stories*, and *My Greatest Day in Baseball* by John P. Carmichael and Others. I would let go of Frank, and he would totter to the bathroom if he hadn't taken care of it outside. I would wait, and he would spritz the back of the john till he found his aim. Out he would stagger and on to his room at the end of the hall. He would plop down on the edge of the bed and undress groggily, groping at his buttons. I would tug off his boots. His shinbones were sharp-edged and gleamed like marble. Zeke would haul himself up one leg at a time, tramp around, and flop at the foot of the bed. Frank would keel over and be asleep in thirty seconds. Sometimes through the open window I could hear the ocean swishing in and out. I could hear it falling up the beach, then pulling back again, dragging pebbles with a hiss and a clatter.

I would go to bed in the front bedroom, now oddly

empty without Joey. The street lamp shone in, helpful as the smile of an old friend. I would lie on my stomach the way Joey used to, watching the empty lighted road. The crickets sizzled in the shaggy grasses under the street lamp. How could Joey, so expert in all he did, run a car into a telephone pole? Why Joey? Why us? I thought and thought and decided there wasn't any answer.

On the first day of school, I walked out of the house and found Lucinda Fragosi waiting for me. Lucinda was now in tenth grade. She was as skinny as ever. The summer had given her a light, wheaty tan. A backyard tan.

"I wanted to talk to you," she began in that dry husk of a voice.

We walked. Lucinda swung her arms like batons.

"I'm sorry about Joe," she said. "I been wanting to tell you."

"I appreciate it," I said.

"I wanted to go to the funeral." Lucinda's face hardened to the stubborn, almost spiteful look it wore when the kids ragged her. I wondered who or what had stopped her from going to Joey's funeral.

"I know you were there in spirit," I said.

"I definitely was," Lucinda said.

"Well, then."

"No one I really liked was ever killed," Lucinda said.

"I suppose it's like losing an arm or a leg," I said. "After a while it's part of things. I suppose you can get used to anything."

"I suppose," she murmured. She brightened. "I want to show you something."

She stopped walking. I waited while she rummaged in her pocketbook, which hung too far from her shoulder, like her dress. She dug around till she found her wallet. The wallet bulged with snapshots of relatives—cousins, I imagined—and magazine pictures of Elvis Presley. It was just like any girl's wallet. Lucinda flipped through the plastic-cased pictures, and there, suddenly, was Joey. It was his senior class picture. In the upper left corner he'd written "Lucinda" and, in the bottom right, "From Joe." She turned the picture over. On the back Joey had written "Hey Lucinda! Always stay as great as you are. Your friend, Joe Malcolm."

I shut my eyes, tight, and drove the pain back down where it belonged, forcing it deep. My eyes watered; I blinked. *Stop it, force it deep down.* Lucinda patted my shoulder. I was being comforted by Lucinda Fragosi, dirty Lucinda, gross Lucinda, washes-her-face-in-the-toilet Lucinda, who was none of those things. I opened my eyes, took a big swallow of the apple-sweet September air, and walked to the bus stop with my friend, Lucinda.

That year again Lucinda rode the bus in peace.

2

Pam Rogers's mother looked down her arrowhead nose at me from the time I began dating Pam. I wasn't good enough. Not anywhere near. Mrs. Rogers wanted a poet for her daughter, or a violin player. A college professor would have been all right. I don't think she ever worried that Pam would marry me, but old Edna didn't want Pam to make a habit of boys like me.

Pam bloomed late, in senior year, and I was her first boyfriend. She lived about a mile from us. She rode my school bus. I'd known Pam casually all my life. She'd never been pretty, never been ugly—a thin, shy, earnest little girl who earned straight A's as effortlessly as Paul built things and I threw a baseball. Senior year, suddenly, Pam had changed. I looked at her standing at the bus stop with the other girls. I looked again. Her thinness was right. She was willowy—pretty. I began wondering if she hadn't always been pretty, and I just hadn't seen it. A couple of times I caught her looking at me, once at the bus stop, once in the cafeteria. I called her and asked her to a movie. She sounded almost scared. She said yes.

On a Friday night I drove over in the Old Man's Ford. Mrs. Rogers answered the door. She sat me down in the living room while Pam fussed with her hair upstairs. Mr. Rogers was stretched out in a big easy chair with his feet on a hassock, a newspaper on his belly. His smile was mild and weary. He looked as if he'd run out of energy years ago. He was a lawyer, Rogers and Hazlitt, in a narrow little office on Main Street. Mrs. Rogers took a perch opposite me. I could feel the prick of her lightless gray eyes no matter where I looked. Mr. Rogers and I talked a little baseball. The World Series was coming up. Mrs. Rogers endured it a few minutes, then inquired out of the blue, "Lee, do you remember the time you and that friend of yours—that dreadful fat boy, what was his name?—hit my windshield with a ball of mud?"

Mr. Rogers chucked his head back and laughed.

"It wasn't funny," his wife said.

"No," I agreed.

"What *was* that dreadful boy's name?" asked Mrs. Rogers.

"Robert Nailer."

"I could have been killed."

She'd been doing about twenty-five, moseying down our road on a warming March afternoon with the snow melting, the ground drinking it. There was mud everywhere. Robert had gotten to playing with this mudball, shaping it idly while we talked by the silvery mica-rich boulder at the edge of the Smalls' apple orchard. He hadn't planned to throw it, as far as I knew. It was sheer impulse. The car came along, and Robert reared back and threw. We took off, shinning through the orchard and across a field humpy with matted yellow winter grasses.

"We didn't know it was you," I said.

"What difference would *that* make?" said Mrs. Rogers.

"None," I admitted.

"Really," she said.

"We were pretty young," I said. Eleven or twelve.

"Not *that* young."

"A cop came over that night—Sergeant Corey—and gave me a lecture about throwing things at moving vehicles."

"The police always say 'vehicle' instead of 'car,' " Mr. Rogers put in. "They always say 'driving under the influence' instead of 'drunk driving.' "

Mrs. Rogers sent him a puzzled, impatient look, but he pushed ahead.

"They always say 'gentleman.' That's the one that really gets me. Everyone's a gentleman. 'And then this gentleman here picked up a beer bottle and hit the arresting officer over the head.' "

Mr. Rogers laughed. I managed a chuckle. Silence.

"Robert moved to Hawaii," I said.

"That's a good place for him," said Mrs. Rogers.

Mr. Rogers said, "If I had a nickel for every time I threw something at a car, we'd be rich, Edna."

Mrs. Rogers let this go. Pam came in, shy, walking on eggs. I bounced up. Her hair was gathered up, baring her swanlike neck. I held her coat for her. Mr. Rogers gave us a cheery wave from his chair, too weary to get up. Mrs. Rogers followed us to the door, hovering like a moth.

"Is that your car?" she asked me.

"It's Frank's," I said.

"Frank?"

"My father."

"You call your father 'Frank'?"

"We don't mean any disrespect," I said.

"How odd," she said.

"Good night, Mrs. Rogers," I said.

"Be home by eleven," she told Pam.

In the car Pam said, "I'm sorry about my mother."

"She doesn't like me," I said.

"She doesn't like anybody. It's a big event when I go out on a date."

"Me, too," I said.

"Really?" Pam said.

"Sure."

I clicked on the radio, cutting into "A Sunday Kind of Love." We listened to the music. It was blue, sweet and sad.

"Can I tell you something?" Pam said.

"Sure."

She drew a deep breath and said, "I feel very comfortable with you."

"Well, you've known me all your life," I said.

"It isn't that," she said.

"No?"

"I don't know what it is." She was like her mother in a way—brisk and direct. My first surprise. I'd imagined her tongue-tied and stammering.

"If you don't know, I sure don't," I said.

"Whatever it is, it's very pleasant," Pam said, settling it.

That's how it all began with Pam Rogers.

I suppose we were like most small-town high school sweethearts in those days. About once a week we went to the movies. We went to the school dances and afterward to the Howard Johnson's at the far end of Main Street. There were parties. Pam's friends' parties were held in bright living rooms with the furniture shoved back for dancing. There would be grown-ups in the next room having a party of their own, drinking beer or maybe martinis. The boys would congregate on one side of the room, the girls on the other. The boys talked sports and politics. My friends' parties took place in paneled basements, usually with no adults on the premises. These basements would be lit by soft red or blue lights, a silky ooze in the swamping darkness. Music blared, electrifying the darkness: Chuck Berry, lots of Elvis. The room smelled of beer and sweet, cheap wine. People danced and they necked—on sofas, in corners, leaning against the wall. Pam and I stood, sat, or lay and kissed till my senses glazed over and an ache squeezed me down below like a fist. If Mrs. Rogers had only known.

Old Edna. Her slate eyes never softened. Your mother ought to drink, I told Pam. She needs to laugh. A few beers might loosen her up. Pam said her mother did drink on occasion. I didn't believe it till the night of our high school graduation, when Mrs. Rogers showed up tipsy. Not drunk. Tipsy.

My discovery of her condition came after the ceremony, on the steps outside the auditorium. We'd all filed out into the dusk. People hugged, wrapped in maroon gowns, weeping shiny tears and smiling. Cameras flashed. I found Frank and Paul. The Old Man was wearing a necktie and a gray-striped vanilla seersucker jacket. I told him he looked like the ice-cream man, but he didn't smile; he just stood, tiny in the crowd, looking jostled and miserable. I told Paulie to drive him home. I said I'd walk, or get a ride with Pam's folks. Paul said he'd be glad to come back, but I said no, and he and Frank slipped away. I wormed through the crowd till I found Pam. Her uncle and aunt had come down from Boston to watch her graduate. Her kid brother was there, lurking behind his mother.

Pam rushed up and pressed a kiss on my cheek. Her large blue eyes were dry but charged with light.

"Congratulations, Lee," said Mr. Rogers, booming it out. He grabbed my hand.

"Lee, this is my Aunt Betsy and Uncle Jim Collins," Pam said.

We all shook hands. Mrs. Collins looked like her sister but not so taut and vinegary. Uncle Jim was chunky, with a ruddy face and very black hair.

"Where on *earth* is your father, Lee?" said Mrs. Rogers. She didn't sound like herself; her voice sailed, feathery. I looked at her. She was wearing white gloves.

"My brother took him home," I said. "Crowds make him nervous."

"Gracious," Mrs. Rogers said, placing a white-gloved hand on her bony breast. "I *do* hope you don't need a ride."

"I don't mind walking," I said. It was only a couple of miles.

"*Walking?*" roared Mr. Rogers. They'd all been drinking, I saw. The men's voices had thickened. "No sir, buster," said Mr. Rogers. "Jim, this boy is one of the best left fielders that ever came down the pike."

"No kidding," said Uncle Jim.

"Jim played for Dartmouth," Aunt Betsy explained.

"Yeah, back in aught-five," said Mr. Rogers.

"Aught-five, my ass," Uncle Jim said.

"*Jim,*" Aunt Betsy scolded gaily.

Mrs. Rogers said, "How we'll fit you in, Lee, I haven't

the slightest. We'll be like one of the lifeboats off the *Titanic*."

"It'll be cozy," said Mr. Rogers. "Don't you want to be cozy, Edna?"

Pam sent me a wink. She looked more like her aunt than her mother, the pretty face cut in neat, straight lines.

"I suppose," Mrs. Rogers crooned, "we should wend homeward."

It took a while to get to the car. Our teachers were going around shaking hands and wishing us good luck. Boys shook hands. Girls gave each other gowned, billowy hugs. It broke up slowly, and I followed Pam and her family to their car. I squeezed in back with Pam, Uncle Jim, and Pam's brother. Mr. Rogers drove slowly, peering over the wheel. The streets were empty, with the lamps shining down through the trees.

"Nice ceremony," remarked Uncle Jim.

"It's kind of sad," I said.

"Sad?" said Mrs. Rogers. "*Sad?*" She gave a tinkling laugh. "It's the beginning, Lee. Just think, Pamela"—she spoke over her shoulder—"in a few months you'll be a college girl. That's when life begins, kiddo."

"Sad in a *nice* way," I explained.

"God, you're going to *love* Bryn Mawr," Mrs. Rogers said.

"Where are you going next year, Lee?" Uncle Jim asked.

"U Mass," I said.

"Lee isn't what you'd call academically inclined," Mrs. Rogers said.

I could feel Pam clench, all the way through the rumple of our gowns.

"What the hell's wrong with U Mass?" asked Uncle Jim.

"Nothing," Pam said.

"Hell, no," Mr. Rogers said. "Don't be such a snot, Edna."

"I really can't afford anything else," I said. "This'll be tough enough."

"You're gonna do fine," Uncle Jim said. "I can see that right now."

"Oh, Lee's not stupid," Mrs. Rogers said.

"This is making me sick," Pam said.

"You're too sensitive, Pamela," Mrs. Rogers said. Then she cooed, "Oh, would you *look* at the moon, everybody?"

Almost full, it had climbed above the trees, bobbing on the still-blue sky. The car went bumpety-bump over the railroad tracks and veered down our road. Our house was the first one, just after the turn.

Mr. Rogers said, "Here you go, Lee, old buddy."

"I'm getting out, too," Pam said.

"You are *not*," said her mother.

But Pam clambered out, close behind me.

"Thanks for the ride," I said.

"You bet," Mr. Rogers said.

Mrs. Rogers said, "We were going to have dessert. And champagne."

"Lee could come," Mr. Rogers suggested.

"Come on back and have a Manhattan," said Uncle Jim.

I looked at Pam. I wouldn't have minded some champagne.

"I want to get to the party," Pam said. The class had rented a restaurant and hired a band for this final night together.

"You just have fun," Mr. Rogers said. "The old folks'll drink the champagne."

"You bet we will," said Uncle Jim.

"I am just devastated," Mrs. Rogers said.

Pam shucked her gown, hauling it up fold after fold over her head. Under it she wore a light blue summer dress and high heels. She bunched the gown and handed it in to Uncle Jim.

"May I ask," said Mrs. Rogers, "what time you'll be home?"

"Mother, for God's sake," Pam said.

"Do not say 'God,' Pamela," said her mother.

"They'll be home when they get there," Mr. Rogers said.

"Correct," Pam said.

"I give up," Mrs. Rogers sighed.

"It was nice meeting you," I said to Jim and Betsy.

"Same here," boomed Uncle Jim.

"Good night," Aunt Betsy said, smiling.

"Don't do anything I wouldn't do," said Uncle Jim.

"Stop at the house," Pam said. "I'm going to get some champagne."

I looked at her. "They won't give it to you," I said.

"Oh yes, they will."

"You'll have to stay," I said.

"Keep the engine running," she answered.

I did. I watched Pam go up the flagstone walk between the tall old lilac bushes. Her parents' house was a good hundred years old, with shingles painted bone white and smart black shutters. On top was a widow's walk, a tiny square porch against the sky. Pam emerged in two minutes, bringing a green, cold-sweating bottle of champagne.

"How'd you do that?" I asked.

"Daddy," she explained.

We drank the champagne in the beach parking lot, handing the bottle back and forth. The sun had vanished below the saucer edge of the ocean. Across the Sound, the moon dangled above the island. Solemnly, stilled by the feeling that we'd grown to some new and mysterious turning point, we passed the bottle back and forth.

"You finish it," Pam said.

There was plenty left. I tilted the bottle and drank the champagne in gulps. Its fizzy sweetness brought to mind the quick, shining water of a mountain stream. It tasted exciting. I dumped the empty bottle over my shoulder into the back seat.

"Can you drive?" Pam said.

"Hell yes, I can drive."

She laid her hand on the back of my neck. It was as if my entire sense of touch had gathered in that one spot.

"I wish we had another bottle," I said.

"I didn't want to press my luck," Pam said.

The restaurant was a summer place by the ocean. The walls were unvarnished wood. Rafters were strung overhead. You could smell the old pine walls and the faint saltiness of the sea. The band was playing when Pam and I arrived. The dance floor was jammed. A man was tending bar, soft drinks only, but we'd seen kids drinking in the parking lot. I bought Cokes for myself and Pam. We found a table.

"I need some more champagne," I said.

"You've had plenty," Pam said and smiled.

She watched me, a champagne sparkle in her round blue eyes. Beyond her, around a large table in a corner, sat the single girls, the eternally dateless. I'd never seen any of them at a dance or party, but here they were. It was graduation night, their night, too. I saw Glenda Jean

Perkins, smiling with wet buckteeth. I saw Corrine Dober, hunch-backed and tiny. I saw gawky Linda Lake and fat Sally Fish. It was like a club. They sat over their half-drunk Cokes, staring at the band. Feeling swamped me, a pleasant, drunken pity.

Glenda Jean Perkins caught me staring at her. She sent me a toothy smile and a wave. She was wearing white gloves.

Pam turned with a graceful dip of her shoulder to see what I was looking at. Glenda Jean waved.

"All the ugly girls at one table," I said.

Pam's blue eyes shone. "Why don't you dance with Glenda Jean?"

"With Glenda Jean?" I said.

"I dare you," Pam said.

"I don't think so."

"Double dare," Pam said.

Why not? I thought. Why not dance with Glenda Jean? It won't make me sick. It won't give me hives.

"No sweat," I said.

I got up, straightened my necktie, and headed for the table in the corner.

The singer, snake thin in a sequined jacket, was singing "Heartbreak Hotel" and humping the micro-phone like Elvis. He wailed the last aching note, then grinned up one side of his face. The dancers unclasped and waited.

"Gonna do one for all you young lovers," the singer panted into the mike.

"Would you like to dance, Glenda Jean?" I said.

Glenda Jean stared, bug-eyed. She smiled, a widen-ing view of moist buckteeth. Eyeing me, she rose slowly, warily, wiping her white-gloved hands on the skirt of her peppermint-pink party dress. She came around the table cautiously, studying me. I waited for her. She led me the short distance to the dance floor.

"I'm not a very good dancer," she said.

"Me neither," I said.

I put my arm around her and took her hand.

Glenda Jean swayed heavily, anchored to the floor. She felt solid, massive in the curve of my arm. She swayed, slower than the sway of the music.

"What are you gonna do next year, Glenda Jean?" I said.

She ignored my question. "You been drinkin'," she said.

"How do you know?" I said.

"You smell like a whiskey factory," she said.

"It was champagne," I said.

"Shame on you," she said.

"Shame on me?"

"Shame on you," said Glenda Jean.

"What are you gonna do next year?" I tried again.

"Nursing school."

"Good for you," I said.

"It's one of the Lord's callings," she said.

"Nursing?"

"Jesus was a healer."

"I guess he was," I agreed. I was beginning to see that Glenda Jean was crazy.

"You *guess*? Don't you read your Bible?"

"I don't exactly pore over it," I said.

"Shame on you."

Glenda Jean had become less anchored. I nudged her back and forth, up and down. People bumped us, ramming me up against Glenda Jean. She wasn't wearing perfume. She smelled like baking bread.

Glenda Jean said, "You'll see the light someday."

"I hope so," I said.

"It's the light of the world," she said.

"Well," I said, "I need all the help I can get."

"Don't you be blasphemous."

I said, "I never knew you were religious, Glenda Jean."

"You never asked," she said.

"I didn't ask tonight," I said. I was actually beginning to enjoy this.

"Yes, you did. You just didn't know you were asking."

"That makes no sense."

"I know it," she said and laughed, a moist rustle behind the shields of her teeth.

We danced. Swaying. Shuffling.

"It's nice of you to dance with me," Glenda Jean said.

"Hell, Glenda Jean . . ."

"Don't cuss," she said.

"Sorry."

"Dance with Linda."

"Linda Lake?"

"Dance with her," Glenda Jean said.

"Why?"

The skinny singer threw his head back and shut his eyes, knees buckling as if he'd been shot, and delivered the last trembling note of his song. The dancers unclinched. Glenda Jean released my hand. Her arm slid reluctantly from my shoulder.

"Thanks for the dance," I said.

"Go dance with Linda. She used to have a crush on you."

"Jesus, Glenda Jean."

"Don't *cuss*."

"Sorry," I said.

I looked for Pam. She'd vanished. Ladies' room, I

figured. I followed Glenda Jean to her table. I held her chair; she lowered herself, ladylike, smoothing her pink dress as she landed. Now she looked up at me, fixing me with those bulging eyes. She jerked her head toward Linda Lake.

"Hey, Linda," I said. "Want to dance?"

Linda gazed past me. "No, thanks," she said.

"No, *thanks?*" I said.

"I don't want to dance," she said.

"I'm insulted," I said.

"Fuck off," Linda said.

Corrine Dober said, "I'll dance."

I thought, *This is going to go on all night.* Corrine bared jagged, rusting teeth in a smile like a cadaver's. Her yellow hair had been set, a neat coil bobbing on her withered shoulders. She wore horn-rimmed glasses. The girls were all staring at me—including Linda Lake, whose oversized mouth was skewed in a smirk. The band had swung into "Why Do Fools Fall in Love?" Glenda Jean was giving me that severe look, an order I couldn't wriggle out of.

"Let's go, Corrine," I said.

Glenda Jean smiled. Teeth. I thought, *You'll make a great mother, Glenda Jean.*

Corrine raised herself, grinning like death itself. Her pixie face came level with my chest. The dancers were quick-stepping, prancing. The music rollicked along, but I slow-danced with Corrine. It seemed appropriate somehow.

She wouldn't come close, and I could reach only halfway around the inverted curve of her back. She felt weightless, hardly more than a feather resting in the crook of my wrist. I could feel the bones of her fingers digging through my jacket, and her arm lay rigid against me, checking me, keeping the distance between us. Corrine smiled; she shuffled her feet mechanically. We drifted, almost motionless in the stamping, prancing turmoil of the dance floor. I looked down and saw Corrine grinning past me.

"Good saxophone," I said.

"Yuh," she agreed.

Then Moose Klingensmith tried a fancy turn, tripped, and rammed Corrine like a freight train from behind. Corrine fell hard against me, all loosely joined bones. Moose plunged past us; someone caught him.

"Sorry, Lee," he said. He grinned boozily.

"Moose, you dumb shit," I said.

Corrine's smile had frozen, turned to fright. Gingerly, she nudged her glasses back up her nose.

"Sorry, man," Moose blubbered.

"Jesus, Moose," I said.

"I'm loaded," Moose explained.

"Corrine," I said, "do you want to finish the dance?"

Corrine nodded. I took her claw hand, and we danced. The moment the song ended, the tiny hands left me.

"Thank you, Corrine," I said.

"Yuh."

"Is your nose okay?" I said.

"Oh yuh."

Leading her to her table, I came face to face with Howie Gladding. Turniphead was almost as drunk as Moose Klingensmith. I could smell the tang of booze on his breath.

"You ol' bastard," Howie said happily. "You really know how to pick 'em."

Corrine waited behind me.

"Yeah," I said, "I know how to pick 'em, all right."

It wasn't so long ago that Joey had challenged Howie on the school bus, shutting him up once and for all. Howie had never bothered Lucinda Fragosi again, but I could see that Joey's lesson hadn't burned deep.

Howie contemplated me woozily. "You're gonna get warts," he said.

"You're gonna get a hangover," I said and pushed by him.

I held the chair as Corrine sat. She was still grinning. I avoided Glenda Jean's gaze; I was afraid she had another assignment for me. I smiled good-bye to the girls and went looking for Pam.

I found Pam out on the terrace overlooking the water. She was sitting alone at one of the tables, which were round with umbrella halos. Her chin rested in her hands. She sat very still. The moon painted her face. She didn't speak when I came out. I pulled a chair and sat down.

"This would be a nice place to eat," I said.

"It would," she agreed.

"You could watch the sun go down," I said.

"I'm sorry, Lee," she said.

"For what?"

"For daring you to do that."

"I didn't mind."

"When I was little, my father taught me that a dare is something you're afraid to do yourself."

"You couldn't dance with Glenda Jean," I said.

"I could have danced with Wally Perry."

"Old Wally," I said. "They used to tease the hell out of him in gym class."

"I bet," Pam said.

"Linda Lake wouldn't dance with me," I said.

"Good for her," Pam said.

"She told me to fuck off."

Pam laughed. Her laugh was trilling. Musical. We sat a while, gazing out over the ink-dark water. You could hear the waves falling. Small, gentle waves. The moon dribbled pearls of light on the water.

"Want to take a walk?" Pam said.

I did. We stood up, and Pam took off her high-heeled shoes. We headed up the beach, strolling close to the water's edge. The music shrank behind us. The restaurant now was a moon-silvered toy at the edge of the bending shore. The waves fell—slow splash, slow retreating hiss.

We found a sheltered place between two low dunes. I took off my jacket and necktie. We sat. The sand was surprisingly cool. After a while we French kissed. Pam's breathing quickened. We lay down, slow at first, then less and less patient, moving, rubbing, humping each other through our clothes until I felt a quick ripple of pleasure and was wet and warm inside my BVDs.

I quit moving and sagged against Pam. I could hear the waves again and smell the kelpy richness of the ocean. Pam's lips were parted, her eyes closed. It was a woman's face—pained now and hungry. Realizing I was through, she sighed. Slowly, slowly, the want in her face subsided. She opened her eyes. She contemplated the stars.

"Sorry," I said.

"It's okay," she murmured.

"I can't help it," I said.

"I know."

"Maybe we ought to just go ahead," I said.

I ached to, of course, but was afraid, perhaps because I knew so little. There was no rush in those days.

Pam shook her head no. I didn't say any more. I was

just as happy to let Pam decide. It was enough to know that one day it would come. We sat up. Shoulders touching, we watched the moon's reflection on the slick surface of the water.

"Are you cold?" I asked finally.

"I'm fine," she said, smiling.

"Want my jacket?"

"I'm fine."

"What time is it?"

She peered at her wrist. "Eleven."

"Early," I said.

"Yes," she agreed.

I thought a while and said, "I wonder how many kids go all the way."

"Some do; some don't."

"How many do?"

Pam only shrugged.

"Do you think Faye Driscoll does?" I asked.

"What do you care?"

"I'm just curious." Faye was homecoming queen and captain of the cheerleaders.

"I *bet* you're curious," Pam said.

"I wonder if Joey did," I said.

Pam looked at me, surprised. "You don't know?"

"He never said."

"You couldn't tell?"

"No," I said.

"Well, I bet he did," Pam said.

"I hope so," I said.

Then we lay on our backs. I saw the dust swirl of the Milky Way: stars, distant beyond understanding. I could hear Pam's breathing. I heard the waves spilling in.

And I slept.

· · ·

When I woke, Pam was bending over me, smiling, and it was morning. Her face was pale and sleep-swollen. The sun had climbed high. I sat up fast.

"What time is it?" I asked.

"Quarter to six."

"Jesus Christ. Oh, Jesus, Pam."

"It's all right," Pam said.

"Your mother'll kill me."

"She'll be asleep. She was blotto last night."

"I don't know," I said.

"Trust me," Pam said.

I hunted for my coat and tie and picked myself up. The water was darkest blue, the distant island green as green silk. There wasn't a breath of wind.

Pam rose beside me. I looked at her, concentrating, as if trying to memorize her face. Her eyes were a dry blue, like the sky this June morning. Her lines were simple; they were classic. She was going to be beautiful, and I was the first to see it. I'd been the first to see she was pretty. You'll always love her, I thought. Somehow, always. I held her and had everything I wanted.

3

The Cape Cod League in those days was composed of local fellows. Today they've got college ballplayers, who can come from anywhere: Maine, Florida, Tennessee—you name it. But when I was a kid, the league really belonged to the towns.

The ballplayers might be anywhere from eighteen to fifty years old. When I was a kid, the ace of the pitching staff on our town team was Eddie West, who repaired lawnmowers in the basement of the hardware store where the Old Man worked. Eddie was the owner's son. Carl Robb, who played the infield, was a reporter for the town's newspaper, *The Covenant*, and after a game Carl would drive over to the office in his uniform and write the game up. He was a very bright boy who'd gone to Princeton. Nuts Peters, part Cape Verdean and the rest Indian, played a beautiful second base and hit a ton— when he wasn't on the bottle. Nuts worked as a handyman: house painter, tree cutter, window washer. He'd do anything. He had a long, bent back and a kindly face that was as brown and cracked as his years-old ball glove. His son was a great athlete. I can still see Nuts on the cold gray afternoons of the football season, slugging whiskey from a pint bottle as he watched his boy scramble for touchdowns. Roger Pires, the third baseman, was another Cape Verdean. He'd quit school to go to work in the cranberry bogs, forfeiting his chance, some said, to be a major-league ballplayer. He was in his late forties by the time I saw him play, and he could dig up a ground ball with such a lack of effort, you'd have thought he could *wish* the ball into his glove. I could go on and on. There was Kenny Scannell, who ran the printing press at *The Covenant,* and Mr. Whipple, who taught math and phys ed at the high school. They kept their gloves and spikes in the trunks of their cars and laundered their own flannel uniforms.

The games were played evenings before dark and every Sunday afternoon. Admission was free, but they did pass a hat. The spectators sat on a rickety bleacher behind home plate or lounged in the tall grass on the hillside along the third base line. The damp summer evenings smelled of the sea. You could see the water from the hillside, glassy on a Sunday afternoon, with the white sails heeling over in the distance.

That was the Cape League, and it was where I began my career as an umpire. I got into it accidentally, like most umpires. I was a pretty good ballplayer—not like Joey, but I could play. I was cocaptain senior year. One afternoon the younger boys were playing a JV game, and the umpires didn't show. The varsity coach, Coach Maretta, sent me and the other captain, Johnny Luce, over to work the game. I strapped on catcher's equipment and went behind the plate.

The first pitch of the game—the first pitch I ever called—was a slow curve. It wandered in waist high, a JV curve ball, swerving gently and visiting the strike zone on the outer edge of the plate. The hitter watched it float by. I called the strike, jabbing my right arm at forty-five degrees. The hitter stepped back with the bat on his shoulder.

"You must be kidding," he said.

Imagine, a JV getting on me like that. I was an all-league outfielder and could have hoisted the kid by his neck like a teddy bear. I took this personally.

"You want to stick around?" I said through the bars of the mask.

"Huh?" the kid said.

"If you want to stick around, keep your mouth shut. The pitch was a strike."

Seeing this jawing going on, their coach came out, giving his belt a tug against the sag of his belly and slamming down his feet like a fat general.

"What's the problem here?" he demanded.

One pitch, and I was in hot water. I'd been right, though. The pitch had been a strike. I pulled off the mask. Coaches, cops, teachers—it was ingrained in me to be respectful to authority.

"Coach," I said, "let me call the game, okay? I know what I'm doing."

He stopped and studied me, frowning. Then he nodded. "All right," he said. "Fair enough."

It was my game then. Mine to ruin or to make right—the difference between noise and music, between a free-for-all and the pretty game of baseball. I never understood, till that moment, what good umpiring means to the game. Baseball can be thrilling, and it can be beautiful—but only if the umpiring is good.

My partner that day, Johnny Luce, stood in the infield with his hands in his pockets, grinning at his mistakes, chatting with the infielders and base runners. Once the catcher whipped a surprise throw to first, picking off the runner, who'd gotten careless, and Johnny didn't see it. He was standing with his arms folded, enjoying a laugh with the shortstop. It wasn't my call, but I saw it. The runner dove late; the tag slapped his arm. Got him. I made the call. It was easy. There is a moment, the tiny part of a second, when a hand or foot meets the base. There is another moment when a tag falls. The trick is to see both moments, to pick them both out in the whirl of time; if you see them both, you know which happened first.

Coach Maretta had strolled over to watch. The coach had played a lot of ball in his time, college and pro. He'd coached our town team in the Cape League and was now league vice-president. After the game, he asked me if I'd ever umpired before and if I'd enjoyed it. Meanwhile, the visiting coach, the fat one, came chugging over to tell me what a fine game I'd called. He grabbed my hand and said it was always a pleasure to run into good umpiring. A few days later Coach Maretta offered me the job umpiring in the Cape League. Fifteen dollars a game—real money in those days. No more pumping gas at night. No more working till eleven. I could even slack off on the lawn jobs. Yes, and lie on the beach with Pam.

The first person I ever tossed was Red Carroll, a onetime minor-league catcher who coached high school as well as his town's Cape League entry. Red was a lean, rawboned giant, with the biggest hands I'd ever seen, brick-pink hands wadded with muscle. I'd played against his high school team. Red would pace in front of the bench, florid face knitted dangerously, spitting past his shoulder and barking, deep-voiced, at the umpires. The umps were afraid of him. They should have walked over and shut him up but did not. Red tongue-lashed his players, who endured it meekly and won for him.

It was my third game, a Sunday afternoon, hot and sticky under a high sky and blazing light. The sails hung motionless in the smoke-blue distance. The game dragged, error-riddled, lurching along without rhythm. The pitchers were wild; the infielders were kicking the ball around. It's hard to concentrate in a game like that. I was working the bases. About the fifth inning, Red Carroll began to nag me.

"*Bear* down, Malcolm, *bear* down. . . ."

I'd always hit well against his team in high school. Maybe he'd taken it personally.

"That one looked fair, Malcolm. Looked fair by a foot—Jesus."

Maybe he was trying to intimidate me, period.

"That's a balk, Malcolm; he's not stoppin'. That's a balk."

After a while I could hear almost nothing else. The harder I tried not to listen, the more I heard. Then it would cease for a few minutes, and I would tell myself it was over, that it hadn't been anything in the first place, just some harmless ragging—water off a duck's back. Then he'd start again.

"What are ya doin', Malcolm, sleepin' out there?"

In the eighth inning one of Red's fellows tried to leg a single into a double. I trailed him, making sure he stepped on first, and sprinted to position for the close play at second. The throw was sweet. The runner slid, hooking like a question mark as the shortstop brought the ball around in his glove, nabbing the runner's ankle. Got him. I watched long enough to be sure and rang him out.

Red Carroll popped off the bench.

"He never *tagged* him, Malcolm, he never *tagged* him."

The deep, rasping voice carried in the stillness, audible to the women lolling in the grass on the hill and to the kids straddling bikes behind the home bench.

Red came closer, prowling with his hands rammed in his hip pockets, his big shoulders squared.

"You weren't hustlin', Malcolm."

My partner waited behind the plate. He'd taken his mask off. The ballplayers watched, relaxing with their hands on their hips. My mouth had gone dry; I wetted it as best I could. I was scared of Red Carroll but more scared of what would happen if I didn't scotch this here and now. It wouldn't have just been Red. Every bully in the league would have come gunning for me. I took a deep breath to steady myself and called time. I went about halfway to Red Carroll.

"Mr. Carroll," I said. "I want you to sit down and be quiet. I've heard enough."

"You have, huh?"

"That's right."

"Well, you're gonna hear a lot more."

"I'm not gonna hear *any* more."

I spun and walked away.

Behind me Red said, "You couldn't ump girls' softball."

A few of his fellows along the bench giggled. I don't blame them, really. I braked and spun back. Red had sat down. His long, muscle-strapped legs were stretched out, ankles crossed. I didn't have the technique yet. I would be taught at umpiring school and would refine it after watching the legendary Bugs Trovarelli throw a few fellows out of big-league games in front of 30,000 people. For now I just aimed a finger at Mr. Red Carroll and said, "Mr. Carroll, you're out of the game."

He smiled. "For what?"

"Out," I said.

He didn't move; he just sat with his legs out and his arms folded, looking amused.

"Mr. Carroll," I said, "you got three minutes to leave, or you forfeit."

He leaned with his arms still folded and spat tobacco juice in the dust by his feet. Slowly he lifted his left wrist and contemplated his watch. I didn't have a watch. I don't know why I said three minutes.

"Is that daylight savings time," he said, "or mountain time?"

Giggles.

"You better be on your way," I said, "by the time I cross the first base line."

I turned and strolled out onto the field. I allowed him some time. When I looked, he stood up. I watched him pick up his windbreaker and a catcher's mitt. He was grinning. He threw the jacket over his shoulder and went slouching off the field, still smiling.

Just about everyone in town knew Coach Joe Maretta. He taught everybody's kid math and science in the junior high. In the summertime he worked behind the window in the post office. He'd been a fullback at Holy Cross as well as a baseball player—a broad, shambling man with no neck, just a head set on square shoulders. He had a voice like a blast of gravel, and when he smiled, the big, flat face broke into a million sunny lines.

His parents had been immigrants. Maretta had earned his way through college lugging a football. His love, though, was baseball, and New York had signed him after graduation. He'd fallen just short of the majors, playing a couple of seasons in Triple A. The dream lay just out of reach, so he came home, got a master's, taught, and coached. Now, he said, he wanted to coach a kid who would make the majors. Just one.

Along came his son, Bobby, who was our bat boy when I was playing. He had his old man's olive skin and dark eyes. Later he caught for his old man. He batted .400 his senior year. Joe must have spent hundreds of hours tutoring him. Bobby played college ball and was drafted by Cleveland. He signed and started playing in the minors. Meanwhile, a blur had appeared on one of Joe Maretta's big lungs, growing fast. Bobby went up to Triple A. Later he made the jump to the big leagues; he came to Boston one day and banged a double off the wall. His mother was at the ball park, but Joe Maretta had died one year before, of cancer.

But all of this was a long way off the night Joe Maretta knocked on our door bringing the ad clipped from *The Sporting News* for the umpiring school in St. Petersburg, Florida. Pam was at the house. She and the Old Man and I were eating dinner. It was late to be eating, or the coach wouldn't have come. The Old Man nodded at the apology and shot me a black look that said, *Who would expect to find people eating dinner at eight-thirty?* Frank was sore because Pam and I had spent the day over on the island and missed the boat we said we'd come back on. The Old Man liked to eat early, though he didn't eat much; he just went through the motions. Pam and I had rented bicycles and ridden all over the island. We'd swum on the outer beach, where the waves charged in high as hills, and biked maybe sixty miles. The sun had scorched us. We both had that pleasant, beach-drugged feeling, the taste of sea salt in our lungs. Coach Maretta sat down, crowding the table. The blond light still washed the tall, old-fashioned windows.

"Get Joe a beer," the Old Man told me.

"Nah," the coach said. "I can't stay, Frank."

He dug in his shirt pocket and brought out the clipping. He didn't say anything, just handed it across the table to me. There was silence while I read it. Pam and Frank had stopped eating. "Nickinello School of Umpiring," it said, and pointed out, as if anyone reading *The Sporting News* wouldn't know it, that Nick Nickinello was a former big-league umpire. He was, actually, one of the greats. Sessions lasted six weeks and cost $400, room and board included. I handed the ad to Frank.

"There's about sixty guys in each class," Mr. Maretta said. "The best ten get jobs in the minors. Guaranteed."

The Old Man passed the clipping to Pam. He looked doubtful.

Mr. Maretta said, "I only mention it because of your God-given talent. You could be a big-league umpire."

My heart jumped. I stared at the wide, square face of the coach, which was knitted up, deadly serious. Pam had finished reading. She handed me the ad very slowly.

"You don't realize . . ." Maretta began. "I don't know what makes a good umpire. Reflexes? Good eyes? I don't know. You've got it, whatever it is."

"It's easy," I said.

"No, it isn't," Maretta said.

"Lee's going to college," Pam said.

"I know," Maretta said. "He *should* go to college."

"Of course he should," Pam said.

She'd never liked Maretta particularly. He was a little roughed-edged for Pam. She said he was dumb. He wasn't.

"If it was me," the coach said, "I'd want to know. I just thought Lee should know."

"Any money in it?" Frank said.

"Decent," Maretta said. "Winters off. Retire at fifty-five with a nice pension."

I could see new, warm color in Pam's already brilliant face.

"Joe, I dunno," Frank said.

"It's a hell of a choice, I know," Maretta said.

"On the other hand," Frank said, "Paul didn't go to college. He seems happy enough."

"Well, I've had my say," the coach concluded. He pushed back his chair.

"Show Joe to the door," ordered the Old Man.

I jumped up.

"See ya around, Frank," Mr. Maretta said. "So long, Pamela."

"Take care, Joe," said the Old Man.

Pam nodded.

I followed the coach through the living room and outside into the dying light and the smoky shadows of the elms. He drove a station wagon, like all coaches, a gray-blue clunker listing on bad springs. He opened the door but did not get in.

"I don't know what to tell you," he said.

"You sure you're right?" I said.

"No question."

He studied me. His face softened, lit with that smile. On the ball field he had cussed me, he had ranted with that blast-of-gravel voice, but always for what I could have done better and had not. I'd been too damn complacent—always. I was a good ballplayer, steady, all-league—but not a great one. I'd be forgotten in three years, whereas Joey's exploits would live for twenty. The time he knocked the third baseman's hat off with a line drive. The time he struck out ten hitters in a row. In school I'd been a B student, all the way down the line. How many A's could I have pulled down? I knew dumber kids who earned A's. I closed the books too early at night. I skimped. I didn't care.

Joe Maretta lowered himself into the car, rocking it. "You're workin' tomorrow night, right?" he said.

I nodded.

"I'll stop by," he said.

Again I nodded. A big-league umpire. The best in the world.

"Thanks for coming by," I said.

"You bet."

Inside the light had died suddenly in the tall windows around the dining table. The Old Man played with his spaghetti, shoving strands of it this way and that. Pam watched me come in. Her mouth was shut tight.

"How *'bout* that?" I said.

"I dunno," Frank said.

"Don't know *what*?" I said. I pretended not to notice the hard look Pam was giving me.

"Joe know what he's talking about?" the Old Man asked.

"Sure he does."

"I just don't know," Frank said.

My plate was empty, and I grabbed it and went out for more. The kitchen was small, with red-brown linoleum worn through at both doorways. In the backyard an elm towered, reaching over the small, tired garage, where our old hoop and plywood backboard still hung. The hoop jutted netless, growing rust. I thought of Joey, darting and feinting, twirling high off the ground as he floated the ball through—*swish*—with just a flick of his wrist. On a dry winter day, a new basketball bounced high off the hard dirt of the driveway—*pang, pang, pang*—with the echo twanging off the board fence. The white paint on the backboard still wore fingerprints where Joey had held it wet and bolted it in place, too impatient to wait another night for the paint to dry. He had to start shooting right away. The damp paint had dabbed the ball all over, but the paint had worn away quickly.

I came back with a hill of spaghetti. The Old Man eyed me, the lines webbing his face. "What about college?" he said.

"I don't know," I said.

"I don't believe this," Pam said.

"I have to work my way through college," I reminded her. "Not like you, Pam."

She glared, her blue eyes spitting light.

"It's true," I said. "I'll be washing dishes, working in the laundry . . ."

"Paulie didn't go to college," mused the Old Man, stroking his chin.

"That's right," I said. "He seems to have survived."

"I don't believe this," Pam said. "*I do not believe it.*"

"It might not be so bad, Miss Pamela," the Old Man said.

"She doesn't know what it's like to be poor," I said.

"We can't afford to be so choosy, Miss Pamela," Frank said gently.

Pam liked the Old Man. She wasn't going to argue with him. She waited and after Frank had gone to bed—he went early when she was at the house, skipping getting drunk—we had our first real fight. We hadn't said one word since Frank had climbed the stairs with the dog clomping behind. We were sitting on the sofa in the flickering light of the TV, watching without seeing, thinking our own thoughts, a mile apart in the softness of the couch. At last, when I figured Frank was asleep, I said, "Why do you want to deprive me?"

"*Deprive* you?"

"Here's my one chance to be somebody."

"An umpire? *Somebody?*"

"You snot."

"Snot? Because I believe in the value of an education?"

"Education isn't everything."

"It is," she insisted. "If you have the brains, it is."

"Maybe I don't have them."

"You *do*. You could amount to something."

"What? A schoolteacher?"

"What's wrong with that?"

"I don't see it at the top of your list."

"I don't rule it out," she said.

"My ass," I said.

"Don't be vulgar."

"I can't help it."

"Try."

"You sound like your mother," I said.

"*You* sound like an umpire," she said.

I laughed. We were like a couple of kids throwing things at each other, grabbing whatever came to hand and letting fly. From the other end of the sofa, Pam sent me a steely sideways look.

I said, "Let me give it a try."

"I can't stop you."

"I can always go to college later."

"People say that, but they never do."

"How the hell do you know?" I was starting to heat up again, but I closed my eyes, waiting it out. Pam was staying silent. Her gaze was glued stubbornly to the TV.

She spoke finally. "We won't see each other, you know."

"Not for a while," I agreed.

"Is it worth it?"

"I don't know," I said and slid over to her. I reached around her. She didn't budge. "Listen," I said. "If I don't do this, I may never get out of this town. I'll be stuck here. Like Paul."

"No," she said. *"No."*

"Let me try it, Pam. Please."

"I can't stop you," she said again.

"You probably could."

She looked at me. She swallowed and blinked, knocking two fat tears over the edges of her eyes, down the slow curves of her cheeks. I pulled; she came.

"I love you," I said.

I hadn't said it till now. I suppose I hadn't been sure it was true, though when I look back, I see it was, maybe from the first date.

Pam sighed and returned it. "I love you, too."

"So there," I said.

"I want the best for you, Lee."

"Maybe this'll be the best," I said.

"I hope so," she said without much conviction.

I made the inquiries and discovered I'd have to hang on in Florida when the six weeks of umpiring school ended. I'd have to go to work because I could only rise by working. There would be fall and even some winter tournaments, college and high school, and then, if fate willed it, a job in professional baseball in the spring. Pam and I decided I'd come home at Thanksgiving—Christmas at the latest. Even Thanksgiving seemed too distant to imagine.

The summer flew by. The leaves turned a darker green, and the evenings now were clear and golden, cool as soon as the sun was gone. Labor Day came, and the town emptied, the cars flowing in a slow and endless river through the intersection by Dimmick's Gulf, creeping along full of kids and luggage toward the bridge in the distance. The next day the beaches were almost empty. Traffic moved easily along Main Street. A hush had fallen, eerie until you were used to it.

On Pam's last night, her parents insisted on having dinner alone with her. I could have her later. I ate supper with the Old Man, getting up every ten minutes to look at the clock on the kitchen wall. The sun was going down in a blaze of gold over the dark tops of the elms. Frank was in a black mood, saying little, stabbing angrily at his food. He was drinking vodka with his dinner, tossing it down like milk or beer. He wouldn't be upright long, I guessed. He thought the world of Pam, and I guess it worried him that we were separating. Eight o'clock came finally, and I grabbed the car keys off the hook by the kitchen door and was on my way.

Pam and her parents were still at the table. Her kid brother had eaten his ice cream and vanished. No one had turned a light on, and the rooms were thick with evening shadows. Coming through, I saw Pam's suitcases at the bottom of the stairs, and a chill pierced me, a feeling like autumn. The time was dwindling; our moments together were racing by. I wanted to grab Pam and get the hell out of there.

"Sit down, Lee," Mr. Rogers invited. "Have a glass of wine."

I did not want to sit down, but Pam sent me a wink and a nod, her promise that there would be time later. I sat down. Her brother's dish was in front of me, smeared with chocolate ice cream. I pushed it back. Pam rose and went to get me a wine glass. She touched my shoulder as she circled past.

"We've been talking about college," Mrs. Rogers said.

There was sugar in her voice. Tomorrow, she was thinking, Pam would be done with me.

"College," I repeated.

"Did you know I was a Bryn Mawr girl?" Mrs. Rogers said.

"Pam told me," I said. I tried the wine. It pricked my tongue, dry and bitter.

"I've been telling Pam all the marvelous things she has ahead of her," Mrs. Rogers said.

"Has Bryn Mawr changed a lot since your day?" I asked.

"Good heavens, no."

"There've been a few changes," Mr. Rogers said. "For instance, the invention of the electric light. It's made an enormous difference, Edna."

Pam giggled, and I set my wine glass down quickly, spitting laughter. Mrs. Rogers stared quietly at her husband.

Pam said, "Just think how much time it took getting down there by stagecoach, Mother."

This set the three of us off again. Mr. Rogers had a throat-clearing laugh, like a cough. Pam's giggle doubled her over.

Very dryly Mrs. Rogers said, "Ha, ha, and ha."

"It was my fault," I said.

"It *was* a rather silly question," Mrs. Rogers said.

"I know," I said.

"Mother," Pam said, "tell Lee about the time President Lincoln came to speak."

"Pamela, *really*," her mother said.

Mr. Rogers winked at me.

"Let's talk about *you*, Lee," said Mrs. Rogers.

"Well, I leave in three weeks," I said.

"Someday, Edna," Mr. Rogers said, "we'll go to Boston and watch this boy umpire."

"I think I'll pass," said Mrs. Rogers.

"Edna doesn't like baseball," her husband explained.

"To put it mildly," Mrs. Rogers said.

"It's not for everybody," I agreed.

"Certainly not." Mrs. Rogers glanced at Pam.

Mr. Rogers said, "Well, we don't want to keep you two."

"Speak for yourself," said Mrs. Rogers.

"We're leaving," Pam said.

"Lee hasn't touched his wine," protested Mrs. Rogers.

I could fix that. I did. It tasted like chalk.

"Gracious," Mrs. Rogers fluttered, watching me chug it.

Pam bounced up, and I did, too. Time slowed. The night was young. Looking again at the suitcases, I felt a nice blend of the sweet and the sad.

"You be home early," Mrs. Rogers said. "You're getting up at six, remember."

"I'm aware of that, Mother."

"Where are you going?" Mrs. Rogers asked.

We didn't know.

"Oh," I said vaguely, "just for a drive."

"Well, be home early."

The door banged behind us, clinking the brass knocker. I held the car door for Pam. She had flicked on the radio when I got in. In those days we all listened to 1010, WINS, in New York City. It traveled up over the water, clear and powerful. Little Richard was singing.

We wandered aimlessly, heading nowhere. I drove by the water; it was dark as blue steel, strafed with the gold of the setting sun.

"What do you want to do?" I said finally.

"We could take a walk."

"Then watch some TV."

Watching TV meant necking on the sofa.

"We'll watch a lot of TV tonight," Pam said.

I left the car in front of my house. It was dark in there; the Old Man was asleep. I offered Pam my hand, and we walked slowly down the gently winding road, smothered now in the evening shadows of the ancient elms. Crickets whirred in the tall grasses and thickets of cherry and bittersweet.

"They gave me a sex lecture," Pam said. "That was the first order of business."

"With your brother sitting there?"

"Sure. They told me not to sleep with anybody. They said I'd always regret it."

"How would they know?"

"Don't ask me."

"I bet your father got laid before he was married."

"Who knows?" Pam said.

I said, "Who'd they expect you to sleep with?"

"College boys."

"If you sleep with anybody, it better be me."

"It will be," Pam said.

We passed Lucinda Fragosi's pastel-green house, and I remembered Joey braced in the aisle of the swaying school bus, telling them all to stop ragging Lucinda. We passed the Hollister place, its shingles painted white, with dormers. An enormous house. I wondered where Martha and Judy were these days. College, I supposed.

We passed a steep hill with a big house planted on its summit. It was a summer house, empty most of the year.

"Remember when we used to go sledding here?" Pam said.

"I don't know why someone didn't get killed by a car," I said.

"How did we stop?" Pam asked.

"I don't remember."

"I don't, either," she said.

"Maybe we just shot right across the road," I said.

"God," Pam said.

We turned down the dirt road, past the field where I'd played sandlot baseball. Kids still played here; the ground was bald at home plate, at the bases, and where the pitcher stood. They'd been babies when I was playing. The field swept downhill to a marsh; a fly ball into the marsh was a home run. The railroad tracks rode across the marsh on a bank of rock and cinders. Beyond the tracks lay a pond, and beyond that, misty in the distance, the ocean. After playing ball all day, we would lie in the grass, swapping dirty jokes and smoking dry leaves rolled in brown paper. It tasted disgusting, but we thought it was smart and funny. Those were nice times. We lay in the grass as the spring afternoons faded, gazing out over the marsh and the pond to the blue mirror of the sound. Once in a while an orange and black New Haven Railroad diesel would putter by, dragging a couple of box cars. Or the silver Budd car would scoot past, finishing its run from Boston. We smoked, farted, laughed, swapped jokes.

Why do bees buzz? You'd buzz too, if you had your honey between your legs.

The jokes always had to do with sex.

Little Boy Blue, but his mother caught him. I heard that one a hundred times and would laugh, pretending to understand it. *The wind blows for free; how much do you charge?* Finally I asked Joey what "blowing" was. Joey explained, trying hard not to laugh.

Now Pam and I sat down in the dark, cool grass along the first base line, exactly where I'd plunked down after a ball game with Joey and Howie Gladding and Robert

Nailer and the rest. When had it ended? What day in our lives had we played here for the last time? There had been one final game, one last swing of a bat, one last out made, and we'd mounted our bikes and pedaled home in a spring dusk for the last time ever, without knowing it. I wished I could remember that time.

We were sitting with our shoulders touching. Pam's legs were folded against her, her arms wrapping her knees. The darkening field fell gently to the tangle of the marsh. This had been a nine-hole golf course once upon a time, continuing across the dirt road where the mown grass had long since gone to wild meadow. People still came to drive golf balls. I never saw them, but we were always finding golf balls nestled in the grass. Anyone who found a golf ball would pounce on it, grab a bat, and fungo it into the blue sky, the little ball soaring as if Babe Ruth had hit it. It was always a treat to find a golf ball to hit.

One day Joey discovered one at the edge of the woods on the first base side. I remember him spitting on his hands, then picking up the ball and our Louisville Slugger. Joey could hit a baseball farther than most of us could hit a golf ball. He hung the ball in the air, stepped, and pounded it. Just then, Howie Gladding emerged from behind the tennis court. What he'd been doing down there, I don't know. Small in the distance, he trudged along, unaware that a golf ball had been fungoed in his direction. No one but Joey could have hit it that far. The ball descended slowly, dropping out of the sky onto the point of Gladding's turnip head. It hit and shot sideways.

Howie kept walking. He did not flinch or fall down or even rub his head. He kept walking and commenced to swear. With his big voice, carrying far as a foghorn on that spring afternoon, he cussed Joey. "Gawdamn," he bawled. "You gawdamn shithead. You fuckhead. You dick." And so on. Joey didn't mind being cussed under the circumstances. Howie traipsed on in, spewing every filthy word he knew, some of which did not apply, like *whore*, for instance, and *cunt*. He exhausted his vocabulary on Joey. Grinning, Joey said he was sorry. The rest of us laughed. The more Howie swore, the more we laughed, till finally Howie was laughing, too. All that cussing had soothed away the pain—if there'd been any in the first place.

The laughter had just died when Mrs. Howland arrived. Mrs. Howland lived at the top of the hill, about a quarter of a mile as the crow flew. She scudded onto the field, a big-eyed wildness in her face that froze us where we stood, everyone preparing to run for it if need be. She marched to the middle of the ball field, stopped, and slapped her hands on her hips. She began to shriek.

She'd been having a tea party on the terrace. One of the ladies was from England. Howie Gladding's tirade had come floating up the hill, every word distinct. Mrs. Howland said she'd never been so humiliated. It had busted up the tea party. Mrs. Howland ranted on, silver-voiced. We were a disgrace, disgusting, our parents ought to be ashamed, et cetera. We listened politely. I remember Joey standing with his arms clamped on his chest, a knee bent, squinting earnestly as if Mrs. Howland was expounding some theory that interested him. She said she hoped we were proud of what we'd done today and departed with her chin in the air.

We waited a safe interval, then laughed till our guts burned. We all fell down laughing. Turniphead laughed till tears came, delighted with the way things had turned out. Joey said he wondered what the word for *cunt* was in England, and we amused ourselves guessing. Maybe, Joey said, the word for *cunt* in England was *cunt*, which started a new roar of laughter. Joey said the odds of that golf ball landing on Howie's head were about a million to one. More, someone added, considering the shape of Howie's head. It was like hitting a pin, he said. Even Howie laughed.

Those were nice times.

The Old Man was up when we got back to the house. I couldn't believe it. I'd left him vodka-woozy and still drinking and was sure he'd gone to sleep. I couldn't remember seeing such a resurrection; when Frank drank himself to sleep, it lasted till sunup. But now the lights were on, and the Old Man was watching TV. Here was one more obstacle to my farewell necking session with Pam, and seeing the Old Man awake sent a jab of irritation through me.

They'd begun showing nine o'clock movies on TV, and tonight Frank was watching *Titanic*, starring Clifton Webb. I wished Frank would go to bed; Pam read the wish in my face and laid a finger to her mouth, saying hush, everything will be fine, only have patience. It was a promise, so I resigned myself to more waiting, and we sat down with the Old Man, one on either side and the dog cramming in as well. After a while I went to the kitchen and found some cookies, which we shared across Frank's lap. Toward the end of the movie, they kept showing the ship sinking, tiers of lights tilting steeper and steeper. I pointed out how flat the sea was, like water in a bathtub. Frank shushed me, the way he'd done years ago when he used to take us to the early show at the Empire. Clifton Webb's son gave his seat in the lifeboat to a woman; Clifton Webb was very proud, though he didn't quite bring himself to say so. It wasn't a bad movie, I guess, but I was so hot to get my hands on Pam that the picture seemed to crawl. I was terrified Frank would want to watch the eleven o'clock news, but when at last the picture ended, he heaved a long, husky sigh and stretched.

"Bed time, Zeke," he told the dog.

I bounced up. "Lift," I said. "Monkey grip."

"I don't need any lift," the Old Man said, but he gave me his hand, fingers hooked, and I hooked mine and whisked him to his feet. He'd sobered up considerably.

"Come on, Zekey," he said, and the two of them clumped outside to pee—out back because of Pam.

In a couple of minutes Frank and the dog came shuffling through, and the Old Man said his good-bye to Pam, shy, offering his hand and not quite meeting her gaze. He was crazy about her, though. She'd been why he'd rallied tonight. Pam took his hand but darted in and kissed his whiskery cheek. Frank smiled the wisp of a smile.

"You come back, Miss Pamela," he said.

"I will."

"Don't you forget us, now."

"How could I?" Tears had sprung to Pam's blue eyes. "Good-bye, Mr. Malcolm."

"So long, kiddo."

He turned and stumped up the stairs with the dog scrabbling floppily at his heels.

"God, I'm fond of him," Pam said. Her eyes still glistened.

"He feels the same about you," I said.

"I hope so," she said.

Then I doused the light. Leaving the TV on, we got down to business on the sofa. We advanced quickly tonight, impatient, moving against each other and groping with a new boldness. We sank down and lay in a tangle. My knee was between her legs. Gradually I tugged her blouse out till I could insert my hand. This much we'd done before. I explored the lovely valley of her back, crossing the bra strap to the humps of her shoulder bones. Down again, always gently, to the softness above her hip bones, and around to the firm, hollow nape of her belly. Then, for the first time, I hunted for the buttons of her blouse. Pam rolled back and took my hand: *Stop right there.*

I sighed. I wasn't embarrassed, really.

"Not yet," Pam said.

"When?" I asked.

She didn't answer.

"Why won't you talk about it?" I said.

"I don't know," Pam said.

"We're the only virgins in our whole damn class," I said.

"We're *not*," she said.

"How do you know?" I said.

"You can tell who is, just the way you can tell who isn't," she said.

"Crap," I said.

"Are we going to fight?" she said. "Are we going to fight on our very last night together?"

"It's not our very last night together."

"For a while it is."

I stared at the ceiling, which was a dirty buttermilk in the daytime but was now a restless white-blue from the TV picture. I began thinking of all the things I would never do again, like eating lunch with Pam in the high school cafeteria and playing baseball, and how odd it was—how incomprehensible—that these experiences were gone forever. The ache was ebbing in my groin. I stared and thought, and suddenly Pam sat up, startling me.

Her face was composed and cool in the fitful light thrown by the TV. I wrinkled my face, inquiring with a look that asked what was up. Pam bowed her head and began unbuttoning her blouse.

My heart went crazy. Pam had called my bluff; now what? I didn't know. I was almost scared. She worked her way down, one button, two buttons, three. She unbuttoned the cuffs, shooting me a smug, proud look that made me love and want and fear her, too. She shrugged; the blouse fell away, light as air. I watched, wild inside, helpless to act. Pam reached behind, arching her back, and unfastened her bra. She hunched, and the bra dropped. I stared. Pam dipped her head, splashing her bare shoulders with the tan cascade of her hair. Her straight-edged profile was pleased with itself and at the same time faintly sad. She was beautiful. I stared. She returned the stare finally.

"We're not going to make love," she said, her voice rustling silk.

I nodded. I was relieved in a way.

"Take your shirt off," Pam said.

I floundered up and undid my buttons with thick, clumsy fingers. The air felt strangely cool on my chest. I tore off my shirt. Pam reached for me, and we lay down in this new way, unlike anything before, a closeness that was more than skin against skin. It probably would have been different next time, but for now this was enough. I was no longer hot and horny. A calm had come over us. This was everything. Pam was soft and warm and dry against me. I moved my shoulders ever so slightly, and my hands went everywhere. Every moment was delicious.

We didn't speak for the longest time. Finally I said, "Are you okay?"

"I'm fine."

"We didn't need to make love," I said.

"We will one day," she said.

"You didn't think I was pushing you, did you?"

"No," she said.

"I wasn't," I said.

"I know."

"I never would," I said.

She giggled. "I know that."

"You won't be sorry?" I said.

"Whose idea was it?"

"Yeah, but you might think I pushed you."

"You're funny, Lee. I love your funniness."

"Tell me when you want to go home," I said.

"I don't want to go home at all. I want to sleep in my lover's arms."

"That'd be nice."

"Remember our night on the beach?"

"Your mother never knew?"

"Nope."

We were quiet for a while. Pam's breasts were half-circles. They were softer than they looked.

"You're so beautiful," I said.

"No, I'm not."

"I don't want you to leave."

"I'll write you as soon as I get down there," she said.

"I'll come for Thanksgiving," I said.

"You may not be able to."

"I'll come if I have to walk."

"I hope so."

"It's not so long," I said. "Thanksgiving comes before you know it."

"At least come for Christmas," she said.

"Thanksgiving," I promised.

.   .   .

A little after one-thirty a car stopped in front of the house. It hesitated, idling, and then the engine died. I untangled myself, rose, and peeked out the window.

It was Pam's father.

"Fuck." I whispered it.

"What?" Pam hissed, snapping up and grabbing her bra.

Mr. Rogers killed the headlights. He did not get out of the car.

"Who is it?" Pam hissed.

"Your old man."

Pam closed her eyes. She swallowed; her shoulders fell. The TV still flickered—some ancient Western—but I'd killed the sound long ago.

"He's still in the car," I whispered, watching out of the corner of the window.

Pam thought a moment. She seemed at ease with her bareness, natural as if she were fully dressed. I was getting used to it myself.

"What the hell's he doing?" I said.

"Mother sent him."

"Yeah?"

"Yeah. I have to go, Lee."

"That bitch. That fucking bitch."

She put one arm and then the other through the straps of her bra. The bra clamped on with a quick, expert lifting of her shoulders. That loss, all in a moment, cut deeper than the years of loss I'd been thinking about tonight. Pam was pulling on her blouse and walking out, and tomorrow she'd be speeding south on a train. And there was nothing I could do about it.

"Why did he have to come?" I said.

"Because Mother sent him."

"Your fucking mother."

"Par for the course," Pam said.

65

"Wait'll she hears," I said. "Oh, Jesus."

"She won't hear."

"She'll hear, all right."

"My father won't tell her."

"Sure he will."

"Leave my father to me," she said, just as wise as anything. I scrambled back to the window. Mr. Rogers sat in his car. "It isn't his fault," Pam said. She'd found her comb and was pulling it through the curtain of her hair, tilting her head over.

"I just wish he hadn't come." I felt drained out, hollow.

Pam opened her purse. She rammed in the comb. I hurried over and sat with her.

"I can't stand this," I said.

"Good-bye, Lee."

"Come to Florida with me," I said.

"Don't be silly." She smiled. I thought, *How the hell can she be smiling?* A flash of anger, like jealousy.

"I mean it," I said, babbling like a crazy man. "Go to college later. We'll both go later."

Smiling, she leaned and kissed my mouth. "Take care, darling."

"*Listen* to me," I said. "I'll support you."

Pam stood up. She bent way down and left a kiss on my forehead. "I love you," she said.

I fell back. Pam wasn't leaving; this was a dream. "Wait," I said.

At the door Pam blew me a kiss. "I love you," she said again, and the door took her, closing with a scrape and a bump.

I pitched forward off the sofa and like a wild man scrabbled on all fours to the window. Pam went briskly to the car, head up. The street lamp shone down. Mr.

Rogers leaned over and pushed the door open. He moved slowly, sadly. Pam jackknifed in. The engine shivered to life, its strong rumble filling the wide, empty night. The headlights burst on. The car lurched, then drifted out into the pale-lit road. The hum of the engine slowly subsided till there was nothing but me and this old, small, strong-smelling house.

The next three weeks did not fly by, but I can't say they crawled, either. My suffering lasted three days, and then the ache softened, turning almost sweet. The days were golden and very warm. Each afternoon I walked down the railroad tracks with Zeke, cut over to the shore, and swam, the ocean and the wide crescent of the beach all mine. Nights, the Old Man and I watched movies. I wrote to Pam every few days, telling her how much I missed her and loved her and so on. There wasn't much else to write about. The second week I got a letter from her. She wrote long ones, I would discover, detailed and chatty in a highly literary way. She talked about her courses at Bryn Mawr, her professors, her roommates. She did not mention boys. I missed her and loved her, but excitement rose in me as my leaving drew near, crowding out the sadness. You could count on both your hands the number of times I'd been off the Cape.

The night before I left, Paul came for supper. He brought a huge steak and two six-packs of expensive beer. The three of us had a fine time, slugging beer out of the bottle and talking about the future. Paulie was learning to cook fancy; the steak came with mushrooms, and the green beans were cooked with bits of almond. After dessert Paul reached around and took a small package off the windowsill, gift-wrapped with a red ribbon. I'd noticed it there and guessed easily enough that it was my farewell present. Frank and Paul watched me unwrap it, leaning forward, eager.

It was a wristwatch. A nice one, self-winding.

"God*damn*," I said, "do I need this!"

"Yeah?" Paulie said, his lank face brightening.

"Jesus," I said, "I'd have had to buy one. I've been putting it off."

"We were lucky, huh?" Paul said to Frank.

"Any moron could have told you he needed a watch," Frank said.

"Do umpires wear watches?" Paul asked.

"They must," I said.

"In the big leagues," said the Old Man, "they got clocks in all the stadiums."

I went out into the kitchen and set my new watch by the clock above the sink. I buckled it on, shaking it to wind it. You could hear it whirr.

"I see somethin' else over there on the windowsill," Frank said.

"An envelope," Paul said.

"You better get that, Lee," Frank said.

I did and sat down. The envelope just said "Lee," written in Frank's small, tight scrawl. It was tucked, not sealed. Inside were three spanking-new $20 bills, a shower of money in those days.

"Jesus Christ," I said.

"Don't drop it all in one place," Frank said.

"It's from both of us," Paul said. He was beaming.

"You guys are super," I said.

The Old Man cooked me bacon and eggs in the morning. I'd lain awake so long, my belly was hollow with hunger, so I wolfed the food happily. Frank hovered, glum, that blackness in his face. We didn't talk. He drove me to the railroad station. I bought a ticket for all the way to Florida. The Old Man waited on the platform with me. We both gazed down where the rails met in the distance. The lines beside Frank's eyes slashed up and down, crisscrossing. I tried to remember when those lines hadn't been there and could not. Sometimes it seemed that Frank had been born old.

"I'll write," I said.

"You better," he said.

"I'm gonna miss you, Frank."

He turned away, tiny and hunched with his hands in his pockets.

I wished the damn train would come.

"Call Paulie when you want company," I said. "Or Doc Jones."

The doc was an old family friend, a widower.

"I bet the doc would watch some of those old movies with you," I said.

The train whistle yowled in the distance.

"You ought to take Zeke on some walks," I said.

The robot face of the Budd car swelled, two square eyes of tinted glass. I would go to Boston and get on a real train. The Budd car slowed, click-clacking. The conductor hopped down as she shuddered to a halt. A few people climbed on.

"All aboard."

" 'Bye, Frank."

"So long, kiddo."

I gave him a hug. He didn't hug back, just fell against me. I took a long breath of his ripe, old smell, then released him. I picked up my suitcase, a monster. Just about everything I owned was crammed in there. From inside the train Frank looked even smaller. His hands were in his pockets. I waved to him through the green-tinted window, but he didn't unholster his hands. The train gave a jerk and commenced to roll. The Old Man stood there with his hands in his pockets, his gaze fixed straight ahead, and slid out of sight.

4

St. Petersburg, Florida
October 11

Dear Pam,
It is a week since I got here, although it seems
like yesterday. The heat is terrific, but I have never
minded heat. There are palm trees everywhere.

The Nickinello Umpire School was a former Catholic elementary school. It had a red tile roof and looked like a
hacienda in a Western movie. Palm trees nodded over it.
The ball field, our laboratory, was the old school playground. It was hard and dusty, with a red-brown clay infield that absorbed the heat till you could feel it through
the soles of your shoes. Nick Nickinello said that the fields
in the low minor leagues weren't much better. He said
we'd better get used to it.

We ate in the school cafeteria and slept on cots in the old gym. Mornings we went to class, cramming ourselves into school desks and jotting notes while Nick lectured. Sometimes Nick brought in a guest speaker, an umpire or a former player. After lunch we went out into the heat and worked on the ball field in simulated games, with the fellows taking turns playing the field and Nick hitting the ball out of his hand. We worked two umpires at a time. The two-man system prevails everywhere in baseball except Triple A and the majors.

After supper most of the fellows headed into St. Petersburg or St. Pete Beach, either to bars or the movies. The idea always was to hunt for girls. A lot of the fellows had cars. Many were in their thirties and even their forties. Many were local. Not all wanted to make the major leagues or even turn pro. Some were college, high school, or semipro umpires who simply wanted to get better.

Many are married, and wouldn't you know it is the married ones above all who want to pile in a car and look for girls in St. Pete? I didn't go. I did not come to Florida to look for girls. I have a girl, right?

Nick Nickinello was, I think, the biggest man I'd ever known. Talking to him, I had the feeling I was speaking up the side of a hill. His hair had grayed. His hands were blunt and thick and knotty. He'd been a catcher in his youth and had jammed and broken quite a few fingers. When he smiled, his eyes narrowed and turned down at the edges, cartoonlike. Often Nick would eat supper with us and then linger to shoot the breeze. He would spin wonderful stories and answer your questions. He was one of the great umpires, and yet not everyone at the school took advantage of the nights he hung around the gym. I did, naturally. Me and my friend, Eddie Snyder.

Eddie was too small to be an umpire. Oh, he could have worked junior high games. High school, maybe. Eddie knew it, but he forgot sometimes. He let himself believe that hustle and good eyes were all an umpire really needed at any level. Eddie loved the game even more than I did. Quick on his feet, he hustled and he ran on every play. He yelled his calls in a thin, girlish shimmer of a voice.

After supper Eddie and I lie on our cots and talk about ourselves and swap stumpers from the Rule Book. I have told Eddie all about you and shown him your picture. Eddie went to a college in Pa. called Franklin and Marshall, which he says is no great distance from Bryn Mawr. Eddie does not have a girl.

Eddie's father was a schoolteacher, and Eddie was going to be one. He would umpire as a sideline, a hobby—high school, he hoped, maybe Pony and Legion. He'd been equipment manager for his college team—anything to be near the game. Eddie plain loved baseball, and Nick Nickinello loved Eddie for it. He loved Eddie's hustle and the way Eddie yelled his calls. Eddie was Nick's pet, which bothered only one person. Just one, and that was enough.

Dave Boyd could have been a good umpire. He was a tall, strong kid, rugged and intimidating. But he wouldn't hustle, wouldn't run. It was beneath him somehow. He wouldn't listen to Nick. He wouldn't listen to anyone. If you told him you batted .350 in high school, he would say he batted .360. If you told him you'd read *Huckleberry Finn* two times, he'd announce he'd read it three or four. He hated criticism. Even more he hated to be ignored. Nick's mistake was ignoring him.

The trouble began a couple of weeks into the session when Eddie walked into the locker room and found his shoes and jockstrap filled with toothpaste. Eddie had no idea who might have done it. I knew. I'd seen Boyd's face when Nick was doting on Eddie—the lofty disgust. Eddie picked up his shoes and the gooey jock and went to the middle of the room.

"Who's the bastard that did this?" he demanded.

I was watching Dave Boyd. Boyd was undressing. He was smiling.

"Eddie, I didn't," someone said.

"I wouldn't do that, Eddie."

And so on. Eddie scanned faces till he found Boyd. Boyd's grin widened. Eddie marched over.

"Clean it up," Eddie said, his voice low.

"Fuck you, Snyder," Boyd said.

Eddie's smooth, oval face was dark as a beet. He hesitated, shoes in one hand, jock in the other. I wondered what he'd do and decided I'd better not wait to find out. Boyd smiled as he watched me drag Eddie away. I pushed Eddie down onto the bench in front of his locker.

"Let it go, Eddie," I said. "Let it go."

"It was a joke," Boyd said.

"That's right," I said.

"You got to be able to take a joke in this world," Boyd said.

"That's right," I said.

Next day my shoes and jock had received the toothpaste treatment. "Let it go," Eddie said sarcastically. I let it go.

• • •

Nick Nickinello's Ten Commandments:

1. Never let anyone call you "horseshit."
2. Be stationary when making a call. It is like taking a picture. If you're moving, the picture blurs.
3. When working the plate, don't let the catcher talk too much. It will distract you, and he knows it.
4. Never confer with your partner between innings after a close call and an argument. It will look as if you doubt your call and have gone for reassurance.
5. Before a close play at the plate, remember to peel off the mask without knocking your cap over your eyes.
6. Never hurry a call. Wait. Be sure. That second of hesitation makes all the difference.
7. Listen to an argument for a minute or so—if there is no cussing. If he keeps it up, walk away. If he follows you, warn him. If he follows some more, unload him.
8. Don't let them jaw at you from the bench. It tarnishes your game. Walk over there and shut them up.
9. Never say, "One more word and you're out of here," unless you're ready to toss the guy. Guaranteed, he will say one more word.
10. Never let anyone call you "horseshit."

As I said, we took turns playing the field and running the bases while two of us umpired. When you weren't umpiring, you were supposed to pay attention to the two who were. Nick would stop every few minutes to explain things and pop questions.

Rain was coming. The sky shed a waxy glare. No breeze stirred, and the air was sticky. It was hot. Eddie was plate umpire. I was working the bases; nobody was on. Nick fungoed the ball down the right field line, past the right fielder. I sprinted down the line, following the ball. I had to see, first of all, whether it was foul or fair. Second, it might clear the fence, and sometimes from a distance you can't be sure whether the bounce is on your side of the fence or beyond.

The ball didn't reach the fence; it landed fair by six inches and skidded. The right fielder chased it. The runner was rounding first. Eddie was trailing him, which was my job ordinarily, except that I was in the outfield. The secret of the two-man system is swapping responsibilities. You have to be fluid. It requires some imagination sometimes. The runner swung around first, with Eddie shadowing him. He hit second base and kept running. Eddie stuck with him and positioned himself for the close play at third. It would have been close—that is, if the ball hadn't struck a pebble and shot by the third baseman. The runner had slid. He hopped up and headed for the plate.

Eddie now had been left behind. He'd lost position. I'd been thinking ahead, however. Suppose the throw got away from the third baseman? The chances were slight. They are in most leagues. But you have to use your imagination. *What if*? So instead of trying to follow the base runner, I scooted straight home. *I got it Eddie; I got it.* You have to talk to your partner; you have to let him know. Now Eddie could relax. I was there. The catcher's mitt swallowed the throw, and the tag fell, nipping the leg of the sliding runner. I waved him out with the gesture we'd all learned: driving a dagger down through a door.

Nick came waddling out, tapping his bat against his thigh. A bat in the paw of Nick Nickinello looked like a little wand. Nick had never taught what Eddie and I had just done. He shambled out to Eddie, stopped, and clapped his thick, sun-darkened hand on Eddie's shoulder. He looked all around the field.

"*That*, fellas," he boomed, "is the way it's done."

Eddie and I walked off the field, giving way to two others. Dave Boyd was standing along the first base line. We had to pass him. He kept his thin, long eyes on us, and as Eddie brushed past, he flipped Boyd the finger. A cold smile stirred in Boyd's face. I grabbed Eddie and yanked him away.

"What'd you do that for?" I whispered.

"I felt like it," Eddie said.

"Leave the guy alone, Eddie."

"Leave *him* alone?"

"Just leave him alone."

"Tell him that," Eddie said.

Ten minutes later the rain struck. Clouds came piling in—hunks of slate—and a sudden wind grabbed the tops of the palm trees. Thunder stuttered in the distance, tore loose, and raced toward us, rattling louder and louder. "Let's get outta here," hollered Nick, but the rain caught us, raking the field. It felt wonderful, beating down so cool, but we ran anyway, laughing giddily like a bunch of kids. We crowded inside, spikes clattering on the cement stairway, and down into the rainy-day-dimness of the locker room. Eddie and I sat down on the bench in front of our lockers. There was the biting odor of hot balm, the yeasty sweetness of talcum.

Across the room Dave Boyd sat down, closed his eyes, and tilted back his head, enjoying the rain still streaking his face. Eddie stripped quickly and vanished into the shower. He always showered and dressed promptly, as if it made him uncomfortable to be naked in the midst of so many hairier, thicker-muscled bodies. I watched him come out of the shower; he was thin and ribby, like a little boy.

Boyd wandered into the shower. I still sat, just my shirt peeled, wondering what Boyd was going to do about

Eddie giving him the finger. Boyd would do something, I knew. Eddie sat with me, arms dangling between his thighs. His shirt was still unbuttoned. His feet were bare.

"Why don't you take your shower?" he said.

"I will."

"I want to go eat."

"Why'd you give Boyd the finger?"

"Here we go again."

"Why?" I said.

Boyd came out of the shower. He took his time dressing. He dashed talcum into his wool socks and sheathed his long, arching feet. He tied his shoes. He was still shirtless; his chest and shoulders were white, his neck and arms red as new brick against the white, as if he'd been painted. He straightened now and looked over at Eddie.

"Hey, Snyder. Did you flip me the bird out there?"

"I sure did," Eddie replied.

"May I ask why?"

"May I ask why," Eddie came right back, "you put toothpaste in my shoes?"

"Who says it was me?"

"Who says it was me that gave you the finger?" Eddie said and let loose an airy, nervous giggle.

"You give me the finger again," Boyd said, "I'll break it off, you little shrimp," adding, "you little girl."

You could hear the fluttering splash of rainwater from a gutter spout outside the high window. Eddie and I were buddies. We were the two most serious candidates in the current crop at Nick's school, devoting ourselves day and night to umpiring. Our determination had made us a pair. Now the fellows all watched me. It seemed I owed Eddie something. I sighed. All right.

"What do you have against Eddie, Dave?" I said.

Boyd considered me with narrow, glittering eyes. The rainwater shimmied down outside the window.

"I don't like suckin' ass," Boyd said. "I don't like the way you guys suck up to Nickinello."

"Who sucks up?" Eddie snapped.

"You. You been kissin' Nickinello's ass ever since you got here."

"We're just trying to learn, Dave," I said.

"He's got a lot to offer," Eddie said.

"He hasn't got shit to offer," Boyd said.

"Neither do you," Eddie said.

"How would you like another shower, faggot?" Boyd said.

"Fuck you," Eddie told him.

"Yeah?" Boyd said and started toward us.

He looked immense to me at that moment—narrow-hipped and broad-shouldered, his arms curving out from his body. It was beginning to look as if he really was going to heave Eddie into the shower, clothes and all. He advanced, smiling a mean squib of a smile. I stood up. I got between him and Eddie. Boyd shoved past me; I grabbed his arm.

"Let's drop it, Dave," I said.

Boyd shook me off with a powerful shrug. I grabbed him again, and this time he grabbed me back and threw me aside. I held on. We went down, bringing the bench over with us. I felt the hard, warm cement against my shoulder blades, bone bruising, and saw Boyd reach back and swing. The punch exploded under my eye, jolting the world to a dark blur. I rolled, half blind, before he could hit me again and pushed up, lifting him on my back. Shadows clogged my vision. Nausea swept my belly. Boyd locked his arm around my neck, squashing my Adam's apple. He was trying to lift and turn me so he could belt me again. I tore his arm away, astonished by my own strength, and realized Boyd was gone.

I climbed to my feet and saw Nick Nickinello. Nick was furious. Pain now was swamping the left side of my face, liquid and throbbing. Woozily I saw Boyd, standing uneasily with his hands on his hips. I was aware, too, that the fellows had all gathered around, hemming us in.

"What," growled Nick, "in the goddamn *hell* is going on?"

The pain blazed in the bone of my cheek. My belly still roiled.

"Boyd started it." It was Eddie.

"Yeah?" Nick said.

"Nick," I said, "can I sit down?"

"You better," Nick agreed.

A couple of the fellows righted the bench we'd knocked over, and I sat.

"It had nothin' to do with Malcolm," I heard Boyd say. "I was gonna throw Snyder in the shower."

"And why," Nick said, "if I ain't bein' too nosy, were you gonna do that?"

"To shut his wise little mouth."

Nick sighed, the sloping hills of his shoulders lifting slowly.

"You okay, Lee?" he asked.

"I guess so," I said. My voice sounded far away.

Nick frowned, considering what he should do. Everyone waited. The side of my face was a sheet of flame.

"All right," I heard Nick say. "Can I see you in my office, Dave?" The voice was gentle, golden. "Get your shower, Lee. Eddie, fetch him some ice from the kitchen. Then I want to see you fellas, too."

He turned, swaying as he walked. The fellows broke up, scattering to their lockers. Boyd finished dressing. Eddie put his shoes on.

"I'll get you some ice," he said.

I nodded.

"I'm sorry," Eddie said.

I just nodded. I could feel my face swelling, stretching the skin and pushing my eye shut. Slowly the locker room filled with the buzz and mutter of voices. In the shower fellows asked me if I was all right. I said yes, though I wondered what "all right" meant. Boyd had really walloped me.

Eddie was waiting with the ice when I came out. It was wrapped in a dish towel. The rain had stopped, and already the sun was honeying the windows of the locker room. Eddie waited while I dressed. Neither of us said anything. We climbed the stairs and crossed the gym, which was cluttered with cots and suitcases thrown open on the floor. I pressed the ice to my face. It froze the pain on the surface at least, stopping that rolling throb.

Nick's office had been the principal's office when this was an elementary school. A bulletin board hung outside the door, plastered with newspaper clippings—clippings slapped on top of clippings until the board had been buried. There were stories about the school and about Nick. There were accounts of great rhubarbs, both in the big leagues and the minors. You could hear Nick's voice punching its way through the door.

"Are you mad at me?" Eddie asked.

I sighed. "No, Eddie."

"Yeah, you are."

"I just don't feel well."

"I didn't want you to get hurt," Eddie said.

I closed my eyes. The ice was melting, soaking the towel and dripping on the floor.

"Eddie," I said, "why didn't you keep your mouth shut down there? Why did you have to push it?"

"I don't know," he said. "I just don't like to be bullied."

"You don't have to antagonize people."

"He antagonized *me*," Eddie said.

I gave up. Eddie folded his arms, leaned back against the wall, and squinted up at the fluorescent light.

"You'd think I was the one that hit you," he muttered.

I didn't answer him. Inside the office the conversation was winding up. The voices grew, coming nearer to the door. I heard Boyd laugh. He sounded satisfied, even happy. The door jerked open. Nick held it for Boyd.

"Malcolm," Boyd greeted me, "you okay?"

"Sure."

"I'm sorry, man. I'm really sorry."

"Don't worry about it."

"Friends?" Boyd stuck out his hand, the one that had bashed me.

"Sure."

We shook. He shook Eddie's hand, too. Eddie didn't say anything.

"See you guys at dinner," Boyd said.

"Come on in, you two prima donnas," Nick said.

The office was littered with cardboard cartons stuffed with papers. There were shelves stuffed with Rule Books, old *Baseball Registers*, and trophies. The yellow concrete walls were busy with photographs of Nick during his umpiring days. One showed him squeezed down in his crouch, hunkering as low as a man that huge can go, peering over the catcher's shoulder while none other than

Joe DiMaggio coiled for his swing. I saw another of Nick in an argument with someone I didn't recognize in a Washington uniform, the two of them rubbing up against each other and hollering. Nick towered over the fellow.

"Sit down, boys," Nick told us.

We did, choosing two wooden armchairs from the little audience arranged in front of the desk.

"How's the eye?" Nick asked.

"It hurts."

"I bet it does," Nick said.

"I'm glad you came along," I said.

"What happened down there?" Nick said.

I let Eddie tell. He gave it to Nick pretty straight. Nick nodded, furrows rumpling his face.

"It's my fault," he said. "I should have paid some attention to Boyd. It wouldn't have killed me."

"He doesn't listen," Eddie said. "He thinks he knows everything."

"Not really," Nick said. "It's all bluff, Eddie. The poor bastard's all bluff."

"Not all," I said.

"Not all," Nick agreed. He looked at his hands, folded on his desk blotter. Nick had short fingers. The hands were oblong and very thick, like cushions. He studied them.

"I was on my way down to talk to you, Lee," he said. "I got a call a little while ago from a fellow over in Sanford, runs a baseball school. His fall tournaments are comin' up, and he needs an umpire. He's in a jam."

I stared at Nick's furrowed, thoughtful face.

"I get a lot of these calls," Nick went on. "You'd be workin' two games a day, every day but Sunday. Six bucks a game. You interested?"

The pain in my face melted and was forgotten. "What

about the school?" I said. We still had another two weeks.

"I'll graduate you early," Nick said.

"What about the test?" At the end of the six weeks came a written examination.

"I'll waive it," Nick said. "You know the Rule Book."

Eddie, silent all this time, said, "What about me?"

"What about you?" Nick said.

"Can your friend use two umpires?"

"I thought you were gonna teach school," Nick said.

"Not till January," Eddie said.

"Stay here," Nick said.

"It wouldn't be the same without Lee." Eddie's voice faltered. "I . . . Nick, I don't want to be here when Lee's gone."

Silence. Nick unclasped the brown wads of his hands, the fingers crooked and knobby where he'd busted them.

Softly he said, "You'll be fine, Eddie. I'll see to that."

Eddie's gaze jumped from Nick to me and back to Nick. "Get me a job over there, Nick. Please?"

Nick sighed.

"Eddie," I said, "you don't know how rough it can be. High school and Legion is one thing, but after that . . ."

"It's true," Nick said. "These tournaments are college teams, and you'd be amazed what foul mouths those college boys have. On the other hand . . ."

"What?" Eddie said.

"Well, the tournaments ain't all that bad. The boys are there to learn, mostly. It's basically an exhibition season."

"Well, then," Eddie said.

Nick thought some more. "Tell me what nine-oh-one-A says."

Eddie piped right up. "The umpire shall be responsible for the conduct of the game in accordance with these official rules and for maintaining discipline and order on the playing field."

"Kee-rect," Nick said. He smiled, tugging his eyes to a warm squint. "Eddie, there's no question you can make the calls. It ain't that. It's nine-oh-one-A. Tell you the truth, I'm a little worried about your buddy here."

"About me?" I said.

"That's right," Nick said.

"I'll be okay," I said.

"They don't scare me, either," Eddie said.

"It's all right to be scared once in a while," Nick said.

"We'll be fine," Eddie said.

"Well," Nick said, "I can get you a job over there, Eddie. Then go home and teach school, okay?"

"I will," Eddie said.

"We're all set, then," Nick said. "You guys can leave in the morning."

"Is Boyd gonna be all right?" I asked.

"Yeah, I got it all smoothed over," Nick said. "I told him to start hustlin', and he could be a good umpire. I'll pay lots of attention to him the next two weeks."

"He might be good," I said. "He's tough enough."

"He might," Nick said. "You got to be tougher yourself, Lee."

"Don't worry," I said.

Nick's smile widened. "It'll be a while before I forget you two guys."

I said, "We'll be in touch, won't we, Nick?"

"You bet," he said.

"Wish us luck," Eddie said.

"I do," Nick said. "Believe me."

You wouldn't have known it was November except by the calendar. The days were warm. Baseball weather.

There is nothing to do but work. Nights, we go to the movies. We see every show that comes to town, sometimes twice.

On Sunday afternoons old men played chess or checkers by the lake, leaning over with their chins in their hands.

I just cannot get away for Thanksgiving—I don't know how I thought I could. I don't have the money or the time.

The baseball school was located in an old minor-league stadium about a mile from the center of town. It was like minor-league ballparks everywhere: roofed grandstand, ten-foot outfield fence, spindly light towers, RC Cola scoreboard. Outside the stadium were two more ball fields so there could be three games going simultaneously. The proprietor, a big lefty pitcher who had hurled briefly for St. Louis, gave evening clinics on hitting and throwing. The games were played at ten in the morning and at two in the afternoon. Eddie and I always worked together. The fields outside the stadium were like the country ball parks of the Cape League. Old men from across the street would drag lawn chairs over and sit in the sun watching the ball games. Working in the stadium was tougher but more satisfying. In the stadium the boys concentrated harder. When ballplayers concentrate, umpires must, too.

Eddie and I lived in a tiny apartment above an electrical appliance store on Main Street. We walked to and from work. We passed the lake and then a neighborhood of houses sitting close to the street, all with shade porches. In the late afternoons people would be sitting on the porches. Some said hello; some did not, though they saw us day in and day out. Conversation would break off as we approached. Everyone would watch us till we were out of hearing.

> *. . . cannot come for Christmas after all. The bus takes three days one way, that is almost a week traveling time. Plus the money. I have begun saving for a car, which I will need if I get a job in the minor leagues. I only hope Nick Nickinello knew what he was talking about. He said it is only a matter of time before someone notices me, which is why I must keep working.*

Closer to the stadium was the black section. Kids would be playing in the weedy dust morning and evening. They would stare at Eddie and me. We'd call out hello, and they'd call it back to us. The black neighborhood was the friendliest, which seemed odd, considering the way white people behaved down here. It wasn't just the segregated restaurants and diners. Eddie and I actually saw a gas station with a sign by the pumps: WE SERVE WHITES ONLY. I told Eddie I wanted to ask the owner why. Eddie said it wouldn't do any good. I said I didn't expect it to, but I was curious to hear what the man would say. I couldn't imagine what he'd say. The segregation sickened Eddie as much as it did me, but we were just kids miles and miles from home, working hard at getting by, and we stayed out of it.

> *. . . to thank you for your Christmas check. Frank and Paul sent money too. I bought two shirts, a Christmas present for Eddie (Brownie camera), and Christmas dinner for Eddie and me at a good res-*

taurant. I also put money toward the car. Eddie gave
me a pair of umpire shoes with the steel tongue to
protect your foot from fouls. I have been working in
baseball shoes all this time—it's a wonder I haven't
busted my foot. Soon Eddie will head north to teach
school.

On New Year's Eve we went to the movie *Shane*, which had come out a few years ago. I'd seen *Shane* the first time with Joey and Paul and the Old Man. Joey had loved it. He'd seen himself, I suppose, in Alan Ladd, who finally declares his own one-man war on the gang that is trying to run the homesteaders out of the valley. Alan Ladd didn't have to get into it. He could have just drifted on. Joey was Alan Ladd—Shane—gunning down Jack Palance in the saloon. It seemed like a century ago that I'd sat in the popcorn-fragrant Empire Theater with Joey and Paul and the Old Man, watching *Shane*.

. . . want you to know I still love you and hope
somehow we can make up for lost time when I finally
get home. Please write.

Three days before Eddie was to leave, we came in from working our morning game and found Les Walker, the ex-pitcher who owned the baseball school, waiting for us at the gate. Les said he wanted to talk to me in his office. He didn't say anything about Eddie, but Eddie tagged along just the same. We followed Les into the warm shade under the grandstand and to the concrete burrow that was Les's office. Les opened the screen door for us, and there, bigger than I remembered, sat Nick Nickinello. A second fellow, thin and vaguely blond, sat next to him. I barely noticed the thin man. Nick hoisted himself to his feet, beaming his crinkly smile. It was wonderful to see him.

"The prima donnas," he said.

"Hey, Nick," I said.

Nick grabbed my hand. He grabbed Eddie's.

"How you been, Nick?" Eddie said.

"No complaints," Nick said. "Fellas, meet Walt Waddell."

Waddell stood up. He was tall and hollow-chested. His yellow hair looked damp. He wore a necktie and a seersucker jacket like the Old Man's. His smile looked like an effort; it was more a grimace than a smile.

"Sit down, boys," Nick said.

He and Waddell sat down in wooden armchairs. Eddie and I took the couch. Les Walker went around behind his desk.

"So," Nick said, "how goes the battle?"

"Great," Eddie said.

"Walt here is president of the Central Florida League," Nick said.

I knew then what was up. Nick sat forward, jacket tight on his round, hunched shoulders, hands clasped between his knees. Mr. Waddell sat jiggling a knee, a nervous wisp of a fellow.

"Walt?" Nick said.

Mr. Waddell cleared his dusty throat. "Nick tells me you're looking for a job in organized ball, Lee."

"Yes, sir," I said.

"I haven't seen you work," he continued, "but Nick and Les have, which is just as good. So . . ." He straightened, placing his hands on his knees. ". . . I want to offer you a job."

I was excited, of course, but not surprised.

"I have only one hesitation," I said. I looked at Nick. "It's so far from home."

Mr. Waddell turned to Nick, arching his straw-yellow eyebrows.

"Take the job, Lee," Nick said. "In the first place, you'll be jumping all the way to Class A. In the second place, Walt's a good league president to work for. He's a stand-up guy. He'll back you. Some league presidents—Christ—they don't back their umpires. They'll let you hang."

"I appreciate that," Mr. Waddell said.

"It's the truth," Nick said.

"All right," I said. "I'll take the job."

Mr. Waddell smiled his pained smile. "Swell. I can pay you two hundred and ten bucks a month, plus expenses. You got a car?"

"Not yet."

"Get one. Get a good one. You can't be breakin' down."

"I've been saving," I told him.

"I'll hate to lose you," Les Walker said.

"It's not till April," Mr. Waddell said.

I'd forgotten Eddie. He was beside me on the sofa, sitting back with his arms folded, drinking it all in. Now he said, "You got any more openings?"

Everyone stared at him. Eddie was sitting back with his arms folded stubbornly, his chin tucked down.

Mr. Waddell said, "Openings for who?"

"Me," Eddie said.

"You're too small," said Mr. Waddell. "Christ, they'd murder you."

Gently Nick said, "You don't want this, Eddie. You really don't."

"Will you quit telling me what I want?" Eddie said.

"What about your teaching job?" I asked.

"The hell with it," Eddie said.

"Don't be foolish," Nick said.

"I'm a good umpire," Eddie said. "Les? Am I a good umpire?"

"He is a good umpire," Les said.

Nick said, "Be sensible, Eddie."

I was watching Mr. Waddell. He'd begun thinking. His watery gaze was on Eddie, and his right knee was jiggling harder. He looked at Nick.

"Can he umpire, Nick? Can this little shrimp umpire?"

"Yes and no," Nick said.

Eddie blushed pink and glared at Nick. Anger squirmed in Eddie's thin face. Nick had betrayed him.

"Can you control a game, Eddie?" said Nick, his voice rising. "Can you do that?"

"Yeah," Eddie said. "*Yeah.*"

"It might create some interest," Mr. Waddell said.

"Jesus, Walt," Nick said, "it ain't a goddamn freak show."

"Freak?" Eddie said. "Am I a freak, Nick?"

"Eddie," Nick said, "go home to Pennsylvania, and do what you were meant to do. You'll thank me for it, kid."

"You're trying to stick a knife in my back," Eddie told him.

"No, I ain't, Eddie."

"Lee? You willing to work with him?" said Mr. Waddell.

I hesitated. It would have been tough for Eddie— and me—even in the Cape League—fellows playing ball just for the hell of it, their futures, their livelihoods not hanging in the balance. I remembered how Red Carroll had tried to break me down that first time he'd seen me work.

Nick, reading my face, said, "You want this, Lee? The minors are no day at the beach under any conditions."

"Don't let him turn you against me, Lee," Eddie said.

"I don't want to force you," Mr. Waddell said. "If you don't want to work with him, that's it. End of discussion."

"Lee?" Eddie said. A light danced in his eyes.

"I can't decide for Eddie," I said.

"I asked you will you work with him," Mr. Waddell said.

"Sure," I said. "I'll work with Eddie."

Nick sagged gloomily back in his chair. Eddie threw him a triumphant half-smile.

"It's settled, then," said Mr. Waddell, slapping both knees.

"Thanks for coming over," I said.

"Hey, don't mention it. Nick, I got to run."

"Gimme a minute, Walt," Nick said.

"Sure," Mr. Waddell said. "I'll be in the car."

He pulled the screen door shut behind him.

Nick said, "Remember who your friends are, Eddie."

"I'm beginning to see who my friends are," Eddie told him.

Nick contemplated him, then turned to me. "Stay in touch, Lee. Lemme know how it goes."

"I will."

Nick lifted his mountain of a body out of the armchair. I got up. Les Walker rose behind his desk. Eddie stood but did not look at Nick.

"Don't let me down, Lee," Nick said.

"I won't," I promised.

"Don't let the bastards tarnish your game," Nick said.

"No," I said.

"You too, Eddie," Nick said. "Hang tough, kid."

But Eddie didn't answer him. He wouldn't look at Nick.

The colleges began their season in February, and Eddie and I soon said good-bye to Les Walker and his baseball school. We bought a car, splitting the price—a bright red second-hand Pontiac with 60,000 miles on the odometer. We were college umpires now, and college ball is serious business in Florida. Eddie performed decently. His confidence was high; his calls were good. The boys went easy on him, I thought. I had a few rhubarbs. Not many.

Eddie reads a lot, and I am beginning to pick up the habit, you'll be glad to know. The apartment is getting cluttered with paperback books. Please write.

In March we got a letter by certified mail from Walt Waddell. Our first game would be on April 8 in Daytona. Mr. Waddell enclosed a list of hotels and rooming houses in each of the towns in the league. The league secretary would send us our schedules every two weeks. It was the same in the majors.

Wish me luck. I miss you.

Love,
Lee

5

On April 8, I walked out of a cheap hotel with Eddie Snyder into a blistering Florida morning and headed for the ball park and my first game as a professional umpire. Daytona smelled of low tide: salt and mud. I got behind the wheel of our Pontiac, and we climbed the main strip with the sea spread behind us. Neither of us spoke. My gut was churning. My heart danced. Everything shone in the hard morning light: the whitened roads, the leaves of the palm trees. We drove to the ball park without speaking.

The parking lot was potholed white dirt. The stadium was a brick horseshoe, the brick smudged and weary looking. Several cars crouched near the players' entrance. You could hear the lazy scratching of crickets. Eddie and I hauled our duffel bags out of the trunk and threw them over our shoulders. We went in through the players' entrance.

The inside of the ball park was a grimy basement gray. The cement floors had been pocked and scraped by cleated shoes. Eddie and I wandered, trying a couple of corridors, till we found a small, bent black man in gray janitor's clothes. His face was deeply seamed, an ashy brown.

"Help you?" he said.

"We're the umpires," I said.

"You a bit early," he said. The voice was dry, dusty.

"We're rookies," I said.

"Ah," he said. Then, "Y'all follow me."

He turned, moving patiently down the dim corridor, silent on his long feet. We trailed him, shouldering our duffels. The door to the umpires' room was propped open. The room was tiny, maybe ten by ten: hooks on the wall, table, two folding chairs. A single shower head peeked down. A couple of windows were propped open with Coke bottles. Eddie and I threw down our gear. The old man eyed us.

"Where's the bathroom?" Eddie said.

"Ain't none."

"What are we supposed to do?"

"Wal . . ." He sighed. The sigh lifted his skin-and-bone shoulders. "You can do tinkle in the shower. Ain't s'posed to, but everybody do. Other business, you got to use the visitin' team locker room."

"I bet they love that," I said.

"Depend how the game go."

"What a pain in the ass," Eddie said.

"Don't be blamin' me."

I prowled closer to the shower; the sieve of the drain blew out a stink of urine.

"Jesus," I said.

"You boys new, all right."

"We're green," I agreed.

"Class A ball," the man said. "A long, long way from the big time." He stared at Eddie. "You awful small for an umpire."

Eddie's face clouded. "That's what they tell me," he said dryly.

"Eddie can take care of himself," I said.

"Didn't say he couldn't." The man stood with his hands in his deep pockets. "My name's Chester," he said.

"Lee Malcolm. This is Eddie Snyder."

"Pleased to meet you."

I went over and shook Chester's hand. Eddie roused himself and did the same.

"You need anything," Chester said, "you ask me."

"Like what?" I said.

"Git you sandwiches and beer after the game."

"All right," I said.

"Maybe rustle up an electric fan."

"Do that," Eddie said.

"We'd appreciate it," I said.

"I'll git onto it." He smiled. It was a kind smile, sad lines trailing down his oval face. "See you boys later. Good luck, now."

We thanked him. He gave us a farewell smile and vanished noiselessly. Eddie and I stripped, silent, thinking our own thoughts. Eddie peed in the shower drain, and then I did. We sat down at the table in our shorts. The varnished yellow top had been gouged all over with initials. They'd used pencils mostly, tracing and tracing till they'd dug through to the wood. I read the initials, wondering who'd cut them. I didn't recognize any big-league umpires. "I call them as I see them," someone had etched, "and they ain't nothing till I call them." Eddie didn't seem interested. He sat parallel to the table, staring at the floor.

"How you feeling?" I asked.

"Nervous."

"It's just another ball game."

"It is like hell."

"I know," I said.

"Aren't you nervous?"

"Sure I'm nervous."

"I hope I don't puke," Eddie said.

He sat a while, naked, fragile, staring at nothing. Worrying about him, I wasn't thinking of myself. The doubts, the perils, all seemed to hang over Eddie's head. My nervousness was for Eddie, not myself.

"Chester seems like a nice fellow," I said.

"Did he have to mention my size?"

"Better get used to it, Eddie."

"Easy for you to say."

"What do you want me to say?"

Eddie sighed. "I don't know."

"Are your parents small, Eddie?"

"Yeah."

"It's funny," I said. "My old man's tiny, and look at me. My brother Joey was built like a Greek god."

"You're lucky," Eddie said.

"I know it."

"Maybe your mother was big," Eddie said.

"She couldn't have been too big."

"Well, you're goddamn lucky, Lee. Being small is no picnic."

"No," I agreed.

The fans were on Eddie from the moment we climbed the dugout steps into the brightness and dry, raw heat.

"Hey, midget."

"Hey, ump, ya mother's callin' ya."

"Hey, who zat, Shirley Temple?"

The voices were close by, just over our shoulders.

"Bastards," Eddie said.

"Forget 'em," I said.

"Fucking bastards."

"You can't let 'em distract you, Eddie."

We walked to the plate and waited for the managers. The little ball park was stuffed: Opening Day. The pitchers were warming up on the sidelines. The sun beat down out of a cloudless sky. I was chewing gum rapidly, around and around. The managers, Johnny Gibbon for Daytona, Gil Jones for Winter Haven, bounced out of the dugouts and came on the jog, both young men. We all shook hands.

"Welcome to the league," Gibbon said.

"Virgins, I hear," said Jones.

"I used to have your baseball card, Gil," I said.

"No shit?" Jones said, grinning.

"What about mine?" Gibbon said.

"I think so," I said.

"I was up longer than Gil was," Gibbon said.

They handed Eddie and me their lineup cards. Over our shoulders someone yelled, "Hey, Gibbon, where'd you dig up them umps, man?" Gibbon stuffed one hand in his hip pocket and, pointing with the other, recited the ground rules. The outfield fence, I remember, was so rickety that the ground rules provided for balls that struck the fence and became lodged between two planks. Automatic double, of course. There was a storage shed in the left field corner; a ball that hit the shed was in play. Eddie and I listened carefully. After a while you learn every ground rule in every park by heart, and the pregame gathering becomes a formality, a kind of social occasion.

Johnny Gibbon finished his spiel. "Any questions?" he asked.

"I guess not," I said.

"Nope," Eddie said.

"Let's play ball," I said.

I stayed where I was while the others scattered, the managers to their dugouts, Eddie to first base. I was sweating richly. My longjohns sponged up the sweat. They would also keep the dust off my skin. The chest protector hugged me warmly, and the dark blue shirt and trousers soaked up the heat.

Applause exploded as the Daytona players spilled from their dugout and went frisking out to their places. The pitcher strolled to the mound and kicked some dirt around, doctoring it to his liking. He threw some warmups; I crouched, jamming down and sighting over the catcher's shoulder to get the feel of it. The ball darted, whapping the big mitt. The kid had good stuff.

The anthem played, an old record, floating scratchy and quavering out of the staticky PA speakers. My heart sped up as I listened. The flag hung limp, as if tacked to the blue sky. The anthem finished tremblingly, and the crowd gave a cheer and sat down. I checked my ball and strike indicator for about the tenth time, making sure it read zero–zero. I looked down at Eddie. He stood with his hands clasped behind him, busily chewing gum, munching it around and around and shooting quick, almost secretive glances at the crowd.

The lead-off hitter ambled into the box. He spat over his shoulder. The pitcher rubbed up the ball, his glove clamped under his arm. I bent down and whisk-broomed the plate, then pocketed the broom against my hip. The catcher sank in his crouch. I pulled down the mask, shutting myself in, and, filling my lungs, bellowed the old command: "Play ball."

•　•　•

Good call, Eddie. Good call.

His silky voice sailed and shimmered, bright with confidence.

"Yeah, he got him, outta there."

"Foul ball, foul foul foul . . ."

The pitchers were good, pouring strikes. The game flowed, rhythmic. Windup . . . pitch . . . *whap* in the mitt . . . *Stee-rahhk!* Two notes, high and low, a down-sliding sound. Don't rush the call. Windup . . . pitch . . . *whap* . . . *stee-rahhk!* A ball is *buh.* You dismiss it, *nuh.* You have to sell a called strike three, and you don't wait, not this time. You whirl immediately; you wave him out of there with body English—no doubt about it. Slam that fist; put the mustard on it.

Eddie was hustling, sprinting to position.

Good call, Eddie. Good call.

No arguments. Nothing. Until the fifth.

The cleanup hitter for Winter Haven bounced one to the third baseman, who gloved it prettily and snapped the throw—high. Eddie was in position, right angle to the throw, and on this routine play did something unexplainable and astonishing, which was to drop to one knee. It might not have mattered had the throw been on the money. But the ball sailed high, and the first baseman leaped, snaring it and twisting as he came down, slapping a blind tag on the runner.

I assume he tagged him. Because when Eddie called him safe, the floodgates opened. Johnny Gibbon, so amiable in the pregame conference, shot out of the dugout, rage twisting his face. Johnny grabbed the hat off his head and ran at Eddie, screaming. Eddie squared to meet him. The first baseman was also yelling. The crowd let go a torrent of boos. Gibbon and his first baseman, a kid named Borders, surrounded Eddie, yelling down at him.

It had been the right call in a sense. Eddie hadn't seen a tag, and you never call what you don't see. However, Eddie *couldn't* have seen the tag down on one knee.

The two men, both big, bellowed their tirades while Eddie tried to reason with them in his soft, smaller voice. ". . . Didn't see shit. . . . Where were ya, for Christ sake," and so on, while Eddie purred, "That's the way I saw it; I'm not gonna change it, fellas."

Eddie turned and walked away from them. They chased him, scrabbling around in front of him. He was going to have to unload them. I pulled off the mask and headed out there. The crowd kept up the dark, windy booing, and a few crumpled Dixie cups came arching out the grandstand.

"Let's break it up," I said. "Come on, John. You've had your say."

"It isn't your argument," Gibbon snapped.

"Oh yeah, it is. I'm in this, too."

"We're talkin' to your partner."

"Talk to me, too," I said.

The crowd was jeering and booing and tossing more Dixie cups. Gibbon and Borders were yelling again at Eddie. It was obvious they had to be tossed, and I was praying, *Toss 'em, Eddie; toss 'em.*

Finally Eddie did. Gibbon first. Eddie reared back and flung the arm around, saying, "Outta here" in a ribbony squeal. Borders still wouldn't leave, so Eddie heaved him, too. Now they had nothing to lose; they could say anything they wanted. They let go, cussing Eddie worse than he'd ever been cussed. Squirt. Choker. Horseshit. Eddie tried to walk away, but they followed him, raining the insults on him. I got between Eddie and Gibbon and began nudging Gibbon backward. I wondered if he'd slug me. It happens in the minors. I was going to slug him back; I'd marked the spot, the middle of his forehead. I had to settle this thing, or I wouldn't have a moment's peace the rest of the season, just as I had had to shut Red Carroll up that first time in the Cape League. Already Eddie was through. He'd taken too much. Eddie was through from that moment. I pushed, and Gibbon gave ground, hollering over my shoulder at poor Eddie.

Borders was coming slowly, walking a few steps, turning and yelling, walking, turning and yelling. Gibbon was in the dugout, and I went to Borders and told him to get the hell off the field. He did. I stood at the edge of the dugout till Gibbon and Borders collected their things and vanished into the tunnel. I was breathing hard and pouring sweat.

"I don't want to hear any more," I said, looking up and down the bench. They answered me with flat, wary stares. I spun away, and a beer bottle plunked on the turf ten feet from me, bouncing and somersaulting. The crowd cheered. I picked up the bottle and tossed it to the Daytona bat boy.

"Get rid of this," I said.

I couldn't visit Eddie. He was chewing his gum furiously. Fellows in the box seats behind first were riding him fiercely. The second baseman was scooting around picking up the paper cups, cradling them against his chest. A new first baseman came out to replace Borders, circling over to tell me his name. I wrote it on the card. The catcher waited in his crouch. I went around behind him. The crowd began to subside.

"Your partner blew it," the catcher said.

"Yeah?"

"He blew it."

The kid spoke without turning, still hunkered in his

crouch. You don't mind a catcher or hitter jawing at you if they don't look back. The crowd doesn't know you're being spoken to; you're not being shown up.

"I couldn't see the play," I said.

"I saw it," the catcher said.

"So did Eddie," I said.

"Tell me about it," the catcher said.

"If you're smart," I said, "you'll drop the subject."

He did.

The game ended on a swinging strike, and Eddie and I headed briskly for the dugout—resisting the urge to run. A cop met us halfway and walked us in. People were leaning out over the railing, hollering at us. Faggot, pansy, Mutt and Jeff. We clattered down the cement steps and into the safety of the tunnel.

Chester had brought the fan. He'd stuck it under one of the flipped-up windows. It turned slowly, nudging down a sluggish current. Quickly we peeled our drenched shirts.

"Go ahead," Eddie said, "ask me."

"Ask you what?"

"Why I got down on one knee."

"It did cross my mind," I said.

"I don't know why," Eddie said. "I was going so good, I was getting cocky. I was trying to be . . . creative."

"You were creative, all right."

"Yeah."

"I think he tagged him, Eddie."

"No shit," Eddie said.

There was a tap on the door, and Chester crept in, arms full with a six-pack of beer and a carton of sandwiches. He set them down on the table, lowering himself on supple knees.

"Be three dollars," he said.

I fetched my wallet and gave Chester four bucks. He pushed the money down into his front trouser pocket and lingered, watching me punch open a beer and drink half of it in one pull. It was burning cold and delicious. Eddie sipped. He would have preferred an RC or a Coke.

"Wal," Chester said, "you boys done all right."

"No," Eddie said.

"Pretty good rhubarb," I said.

"Yeah, ol' Gibbon, he'll get goin' sometimes."

"He sure does," I said.

"Wal," Chester said, "won't be your last beef."

"He's right, Eddie," I said. "We got to get used to it."

"Can't let folks get you down," Chester said.

Eddie nodded.

"Take care," Chester said. "Tomorrow's a new day."

"He's right, Eddie," I said again.

Eddie nodded. I reached over and gave his shoulder a comforting swat. He managed a smile, but tears had come. Eddie lowered his head and cried silently into his lap, and I wished he'd listened to Nick Nickinello.

If this was Class A, I would have hated to see Class D. The parks were run-down. The lighting was miserable. The crowds were mean. One reason they came, I guess, was to rag the umpires. They were moody, too, sometimes turning on the home team the way a cat will suddenly twist back and claw the hand that's been stroking it and making it purr. There were regular customers at every ball park who had their favorite targets for ragging. It might be a player; it might be an umpire. It might even be a coach. At certain parks there were loud-mouthed, beer-swilling morons who would sit close down and ride Eddie or me the whole game long. I never could figure how these people selected their victims; it was as if the names came out of a hat. The ragging could be good-natured. It could also be ugly. I'll never forget some of the abuse thrown at the black ballplayers. I don't know how they stood it.

I had some rough times myself. One night in Clearwater, I was working the plate when the catcher gunned a pickoff throw to first. Distracted by the throw, I forgot to register the pitch on my indicator. It wouldn't have mattered if the batter had hit the next pitch, but he didn't. A couple of pitches later, I called ball three on what was really ball four. The hitter started to chuck his bat and trot to first; I summoned him back. The scoreboards in those old Class A ball parks didn't show balls and strikes, although that probably wouldn't have mattered, as the scoreboard can be wrong. The Clearwater bench erupted, and the manager, snowy-haired Mike Kirkpatrick, came bounding up the dugout steps. The catcher had whipped off his mask and was yelling. They were telling me to ask Eddie, which I did. Eddie hadn't clicked the pitch, either. It did seem to me it was ball four, but the indicator said three and one. I had to trust it. Besides, if I'd changed the call now, the other team would have descended on me, just as furious. I had to toss Mike Kirkpatrick, a decent fellow who happened to be right this time. It wasn't till after the game that I figured out what had happened.

I had my share of rhubarbs, and I kicked plenty of calls. My trials, though, were nothing compared to Eddie's. The players learned soon enough that they couldn't tangle with Eddie without taking me on as well, but that didn't stop them from nagging him and snarling just a little on the close plays. There was nothing I could do about the fans. I began to wonder if Walt Waddell wasn't right about Eddie bringing in the customers. Sometimes I fantasized about jumping the barrier and grabbing some sweaty drunk by his neck, but it would not have paid off, and the fans knew it. It is easy—and safe—to ride an umpire from the stands.

The strip joint sat along the state highway outside Clearwater, a pair of domes that looked more like silos than what they were supposed to represent. Eddie and I had passed it often, driving back and forth across the crooked trunk of Florida. At night the frilly pink neon sign would be flashing off and on, playful. Come on in, it said. Try us. The Booby Hatch. Eddie and I would laugh at the name and at the two silo-boobs, which Eddie said looked like spaceships or guided missiles.

It was early July now. I hadn't been with a girl, hadn't touched one, since Pam. I hadn't talked to one except the waitresses in the diners and the girls selling tickets and popcorn in the movie theaters. Until lately I hadn't minded. All my energies, every drive in me, had been spent on my work. And there was Pam. At least, there was the memory of her. Pam had become part memory, part promise. It had been enough.

Then we drove past the strip joint one night, and I looked at the lacy pink sign and did not laugh. It was like waking up and realizing I'd fallen behind, maybe hopelessly, in some crucial duty like school or taking care of the Old Man. I felt a flicker of panic, then a familiar ache returned in a great surge. We worked a game in Clearwater the next night, and as we undressed afterward, I asked Eddie if he wanted to go to the strip joint.

Eddie was stepping out of his trousers. He straightened and stared at me. "You're crazy," he said.

"It'll get us out of our rut," I said.

"What rut?"

"Jesus, Eddie. We umpire. We go to the movies. We drive the goddamn car from town to town. What else do we do?"

Eddie shrugged. "I'm happy," he said.

"Look," I said. "It'll be an adventure."

"You're underage," Eddie said. "They won't let you in."

"Sure they will. The guys at Nick's school all said I could get served anywhere."

"I don't want to go," Eddie said.

"Why, Eddie? Why?"

"I just don't."

"Aren't you horny, Eddie?"

"Yeah," he said. "Sure I am."

He looked scared. I saw then that I'd scratched some painful secret of Eddie's—a wound, maybe, left by a girl or by many girls. Eddie wasn't homosexual, I knew that. Maybe he simply didn't crave women, sex, any of it. I never found out. It was Eddie's secret, and I left it alone. But I still wanted to go to the strip joint.

I said, "We'll have one beer, Eddie."

"No."

"Tell you what. I'll work the plate the next four games."

"Look, Lee . . ."

"Five games," I said.

"You'd work the plate five games in a row?"

"Sure."

"You're crazy," Eddie said.

"Please, Eddie," I said.

"All *right*," Eddie said. "If it'll make you happy."

"You're a pal," I said.

• • •

It was a twenty-minute drive. The sign winked, a pink scribble against the blue-black sky. A long awning with a red carpet underneath led you to the door, which was positioned between the two domes. My insides went soft. I didn't know what to expect. I wore my youth and inexperience like a tweed suit of clothes short at the wrists and ankles. I pulled the door open for Eddie.

"You first," he said.

I walked in ahead of him. The lobby was small and dark, with the two large boob-rooms on either side. One boob was empty and unlit. The other roared music and spat flickering colored light. A waitress stepped smartly up to greet us. She was smiling.

"Hi," she said.

"Hello," I said.

She looked very young. She wore a short skirt, black tights, and black high heels. Her hair fell like black rain to her shoulders.

"Sit anywhere you like," she said. "I'll be right with you."

"Thank you," I said. You could barely hear yourself through the blasting music. I plunged into the noise and the fluttering, changing rainbow light.

A round stage nearly filled the room, with little tables around the wall. On the stage a naked woman was dancing. She wore high heels and a G-string. She danced unhurriedly, as if conserving her energy, moving her arms like snakes. I stared. She seemed enormous, bigger than life. She was ripe. Golden. She saw me ogling her and returned the look. Her lush mouth curled faintly. Eddie gave me a nudge. I tore my gaze from the stripper and found an empty table. We sat. Already the dancer had turned and was flaunting herself in another direction. There were men on all sides of her. I watched her. So did Eddie. The waitress arrived.

"What can I get you guys?"

She was smiling. Her mouth was small, her face a perfect heart. She was small-breasted, girlish—especially in the presence of the big woman on the stage.

"What do you want, Eddie?" I asked.

"Beer."

"Two Budweisers," I said and watched her whisk away. I thought she was very pretty.

We watched the stripper. There wasn't anything else to do. It would have been rude to talk. The stripper danced. She looked bored. The rest of the customers had come alone. They sat with their arms folded, their drinks waiting in front of them, some gazing solemnly, some smiling foolish smiles. I felt sorry for them. I felt sorry for the stripper, though I didn't know why. The whole thing made me uneasy.

The waitress arrived with our beer. I paid and tipped her fifty cents. She had green eyes. Black hair and green eyes.

The music crashed and died. The stripper broke off in mid-squirm, and the men applauded politely. No cheering, no whistling. The woman flung her head back and closed her eyes. Then she reached down and snatched the clothes she'd begun in before Eddie and I came and descended gingerly in her high heels. From the middle room came jukebox music, just a murmur after the squall of the dance music. A few lights went on, pale, whiskey yellow.

"What do you think, Eddie?" I said.

"I don't know," Eddie said. "She's awful big."

"Lush," I said. I didn't desire her and didn't know why. "The waitress is pretty," I said.

"She's okay," Eddie said.

"Buy me a drink, boys?"

It was the stripper. She'd covered herself in a red

silk blouse that hung past her hips. Her thighs were at our eye level, honey colored.

"Whaddaya say?" the woman said. She wore that faint, cold smile.

"Uh . . ." I didn't know what to say.

"No," Eddie said firmly.

The golden thighs didn't budge. "You don't like me?" the woman said.

"We like you," I said.

"Leave us alone," Eddie said.

"Leave you alone?" The woman's voice rose, hoarse, sour. Heads turned. "You came *in* here, didn't you?"

"Leave us alone," Eddie said. He sounded pouty. Stubborn. It was the way he'd talked to Dave Boyd, and it had the same effect.

"You cheap bastard," the woman said.

"Fuck you," Eddie said. His arms were folded. He smirked, eyes narrowed.

"You'd like to," the woman said.

"No, I wouldn't," Eddie said.

The woman's face, which might have been good-looking, maybe even beautiful, was warped with anger. Up close she looked older. Eddie stared past her, his arms clamped on his chest. The woman leaned over off her high heels, picked up Eddie's glass of beer, and dumped it in his lap. Eddie shot to his feet.

"You cunt," he said.

The stripper swung with an open hand, catching him on the chin. I bounced up and yanked Eddie out from behind the table, keeping myself between him and the woman. Her face looked fierce. It looked tragic. She stuck her hands on her hips.

"Too good for me?" she said.

"No," I said.

"Whyn't you take your little faggot friend and beat it?"

"I'm going to," I said.

I pulled Eddie by the arm. A man stepped in front of me. He was wide as a door, with a sweaty, reddened face and blond hair. He was a customer; I'd noticed him across the room. He wore an untucked, half-buttoned shirt, white with green alligators printed over it.

"What's goin' on here?" he said. He spoke in a syrupy drawl.

"Nothing," I said. "We were just leaving."

"They botherin' you, Gloria?"

"They're too good to talk to me, that's all," said the stripper.

"You boys better show some respect," the fellow said. His breath reeked of hard liquor. "Gloria's a lady, understand?"

"I do," I said. "I understand. Now I want to get out of here."

I started but the man put his meaty hand against my chest, stopping me. "You best apologize," he drawled.

Now Gloria threw her head back and shut her eyes the way she'd done when the music had ended and the applause had rattled thinly around her—a weary look, I realized, sick of it all. She opened her eyes and said, "Forget it, Jim Bob. The hell with it."

"Wait a minute," said Jim Bob. "They're gonna apologize, Gloria."

"They're rubes, Jim Bob. They don't know better."

I headed for the door, throwing the fat man's hand away and shouldering past him. Eddie stuck at my heels. The waitress was standing in the doorway, resting her tray against her knees. I blew by without looking at her. I was damn sore, even at her. I shoved through the door into the woolly sweetness of the Florida summer night. I was halfway down the red carpet when the door banged again.

"Hey, sucker." Jim Bob. "I want you out back, motherfucker."

"I'm going home," I said over my shoulder and kept walking.

"Not yet, you ain't."

He followed us to the car. When I grabbed the door and turned, he was breathing on me, his face red and flat and seemingly noseless, moist with sweat. Blond curls played along his forehead.

"Yankee pansy," he said.

"That's right," I said and lowered myself into the car.

I did not reach the seat. Jim Bob grasped my shirt collar with both his fat hands and yanked me to my feet. I stumbled as he threw his first ham-fisted punch, which only grazed the side of my head, or I would have been knocked ice cold. I found my balance. He charged, trying to grab me with his left hand and hit me with his right. The punch caught the back of my head. Jim Bob kept coming, bulling me backward till he had me pinned against a car. He smelled of sweat and booze. Again he held my shirt collar. I freed my right arm and hit him in the gut with everything I had.

His wind left in a gush. His big, round fist still clutched my shirt collar. I hit him again, higher, and felt ribs under the jelly of his flesh. He began to cough. His knees were melting. The fist still held. I hit him hard, again in the belly. Jim Bob coughed. He hacked. He let go of my shirt and doubled over, hacking. Eddie and I watched. Jim Bob toppled forward, rolled, and lay on his back on the asphalt, eyes shut, mouth wide.

"Let's get out of here," Eddie said.

"All right," I said.

"Someone's coming," Eddie said.

I turned. It was a tall, good-looking young man with wide shoulders wearing a white silk shirt.

"I didn't start it," I said.

"I know," he said. He leaned down. "You okay, Jim Bob?"

Jim Bob didn't answer. He was rolling around, sucking air.

"Hey, Jim Bob. You okay, man?"

"What the fuck does it look like?" said Jim Bob.

The tall man straightened. "I'm the bartender," he said.

"I'm sorry about this," I said.

"You guys should have bought Gloria a drink," the bartender said.

"I didn't mean to offend her," I said.

The bartender gazed at me. His face was long and shadowy in the darkness. "What did you come in for if you didn't want to have a drink with one of the girls?"

"I don't know," I said.

"I don't see why we have to buy them drinks," Eddie said.

The bartender looked at him. He studied Eddie a moment. He smiled briefly, a flicker. It wasn't unkind.

To me he said, "Gloria's sorry."

"She ought to be," Eddie said.

"Shut up, Eddie." I really snapped at him.

Eddie sent me a simmering look.

"We really didn't mean to offend her," I said.

"I believe you," the bartender said.

Jim Bob had sat up. "You two faggots still here?" he said.

"Drop it, Jim Bob," said the bartender. "The fight's over."

"You're lucky, boy," Jim Bob drawled at me. "He's a fuckin' gut-puncher, Steve."

"It worked," said Steve, the bartender.

"It's chickenshit," said Jim Bob.

"I'm sorry, Jim Bob," I said.

"Fuck you," Jim Bob told me.

"Same to you," Eddie told Jim Bob.

I spun on Eddie. "Goddammit, Eddie, *drop* it!"

"You make me sick," Eddie said.

He got in the car.

The bartender gave me a sympathetic half-smile. Jim Bob labored to his feet. He gave me a last, mean stare and went stumping back to the strip joint. The stare said he wasn't afraid of me.

"What do you guys do?" asked the bartender.

I told him.

He peered into the car. Eddie sulked, staring straight ahead. "That's the little umpire?"

"That's him," I said.

"I'll be damned," said the bartender.

I thanked him for his help and slid into the car. He waved as we wheeled out.

"He's a nice fellow," I said.

Eddie didn't answer.

"You know, Eddie," I said, "you ought to be a little more grateful."

"Grateful for what?"

"Maybe," I said, "I ought to let you fight your own battles."

"Go ahead."

"I will."

"Go ahead."

I was driving. I watched the road.

"All right," Eddie said. "I'm sorry."

He didn't sound sorry. I stayed quiet.

"I'm *sorry*," Eddie said.

"Okay," I said. "Okay."

We didn't speak to each other again till morning.

The waitress was at the ball park alone the next night. I didn't know it till the game had ended and the small crowd was dissolving. She was standing at the barrier between the screen and the first-base dugout.

"Hey," she said in a loud bright way that made me turn.

She waved, then summoned me with a sassy toss of her head. I could feel my face lighting up as I walked over, carrying my mask. She waited, smiling.

"Hi," she said.

"Hi."

"I came to apologize."

"For what?" I said.

"For what happened last night."

"It wasn't your fault," I said.

I looked around for Eddie, but he'd gone in.

The girl said, "I felt bad about it."

I shrugged. I was trying to figure out what she was doing here. She wore a white shirt with the collar lifted, a gray skirt snug on her hips. Her pocketbook rested against her hips; she had a hand on the pocketbook, her elbow cocked. She looked me straight in the eye.

"You licked that big slob, I hear," she said.

"Sort of. He was pretty loaded. I'm not much of a fighter."

"No?"

"I just knocked the wind out of him."

"There was a lot of it," she said.

I laughed. The lights had been snuffed, except for one tower. Two fellows, both black, were dragging the tarp over the infield. The ball park swam with shadows. It looked haunted.

"I never saw anything like that happen in there," the girl said.

"How long have you worked there?"

"Two weeks."

"Oh," I said.

She read my mind. "It's a job," she said.

"I suppose," I said.

"You religious or something?"

"No," I said.

"You came in there," she pointed out.

"My first time ever in a strip joint," I said.

"You must be religious."

"I'm not," I said.

"Look," she said, "my brother set it up. He plays for Clearwater . . ."

"No kidding? Who?"

"Bobby Vadnais?"

"Sure."

"Anyway, one of the girls told Bobby they were looking for a waitress. It didn't involve any stripping or hankypanky. I'd been wanting to see Florida, and Bobby called me. Said he'd found me a job."

"There are loads of jobs," I said.

"You're religious," she said. "I know you are."

"I'm not."

"I was curious," she said. "I wanted the experience. Okay?"

"Where you from?"

"Detroit. You?"

I told her.

"I'm Vicky," she said.

"Lee Malcolm."

"I know. The bartender, Steve, told me."

I reached across the barrier, and we shook hands. I could feel it all the way up my arm. Vicky Vadnais never stopped looking me in the eye.

"Do you have a car?" she asked.

"My partner and I share one."

"I was thinking I could drop you off. If you're not busy."

I was so surprised—stunned, really—I didn't answer right away. She was so pretty.

"You're busy," she said.

"I'm not."

"I can tell," she said.

I laughed. I felt light-headed. "Will you wait while I take a shower?"

"Sure. I'll be in the parking lot. A blue Fairlane."

I hurried through the tunnel, my spikes scraping and pecking the gouged concrete. Under a bare light bulb in the umpires' room, Eddie sat dismally in his longjohns, nursing an RC Cola.

"Guess who I just saw," I said.

"I know who you saw. The bimbo from the Booby Hatch."

"What do you mean, 'bimbo'?"

I began to tear off the protector and my blues.

"She works in a strip joint, right?" Eddie said.

"She doesn't strip," I said.

"How do you know?"

"Jesus, Eddie." I unpeeled my longjohns. "I'm going out with her tonight."

"Swell," Eddie said.

"You take the car," I said.

"How thoughtful of you," Eddie said.

I got rid of my shorts and jock and headed for the shower.

"It bothers me," Eddie said. "You going out with a girl like that."

I leaned out from the hot spritz of water. "A girl like what?"

"Works in a strip joint."

"Fuck that, Eddie. You don't even know her."

"You don't either," he said.

"I think I do," I said.

Eddie was still in his longjohns, sipping his RC. I came out of the shower.

"What about Pam?" Eddie said.

What about her? I didn't know. Right now, there was only Florida and the loneliness that had been slowly, slowly, darkening me inside.

"What about her?" Eddie insisted.

"I don't know," I said.

Eddie drained his soda. He stood up and plodded to his dressing cubicle. "I guess I'm on my own," he said.

"Tonight you are. Big deal."

"Tomorrow night and the next and the next. I can see it."

"Don't worry, Eddie. Just please don't worry." I was pulling on clothes as fast as I could.

"Good luck," Eddie said, doleful as an undertaker.

I peered into the cracked mirror and gave my wet hair a few comb flicks. Eddie stood in the sallow light of the bare bulb, slowly, mechanically, unbuttoning his damp longjohns.

"I'll see you, Eddie," I said.

"Yeah."

"I'll see you soon," I promised and yanked myself out of there.

. . .

The Fairlane waited in the dark, nose in to the ball park. The parking lot was gauzily lit by the stars and by the lights of the houses across the street. The crickets sang. The crickets sing all year in Florida. A couple of ballplayers, one black, one white, lolled against a car, sipping cans of beer. They watched me get into the car beside Vicky Vadnais, who was also drinking beer. On the seat there was a six-pack, minus one can.

"Help yourself," Vicky said.

I found the opener.

"Hungry?" she said.

"We don't eat before a game," I explained.

"The players don't, either," she said.

I pulled at my beer, trying to act knowledgeable. A group of ballplayers spilled out through the archway. Grins cut their faces. Doors slammed and cars started, clawing dirt and pebbles. Another bunch emerged. One of them was Vicky's brother. He was small and black-haired. He grinned and waved.

"You told him?" I said.

"Sure. We're roommates."

"You told him about last night?"

"Sure."

"I could get in trouble with the league," I said.

"For what?"

"Going to a strip joint. Fighting."

"What do you think the players do?" she said.

"I didn't see any last night," I said.

"They go there plenty," she said. "They go to worse places, too."

"Do they sleep with the strippers?" I asked. I thought of Gloria.

119

"The girls charge money for that," Vicky said.

"How do you know all this?" I said.

"I work there. Listen, I'm not like that. Know what I mean?"

I nodded. We drank.

"Bobby says the guys really respect you," she said.

"They do?"

"Yup."

"They don't act like it."

"Well, they're very immature," Vicky said.

I had to laugh. "How old are you?"

"Twenty-one. You?"

"Nineteen," I admitted.

"Jesus," she said. "A kid."

"Yeah," I agreed.

"You got a girl?" She shot it at me, eyeing me. Her boldness kept surprising me.

"I did, up home."

"Yeah?"

"I haven't been out once since I got down here."

"Bull," she said.

"It's true."

"I knew you were religious," she said.

"I haven't had a lot of opportunity," I said. "How come the ballplayers have so much fun?"

"The girls go to them," Vicky said.

"Bobby must have introduced you to a few," I said.

"Yup." She swigged her beer.

"So?" I said.

"So nothing," she said. "They were assholes."

"Who?" I asked.

"Never mind."

She dropped her empty beer can on the floor and lifted down the six-pack. She slid out from behind the wheel and reached around me. The kiss was shy at first but grew. She was relaxed, sure of herself. Finally she leaned back, still holding me.

"I'm not easy," she said. "It looks like it, but I'm not."

"I believe you," I said.

"I just like you," she said. "Why fool around when you like somebody?"

"I agree."

"I'm true blue," she said, "and I'm not easy."

I looked into those bright, smart, green eyes and knew it was true.

There were six teams in the Central Florida League, so I was in Clearwater, where Vicky shared an efficiency apartment with her brother, a sixth of the time. The other towns in the league were anywhere from one to three hours distant, so she and I were almost always in range of each other. I began seeing her whenever I could, which was nearly every night or day.

After a while she quit her job at the Booby Hatch. She knew it bothered me, her working at a strip joint. It wasn't only the principle but all those hungry men getting their eyefuls. Vicky said they didn't look at her. "I have no boobs," she said. I guessed some of them did, though. If they had any taste, they did. She wouldn't have quit if I'd asked her to. She wasn't a girl you could dictate to. There was plenty of fire in her; she was proud and could be stubborn. I had too much sense to ask her to quit her job, and so one day, quietly, she did and let me know in an offhand way. I knew better than to make a big deal out of it. She found a part-time job at a Howard Johnson's. We had more time together now.

Sometimes we went to the beach, where we would lie close to each other, whispering sweet nothings and thinking steamy thoughts. A beach is no place for deep conversation, especially in Florida. This one, Daytona, was wide and flat, the sand a dark, muddy brown. The surf stretched knee deep for what seemed a mile. The water was pea green and warm as soup.

Often in the long day before a night game, we just drove, cruising the sun-bleached roads with the car radio churning out good rock-and-roll. Sometimes we would stop and take a walk in an orange grove or sit in the shade with the fallen oranges scattered in the grass.

Vicky had grown up in Detroit in a mostly Polish neighborhood. Her mother was Polish. Her old man was French and owned a neighborhood barroom. Vicky had waitressed there, underage; the cops knew all about it and didn't care. She said the only people who were particular about goings-on in the barroom were the fathers at the Catholic church up the street and that her old man had to donate to the church every year to keep them from complaining about the betting that went on and the times the place stayed open after hours. Vicky's mother clerked in a discount clothing store. There were two brothers besides Bobby, both still in high school.

She'd come close, I gathered, to marrying her high school sweetheart. He'd gone to college in Detroit—Wayne State University, which I'd never heard of. But then, I probably wouldn't have heard of Bryn Mawr if Pam hadn't gone there. Vicky wouldn't talk about him. She wouldn't say what had busted up the romance. She did say once that he was older than she was. One day I asked her point-blank if she'd slept with him. She stared at me, big-eyed and solemn, and finally nodded her head yes. Then softly she asked me if I'd done it with Pam. I'd have liked to have said yes but was afraid to. I'd have been found out, you see. I admitted I hadn't. Vick said she'd thought as much. We dropped the subject. It was up to Vicky now. All I could do was wait.

We included Eddie as much as we could. We took him to the diners with us after night games; we persuaded him to go with us to the movies. We always had to talk him into it. Three's a crowd, he said. But Eddie couldn't help liking Vicky. She was proud and she was stubborn, but in the end she aimed to please—me, Eddie, everybody. She made Eddie feel at ease; she was just as likely to grab his arm as mine when we climbed the steps to a movie theater or walked out into the dark after eating. She made Eddie laugh with her off-color remarks.

Still, we wanted some privacy, too, and Eddie lay in our hotel rooms many evenings, alone with the jiggling whir of the electric fan, reading paperback novels. Or he would find himself with a long, blazing summer day to kill. I don't know what he did with himself. I wished I could be two places at once.

They were wearing Eddie out now, fast. Sometimes he didn't seem to hear the ragging. When you've been in the pouring rain, wet to the skin, you get used to it after a while—so drenched that it no longer means anything to get rained on. Eddie had reached that stage. He'd become numb to the abuse, which intensified as he ignored it. Then, with a month left in the season, Eddie packed his suitcase on the sly and vanished.

I would have urged him to stay. Stick it out, I would have said. One more month—we could have managed. Maybe Eddie knew. Maybe he didn't have the strength to argue with me. We were in Daytona, where we'd worked our first pro game. It was an off-day, a Monday. Vicky had driven over, and the two of us had spent the afternoon on the beach. We'd walked up to the hotel in our bathing suits at five o'clock.

The room was locked. I let us in. Eddie's things were gone—suitcase, gear, books, alarm clock. I went into the bathroom; he'd cleaned out his toothbrush and razor. Vicky, meanwhile, spotted a note on the bedside table.

> *I didn't even have the guts to tell Mr. Waddell I was leaving. I was afraid he'd blow up at me or, even worse, try to talk me into staying. I just wanted to leave quietly, Lee. I didn't want any scenes. I decided suddenly. You were on the beach. Just go, I decided. Tell Mr. Waddell the truth. Tell him they ran me out of the league.*
>
> *Keep the car. I mean it. It is my way of repaying you. You took a lot of heat for me. I think you'll make it. I think you'll be a big-league umpire. I'll stick to high school and Legion ball.*
>
> *So long, old buddy. I feel better already. Come see me in York, Pa. We're in the phone book. Say good-bye to Vicky. You were right about her.*

I'd sat down on the bed to read Eddie's letter, and as I was reading, Vicky lowered herself beside me. One bed—Eddie and I always took a single room. We would get a second pillow and take turns sleeping on blankets doubled on the floor. I handed the note to Vick.

"Poor kid," she said.

"What'll I do?" I said.

"You better call Waddell," she said.

"Yeah."

"Call collect."

"Think so?"

"Sure. It's his problem, not yours."

So I dialed operator, and placed a collect call to Mr. Waddell at his home in Orlando. I'd talked to him quite a few times over the season. You had to make a report, both oral and written, when you tossed someone out of a game. The familiar, raspy voice came on. He accepted the collect call and asked me what was up. I told him. I could hear him draw a breath.

"Jesus H. Christ," he said.

"I'm sorry," I said.

"You're in Daytona, you say?"

"Yeah."

"Well, shit. All right, kid. I'll get someone over to you. I'll see what Nickinello's got."

"I'll work with anybody," I said.

"You might have to."

"I'm really sorry," I said. "He didn't give me a chance to talk him out of it."

"It's not your fault, Christ knows. You've done a hell of a job. The ratings on you are sky high."

"Really?"

"Hell, yeah."

"They just wore Eddie out," I said. "Nick was right."

"Well, it stirred up some interest. What's to regret?"

"Nothing, I guess."

"I'll dig up an umpire before tomorrow night."

"So long, Mr. Waddell."

"You hang in there, kid."

"I will."

The phone clicked dead. Vick was beside me, close. We both wore the sticky smells of tanning oil, sweat, and sea salt. Vick's charcoal hair was damp and tangled. She wore a black bathing suit, and her skin was as brown as varnished wood. The afternoon was fading slowly, a lazy, golden time of day, a long way still to darkness. Traffic groaned distantly. The hallway outside the locked door was empty. There was no sound, no movement, in the next room.

"Poor Eddie," I said, but my mind wasn't on Eddie anymore.

"He'll be okay," Vick said.

"Think so?"

"Sure he will."

"He does have a college education," I said.

"He'll be fine."

I stared at the floor. My hands dangled between my thighs. I didn't know what to say now. An odd chill played over me.

"I'm gonna take a shower," Vicky said.

I nodded. She rose and went into the bathroom. The door shut. I sat on the bed, listening to the spritz and slap of the shower. My gaze strayed to my watch: 5:26. I thought of Paulie and the Old Man, how they'd given me the watch before I'd left. My brother and my father— they seemed to belong to another world, another life. I thought, *There is no way of imagining what is about to happen.* I looked at my watch again: 5:30. The shower stopped running.

Silence. 5:33. The bathroom door opened noiselessly, and Vicky strolled out wrapped in a towel. Her black hair glistened. She sent me a glance, composed and prideful, eyes all green heat, as she crossed the room to the windows. She yanked down the shades and turned on the electric fan.

I popped up.

"I'd better take a shower," I said.

"No," she said.

"I'm all sweaty."

"No shower. Not yet."

I sat down again, glad to be told. Vicky landed weightlessly beside me. That chill held me; I trembled. Vick smiled. She reached with both hands into the small of her back, and the towel floated to the floor. I had an eyeful of white skin where her bathing suit had covered her all summer, and of small, soft breasts. She lifted her brown arms around me, and finally I began to burn deep down and to race to hardness in the cool damp of my bathing suit. Vicky pulled me gently, leading, and we lay down in the slow, warm stream of the fan.

Now we lay in the sleepy brook of warm air, staring at the ceiling. Peace flooded me, a rinsing lilac-sweetness. Wisdom grew in me. I was a new man. By and by Pam stole into my mind, harmlessly, bringing no guilt, no regret. It didn't even trouble me that I was going home in a month and that Pam would be there. This had happened. It had to. I remembered something Pam had said once about good novels; you can't guess or imagine what is going to happen, she'd said, and yet when it does, you see that it is the only way it could have happened. It seemed to me now that life was the same way.

Beside me Vick rolled her head on the pillow and smiled at me. I rose on my elbow and examined the slender body, the flowing woman's lines. She watched me look at her.

"I told you I had no boobs," she said.

"You're a knockout," I said.

"Me?"

"Jesus, yes."

"You're not so bad yourself."

"Why don't you spend the night here?" I suggested.

She smiled. "Listen to him," she said. "You sound like an old hand."

"I'm not."

She kissed me.

"Was it okay?" I said.

"Sure."

"Really?"

"Everything you do is okay."

"Spend the night," I said.

"Maybe."

"Come on."

"All right," she said.

We had all night and most of the next day. I wondered how many times you can make love in a night. I had no idea. Time now took on new value. Time for making love. I wanted to fuck this girl, fuck her and fuck her and fuck her. Love her and love her and love her.

I was leaving Florida in a month.

"Vick? Why don't you come home with me?"

She stared. "You're kidding."

"I'm serious."

She thought a while. "Do you want me to, Lee?"

"Absolutely."

"I'd have to get a job," she said.

"You can."

"It's quiet up there, huh?"

"In the wintertime."

"I've never been anywhere but Detroit in the wintertime."

"You'll like this."

She rolled against me. "Oh, Lee."

"How 'bout it?" I said.

"I'd have to go home first. Spend some time."

"That's fine."

She snuggled. "My babe," she said. "My guy."

She touched me below, gentle and sure of herself. I was starting again. Hardening.

"Show me what to do," I said.

"You're doing fine."

Then, afterward, I dozed, exhausted by sunshine and loving. I dreamed of Eddie Snyder. Eddie was getting married. The bride was very pretty, with pearl-bright skin and long, glossy black hair. The hair fell, luxuriant, to her waist. The girl held Eddie's arm, smiling, and I realized with a jolt of surprise and pleasure that it was Lucinda Fragosi. Eddie was marrying Lucinda Fragosi. Yes, and she was pretty. *Lucinda Fragosi was beautiful.* You've changed, Lucinda, I said. Oh, I guess I have, she said, as if it had happened a long time ago, and she hardly thought about it anymore. It was a big wedding, held in our house. The Old Man was there.

I woke up.

Dusk had arrived. I could hear the traffic. I could hear the waves scooting up the beach. Beside me, wide awake, Vicky Vadnais watched me open my eyes. I remembered. I smiled.

6

I didn't believe I was going home. I didn't believe it right up until the day I left, which began at five-thirty in a Lakeland hotel room with a farewell fuck, a drawn-out job, double orgasm for Vick, which went to show how far a virgin can advance in a month with practice. It wasn't a tragic good-bye; we'd be together soon enough. My only real sorrow was the prospect of going without sex for a few weeks. Vick and I ate breakfast in a diner noisy with truck drivers' voices. Vick wanted to hold hands across the table of our booth. We twined fingers. Vick's hands were warm; her palms would dampen warmly when we held hands, a woman-wetness that excited me. We said good-bye in the parking lot. We kissed lingeringly. Vicky stood with her hand resting on her pocketbook, her elbow bent, and watched me climb inside the Pontiac. She touched her fingers to her lips and blew me a kiss and a smile as I drove out. I turned on the radio and headed home.

. . .

I arrived at suppertime on the fourth day. The evening was cool and golden, and I thought of the last nights before school began, sad with the death of summer in the air. Excitement began to build in me as I drove into town. I couldn't wait. The town and everybody in it had stayed the same (I thought), while I had aged and lived through great experiences. I loved this town, and I wanted to stand tall in its eyes. Going home, I've since realized, is like returning after a long absence to an old lover.

I swung through the intersection past Dimmick's Gulf. Now the elms arched overhead, and the houses were large and old, many with widow's walks scraping the sundown sky above the trees. I drove past the old bus stop with the same tree we used to stand under, the same bench the girls sat on. Railroad tracks. The Pontiac bumped gently over them. I veered left, and I was home.

I went slowly up the front walk, savoring the moment. The Old Man was on his feet when I walked in. He stood in the middle of the room, halfway between the sofa and the TV, a sideways grin snuggling up his creased, yellow-brown cheek. The dog rushed at me, his floppy bag-of-bones body shaking, his tail whirling. Zeke shoved his head up my crotch while I grabbed Frank's hand and threw an arm around his shoulders, pulling him against me hard. Then I dropped to one knee and let Zeke tongue my chin. His fishy, old-dog breath woke something in me, thrilling as the peat and mildew smell of the house.

"Lemme look at you," Frank said.

I stood up.

"Jesus," he said, "you look like a goddamn Indian."

"Everyone in Florida does," I said.

"You look like a Portuguese," he said.

"Where's Paulie?"

"He's home. You're supposed to call him."

"All right." I started toward the kitchen, but Frank grasped my shoulders with both hands.

"Lemme look at you," he said again.

I stopped. He kept his hands on my shoulders. I'd almost forgotten how much bigger I was than the Old Man.

"I had a good year, Frank."

"You look it."

"Frank?"

"Yeah?"

"I'm gonna make the big leagues."

He studied me, a smile leaking through. "Who says?"

"No one says—yet. But I know it. It isn't gonna take long, either."

"Don't you get cocky," he said. He released me, giving me a clap on the arm. "Go call your brother."

I was dialing his number when Paul came through the front door. I heard him speak to Frank. I banged down the phone and gave a yell. Paul smiled when he saw me—that shy, gentle smile. He wore a blue work shirt. I grabbed his strong, bony carpenter's hand. Paul turned to Frank.

"I think he's grown," said Paulie.

"Could be," Frank said.

I wondered if it could be true.

"I like your car," Paul said.

"It needs work," I said. "You want to work on it?"

"Sure."

"I'll pay you."

"You don't have to pay me," Paul said.

"Let's quit yakkin' and start drinkin'," said the Old Man.

We piled into the kitchen and broke out the beer. Then, while Paul cooked, Frank and I stood with our butts against the counter, and I told them all about my year. Some of it I'd written in my letters, but I went through it all again. I told them about Nick Nickinello and about Eddie. I talked about steamy nights and white-hot afternoons in rickety ball parks and how I'd defended Eddie and how they'd beaten him in the end. I described a few of our big rhubarbs, which seemed funny now, though they were anything but humorous at the time. Dinner was ready, and I was still talking. I told them about the night at the strip joint and how the stripper had tossed the glass of beer in Eddie's lap. This, too, seemed funny from a distance. I told them about the fat man, Jim Bob, and our scuffle in the parking lot. I did not tell them about Vicky.

I meant to. And yet when I reached the time, I shied away from mentioning her. A sudden uneasiness had crept over me, a squirmy feeling, like guilt. I told them how Eddie had slipped away in the afternoon, and broke off talking.

We all ate, hunching over our plates. Forks clinked on the thick, cheap china.

The Old Man said, "When you gonna call Miss Pamela?"

I felt caught, as if a strong hand had seized me by the collar. "I don't know," I said. "I'll call her."

"I saw her just the other day," Frank said. "She said she ain't heard from you in a while."

"It got pretty busy down there," I said. I looked at my food. Fresh fish, flounder. Moist white petals.

"You better call her," Frank said.

"I will."

"She's goin' back to college," he said.

"I know."

"You better call her tonight," the Old Man said.

"Look . . ." I had to tell them sooner or later. Vicky would be here in three weeks. The Old Man and Paulie stared at me. "I've been dating someone," I said.

"Didn't tell Miss Pamela, huh?" Frank said.

"Why should he?" Paul said.

"I was away a damn year," I said.

"So what?" Frank said.

"It's a long time," I said. "I'm not a monk, Frank."

"Who said anything about monks?" Frank growled.

Paul said, "Lee isn't engaged, you know."

"Yeah, well, if you let Miss Pamela get away, it'll be the dumbest thing you ever did," said Frank.

He got up and went into the kitchen. Paulie and I exchanged looks. I shrugged. Thanks, I was saying. Paul shrugged. I'll do what I can, his shrug said. The Old Man returned with a glass of whiskey.

"What's this?" I said.

"It's Old Crow," Frank said. "Want some?"

"I thought we were drinking beer," I said.

"I need somethin' stronger."

"Come on, Frank," I said. "I haven't done anything wrong."

"What'd you do," he said, "meet some floozy down there?"

"I met a nice girl."

"Yeah?"

Paul said, "What's the big deal, Frank?"

The Old Man slugged his bourbon. "I told Miss Pamela you'd call her."

"I will," I said.

"When?"

"Tonight."

He seemed at least half satisfied with that. I asked Paul how he was doing. The Old Man drank gloomily while Paul answered my questions. He was thinking of starting his own business. He talked about the difficulties of raising capital and so forth. I didn't understand everything he said—I have no head for business—but I pretended to. Frank gulped his whiskey. He ate half his ice cream, pushed the dish back, and stood up.

"Hey, Zeke, let's go do our business."

The dog understood. He lolloped to the front door, Frank shuffling after him in his high-laced yellow boots. The door bumped.

"I wish he wouldn't do that," Paul said.

"He's always done it," I said.

"It always bothered me," Paul said.

"Joey used to laugh about it."

"I know it."

We got up and started clearing off.

"Frank's glad as hell you're back," Paul said. "He gets pretty lonesome."

"What's the big deal about Pam?"

"It's his way of worrying about you. He wants you to find a good, solid woman."

Frank and the dog came back in.

" 'Night, Frank," I said.

" 'Night yourself."

"Try not to make too much noise in the morning," I told him.

"You go to hell," he said.

"Catch you later, Frank," Paul said.

"Yeah," Frank said and trudged up with the dog plodding patiently at his heels.

"We ought to do the dishes," Paul said.

"All right."

I rolled up my sleeves and filled the sink. Paul finished clearing.

"What about this girl?" he asked.

I told him. I told him how I'd met her and about some of the good times we'd had. Paul was drying the dishes as I washed them.

"Guess what?" I said.

He paused and looked at me.

"I'm not a virgin anymore," I said.

"I didn't think so," Paul said.

"You could tell?"

"No. I always wondered about you and Pam."

"She wouldn't," I said.

Paul nodded.

"Vicky's no tramp," I said.

"I never thought she was." He thought a moment. "You gonna call Pam?"

"Jesus, I have to."

"Yeah."

"What'll I tell her?"

"Depends."

"It was a whole year, Paul."

"You didn't do anything wrong. Things change."

"For nine months I didn't look at a girl."

"Nine months is an achievement," he said.

"I think so, too."

"You don't think Pam went that long, do you?" Paul said.

I looked at him. "Pam? Sure."

"A good-looking college girl like her? Shit, the boys must have been all over her."

"What boys?"

"College boys—who do you think?"

"Pam isn't like that," I said.

"Those college girls don't stay virgins long, believe me."

"Yeah, but Pam wasn't ready."

"I bet you five bucks she beat you to the punch."

I washed the dishes, thinking. I couldn't imagine Pam Rogers doing it with anyone but me.

The clock said nine-thirty.

"Maybe I should call her," I said.

"Go ahead and get it over with," Paul said.

"I shouldn't wait till tomorrow. It'd be an insult."

"Get it over with. Just remember, you didn't do anything wrong."

I nodded, dried my hands, and went to the phone in a sudden, crazy turmoil. My finger shook as I dialed. Paulie was finishing the dishes. Three long rings, and Mrs. Rogers answered.

She did not recognize my voice. Or she pretended not to. She gave me a brusque "One moment, please," and dropped the receiver on the table. I heard her call Pam. I heard the muffled thumps of Pam's footsteps, and then the phone rustled to her ear.

The sound of her voice—one simple word, "Hello"— tore through me.

"It's me," I said.

Pam hesitated. "Lee?"

"Who else?" I said.

"Well," she said, careful sounding, "when did you get here?"

"A little while ago."

"And how are you?"

"Pam, I'm good. I'm fine. I want to see you."

"Of course," she said.

"Tonight?"

"It's sort of late," she said.

"Pam, Jesus, it's me."

"All right," she said. "Come on over."

"What's the matter?" I said.

"Nothing."

"You sound so . . . distant."

"We have a lot to talk about," Pam said.

"I'll be right over."

I hung up. Paulie was eyeing me.

"I'm on my way," I said.

"You better tread easy," Paulie said.

"Meaning what?" I said.

"Meaning," he said, "you can't have your cake and eat it, too."

I didn't know what he was talking about. I didn't want to know. I flung out of the house, impatient, and gunned the car engine. I was feeling the excitement of seeing an old lover, that tantalizing curiosity and a certain reck-lessness, a readiness for almost anything.

The porch light burned as before, Halloween orange against the white shingles. I approached slowly up the flagstone walk. The old lilacs nodded close on each side. I remembered my old self coming up this same walk and smiled. I rapped with the brass knocker, still smiling. *You've changed, Lee.* I could hear Pam, could see her gazing at me. *God, you've changed.*

She opened the door. There was a quivering moment, a silence, as we stared at each other. Pam looked deep into me with those dry blue eyes, then stepped up and gave me a brief hug. The smell of her perfume pierced me like a bullet. This is why, I thought, they make so many different perfumes. A perfume for every woman. Pam pulled back.

"You look wonderful," she said, finally smiling.

"So do you," I said, with energy. For she did. Her face was radiant with the burn of the summer sun. There was a new fineness about her, the chiseled bones ever more delicate, ever more precise. Her shirt was open in a deep V, showing breastbones, and I remembered what she'd looked like the last time I'd seen her, when the two of us had stripped to the waist on the sofa. I wanted her, ached for her, from that moment. The new me.

"Everybody's in bed," Pam said. The house was dark behind her. "Let's get out of here."

She grabbed a sweater off the banister and shut the door quietly behind us. I followed her down the walk, watching her so smart and graceful in her tight skirt.

"So this is the famous car?" she said.

"You like it?"

"It's on the loud side," she said.

I held the door for her. She jackknifed in. Swift. Neat. I got in and gunned her up. I'd left the radio on.

"Shall we go to Howard Johnson's?" I said.

"There's a new pizza place," she suggested.

"Howard Johnson's is our place," I said.

"All right," she agreed.

We drove by the water, the long way around to Howard Johnson's. It was a fine, starry September night.

"What about your friend?" Pam said. "Eddie. The car's half his, isn't it?"

"He let me take it."

"How come?"

"Eddie left," I said. "With a month to go, he quit and went home. He told me to keep the car. I suppose I should pay him for his half."

"This must have been after you stopped writing me," Pam said.

I didn't say anything.

"You shouldn't pay him if he gave it to you," Pam said. "A gift's a gift."

We drove by the harbor. The yachts were berthed

along the marina. Some were lit inside, and you could glimpse people sitting around, playing cards or thumbing through magazines.

"They always look so bored," I said.

Pam said, "What else happened that I don't know about?"

"Hey," I said, "you didn't exactly shower me with mail, either."

"No," she agreed.

"What happened with you?" I said.

"We have a lot to talk about," Pam said.

"Don't dodge," I said.

"I won't if you won't."

I got quiet. I didn't want to answer a lot of questions.

"Why did Eddie quit?" Pam said.

"He couldn't take the abuse. It wore him out, just like Nick Nickinello said it would."

"Swell," Pam said. "Sounds like a fun way to make a living."

"Eddie was too small."

"Sounds like a jungle."

"You know what it's like," I said.

The parking lot at Howard Johnson's was nearly empty. Across Main Street stood the clapboard Community Center, with its huge dirt parking lot where they held the football rallies on Friday nights throughout the fall. Pam and I went into the restaurant. Our old hangout. At the counter an old man sipped coffee, lifting the thick white mug with two hands. A couple of men in brown work shirts with their names stitched in yellow over the pockets sat in a booth, silently keeping each other company. One of them was digging into a banana split. Pam and I slid into a booth we'd sat in often. I remembered how the kids would come crowding in here after a dance or a movie, filling the place with talk and laughter and jukebox music. It was a game to see how many people could cram into one booth.

Pam laid her arms on the table, craning forward gracefully. I kept rediscovering her long neck, tannish hair and blue eyes.

"You look terrific," I said.

She eyed me. I was beginning to feel clumsy. Not like someone who had traveled, who had held his own and then some in the dog-eat-dog world of minor-league baseball. I felt younger than Pam. I did not, however, feel like a virgin.

"You do," I said. "You look terrific."

"Thank you," she said.

The kid arrived to take our order. I didn't know him. Pimples spattered his thin face. His apron was streaked and daubed with different colored ice cream. Pam ordered a strawberry sundae. I asked for a cheeseburger.

"Can I play the jukebox?" I asked him.

"Why not?" he said.

"I didn't want to disturb anyone," I said, glancing at the old man.

"He don't own the place," the kid said.

It was a nickel a play in those days. I fed the machine and chose five songs that had been popular last year, our year. The jukebox whirred and clunked, and Elvis let go with "Heartbreak Hotel."

"Remember this?" I said, folding myself in again.

"Of course."

"Try to enjoy yourself," I said.

Again she said, "We have a lot to talk about."

"You sound like a broken record," I said. "I'm here and you're here. Why don't we just make the most of it?"

I didn't look at her when I said this. I shied from her steady blue gaze. I could feel it, though. I could feel its probing light.

The waiter brought her sundae. Pam stopped studying me and contemplated the sundae. I watched her push the spoon into the rose-pink sauce, peering as if she'd never seen a strawberry sundae before. She carved a dainty spoonful, waiting thoughtfully while the ice cream melted on her tongue. Elvis sang, painting an image of that desolate building at the end of Lonely Street, ornate and silent, the mournful desk clerk dressed like an undertaker.

Pam slowly licked her spoon and said, "Who is she?"

"Who's who?"

"Did your brain go soft down there?"

"Lower your voice," I said.

"If you start telling the truth, I'll lower my voice."

The two fellows in work shirts turned and stared. They went back to eating.

"All right," I said. "I went out on a few dates."

"You did more than that," she said.

"How do you know?"

She glared at me, her eyes sizzling.

"Look," I said. "I met someone. We went out. Didn't you?"

"Yes, but I didn't lie about it."

"Who lied?"

"You."

"I didn't."

"Mr. Smooth," she said. "You're so transparent, Lee."

"I'm crazy about you," I said.

"This is making me sick," Pam said.

"What do you want me to do, get down on my knees and . . ."

I stopped; the kid had arrived with my cheeseburger and a Coke. He set them down and wiped his hands on that disgusting apron. The two men in work shirts got up and tossed some coins on the table. They sauntered out of the restaurant, each chewing a toothpick.

Pam said, "Did you sleep with her?"

"No."

Pam fixed me with her blue gaze. I looked away. The old man at the counter sat with his legs crossed, cradling his coffee mug in his hands. The jukebox was playing Buddy Holly.

Slowly Pam said, "You fucking liar."

"They teach you to talk like that at Bryn Mawr?" I said.

"I'll talk any damn way I want to," she said. Her voice was rising, powered by conviction. "You liar," she said.

"Will you lower your voice?" I said.

"You bastard," she said. "You liar."

The pimply kid was gawking. The old man frowned.

"Listen," I said. "I'll tell you what happened."

"You already have," she said and shot to her feet. "Now take me home."

"Sit down," I whispered.

Home." It was a shriek.

"Jesus, Pam . . ."

But she whirled and strode out, her heels whacking the floor. The old man and the kid were taking it all in with slack, astonished faces. I got up and groped for my wallet. I hadn't eaten my cheeseburger. The boy scooted out from behind the counter as if he was afraid I might walk out without paying. I dropped two bills on the table.

"I'll get your change," he said.

I didn't answer but chased Pam into the rinsing autumn night. She was waiting in the car. She didn't speak, didn't look at me as I slid in beside her. Her straight-edged profile looked immovable.

"Pam," I said, "listen to me."

I still wanted her. The thought of it was making me crazy. I saw us sneaking shoeless up the stairs to my bed-room, where I would undress Pam Rogers at long last, which I should have done last year. A glorious, sneaky screw in the old bedroom with the street light glazing Pam's glorious body.

Pam sat with her arms folded. She stared straight ahead.

"Pam."

"Take me home," she said.

"I want to talk to you."

"Take me home, Lee Malcolm, you filthy liar."

"What about you? Didn't you sleep with someone?"

"None of your business."

"I told *you*," I said.

"You did *not* tell me, you lying son of a bitch."

"College has done wonders for your vocabulary," I said.

"Take me home," she said.

"Not till you listen to me."

"See you later," Pam said and flung open the door.

I lunged across her and yanked the door shut; she tried to bite my arm. I whipped it away from her. Pam started to open the door again, and I sparked the en-gine, fast, and drove out of the parking lot as Pam pulled the door shut with both hands.

"Come home with me," I said. "We'll talk."

"Not on your life," she said.

"It's nothing we can't talk out," I said.

"I feel sorry for her, whoever she is," Pam said.

"Feel sorry for who?"

Pam yelled. She screeched. *"The girl you've been screwing and lying to down in Florida!"*

"I didn't lie to her," I said.

"You're lying to her now," Pam said.

I'd run out of ideas. I was beginning to see it was hardly likely that I was going to entice Pam to bed with me. The moon was up, I remember. I remember its snowy reflection on the pond that stretched to the marsh below our sandlot ball field. I sighed. It was over.

"I want you to know one thing," I said.

My voice had changed; Pam looked at me.

"I didn't lie to the girl in Florida," I said.

Pam studied me. I waited. "All right," she said. "I believe you."

"I really didn't," I said.

"I believe you."

"Seeing you brought everything back," I said. "You're so damn . . . gorgeous, Pam."

"Thank you."

"You are."

"You and I were a long time ago," Pam said.

And I knew it was true. College had come between us. So had Florida, Vicky, baseball, life. Life had thrown Pam one way, me another.

In front of her house I pulled the emergency brake and let the engine run. A rush of pride stiffened me, a deep-down sense that Pam wasn't any better than I was. I didn't offer to walk her to the door. She hesitated.

"I'm sorry," I said.

"You're such an inept liar," she said, smiling. It was her old smile.

"When are you leaving?" I said.

"In three days."

"I'll say good-bye now."

"I suppose it's best," she said, then ventured, "Is your girlfriend nice?"

I nodded.

"Be good to her," Pam said.

"Be good to your college boy," I said.

"Always," she said and smiled. She opened the door. I got one last look at her in the dirty-yellow glare of the overhead light.

"Good-bye, Lee."

"You take care," I said.

"You, too."

She slammed the car door. She'd entered the dark alley between the lilacs when I called to her.

"I'm gonna make the big leagues," I said.

She stopped and turned. I could see her smile, a softening, in the shadows. "I'm glad for you, Lee."

She spun and walked quickly to the house. The porch light torched her hair a brief moment as she jerked open the black door with the brass knocker. The door shut with a bump, gulping Pam; the knocker clinked, the period at the end. The porch light died. Moonlight splashed the white shingled face of the sleeping house.

I didn't sleep that night. Not a wink. I didn't blame myself for getting so hot for Pam. Might as well blame yourself for becoming dizzy on top of a mountain or going woozy drinking gin. But I didn't have to give in as easily as I did. When I closed my eyes, I saw Pam, I saw Vicky. Pam was pale fire; she was slippery moonlight. Vick was warm, red earth. After a long while I thought, *If I were lost in a blizzard in the Alps, who would I want rescuing me? Pam Rogers or Vicky Vadnais? Who would I want struggling through the drifts with food and brandy? I'd want Vicky, that's who.*

At long last the sky lightened to gray milk. It hardened to electric blue. The birds began singing. I heard some crows cawing in the distance. I looked out and saw the wrinkly trunks of the elms and the thickets of viburnum drawing color out of the new day. Sunlight struck the tops of the trees like melted gold.

At six the Old Man got up. I heard him go into the bathroom. Every morning he took a bath. He was in there a long time. Eventually he clomped downstairs in his boots, with Zeke behind him. Zeke's nails rattled on the smooth, worn wood of the stairs. His metal tags jingled. In the kitchen Frank talked to the dog and whistled "Stardust." By and by I could smell coffee and bacon. Lying awake all night builds a terrific appetite.

Vicky came east just before Thanksgiving. The Old Man was against it. Stubbornly he blamed Vick for Pam's exit from my life. Once an idea took hold in the Old Man's head, it was hard to dislodge it. Paulie advised me to be patient. He said it was hard for Frank to trust women after what our mother had done.

I should have known that Vick would solve it soon enough. She sized the Old Man up—he was a man, wasn't he?—and went to work on him. She handled him the way she had Eddie Snyder, attentive to him, listening when he spoke, taking his arm when we went to the movies. It was her gift. Frank thawed, of course. Vick couldn't move in with us—not in those days—but she began coming for dinner, until the Old Man counted on it. Vick cooked. She insisted.

I was working at the Community Center, reffing basketball games, taking nickels from the kids who piled around the counter for candy bars after school, keeping track of the basketballs and Ping-Pong paddles. It wasn't much of a job, but it suited me. I wanted to spend time with Paul and the Old Man. I wanted to walk on the beach with Vicky. There were pickup basketball games at the Community Center, and I often joined in. A few of the fellows were high school teammates of mine. They'd never left town.

Vicky was renting a room from an elderly woman who wanted the company. The rent was a song, and Vick understood the obligation that went with it. She ate breakfast with the old lady. She had tea with her.

Vick found a job waitressing at a Main Street restaurant called the Town House, where the local merchants and Town Hall crowd ate lunch and hung out after work. Vick would listen to their stories and laugh at their jokes. She gave them hugs on their birthdays. They were the selectmen, the Main Street lawyers, the owners of small stores that had been owned by their fathers. Vick made them feel like men without compromising herself. When she received a proposition, she flicked it aside expertly and kindly. The man's pride wouldn't suffer a scratch. It was her gift, and it was genuine.

I worked one more season in the Central Florida League. Vick came with me, and we lived together, masquerading as husband and wife, in a trailer camp midway between the coasts. I could drive to every town in the league. It was hard on my partner, existing alone in those fleabag hotels, but he couldn't complain, me being a married man. I was taking a risk. Living in sin hadn't even begun to gain the respect it enjoys today. I could have been fired. To be safe we bought Vick a cheap wedding ring.

Our neighbors in the trailer camp were from all over Florida, as well as out of state. They were white and poor. They had flocks of kids who spent the long, blazing days playing half naked in the dust outside the trailers. The men worked for orange growers and did construction. They couldn't have been union; they were too poor. The women sat around on their steps or in their tiny kitchens, gossiping and sipping RC Cola or Dr. Pepper.

Vicky, of course, made friends with all the women. They were sad and bored. Their faces were heavy and slack, their eyes hooded and sharp with loneliness and suspicion. Vicky knew, with that instinct that never failed her, how to inquire about their kids, how to chat with them about the game shows and soap operas they watched on their fuzzy TVs. She knew, too, how to flit away before they could snare her for a game of cards and how to slither out of having to choose sides in their never-ending feuds. "I feel sorry for them," Vick said. I did, too, but not as sorry as Vick felt.

No longer new, Florida seemed heartless: so hot, so flat, so dry. Vicky made it all right. After the night games she rubbed my back, fed me icy beer, and made love to me in the natural, smiling way she had.

My partner was a good umpire who could take care of himself on the field. I only had to fight my own battles, which seemed simple after defending Eddie Snyder. My partner's name was Mike Kilroy, and I thought he'd make the major leagues someday. He never did.

Only once did the subject of marriage arise. It was the Old Man who brought it up. Vick had come for a second winter. She'd gone back to her old job at the Town House. I was working for Paul, banging nails. Paulie was teaching me the art of building. One night at dinner—Paul had come over—Frank turned to me and said out of the blue, "When are you two gonna tie the knot?"

Vick smiled, amused by the way the Old Man said

whatever popped into his head. Then she sent me a questioning look, wondering if I'd said something to Frank.

Paul said, "They'll tell us when the time comes."

I was sure of just one thing: I was too young to be married.

"Just gimme an idea," Frank said.

"After I make the big leagues," I said.

Vick's green eyes bulged.

"I guess that makes sense," Frank said.

"We'll have money," I said.

"That's true," Frank agreed.

"How long will it take you to get up there?" Paul asked.

"Three or four years," I said.

Little did I know. I was going into Triple A in the spring. I would spend one year in Triple A, then jump to the majors.

"That's a long time to wait," Frank said.

I shrugged.

Frank said, "What do you think, Miss Victoria?"

Vicky was watching me. "I think we'll see," she said.

The Old Man nodded. I could see he wasn't satisfied, but he let the subject drop.

That night Vick and I made love as usual in my old bedroom. Afterward she pondered the ceiling a while, then said, "After you make the big leagues, huh?"

"Sure," I said.

"Are you proposing?"

"You can't propose three or four years in advance," I said.

"No," she agreed.

"We're too young, anyway," I said.

"I suppose," she said.

We were quiet a while.

Vick said, "From now on it's up to you. I'll never mention it again."

It was a promise I knew she'd keep.

PART 2

7

Ron Chapman was a rookie with the New York Barons the year I broke into the league. We'd both come fast. Chapman had spent a year in an A league and a year in Triple A, where he'd slugged fifty-two home runs and stolen sixty bases. Not only were he and I rookies together; we both made our major-league debut in the same game. On that opening day in New York, I had my first run-in with him.

Chapman was not your average ballplayer in any sense of the word. He'd gone to UCLA, like Jackie Robinson. The year before he turned pro, he was arrested in Montgomery, Alabama, for sitting in the whites-only section of a city bus. He'd intended to get arrested. He was, I'd heard, a personal friend of Dr. Martin Luther King, Jr., who was just beginning to attract national attention.

A couple of weeks before the season opened, Chapman had made news with a spat with the New York sportswriter Tommy Shannon. This was down in Florida during the exhibition season. Shannon had been singing Chapman's praises in his column. Chapman was the new Willie Mays, Shannon wrote. Chapman, like Mays, was fleet, strong, and graceful. There was some Jackie Robinson in Chapman, too—that fire.

Chapman read the column and waited for Shannon to come into the clubhouse. Shannon came; Chapman got up and blocked his way. Chapman stood about six-two. He had nervous ballplayer's legs and shoulders crammed with muscle. His mahogany face looked charred—charred by his own anger. Tommy Shannon stood maybe five-eight. He was graying, dough-soft, and fearless. He didn't like finding his way obstructed.

"Mr. Shannon," Chapman said. His voice was deep and smooth. It was like dark honey.

"Whatsa problem?" Shannon said.

"Why not the next DiMaggio? Why not the next Babe Ruth, for that matter?"

"What in the hell," said Shannon, "are you talkin' about?"

"You compare me to Willie and Jackie. Why not to Ted Williams?"

Shannon squinched his owl face. "Ya don't look anything like Williams, for Christ sake."

"Exactly," said Chapman.

"Kid," said Shannon, "will you mind tellin' me what the fuck you're gettin' at?"

"Racism."

The half-moon of Shannon's jaw fell. He stared at Ron Chapman. "Run it by me one more time," he said.

"It wouldn't occur to you to compare a black man to DiMaggio, would it?"

Tommy Shannon contemplated Chapman for a long moment. Then slowly he said, "You . . . are . . . fulla . . . shit."

Chapman stood his ground. Shannon sent the tall man a fierce scowl, then whirled away. He marched to the elevator, rode up to the press box, and began to write. Other writers who were up there told me he wrote nonstop, fingers snapping at the typewriter keys. The column was nationally syndicated. It said, in part:

> *Ron Chapman is a punk. Oh, the veneer is fancy. The vocabulary is sprinkled with $5 words. But when you dig underneath the airs and the education, you find a punk who thinks the world owes him a living because he happened to be born with brown skin. You find a talented young man, blessed by God, who is spitting at the game and the country that have given him a chance to be rich—and immortal.*

As far as I know, Chapman never responded. Disdain and silence were his answer.

I didn't meet my three partners until that Opening Day in New York. During the exhibition season you work the three-man system, and the groupings are haphazard. For the regular season the leagues construct the umpiring crews carefully. They will try, for instance, to blend youth with experience. They look for harmonious combinations. Our crew mixed two veterans, Bill McKnight and the great Bugs Trovarelli, with Roy Van Arsdale, a second-year man, and me. I met the three of them in the hotel lobby just before we left for the stadium.

I'd ridden the train down the day before. My partners had checked into the hotel and gone out again, and

Bugs, who was the crew chief, had left a message at the desk saying we would meet in the lobby at eleven-thirty in the morning. This hotel was a long way up from the hotels of my minor-league days, even Triple A. The city, too, was far from what I was used to. I'd never seen streets so clogged, sidewalks so teeming. I'd never heard such noise—screech, growl, clang, and the constant, groaning wind that is the sum of it all, the undying echo, a tremble of concrete and steel. In the city air I smelled spices, yeast, rot, sweat, gasoline, and spring flowers.

I ate supper alone at a restaurant around the block from the hotel. I was in my room at nine. I tried to read. The words wriggled and danced; I couldn't wrestle them still. I watched TV for a while. Then I lay in bed with the window open, listening to the city breathe, moan, chuckle, and belch. Horns beeped; sirens streaked across the night. I felt tiny and I felt lonely, but it was a thrilling loneliness, a brief pause before this and other great cities opened their arms to me.

I woke to a lead-gray morning. The city was busy. The growl of the traffic played up the faces of the buildings. I didn't know about room service, so I went out and hunted around till I found a delicatessen. I ate a big breakfast that my stomach didn't want. The expense money, more than $25 a day, seemed fabulous to me, though I later heard Bugs and McKnight gripe about it. I lay around the room, trying to read, but I kept seeing a crowd, big as a sea, loud and wild as a hurricane. My stomach squirmed, churning that heavy breakfast around. I wondered if I would vomit. At eleven-fifteen, I rode the elevator down to the lobby.

I strolled around, watching the people come through. They all hurried. In New York everyone hurries. Under the awning in front, the doorman waved taxis over for the people who came gusting out through the revolving door. He was a stocky fellow, his uniform buttoned tight over his broad chest and shoulders. A few people shook their heads no, they didn't want a taxi, and strode briskly away on the wide, scrubbed sidewalk. I kept glancing at the elevator.

I saw a fat man with white-blond hair get out—a smiling, radiant cherub with tiny feet and no neck. I turned away; this was no umpire. I'd begun pacing again, watching the doorman, when a bright, creamy voice piped up behind me: "Lee Malcolm?"

It was the fat man. His smile bent like a crescent moon across his round, baby-smooth face.

"Welcome to the crew," he said. "I'm Roy Van Arsdale."

I took the fat pink hand, which had a surprising, biting strength. "When did you get here?" he asked me.

"Last night."

"Did you meet Bugs and Bill?"

"Not yet."

"I guess they were out on the town last night. They're buddies. Very tight."

"What's Bugs like?" I asked.

"He's a hard nut," Van Arsdale said. We stared out at the busy avenue. I kept glancing at the elevator.

"I understand you spent only three years in the minors," Van Arsdale said.

I nodded.

"Amazing," he said. "I spent five, and they thought that was quick."

"It was," I said.

"Three is incredible. You must be good."

"I think I'm ready," I said.

"Here they come," he said.

Some will tell you even now that Bugs Trovarelli was the greatest who ever pulled on the blues. They will say he had a better eye than Bill Klem and was every bit as tough. I knew Bugs from newspaper pictures and from TV games going back as far as I could remember. Bugs had broken in about the time I was born.

He wasn't big—not for an umpire. His chest jutted like a bulldog's. He walked with his shoulders thrown back, advancing impatiently on bowed legs. He wore a cool-green blazer and a yellow tie. His shoes were expensive. His face was sun browned, his features bulbous. Bugs strutted bowlegged across the hotel lobby, a tough, impatient man with a bad-boy glint in his eye.

McKnight was of Bugs's era but nowhere near the umpire that Bugs was. McKnight was an ex-pro football player with a thick trunk of a body and big slab feet. His hair, parted in the middle, was graying. He dressed conservatively, not with Bugs's flair and imagination. Moroseness shaded the crags of McKnight's face; a look of edginess and gloom.

They greeted Van Arsdale first. Bugs smirked as he squeezed Roy's hand.

"Thought you were gonna drop some weight over the winter," he said.

"I did." Van Arsdale grinned.

"Like hell," Bugs said.

"I think you gained, if anything," said McKnight. He had a bigger voice than Bugs's, thick and booming.

Finally Bugs turned to me.

"This the new boy?"

"Lee Malcolm," I said. "It's a pleasure to meet you." I offered my hand.

Bugs gripped it hard. "I hope you're good, Malcolm. When the league secretary told me I was gettin' a kid who did three years in the minors, I 'bout shit my pants."

McKnight opened the cave of his mouth. "Three years?" he said. "That's all?"

"Afraid so," I said.

"Christ," McKnight said.

"I'm ready," I said.

"Let's get goin'," Bugs said, shooting a glance at his watch. He barged through the spinning door. McKnight pushed through next. I waited till last.

The doorman grinned, lighting up at the sight of Bugs. "How are you, Mr. Trovarelli?"

"Too fuckin' old, Jimmy. I shoulda stayed in St. Pete; shoulda quit while I was ahead."

"Hell, ya got ten good years left in ya," said the doorman.

"Jesus," McKnight rumbled gloomily.

"You, too, Mr. McKnight," said the doorman.

"Get us a cab, will you, Jimmy?" Bugs said.

"You bet," Jimmy said.

He stuck two fingers in his mouth and blew a piercing whistle. A cab in the far lane slowed, found a break in the traffic, and scooted over. We piled in. Bugs sat in front. The doorman leaned down and touched his forehead.

"Good luck, fellas," he said.

Bugs thanked him. "Stadium," he told the cabbie. We dove into the fast river of traffic.

"Here we go again," McKnight said.

"I wish to hell it was warmer," Bugs said.

"It's never warm on Opening Day," McKnight said. "How many years before you learn that, Bugs?"

"I love Opening Day," Van Arsdale said.

"You would," Bugs said.

"That feeling of beginning," Van Arsdale said.

"I don't like the pressure," McKnight said. "I get tired of the pressure."

I looked out at the dove-gray canyon walls of New York City. I watched the people, floods of them.

"You been readin' about this Chapman?" Bugs asked over his shoulder.

"Ain't he somethin'?" growled McKnight.

"You hear about that run-in with Tommy Shannon?" Bugs said.

"Crazy bastard," McKnight said.

"He's got an attitude," Bugs said. "You notice that in Florida, Billy?"

"I did," McKnight said.

"He's a troublemaker," Bugs said. "I tell you, he better not start anything with me today."

"I hear his own teammates can't stand him," McKnight said.

"They'll like him better," Van Arsdale said, "when they're in first place in mid-August."

"He can play," Bugs admitted. "You're right about that, Fat Man." He turned and gave me a smile. The grin showed a neat space between his two upper front teeth. "You got to establish yourself today, Malcolm. You know what I mean?"

I nodded. I'd jumped leagues so often, come up so fast, I was always having to establish myself. No sooner had I established myself than I'd moved up.

"Show 'em you got it *here*," Bugs said, whacking his belly.

"I will," I said.

"It isn't as if he's never umpired," Van Arsdale said.

"I've seen minor-league umpires before," Bugs said.

"This ain't the minors," McKnight rumbled pointlessly.

We'd reached the stadium, gigantic and deserted, the grills of the light towers bumping the slate sky. My insides were churning. My legs weren't good.

"Rookie pays," Bugs says, ramming his door open.

"Opening Day, that's right," McKnight said.

The fare was almost $8. I took their word for it and paid. I tipped the cabbie a quarter.

"After this we divide it," Van Arsdale said.

Single file, me last, we entered the stadium through the press gate. The guard waved us through with a smile. We passed through concrete tunnels with Bugs pushing along rapidly in the lead. It was two hours till game time, and the concrete and steel seemed frozen, waiting to be thawed by the trampling and roar of the crowd. The tunnels wore decent coats of paint, yellow and pale green, and were not so dark and narrow as the bottoms of the minor-league ballparks. We passed the visitors' clubhouse. The door was open, and a radio spewed a Chuck Berry song, which brought sweet memories of home, of Zeke and the Old Man, and I saw the road winding past our house, the grasses beginning to spring up beside it, and the elm leaves unfurling overhead. Soon the lilacs would be blooming all up and down the road, and I could almost smell their dizzying fragrance.

The umpires' room awaited our arrival, door propped open. Our gear had been shipped ahead. The clubhouse boy had hung our blues on hangers in our cubicles and laid rolled socks, folded longjohns, and clean jocks on our shelves. This was the big leagues. The room was spacious; with concrete walls and a rug on the cement floor. There was a plywood table, folding chairs, TV, and a refrigerator. I dragged a chair to my cubicle and plopped down.

Bugs and McKnight began immediately to undress. Van Arsdale lowered himself onto a chair by the plywood table, burying the little chair under his round bulk. The New York newspapers had been laid out on the table. Van Arsdale rustled one open and began to read. Bugs unbuttoned his shirt, watching me. He grinned his tricky, boyish grin.

"You nervous, kid?" he asked.

"Yeah."

"You got the runs?"

"I don't know."

"Better hit the can before you go out there. Don't want to shit your pants." He looked over at McKnight. "Remember when that happened, Billy? Remember when that rookie we worked with in 'forty-six shit his pants?"

"Jesus, yeah," McKnight said.

"What a mess," Bugs said. "What was that guy's name, Bill?"

"Richardson," McKnight said.

"That's right," Bugs said. "He didn't last long."

"About three years," McKnight said.

Bugs had hung his shirt on a hanger. He stepped out of his trousers. His body was white as ivory where the sun didn't reach it, while his face, neck, and hands were a rich, shiny bronze. In his shorts he strutted to a high shelf and pulled down a tin can. The can had once held cookies. Now it was half full of black mud from the Delaware River. Bugs carried it to the table. He went to the sink, drew some water in a paper cup, and dumped the water onto the mud. Under the table a cardboard box full of new baseballs waited. Bugs ripped it open. The baseballs, shiny white, snuggled in orange tissue paper. Bugs was rubbing them today because he was working the plate. Van Arsdale was leaning down over his spread-out newspaper. McKnight had begun slowly to dress. I watched Bugs. I watched him grab the first baseball, scoop mud on two fingers, and smack it onto the shiny cheek of the ball. He commenced to rub, chafing the ball between his strong hands, kneading till the leather had drunk the mud, dulling its waxy gloss. I'd seen this done and done it myself a thousand times, but Bugs raised it from a humdrum chore to something stylish. Bugs gave it flair. He frowned as he worked. He had black eyebrows, and when he frowned, they arched down, shuddering to the bridge of his nose. Bugs dropped the finished baseball into a tin wastebasket and reached for another.

"So, Malcolm," he said, "you worked in the Central Florida League, I hear."

"Two years," I said. "One year in the American Association."

"Is Walt Waddell still the president down there?"

"He hired me," I said.

"Billy," Bugs said, "remember that banquet in Orlando?"

"Oh, Jesus," McKnight said, smiling faintly. He was dressing very slowly and mechanically, as if his mind was somewhere else.

"I was givin' a speech," Bugs said. "Waddell introduced me as Babe Pinelli."

"Babe Pinelli," McKnight said. "Christ."

I forced a smile. I'd begun unbuttoning my shirt.

Van Arsdale closed the newspaper, sighed, and hoisted himself to his feet. He plodded to his cubicle and began to peel his clothes. Every fifteen seconds or so Bugs would finish rubbing a ball and drop it into the wastebasket. In his longjohns McKnight trudged to the refrigerator. He opened it, and I saw that it had been loaded with beer. Bugs paused in his rubbing and watched McKnight pull out a can of beer. McKnight sat down and took a long swig. Bugs reached down for another base-ball. Van Arsdale stepped out of his trousers. He stepped out of his shorts. He was fat, all right, an eruption of flesh, a creamy flood. His skin had an odd brightness, as if a light burned inside. Roy Van Arsdale padded on lit-tle feet toward the john.

"I thought you'd dropped some weight," Bugs said.

"I did," Van Arsdale said.

"He dropped an ounce and a half," McKnight said.

"That's about right," Van Arsdale said.

McKnight crushed his emptied beer can in his heavy mitt. He set the doubled-over can on the floor.

"No more, Billy," Bugs said gently.

McKnight nodded.

A spasm tore through me, slashing my insides. Sweating, I headed for the bathroom. Bugs watched me, and I saw the grin again, with its neat, thin gap in front.

We followed Bugs through the tunnel to the distant square of pulsing, silver-gray light, our cleats rattling on cement. The light patch swelled as we neared it, and you could hear the molten noise of the crowd. We came out in the visitors' dugout, and I could feel the air tremble. The stadium was packed, upper and lower decks. My mouth was dry. My tongue felt swollen. The PA was giv-ing the lineups; each name brought a cheer, swamping the bowl of the stadium. The players milled nervously up and down the dugout. They didn't look at us. We weren't supposed to look at them, I suppose, though I did. I looked at every taut face as I moved the length of the dugout to the water cooler. I drank, slicking my throat and stone-dry mouth with water. I was still drinking when Bugs climbed the cement steps. McKnight and Van Ars-dale scrambled up after him. I was left behind; I had to run to catch up.

At the plate Bugs said, "Stick with us, Malcolm. Don't be makin' detours."

I nodded. The noise of the crowd arched close above our heads like currents of electricity. Bugs's face seemed to have sharpened—as if the knobby bones had lengthened, thrusting against the tough leather of his skin. The glint was gone; Bugs was all business. McKnight's frowning face was all crags and shadows. Van Arsdale glowed, pinkish porcelain cheeks lit from within. Bugs looked down and kicked the dirt.

"Let's go, you bastards," he said. He meant the managers.

McKnight spat sideways.

Van Arsdale smiled at the crowd.

Then Dusty Wilson, the Chicago Blades manager, bounded up the dugout steps and jogged over, jostling his heavy belly. I heard a great, molten cheer: Whit Stahl, the New York manager, was coming. Whit smiled, lifted his cap, and scrawled a circle in the air. I knew both managers from the exhibition season. Everyone said hello.

The ground rules were pretty straightforward, not like the playground rules in the quirky ball parks of the minor leagues, with their sheds and rickety fences and picnic tables in foul territory and trees reaching across outfield fences. In the wide, serene spaces of the big leagues, everything made sense. Each ball park had its own flawless geometry. Whit Stahl recited, pointing, the way managers always do. His gray eyes twinkled in the wrinkly bag of his face. He had old man's ears—long, with fleshy lobes. He and Wilson exchanged lineup cards. They gave a card to each of us.

"How many opening days does this make for you, Whit?" asked Wilson.

"I broke in in nineteen-twelve," Whit said. "I got drafted into the war in nineteen-seventeen. I spent some years out of baseball in the thirties. Shit, I don't know. I never added 'em up."

"I never added mine up," Bugs said.

"I hate this fuckin' weather," McKnight said. "It makes my bones ache."

"You guys tell your pitchers to keep it movin' today," Bugs told the managers. "I don't want to freeze my nuts off till six o'clock."

"Let's get goin'," McKnight said gloomily.

"Good luck, sonny," Whit Stahl said to me.

"Let's play ball," Bugs said.

We broke up. The managers headed for their dugouts. McKnight trudged to third base. Van Arsdale, who was working second base, walked with me to first. The Barons took the field, romping to their positions in a cloudburst of applause. My mouth had gone dry again. My legs were uncertain; I was worried about them.

"How do you feel?" Roy asked me.

"Nervous."

"You'll be all right. Get an early ground ball; you'll be fine."

The first baseman was rolling the ball to the infielders. They would bend nonchalantly, shovel it in their gloves, straighten, and snap the ball to first.

"It's a nice life," Van Arsdale said, gazing around at the crowd. "It beats teaching school."

"Teaching school?" I said.

"That's what I used to do. Teach school."

A schoolteacher. I wondered how he'd gotten into umpiring.

They played the anthem. It seemed to go on and on. There was a slow wind; the flag writhed against the gray sky. I thought again of the Old Man, who I knew was listening this very minute in the hardware store. Probably Mr. West was listening, too. Maybe other people were listening in other stores. It would be like the World Series, when radios crackled in the stores and barber shops up and down Main Street, the announcer's voice sounding sharp and urgent in the silent, shadowy fall afternoons. The anthem finished; the crowd cheered and settled down.

I walked to my position down the line. The pitcher threw his final warm-ups. The catcher pegged to second; the second baseman ladled the ball underhand to the shortstop, who whipped it to first, who gunned it across to third. The third baseman walked the ball to the pitcher, rubbing it as he went. Bugs bent over and whisk-broomed the plate. I chewed my gum, trying to work up some moisture. The willowy pitcher stood on the mound and read his sign. The Blades' leadoff hitter cocked his bat. The pitcher reared gracefully and threw. The hitter watched it; Bugs shot the right arm straight out—*stee-rahhk*. The crowd roared, and the season had begun.

Ground ball to the third baseman. Position: ninety degrees to the throw. The third baseman scooped and threw; the ball seemed to slow, drifting across. I couldn't hear anything; the world held its breath. The runner pounded down the line. The ball sailed true, and I watched the bag and listened, watched and listened till I heard the ball hit the glove—whap—and saw, a sliver of a second later, the runner's foot slap the bag. Pause. Then I flung my fist and bawled the out: "He got 'im," selling the call. Noise again. Cheers fell; the air shook. I'd forgotten the Old Man, the hardware store, Main Street, home. There was nothing but this baseball game. There was no time, only innings, a lengthening string of white digits on the slate-black scoreboard.

Behind the plate Bugs ruled with an iron hand. He used his voice like a hatchet. Bugs didn't have to holler. No hitter dared turn to argue a call. A few grumbled, eyes front, and Bugs usually ignored them. If they mouthed too long, Bugs raised his mask and told them, "Shut up and hit." He didn't yell it, yet I could hear it all the way down at first, through the din of the crowd.

McKnight enforced his calls with a thunder-dark scowl and a voice like a roar from a cave. It was as if close plays made him mad. You put me to this trouble, his scowl said, don't make it worse by arguing with me. And yet they did. Nothing big, not this game, but there were shakes of heads, a few testy cracks. McKnight would yell back at them, bellowing till he had the last word. He looked and sounded ferocious, but the players didn't seem cowed.

Van Arsdale smiled, hustled, and danced, unbelievably light on his feet. He would scuttle into the outfield to follow the flight of a fly ball, then spin and scoot back again to be where he had to be. His little feet flickered as he ran. He made his calls with huge flourishes, twisting, waving, and punching the air. The thin, musical voice eddied and skated. He sweated, even on this cool day, and the sweat shone on him like a rich lotion.

In the bottom of the eighth, Ron Chapman rammed the ball into center field—base hit, his second. New York had the lead, 2–0, and there were two out, which meant it was a good time to try to steal second. Chapman edged sideways off the base, crouching on the balls of his feet, studying the pitcher, Rob Kidder. Kidder was a righty. He watched Chapman over his left shoulder. I remember Kidder's tall number 16. Chapman sneaked out farther and farther. Kidder watched him, back squared, over his shoulder. Pause. Kidder whirled and threw to first; Chapman dove and grabbed the bag as Scott slapped the tag on his shoulder, just late. I spread my arms out— *safe*. Scott lobbed the ball back to Kidder. Chapman got up and slapped dust from his legs and chest. Kidder took his place again, spread-legged, watching Chapman over his shoulder. Chapman crept sideways toward second. Kidder threw again, gently this time, a tired throw, and Chapman flitted back without having to dive. There were some boos for Kidder. Kidder got the ball back and once more placed his right foot on the white slab of the rubber. Again he put his chin to his left shoulder, contemplating Chapman over his back. Chapman crab-stepped out, gaining confidence, inching, inching, inching. Kidder waited. Chapman dared one more half-step, and Kidder spun and threw. Chapman dove, plowing up the dust; the glove gulped the throw and fell, almost simultaneous with Chapman's reach for the bag, but—yes—a split second sooner. I was sure. I pointed to the spot where the tag had nipped him, my hand became a fist, and I straightened and slashed him out.

It was as if I'd yanked a cord, bringing down a storm of boos. Chapman remained stretched out in the dirt. He was grimacing. The booing groaned on. Chapman climbed to his feet, taller than me by half a foot or more.

"No *way* I was out."

"Yeah," I said, "he got you."

"No damn *way*."

"He got you, Ron. Let's play ball."

"Don't 'Ron' me," he said.

"You better get away from me," I said.

"Don't 'Ron' me. I don't even know you."

"Suit yourself," I said.

I was moving away from him now. The teams were

changing sides. The booing groaned on. Behind me Chapman said, "I know I was safe, ump."

I kept walking. I reached my position down the line, turned, and folded my arms. The bat boy scampered out with Chapman's glove. Chapman accepted it without looking at the kid. Chapman was glaring at me, giving me the evil eye. His eyes were slitted; his face looked fire-blackened. He shook his head slowly, saying, *You are wrong, wrong, wrong.* The booing was subsiding. Chapman sent me a final burning glance and trotted toward the outfield.

Bugs and McKnight went their own way that night, and Van Arsdale invited me to have dinner with him at a restaurant he knew not far from the hotel. I didn't know New York. I didn't know the boroughs. I didn't know Manhattan, upper and lower, east and west. Roy said it was easier to learn New York than a lot of cities—Boston and Detroit, for instance.

The restaurant was French—small and dark and homey. We drank wine, my least favorite alcoholic beverage. Roy ordered it. Wine seemed to go with the place. We told each other about ourselves. Roy was a good listener. I told him about the Old Man and Paul and how Joey had been killed. I told him how I'd changed my mind about going to college.

Roy came from Maryland. He'd been an English teacher before his umpiring days. A twist of fate had brought him to umpiring; Roy talked about it that first night and on other nights till I knew the story as if I'd been there. Six years ago, he'd been teaching at a private boy's school in Virginia, not far from Washington, D.C. One summer afternoon, a Sunday, he found himself in the city, strolling and drifting. He came to a park, where some fellows were playing softball. Roy hung around. The game, it turned out, was a serious matter. Two offices—law firms, maybe—were playing.

There were no umpires. It worked this way: The catcher called them foul or fair, and the coaches at third and first, players taking turns, made the calls at the bases. This system may have worked well enough under normal circumstances, but this game was supposed to decide which team went to some tournament, and both wanted it. Roy hadn't been watching long when an argument broke out.

One of the infielders had thrown wild past first, and the teams couldn't agree on how many bases the runners were entitled to advance. There were two runners on, so it was complicated. Finally, after a lot of jawing, they decided to do the whole thing over—send the runners back and let the hitter try again.

Roy had never umpired. He'd played some sandlot ball as a fat kid. He didn't know the intricacies of the game or all of the rules. But on this sunny summer's day in a city park, he felt an odd attack of alarm; he'd been enjoying the game, had become interested in the outcome, and now it was being ruined. He felt cheated. If you can wipe out a fellow's at-bat and let him hit again, what can't you do? Suddenly the game had been made childish. Roy had a teacher's inclinations, and in spite of his obesity, a large endowment of aplomb. He decided he wasn't going to let them spoil the game for him. He marched out and asked one of the team captains if they wanted an umpire. This was the action, deliberate and totally self-assured, that changed Roy's life forever.

The captain yelled out to everybody, "Do we want an umpire?" They did. They all thought it was a swell idea. Roy borrowed a catcher's mask. Then, to begin, he ruled on the play just ended, sending the batter to second, one of the runners to third, and allowing a run. Then he went behind the plate and told them to play ball.

Everything went fine—for a while. Then, in the next to last inning, Roy called a fellow out on strikes. The game was slow-pitch: no one had struck out; no one expected to strike out. But this fellow looked at a pitch that drifted down knee high on the outside corner. Strike. There was no other call.

The fellow exploded. The whole team did. It was a regular argument, a major-league argument.

"You're crazy," the hitter told Roy. "You're *crazy*."

"Caught the corner knee high," Roy said.

"Bullshit."

"Now, now," Roy said.

"You can't *do* this," the fellow said.

"Sit down," Roy said, "or I'll have to eject you."

The fellow's eyes bulged at this announcement. "Eject me? I'll eject *you*, asshole."

Roy gave him his mild, cherubic smile. "Don't swear," he said. "Don't swear at the umpire."

"Oh, fuck you."

Roy unloaded him.

Now his teammates came swarming out like hornets. Roy stood massive and serene in the midst of them.

"You can't throw him out," they kept shouting. "You can't throw him out."

"I just did," Roy said.

"Well, you can't."

"Well, I did."

"We don't want you," they said. "You're fired."

"Yeah, you're fired," said others.

"He's fired."

"So long."

174

"Wait a minute," Roy said. He pumped his voice up. *"Wait just a goddamn minute!"*

Silence. Roy stood there, surrounded.

"If you want me to leave," he said, "I'll leave. I'll go. But if you do this—if you dismiss me in the middle of a game—you make the game meaningless, do you understand? Whoever wins, it'll mean nothing. The score will mean nothing. Your man here took a good pitch and struck out. He swore at the umpire; he's out of the game. That's baseball. Those are the rules. Do you want to play the game right, or do you want to play a made-up game that'll suit your tantrums and your mistakes?"

They listened, both teams. They listened spellbound. Roy finished the speech and waited. The fellows all looked at each other. Roy could see the logic of his sermon sinking into the smart, youthful faces—these were lawyers, remember—like oil softening leather.

Finally someone said rather meekly, "Well, could you leave Clark in the game?"

Clark was the fellow Roy had tossed.

"No," Roy said. "I cannot *leave* Clark in the game, because Clark is no longer *in* the game. What did I just finish saying?"

There was more discussion. This fellow Clark was in no mood to depart. He apologized for cussing Roy. He said if he'd realized, he would not have. Realized what? Roy said. Rules are rules. So serene and certain was Roy, so smilingly unyielding, so *right,* that they finally gave in. They began abandoning Clark, dropping away one by one till he alone insisted he be allowed to play the game out. I couldn't have pulled it off. Roy worked a spell on them, turning them docile as children. He was one of the few umpires I ever saw whose authority flowed from some deep place that had nothing to do with brute toughness. Even in the big leagues Roy didn't get many arguments. He got fewer than Bill McKnight, who had played pro football with Bronco Nagurski.

Roy bought a Rule Book—baseball, not softball—memorized it, and applied for work in an industrial league in Maryland. It may have been his angelic self-assurance, or maybe there was an umpire shortage; they hired him. He went into it without self-doubt and found he was in his element. One night the manager of the Alexandria club in the Carolina League, a fellow named Clyde Farnsworth, drove over to look at a kid who was supposed to be a hot prospect. The kid ushered a couple of ground balls through his legs, and Clyde was disgusted. But he noticed Roy. Roy was flamboyant, even then. Farnsworth called the president of the league and told him he'd discovered a good umpire. Unbeknownst to him, Roy was scouted. The president of the Carolina League offered him a job. Roy never went to umpiring school.

We'd finished our dinner and the wine and for now had talked ourselves out. Roy looked at his watch.

"I have to run," he said. "I have to meet some people. Can you find the hotel?"

I said I could. Up one street, then over.

Roy picked up the check. "I'm buying."

"No," I said.

"Your first big-league game. My pleasure."

"Well," I said, "okay."

"You can take me out on my birthday or something."

We drifted out into the chill city night, the charged, odor-rich air of fabulous Manhattan. Roy flagged a cab in front of the restaurant. Before he got in, he shook my hand. I thanked him again for dinner, and his moon face widened with that crescent smile, his eyes shining like blue stars. I watched him scrunch down into the cab. There goes a happy man, I thought.

I drifted back to the hotel, loitering with my hands in my pockets by the brightly lit store windows with their women's clothes, jewelry, and beautiful furniture. The traffic raced up and down, hurtling through the big intersections. I wondered where everyone was going. I was mildly drunk and feeling a sweet ache of excitement at being in New York City. I didn't want to go to bed yet. Nobody had gone to bed yet. I wandered into the hotel bar.

I chose a table in a corner and ordered a beer. There were couples seated here and there and several solitary men hunching meditatively over the bar. I drank my beer and began feeling lonesome but in that temporary way, an excitement like the smell of spring in March. I was drinking a second beer when Bugs and McKnight walked in.

They didn't see me. I watched them climb onto bar stools. They planted their elbows on the bar emphatically, as if they were claiming the space for a good, long time. Half drunk, sweetly aching, sad, happy, and curious, I picked up my glass and bottle and went over to them.

"Hi," I said.

Bugs turned, swiveling on the stool. "Well, well, well," he said.

"Can I join you?" I said.

"Why not?" Bugs said.

I lifted myself onto the stool next to Bugs. He and McKnight were drinking whiskey on the rocks. McKnight was smoking a cigarette.

"Did you have a nice dinner?" I asked.

"Yeah," Bugs said. "We'll have to take you with us sometime. You like Italian food?"

"Sure," I said.

"We'll take you with us sometime."

"Where's Fatso?" McKnight asked. The glass of whiskey looked like a thimble wrapped in that big paw. He held his cigarette in the same hand, wedged between two thick fingers.

"I don't know," I said.

"Didn't he eat with you?" Bugs said.

"Yeah, he ate with me. Then he went somewhere."

"Good," Bugs said. "I want you two to get along. We don't want to have to babysit you, Malcolm."

"I don't need a babysitter," I said.

"See, Van Arsdale was kind of a loner last year," Bugs said. "He didn't hit it off with Chris Vale, our other partner."

"Chris ain't easy to get along with," McKnight said.

"Yeah, that Chris, he's a tough kid," Bugs said, smiling.

"We hadda let him hang with us," McKnight said. "By the middle of the season, he wouldn't have nothin' to do with Van Arsdale."

"We didn't mind, understand," Bugs said. "Sometimes, though, the old-timers like to be alone. You understand, Malcolm?"

I think I nodded. I'm not sure.

"Chris and Van Arsdale," Bugs resumed, "were as different as night and day."

"That Chris is some rough bastard," mused McKnight. "Remember when Buddy Driscoll shoved him, Bugs?"

"Yeah. Jesus."

"What happened?" I asked.

"Chris busted him in the mouth," Bugs said.

"Loosened his teeth," McKnight said. "Buddy needed all kinds of dental work."

"I read about that," I said.

"The league suspended Chris for a whole week," Bugs said, "which I don't think was right. Buddy did shove him, after all."

"If a ballplayer shoves you, you got to take recourse," McKnight said.

"Anyway," Bugs said, "the league secretary knew the situation with Chris and Van Arsdale and transferred Chris to another crew."

"Too bad they didn't take Fatso," said McKnight.

"In a way," Bugs agreed, "but Chris was difficult, Billy. You forget."

"He was difficult," McKnight agreed. He flipped his glass, down the hatch, and motioned for two more whiskeys.

I called to the bartender for another beer.

"And yet," Bugs mused, "he was like the old-timers. Bill Klem, Bill McGowan, Beans Reardon—fellas like that. If you think we're tough, Malcolm, you shoulda known those guys. You don't know what tough is."

"They wouldn't have put up with Van Arsdale," McKnight said.

"Put up with what?" I said. "He doesn't bother anybody."

"His style, for one thing," Bugs said. "All that dancin' around like a fuckin' clown out there."

"You couldn't have gotten away with that shit in the old days," McKnight said.

"Never," Bugs agreed.

"I don't know why the players don't mind it more," McKnight said. "I can't understand it."

"They would have in the old days," Bugs said. "Can you see Pepper Martin gettin' a dose of it?"

"The ballplayers ain't like they used to be," McKnight said.

"You got a few but not many," Bugs said.

"The whole fuckin' country's goin' soft," McKnight said. The whiskey had begun to thicken his voice, I noticed. "That's why the Communists are gonna win this thing."

"What thing?" I said.

"Bill's a worrier," Bugs explained.

"The war that's goin' on," said McKnight. "It don't take guns to make a war, Malcolm."

"I suppose," I said. I never could get worked up about the Communists.

"The old pessimist here," Bugs said.

"It's goddamn true," said McKnight.

"Let's finish up, Billy. We got a game tomorrow."

"And the next day and the next," McKnight said gloomily.

I didn't want to finish my beer but felt I had to, or Bugs and McKnight would say something. I sloshed it down. Bugs and McKnight drained their glasses, threw some bills on the bar, and slipped heavily off their stools. They strolled out, not waiting for me, moving stiffly. I paid quickly and chased them, catching up just in time to scurry through the shutting doors of the elevator.

I slept like a dead man that night.

8

Bobby Vadnais also made the big leagues that year. Detroit had brought him north as a reserve outfielder, so Bobby was playing in the town he'd grown up in. It occurred to me, with a series in Detroit looming, that I ought to notify Bugs that I was dating (if that was the word) Bobby's sister. I made the mistake of bringing it up in the dressing room with all four of us sitting around waiting to go up.

"No kiddin'?" Bugs said. "What's she like?"

"She's nice," I said.

"That doesn't tell us squats," Bugs said.

"He means," McKnight said, "is she a looker?"

"I would say so. The point is . . ."

"I know what the point is," Bugs said. "Don't worry about it. Just do your job"

"I shouldn't tell the league president or anything?"

"Jesus," Bugs said. "What do you want, his permission?"

"It's fine, Lee," Roy said, coming up out of his newspaper.

"Roy here never tells us about his girlfriends," McKnight said.

"I don't know that he has any," Bugs said.

"He ain't sayin'," rumbled McKnight.

Roy smiled gently, reading his newspaper.

This was in Philadelphia. We went from there to Detroit on the overnight train. It was a fine way to travel, I discovered: being rocked to sleep with the wheels' fast rhythm whispering up from below, the darkened world and the lights of empty towns flashing past the long window. I didn't draw the curtain. When I woke, I was an hour from Detroit, and the world was soaked in spring sunshine, exposing the plowed fields and the brown and faintly green hills. I shaved and dressed in a hurry. We were in on time, and when I swung down off the train, lugging my suitcase, Vicky was waiting. I hadn't seen her in almost two months.

She was wearing dungarees, snug and right, and a white shirt with button-down collar. Her smile opened out, and I pulled her up against me and kissed her.

"Hi, kiddo," she said.

"Hi yourself," I said.

The rest of the crew came spilling down out of the train. They gathered around, staring at Vicky. I introduced them, beginning with Bugs.

"How *do* you do?" said Bugs.

"Pleased to meet ya," warbled McKnight.

"Delighted," Roy said.

Vick offered them each her hand and a brief smile. Then she stepped sideways to me and took my hand.

Bugs said, "Well, Malcolm, you were right; she's a looker."

"The kid ain't such a dope as we thought," said McKnight.

"Oh, to be young again, huh, Billy?"

"That's the truth," said McKnight.

"How'd you get here?" I asked Vick.

"I've got my car," she said.

"Say, how 'bout a ride to the hotel?" Bugs said.

"I'd love to," Vick said, "but we've got to meet my folks."

"Now?" I said.

"Yup."

"You should have warned me," I said.

"What's the matter?" Bugs said. "They'll love a nice boy like you."

Roy had stood quiet all this while. Smiling. His hair looked almost white in the spring light seeping in through the dirty station windows.

"You bet they'll love him," Vick said.

"Why don't we all have dinner tonight?" Bugs said.

"No, thanks," Vicky said.

We were moving now. Vick kept her hand in mine, and we walked out ahead of the others.

"Oh, to be single again," Bugs said.

"Yes, sir," said McKnight.

"Go easy, you two," Roy said softly.

In front of the station we left them in the taxi line. When we'd gone around the corner, I said, "Where are we meeting your parents?"

"We're not meeting them till tonight."

"Then why did you? . . ." I stopped walking.

"Because I didn't want to drive those creeps anywhere."

"Oh."

"You didn't catch that?"

We were walking again. "No," I said, then added, "Are they really creeps?"

"Jesus, Lee. Did you see how they were looking at me?"

"Not Roy," I said.

"The fat one?"

"Yeah."

"He was okay. It was the other two."

"Bugs and McKnight."

"Yeah. Are they married?"

"Sure. Why?"

"Do they play around?"

I looked at her. "Who would they play around with?"

"Anybody."

"They're too old to play around," I said.

"They're not too old to try."

We found the blue Fairlane. Vick opened the trunk, and I heaved in my suitcase.

"Anyway, Roy's nice," I said.

"He's shy," Vick said.

"Not Roy."

"With me he was."

We got in the car. Today, Monday, was open. I didn't work till tomorrow night. The time seemed vast. Vick stuck the key in the ignition but did not fire up the car.

"Well, what's the schedule?" I said.

"This."

She lifted her arms around me. Maybe it was because it was her city, but I wasn't embarrassed kissing in broad daylight with people streaming past the car. They must have stared, but I didn't mind.

I was nervous about meeting the family and would have liked to get it out of the way, but we weren't going out

184

there till suppertime. Vick's old man and mother were at work and the boys at school, so we couldn't have said hello anytime soon even if Vick had wanted to, which she did not. We larked around, following our noses. We walked along the river and explored Hudson's Department Store. Vick told me how her old man used to take her there when she was a kid, just the two of them, and how grand it seemed, particularly around Christmas. For fun we ate at the lunch counter where Vick's father used to treat her. At five I checked into the hotel. After the bellhop had gone, Vick came up for a quick one on top of the bedspread. The room was high up, and I didn't pull the curtains. The spring light was a soft yellow, and you could see the gray buildings of Windsor, Canada, rising square against the pastel sky. Vick made love with a smile till her face steamed and melted and she cried out. Then she smiled, wet-eyed. We both took showers and went, love-drugged, to meet Vick's family.

With the rush-hour traffic flooding the wide avenues, it took a while to get out there. We drove through a lot of black neighborhoods; then there was a sudden change to white. The Vadnais house was yellow clapboard. It owned a handkerchief-patch of front lawn. Old trees lined the street, and cars were parked almost solid along both sides. We found a space, and Vick snaked the Ford in expertly. She kept glancing at me as we walked to the house. I was pretty nervous. In the living room two long, rawboned boys lay on the floor gazing up at a big TV.

"Hey, you guys," Vick said.

The boys climbed shyly to their feet. Vick introduced them: Steve and Mike. Teenagers. They mumbled hello, stuffed their hands in their dungaree pockets, and looked at the floor. Vick led me into the kitchen.

Her father was sitting at the red Formica-topped table, nursing a beer. Mrs. Vadnais stood at the stove, cooking. Mr. Vadnais glanced at me casually, as though he'd known me all my life.

"Lee," he said, "when's my boy gonna get some playin' time?" You would have thought I'd been in the room right along. "We sit in front of the TV all weekend, we never see him."

"Daddy," Vick said, "this is Lee."

"I know this is Lee."

"Nice to meet you," I said and gave him my hand. He was a small man, thick and square, with very black hair. His face looked doleful but in a way that made you want to smile. I liked the little man from the minute I met him.

Mrs. Vadnais looked older than her husband. She was more reserved, more careful. She put down her spatula and shook my hand, looking me over.

"Sit down, buddy," Mr. Vadnais said. "Victoria, get him a beer."

I sat down. The table was set for dinner. Vick opened me a beer, then flitted from the room. Meat hissed and spat on the stove.

Mr. Vadnais said, "I told Mary, I says, 'He'd be better off in the minor leagues. At least he'd be playin'.' "

"He's got time yet," I said.

"Everyone can't be a big star right away," Mrs. Vadnais said.

"I guess not," said Mr. Vadnais.

"Your son's in the big leagues," I said. "That's every kid's dream."

"My husband's a worrier," said Mrs. Vadnais. "He enjoys it."

"When I had Bobby in the Central Florida League,"

I said, "he was a sweetheart. Never gave me any trouble."

"You ought to be his mother," said Mrs. Vadnais.

"He's got a temper," Mr. Vadnais admitted.

"Remember when he hit Vicky with the rock?" said Mrs. Vadnais.

"Busted her in the forehead. Christ, did she scream."

Then Bobby himself walked in. He lived at home when the team was in Detroit. Bobby was small for a ballplayer, and yet in a room you did not see him that way. He was a little better than my height, strong, with immense wrists and hands. We shook hands, and he grabbed a beer out of the refrigerator.

"We were talkin' about the time you tried to kill your sister with a rock," his father said.

Bobby grinned. He joined us at the table.

"Lee and I got to be careful here," he said.

"Why's that?" asked Mr. Vadnais.

"We're not supposed to associate off the field," I explained.

"League rules," Bobby said.

"You guys can't avoid it," said Mr. Vadnais. "You might be related someday. Then what?"

"Daddy, Jesus." Vicky had just walked in.

"Don't say 'Jesus,' " her mother told her.

"We'll cross that bridge when we come to it," I said.

"Can I help you, Ma?" Vick asked.

"Just talk to the men," said Mrs. Vadnais.

Vick grabbed a beer and sat down with us. "I met Lee's partners, Bobby," she said.

"Yeah?" Bobby's black eyebrows arched up. "You met Trovarelli?"

Vicky wrinkled her face. "They're creeps."

"The butterball?" Bobby said.

"Roy," I said.

"He was okay," Vicky said.

"What's their problem?" Bobby said.

"They got bedroom eyes," Vicky said.

Bobby's swarthy face split with a laugh. He had fine teeth. He was a good-looking kid.

"I guess I should have told them to mind their manners," I said.

"No," Vick said.

"She can take care of herself," said her father.

"I didn't realize it was so bad," I said.

"It wasn't," Vick said.

"Yeah, it was."

"That Trovarelli," Bobby said, "is a tough nut."

Mrs. Vadnais now was setting the food on the table. Vicky jumped up and helped. There was an enormous platter of fried pork chops. The fried-meat smell took me back to my childhood. The two boys loitered in. We'd just begun to eat when the phone rang in the living room. Steve Vadnais ran to answer it. It was for Bobby. We were eating full speed when he came back, especially the boys, bending down and shoveling it in. Bobby reappeared silently. He stood in the doorway with his hands shoved in his pockets and his face glazed and distant.

Vicky broke the silence. "What's the matter, Bobby?"

"I been traded," Bobby said dumbly, as if the word, the concept, was brand new to him.

"Traded?" said his father, in the same voice.

"Yeah." Bobby shook his head and moved to the table.

"I don't get it," said Mr. Vadnais. "How could they trade you?"

"They traded me, all right."

"Sit down, Bobby," Vicky said.

He did. "Jesus," he said.

"Who to?" said his father.

"New York."

"New York?" said Mr. Vadnais, squinting unbelievingly, as if New York was out somewhere at the farthest reaches of the earth.

"It isn't the end of the world," Vicky said. She and the boys were eating again, though with a little more decorum.

"Who'd they trade you for?" asked Mr. Vadnais.

"Straight up for Freddie Chase."

"Chase?" Mr. Vadnais wrinkled his face again. "That bum?" he said.

"He isn't a bum," Bobby said, "is he, Lee?"

"Oh, no," I said.

"Jesus, I could hit Chase," Mr. Vadnais said.

"You couldn't hit Ma," said Steve.

"Yeah?" said Mr. Vadnais.

"Daddy played in high school," Vicky told me.

"What position?" I asked.

"Left out," Steve said.

"And who taught you to play, smart guy?" said Mr. Vadnais. "Who bought you your first mitt and taught you how to use it?"

"You did, I guess."

"My brother taught me," I said.

"New York," Bobby said dreamily.

"I wouldn't mind living in New York," Vicky said.

"Beautiful girls in New York City," said Mr. Vadnais.

"How would you know?" said his wife.

"Mr. Vadnais," I said, "it's no insult to be traded for Freddie Chase. He's a good pitcher. Has a great fork ball."

"I believe you," said Mr. Vadnais.

"When do you leave, Bob?" asked Mrs. Vadnais.

"I got to be in New York tomorrow night."

Mike, who looked about fifteen, said, "You'll be teammates with this guy Chapman."

"That's all I need," Bobby said.

Mr. Vadnais turned his doleful frown on me. "What do you think of him, Lee? What do you think of Chapman?"

I considered a moment. "I don't know. I don't know what I think."

"Don't you think he goes too far?"

"I don't know. I try to imagine what I'd do in his place."

I thought of the signs, WE SERVE WHITES ONLY and the shacks with the gray-skinned black children playing in the weedy dirt.

Mr. Vadnais shook his head mournfully. "What does the guy want?"

"He probably has what he wants," I said. I wasn't sure, though.

"He doesn't have many friends around the league, I know that," Bobby said.

Mrs. Vadnais said, "You eat your dinner, Bob."

He did, hunching over and stabbing disconsolately at it.

"It could be worse," Vicky told him.

"It's a slap in the face," he said.

"It's a trade," I said. "Value for value."

"Could be the best thing ever happened to you," said Mr. Vadnais.

"Could land you in the World Series," I said.

"Think of that," said Mr. Vadnais, smiling for the first time all evening.

After dinner the two boys vanished into the living

room to watch TV, and Bobby went upstairs to pack a suitcase. He was going to fly to New York in the morning. Vick and her mother cleared the table and washed the dishes while Mr. Vadnais and I sat drinking beer. He wanted to know what I really thought of the trade, what I *really* thought of Freddie Chase, and if it was a slap in Bobby's face after all. I had to repeat everything I'd said and swear I meant it. Then he asked about me, my home, and how I'd gotten into umpiring, and, loosened by the beer, I gave him a short account of my life, including Joey's death and the disappearance of my mother. He seemed very concerned, drinking in every word I said.

By and by Vicky sat down again, laying her hands and forearms on the now bare red Formica.

"Have a beer," said her father.

"We're going out, Daddy."

"Yeah?"

"Darn right," she said.

"It was a terrific dinner," I said.

Mrs. Vadnais was hanging up her apron. "Glad you enjoyed it," she said.

Vicky stood up, so I did, too.

"Isn't she somethin'?" said her father. "Is she a doll, or what?"

"She is," I agreed.

"You better marry her 'fore someone else does."

"Ma, will you put a gag on your husband?" Vicky said.

"I been tryin' for twenty-five years," said Mrs. Vadnais.

"Seriously," Mr. Vadnais said, "I'd hate to see you lose out."

"I won't lose out."

"Daddy, will you muzzle yourself?"

"Thank you, Mrs. Vadnais," I said, giving her my hand.

"Come back," she said.

Mr. Vadnais followed us to the door. I said good-bye to the boys, who mumbled from the floor. It was dark in the living room except for the nervous, snowy light of the large screen.

"You come back, Lee," said Mr. Vadnais.

"I'd like to," I said.

"Isn't she a doll?" he said.

"She is."

"Go to bed, Daddy."

"Thank you, Mr. Vadnais."

"Come anytime."

"I'll be in Detroit an awful lot."

"The door is always open."

He watched us go up the walk and along the wide, notched sidewalk. The door shut with a reluctant clunk. The street lamps shone down through the budding branches of the trees. A faint, sweet smell of moist earth mingled with the city fumes. Spring.

We drank more beer in a bar farther out from downtown. On a tiny stage three fellows played country music on guitar, fiddle, and bass. They did "Your Cheatin' Heart" and "Please Help Me, I'm Falling," I remember. Then Vick drove me in on what I would know later was Woodward Avenue. Again I noticed the sudden change from white to black. The Avenue was crammed with bars, movie theaters, record stores, roller rinks, and, I guess, whorehouses. I watched the loiterers; the fancy, strutting women; the groups of angry-looking kids with their thin, curved backs and long, skinny legs. Vicky did not seem interested or even to notice. She'd grown up with it.

We went carefully to my hotel room, darting into the elevator and checking up and down the hallway when we got out. I didn't want to run into any of my partners, even Roy. In bed we went slowly. Later we tried again, but with all the beer I'd drunk and a sudden fatigue that had come over me, I had to give up. I was almost asleep. I told Vick I'd see her to her car, but she said no and kissed me. I said yes, absolutely, and the next thing I knew, she was gone, and I'd been sleeping. I could smell her perfume in the pillow. I went back to sleep, wondering whether the Old Man would get along with Mr. Vadnais, and guessing he would.

The ball parks were half empty at night before the weather turned warm. There would be no one in the sections out beyond the foul poles, the freshly painted blue and red seats sweeping up into the dark beneath the grandstand. The ball parks seemed small then. They seemed more intimate. It was like being indoors, in a ballroom, perhaps, with the night sky for a ceiling above the diamond grills of the light towers. When someone hit one into one of those empty sections, the kids would chase it in packs, clambering over the seats and flurrying down the chutes of the aisles. Cheering on those nights was restrained and conversational; you could hear sentiment in it: surprise, awe, laughter, sarcasm. A big crowd swells a ball park. It depersonalizes it.

Quickly old injuries flared in McKnight's big, gnarled body. He'd played football for Chicago back in the 1930s; his nose had been broken many times and had that squashed, lumpy look. His legs had been punished. His career had been finished by a knee injury: "A big dumb fullback, name of Lenkowski, blind-sided me in the rain one day. Fuckin' knee tore like a piece a celery." Sometimes his legs hurt him so badly, he could not crouch for nine innings, and then Bugs would take his turn behind the plate. Roy and I both offered, but Bugs said no, without thanking us. The cold nights were especially hard on McKnight. He said he'd be fine by mid-May, and then it would begin again in September.

The nights warmed; the ball parks filled. The Barons, thanks to Ron Chapman, ran out ahead of the pack, with Boston and Philadelphia biting at their heels. McKnight's aches subsided, but then he hurt his back, which seemed to trouble him more off the field than on. When we were in Boston, I made the long drive home and slept in my old bedroom. In Detroit I saw Vick and her family. The league hadn't expanded yet; there were only eight teams, eight cities. We were in Detroit every couple of weeks. Vick never went on the road with me. She was waitressing again for her old man, and besides, I wanted to keep her clear of Bugs and McKnight.

In Chicago, McKnight vanished to be with his folks, and in Philly Bugs did the same. Roy's parents were divorced. I don't know where his old man had gone, but his mother lived near Baltimore, and Roy often, though not always, went to see her when the crew was in town.

We all had our rhubarbs, of course. In Chicago McKnight unloaded Terry Conlan for calling him "horseshit," which is automatic, though Conlan was in the dugout when he said it. In Boston I chased Angel Manuel after I rang him out on a slide into home. He kept yelling "boolsheet" at me. "Ees boolsheet, omp, ees boolsheet." He wouldn't stop. I don't think he knew any other English. How he got along in the hotels and restaurants that year, I don't know.

In Washington Roy tossed Clyde Farnsworth, the manager, which was ironic, Clyde being the fellow who discovered Roy when Roy was working in the industrial league in Maryland. Roy was working the plate the night he chased Clyde. Technically, you're not allowed to argue balls and strikes, though they all do to a certain extent. When they really want to let you have it, they visit their pitcher, stall till you come out to tell them to break it up, and then tell you what they think of your strike zone. Which is what Clyde Farnsworth did. Roy peeled off the mask and waddled out to adjourn the conference, and Clyde commenced to bark at him. Roy listened for a minute, smiling like a cherub and, still smiling, heaved Clyde out. Roy's face did flush deep red, I noticed. Clyde called him a "fucking clown" and departed.

Bugs and McKnight didn't invite me to have dinner with them as Bugs said they would. Maybe they changed their minds. Maybe they never meant to in the first place. They never invited Roy, either. They continued to rag him—little things, which Roy didn't seem to resent. He'd be heading into the shower, and McKnight might say, "Don't do nothin' naughty in there." Bugs would snicker. We'd be riding an elevator, and Bugs would notice the weight limit posted on the wall and make some crack about how Roy should have ridden the freight elevator. That sort of thing. Roy would twinkle, as if these schoolboy remarks amused him. I was getting sick of it, myself.

The first collision took place in the dining room of our hotel in Boston. We'd arrived in the city late the night before, and instead of going home I'd stayed in the hotel. It was a fine, warm spring morning. Daffodil light flooded the hotel dining room, which was ornate and old-fashioned, with plum carpeting and poker-faced waiters.

I came in and found Roy alone with his breakfast and the newspaper. The starchy white tablecloth was crowded with plates and bowls. There were eggs, sausages, hashbrowns, pancakes, and fresh fruit. Roy smiled good morning. I sat down.

"Coffee?" he offered.

"Absolutely."

I'd brought a paperback novel, *The Old Man and the Sea*, in case I had to eat alone. I laid it on the edge of the table and borrowed a cup from another table. Roy poured for me, holding the silver pot with both plump hands.

"What are you reading?" he asked.

I showed him.

"Ah," he said.

"What do you think of Ernest Hemingway?" I asked him. Roy was the English teacher.

"A beautiful writer but a bad thinker," Roy said.

The waiter arrived. He was a morning waiter, brisk and aloof. I ordered a couple of eggs, over light, and bacon.

"He doesn't like baseball," Roy said. He'd begun eating again.

"No?" I said.

"DiMaggio and the bone spur. Have you got to that yet?"

"The kid and the old man love DiMaggio."

"DiMaggio's on the sidelines with a bone spur. The boy and the old man wonder what a bone spur is. They assume it's horrendous, to keep the great DiMaggio down, whereas they're the ones who know true pain."

"I missed that," I said.

"In one of the short stories, Hemingway says, 'Baseball is for louts.' "

"Louts?"

"Louts."

"No," I said. "Ice hockey is for louts."

"I agree," Roy said.

"I remember Nick Nickinello saying baseball is the most beautiful game in the world. 'And yet,' he said, 'no badly umpired game has ever been beautiful.' "

It was then that Bugs and McKnight walked in. I saw them before Roy did and guessed that there would be some nastiness. It was scrawled in Bugs's face, the ugly lines of a black mood that might have come from anything—a fight with his wife, a hangover, dreams, anger at being a day older. He and McKnight looked around the way they always did on entering a room, checking everybody with their bold stares, and came over to say hello to Roy and me.

"Sit down," Roy invited them.

"I don't think the table'd hold any more plates," Bugs said. "I think the goddamn legs would give way."

Roy put down his fork. He wiped his mouth with the big linen napkin and smiled.

"I mean, Jesus," Bugs said, "you think you got enough to eat?"

The waiter breezed up with my order. He said, "Excuse me," to Bugs and McKnight, who retreated out of the way while the fellow placed my eggs and coffee on the table. He nodded and was gone.

"How's your back feeling, Bill?" I said.

"Like shit," McKnight said. He wasn't in any sunny mood, either.

"You know," Bugs said, "you're gonna kill yourself, eatin' like that."

"Think what you're doin' to yourself," McKnight grumbled.

"Where's your pride?" Bugs said.

Roy held on to his smile, but some of the radiance had gone out of it. For once the smile seemed to take some effort.

"Do you need all that?" Bugs said. He couldn't drop it. Roy's breakfast had become the focus of Bugs's dirty mood.

"Nobody needs all that," McKnight said.

"Christ, no," Bugs said.

I'd heard enough. For over a month I'd listened to these two and traveled all the way from awe to disgust. I was an umpire; young as I was, I could tell a ballplayer to shut up, and he would. I could order a scrappy, foul-mouthed, street fighter of a fifty-year-old manager to leave the premises, and he would. I knew one thing at the moment: I'd heard enough.

"Why don't you drop it, Bugs?" I said.

Bugs's head snapped around. He stared at me, black eyebrows shuddering together.

"What'd you say, Malcolm?"

"Why don't you leave Roy alone?" I said.

Bugs placed his hands on his hips. The faintness of a smile worked its way up his hard, knobby face.

"Why don't you make me, kid?" he said softly.

"This is ridiculous," Roy said.

"It is," I agreed. I wondered if Bugs could still fight. Probably.

Bugs said, "Don't cross me, Malcolm. I'll clean the floor with you, kid."

"Yeah?" I said.

"Don't cross me," Bugs repeated. "Don't ever cross me."

I didn't look at him.

McKnight said, "Come on, Bugs. Let's eat." He spoke

soothingly, the way Bugs gentled him when he flew into his rages on the ballfield.

"Let's go somewhere else," Bugs said. "I don't like the smell in here."

He gave me a fierce look and turned on his heels. I watched them stalk out. Bugs's shoulders were pushed way back, stretching his jacket.

"Good riddance," I said. I began cutting my eggs.

Roy's hands were in his lap. He stared at his food, suddenly thoughtful. He stared at his food without seeing it.

"Eat," I said.

Roy drew up a sigh. The smile crept partway back. "I really shouldn't eat so much," he said.

"If you want to, you should."

"No, I shouldn't."

"Don't listen to those two stupid bastards," I said.

"All right," he said. He found his fork.

"It's your life," I said. "It's your body."

Slowly he began shoveling it in again. "I wonder what set him off," he said.

"It wasn't you. Bugs has problems."

"You shouldn't have crossed him," Roy said.

"The hell with him."

"You shouldn't have crossed him. It's a long season."

"He'll get over it," I said.

"No, he won't."

I shrugged. "I don't care."

"They don't bother me," Roy said.

"They bother *me*," I said.

"It's a long season," Roy said again.

"Don't worry about me," I said. "I can take care of myself."

"It's easier to get along," Roy said.

"Not always," I said.

That afternoon Bugs had his worst game of the season. He was working second base. Seventh inning, one out; Chuck Webb at first; three balls, one strike, on Amos Sinclair. Next pitch, Webb ran. Ball four. Webb, of course, didn't know it was ball four. He slid into second, and the catcher for some reason threw down there. Bugs didn't know it was ball four. He made the call—out—at second. Webb jumped up and headed for the dugout. The batter had walked, and Webb had been entitled to second, but now he was trotting to the dugout. Russ Gabriella, the shortstop, had taken the throw from the catcher and made the tag. Now Gabriella saw Sinclair jogging to first. He realized what had happened. I was working first, and I caught on at about the moment Gabriella did. I saw him chase Webb, and my heart plummeted like a stone, for I knew what the result of this would be, and I was powerless to prevent it. I couldn't warn Webb. Gabriella slapped the tag on him, right in front of me. Out. There was a long, blank moment of incomprehension, and then Webb understood what had happened. Bugs understood. The Boston bench understood. The crowd of 20,000-plus understood. And the sky fell on Bugs Trovarelli.

It wasn't Bugs's fault, really. At least, it was no more Bugs's fault than Webb's. Why hadn't they looked? Why hadn't Bugs looked? Well, Boston blamed him for not informing Webb that it was ball four. The Blues crowded around him, and the booing was a hurricane. Bugs hated to be booed. It might have been his only weakness as an umpire. The booing worked its way under his skin.

Webb was the first to be unloaded. Bugs threw him

out with a grand fling of his arm, punching a tunnel in the air. He got rid of Phil Nagle, the Blues' big catcher, and, finally, Lou Maples, their manager. Roy, Mc-Knight, and I helped restore order, shoving the fellows away from Bugs and telling them to shut up, what's done is done, and so on. We would nudge them away, and they would holler torrents at Bugs over our shoulders. Bugs yelled back, bawling like a wounded lion. I loved every minute of it.

After the game Bugs spoke to no one, not even McKnight. The dark eyebrows seemed to have knocked together so hard, they'd become attached. His eyes were slitted; he looked oriental in his ferocity. Fortunately, I didn't have to wait for them. I was going home. I left the dressing room with only a nod to Roy, whose nod to me was reassuring, and lugged my suitcase out through the press gate.

I was still driving the red Pontiac. Paulie had rebuilt the engine. I paid a service station near the ball park to keep the car ready, sweetening the deal with free tickets and baseballs for the owner's kids. I hustled over there now, threw my suitcase in the back seat, and flew home.

The Old Man had listened to the game on the radio. He could only hear the games I worked in New York and Boston, but when I was in either city, Frank never missed an inning. Occasionally he could watch me on the TV. He was very sympathetic with Bugs's predicament today. The Old Man assumed Bugs and I were great chums, and I let him think so. The truth would only worry him. I drank some beer; Frank tugged at his whiskey; and we shot the breeze till I cooked dinner. He told me Paul was in love. The lucky girl was Ginny Crocker, whom I remembered from high school. Frank said Paulie would be over later. We had a nice dinner, the Old Man and I. He got smashed. I helped him to bed early, flicked on the TV, and waited for Paul.

Paulie walked in a little before eleven, wearing the smug, tranquilized look of a man who'd just been laid.

"Congratulations," I said.

"On what?" he said.

"On a nice, sticky screw," I said.

Paulie wrinkled his gentle face. He didn't talk that way. Joey did.

"How do you know?" Paul said.

"It's written all over you," I said.

"Yeah?"

"Sure."

I was happy for my brother. I remembered Ginny Crocker as dark-haired and silent, lanky but not ugly. Paul and I opened a couple of beers and sat down at the old table, with its scorch rings and peeling varnish. The tall windows were open, bringing a scent of lilac through the screens.

"So what's new?" I asked.

Paul smiled, blushed, and shrugged.

"You're in love," I said.

"Maybe," he said.

"Gettin' laid every night."

"Not every night."

"Oh, yeah?"

"How's Vicky?" he asked.

"Terrific. I see her when we're in Detroit. I love her old man."

"You gonna marry her?" Paul asked.

"I guess."

"When?"

"I don't know," I said. "In the off-season, I suppose."

"Don't wait too long," he cautioned.

"I can't seem to keep my mind on it," I said.

"Well, as long as Vicky doesn't mind . . ."

"I don't think she does."

We drank. Paulie pushed his chair back. "You want another beer?"

"Sure."

He came back with two more moist bottles.

"I saw Crazy Henrietta today," he said. "I gave her a ride home."

"Was she shopping?" I said.

"Yeah."

Crazy Henrietta was the sister of Mrs. Barlow, the widow who lived down the street. Crazy Henrietta was retarded. Every now and then Mrs. Barlow would give her a purse full of money, and Henrietta would put on a print dress and amble, splay-footed, to town, gawking happily at the cars cruising by and at anyone she might see trimming a hedge or watering a front lawn. She would spend her money up and down Main Street on anything that struck her fancy, which might be stuffed animals, straw hats, sunglasses, balloons, or candy. She would spend till she had no more, then carry her acquisitions home in a shopping bag. Crazy Henrietta had been going shopping for as long as I could remember.

"I haven't seen her for years," I said.

"She looks the same," Paul said. "The kids tease her."

"Do they?"

"They look into her bag and laugh. They pretend they're going to take it from her."

"Little bastards," I said.

Paul's face, which had worn the radiance of love when he'd walked in, had shed its glow, and I saw nervous lines fretting his high, fragile-looking forehead.

"I keep thinking I ought to speak to them," he said.

"Catch 'em in the act, and kick their asses," I said.

"I don't think I could. I mean, I've seen it, and I didn't do anything."

"Just walk over there, and kick the first one you come to in the ass. Kick the little bastard five feet in the air."

"They aren't that little."

"I don't care what size they are."

Paul sighed.

I reached over and gave him a fond swat on the arm. "You can do it," I said. "You'll enjoy it. Hell, I'd love to catch the little bastards ragging Crazy Henrietta." I'd forgotten all about being afraid. I'd forgotten how your insides turn watery and your legs go cold and boneless. I believed, after this morning, that I could lick Bugs Trovarelli, one of the meanest men who ever walked, even if he was in his forties. I'd become contemptuous of McKnight, a gray granite mountain with no brains.

"I was never like you or Joey," Paul said.

"You're fine," I said. I'd forgotten that I wasn't like Joey, either.

"I've never been in a fight," Paul said softly.

"If you had to, you'd do fine," I said.

"I'm not sure."

"Don't say that," I told him.

"It's the truth," he said.

"What's the matter with you?" I said. "What started all this?"

"I don't know."

"Jesus, Paulie."

He smiled. "What the hell," he said. "We do what we can, right?"

"Next time you see those kids bothering Henrietta, you just wade right into 'em," I said.

Paul smiled again. The lines of struggle had evaporated from his face, and he was the same wise, gentle Paul as before. "You're riding high, aren't you?" he said.

"It isn't easy," I said.

"I know it isn't."

"I got to bear down, every game."

"They ought to pay you more," he said.

I pulled down a final gulp of beer. "Kids are rotten, aren't they?" I said.

"A lot of 'em are."

"Why would they tease Henrietta?"

"I don't know," Paul said. "I guess nobody teaches them."

"Listen, Paulie. Don't say you're afraid, okay?"

"Why do you care?"

"Just don't say it. It isn't true."

"How do you know?"

"Because I know you," I said. "And I don't want to hear you talk like that."

"All right. We'll talk about something else."

"Tell me about Ginny," I said.

And he did.

That night, late, I lay in bed on my stomach with my arms wrapping my pillow, staring down at the lighted street. The sidewalk, which wandered along our side of the street, rolled up over the bulging roots of the elms. The road curved lazily under the street lamp. The grasses on the other side of the street were long and ragged. Farther back the land rose, with trees growing on the side of the hill. The road in its milky bath of lamplight looked like a stage set waiting for an act to begin. I hugged the pillow and gazed down, thinking myself to sleep the way Joey used to.

9

We'd come west from Boston: St. Louis, Chicago, Detroit. In Detroit I had my second run-in with Ron Chapman. This one was a beauty—loud, long, and bitter. Chapman had a reason, if not a right, to be angry. I took a home run away from him. A gigantic home run. I took it away by invoking 6.03: "The batter's legal position shall be both feet within the batter's box."

I didn't have to make the call. Some rules are discretionary. I suppose 6.03 gets violated all the time. No one cares. Chapman didn't gain anything by stepping out of the box. If anything, his stride was too long. He might have hit the ball even harder with a shorter, smarter step.

People asked me why I made the call. A lot of writers wanted to know. The truth was, I didn't know. The call was out of my mouth before I'd thought about it. I saw Chapman's foot nip the edge of the plate; I made the call. Why? I wondered then; I wondered now. It was as if Chapman and I were caught in the same spider's web that summer. We could never quite escape each other.

The Barons and Ravens were playing a night game. The score was 2–2 in the eighth. Wes Wheeler was throwing for Detroit. Wes had been in the bigs as long as I could remember. I'd owned numerous editions of his bubble gum card, seen him pitch in Boston, watched him on TV, and rooted for him in a long-ago World Series. He threw the knuckle ball, which is why he'd survived so long. The knuckler is easy on the arm.

Wes was throwing those butterflies tonight, putting them where he wanted. The ball veered, dipped, and hopped, and the Barons swung hard and never quite hit it square. They swung over it, chopping ground balls to the infielders. They scooped mile-high pop-ups. Then in the eighth, Chapman nailed one. There were two out. Wheeler had walked a couple of fellows. He sent a knuckleball to Chapman, who waited, cocked his left leg, stepped to the butterfly, and hammered it. Home run— you knew it instantly. The ball soared like a rocket, flaring high into the upper deck in right. The home crowd let out a low, bruised sound.

I don't know how I saw the ball and Chapman's foot simultaneously. The moment is layered with mystery. Distinctly, I heard the groan of the crowd, a lament not just for the home team but for aging, gallant Wes Wheeler, who had just seen his masterpiece destroyed. Chapman had flipped away the bat and begun his home run trot by the time I made the call.

"Batter is out; he stepped on the plate."

Chapman stopped. He turned. He looked at me as if I'd suddenly started raving in a foreign language.

Confusion clouded the long, fine face. For a moment Chapman looked lost.

Then he got it.

"You are *joking*."

The crowd buzzed. The base runners had stopped. Whit Stahl, the Baron manager, came scuttling out to inquire just what the hell was going on. Meanwhile, I'd walked back carrying the mask and yelled the ruling up to the press box. It came booming out over the PA system, and the crowd released a delighted cheer.

Chapman had followed me. He never scooted after you; he didn't snatch off his hat, herkyjerkey and comical, like most ballplayers in their tantrums. Chapman was all molten dignity. He grew taller.

"You can't make that call," he said.

"I just did," I said.

Whit Stahl had ripped the cap off his elfin head, lifting a snowy sprig of hair.

"Son," Whit babbled, "you ain't got no blessed business bein' an umpire in these major leagues."

"You can't make that call," Chapman said.

He was so close to me, I could smell the soap and sweat of his body. His voice grew and deepened, the words always distinct, always biting. Whit's raspy lecture and Chapman's burning sermon came from opposite directions, garbling each other. It was impossible to listen to both at once. I held my ground. I threw out my chest. Let them yell a while. As long as they don't cuss me. I yelled back. Read the Rule Book. Stop whining. You ought to know better, Whit. (Whit told me *I* ought to.) Chapman was roaring. The crowd cheered, loving it. The three of us hollered louder.

"Okay, Ron, you've had your say. Let's play ball."

"Don't 'Ron' me. I don't know you."

"Whit, get him outta here, or I'll unload him."

Bugs arrived and began tugging Whit, an old friend, toward the dugout. Whit wagged a pale, knuckly finger at me, but I couldn't hear what he was saying now.

"Throw me out," Chapman said. "Be a hero."

"You got about five seconds, or I will."

"Throw me out, white meat."

I did. The crowd cheered me and booed Chapman, who instead of lingering to cuss me, gave his shoulders a haughty shake and walked off the field. Whit Stahl followed him. The crowd booed Whit, too, but Whit paused, lifted his cap high, and grinned, and the booing fragmented, broke off, and they doused the old man with a cheer. Chapman had disappeared into the tunnel. As Whit went down the dugout steps, I glimpsed Bobby Vadnais in the corner, grinning under the brim of his cap.

In the dressing room Bugs sat down with his first beer and sent me a sly, pleased look.

"You got guts, or you're stupid, Malcolm. Or both."

The beer was in bottles, not cans. McKnight pawed one out and twisted the top off bare-handed. "Did you see the look on Chapman's face?" He smiled, lighting the gray gloom below his eyes.

"It was the right call, Lee," Roy said.

"Oh, you think so?" Bugs said.

"It's a rule, isn't it?" said Roy.

"Do we always go exactly by the rules?" said Bugs.

"Don't we?" I said.

"Oh, Jesus, Malcolm, *think*," said Bugs. "Catcher's balk, you always call that?"

"No," I admitted.

"Phantom double play, what about that?"

"I shouldn't have called him out. Is that what you're saying?"

Bugs tipped his bottle up and swigged. He squinted fiercely into space, thinking about it. "I don't know, kid," he said. "Probably not."

"Shit," I said. I wished Nick Nickinello were here. Nick could have told me.

"So what?" Bugs said. "You kick a call, you kick a call. Die with it. Be a man."

"Won't hurt the loudmouth nigger," McKnight said. "Be good for him, in fact."

"That's intelligent," I said.

"Go fuck yourself," McKnight snapped.

"Easy," Bugs said. He was grinning. "Easy, Billy. Easy. Malcolm, it's not what you think. Billy's not prejudiced."

"Oh, no," I said.

"There are colored boys, and there are niggers," McKnight said.

"That's tolerance, if I ever heard it," Roy said.

"Fat clown," McKnight said.

"Easy," said Bugs, grinning. He seemed amused.

"Yeah, Bill's all tolerance," I said. "We'll send you down to Mississippi, Bill, to join up with Martin Luther King."

"You shut his mouth, Bugs, or I will," McKnight said.

I'd stripped by now, and I gave them both my back and went into the shower. Tonight, Vicky. In the shower I dismissed Bugs and McKnight from my mind and began worrying again about my call on Chapman. I couldn't find the answer to what I'd done. I went over it and over it. Pretty soon Roy came waddling in, round and radiant as a peach. I asked him if he'd ever used 6.03.

"Sure," he said.

"But you never took a home run away from anybody?"

"No. I've seen guys leap out of the box to hit the ball. I was working a game in Waterloo one time, and a hitter practically jumped across the plate to reach the ball. They were trying to walk him intentionally. He whacked the pitch into left field."

"Did he argue?"

"How could he?"

"How could he?" I said. "Jesus, how can any of 'em?"

"Malcolm," Bugs called from outside the shower, "die with the call. Have some balls."

I didn't answer him.

"You want to have dinner with Vick and me?" I asked Roy.

"Some other time," he said.

"Why don't you invite us?" Bugs said.

"We like pretty girls, too," McKnight said.

"Tough," I said.

In the restaurant Vicky said, "What's the matter, hon?"

"Nothing," I said.

"Something," she corrected.

"Chapman," I said.

"Put it behind you."

"I can't seem to."

The restaurant was dark. Quiet. A man played the piano. All restaurants were beginning to look the same to me. Vicky and I were eating sandwiches and drinking beer. It was that kind of place.

"Listen," she said, "Bobby can't stand Chapman. Almost no one on the team can."

"I know it."

"Well, then."

"He hates me," I said.

"You took a home run away from him."

"It isn't that," I said.

"He hates white people," Vicky said.

"That's exactly it," I said.

"He's got a problem," Vick said.

"It's like white people hating Negroes," I said.

"Sure it is."

"Except that the white people started it," I said.

"Started what?"

"The hating. Remember Florida? All those laws?"

"You didn't make the laws," Vick said.

"White people did."

"So?"

I thought a while. "Why did I call him out, Vick?"

"Because he left the batter's box."

"Is that all?"

"Sure that's all."

"I remember watching Wes Wheeler when I was a kid. He was with Boston the last time the Blues won the pennant. I remember charging home from the bus stop after school to watch the Series. I'd get home about the third inning. A couple of times Frank was there, playing hooky from work. Of course, everyone was going crazy because the Blues were in the Series."

"The Ravens haven't been in the Series for years," Vicky said.

"I just wonder," I said, "if Wes Wheeler had anything to do with my call."

"This is making me tired," Vick said.

I thought some more. "I don't like Chapman," I said.

"Why the hell should you?"

"I'd like him if he liked me," I said.

"You goof," Vick said.

"I wish I could talk to him."

"It wouldn't get you anywhere."

"I'd tell him I hate those laws, too."

"Lee, he doesn't care what you think."

"No," I agreed.

"Try to forget it," Vick said.

"I will."

"I'll help you," she said.

The crew went east, and in New York the Baron fans were waiting for me. *Ladies and gentlemen, the umpires for this afternoon's game . . .* The booing would begin at the mention of the word *umpire*, thickening till my name was announced, when it would crescendo, a sooty wind roaring through the stadium. The writers had dug around, trying to find other instances when 6.03 had been invoked. Someone remembered that a second baseman by the name of Abe Terrell who played for Washington had been called out for stepping out of the batter's box after belting a twelfth-inning, game-clinching double in 1949. A columnist wrote that Ty Cobb had jumped out of the box while being walked intentionally and whacked the ball like a fellow serving tennis, just like what Roy had seen happen in Double-A ball in Waterloo. None of the writers criticized me for my call, but the Baron fans took another view. At any rate, it was a golden excuse to boo an umpire. Every time I called a close one against the Barons, the crowd would let loose. They booed me when I called time out. They even booed me when I whisk-broomed the plate.

I didn't mind. After a few innings the intensity would dissipate and the booing would take on a lighter, almost friendly tone. Between innings when I'd been catching it good, Roy would stroll over.

"Shake it off," he'd say.

"It doesn't bother me," I'd say.

"That's the kid," Roy would say and squeeze me a wink.

A few innings later I might catch it again, and again Roy would drift over. We'd repeat the conversation.

Bugs was convinced I was suffering the way he would have if it had been him they were booing. "How ya holdin' up, Malcolm?" he would ask, not bothering to hide his smile. Bugs was loving every minute of this.

"It really doesn't bother me, Bugs," I would say.

"It bothers everybody," Bugs would correct me.

"No," I would say, "it doesn't really get to me, Bugs."

"Yeah, and the Pope's Jewish," Bugs would say.

Chapman ignored me. I was no longer worth looking at or speaking to. If I called him out, he accepted it expressionlessly. I believe I could have called him out on a pitch over his head and he would have spun away stone-faced; given those wide, beautiful shoulders a shake; and strode to the dugout without a word. I was boiling inside. I hated the man.

We concluded the New York series with a Sunday doubleheader, and that evening Bugs and McKnight left by train for Philadelphia. Roy and I stayed over; it was late to start traveling. Bugs's wife lived in Philly, and he pushed ahead to have the extra night with her. McKnight left with him rather than ride with Roy and me in the morning.

Roy had a lot of friends in New York. I'd never met any of them. Roy would go his own way, which isn't as odd as it might sound. An umpiring crew is together so constantly that you need the escape. You need a life outside baseball. It's an unwritten rule. McKnight seldom took Bugs home with him when we were in Chicago. Bugs almost never took McKnight. I'd never brought Roy home to meet Paul and the Old Man. That night in New York, Roy excused himself. He said he had friends out on Long Island. I didn't want to leave town with Bugs and Mc-Knight. I thought I might as well be alone in New York as in Philadelphia.

I ate dinner near the hotel and loitered up and down the wide, busy sidewalks, looking in the windows of the fancy stores. I was resisting going back to the hotel. I always felt I was missing out by going to bed in New York; there was so much happening out there, and though it did not concern me, I wanted to see, to wander around and gawk like a kid at a carnival. We did get carnivals when I was young, and the Old Man would give us curfews—ten or eleven—and I remembered lying in bed while the carny ground on deep into the night, wanting to be there so badly that I itched all over. If this had been any other city in the league, I would have gone to bed. But it was New York, the biggest carnival in the world, and I hailed a cab. I told the fellow to take me to Greenwich Village.

"Where inna Village?" said the cabbie, speaking out of the side of his mouth.

"I don't know," I said. "I've never been there."

"Ya lookin' for action? Thrills?"

"No. I just want to walk around and see the place."

"What is this, your first time in New York?"

"No," I said and let it go at that.

"I'll let you off on Bleecker Street, how zat sound?"

"It doesn't sound like anything. I've never been to Greenwich Village."

"Good luck, pal," he said.

The Village on this hot June night was like nothing I'd ever seen. Start with the smells: richer, ranker, filthier, and sweeter even than uptown. I smelled fruit, things baking, and things rotting; sweat, cabbage, coffee, dog shit, leather, and ginger. The sidewalks here were narrow, and the crowds seemed to snake-dance as they churned along. The sidewalk stalls offered fruit, flowers, books, and tomorrow's newspapers. Music poured from the open doors of the record stores. I wandered around, nudged by the human tides, dazed and happy. I bought a banana ice cream cone, the best ice cream I'd ever tasted. I sat down on a bench in a cobblestone square, beside a young fellow in glasses who sat hunched over, reading a paperback book. He didn't seem to want to chat, but that was all right. I drifted some more and on a street corner found a black man singing folk songs and playing a guitar for the money people would drop in a felt beret on the sidewalk. His voice was weary, dusty, sad, and sweet, and he played beautifully, better than people I'd paid to hear in clubs in other cities, picking sharp, clear, tuneful notes that flowed like a stream under his voice, lifting and floating it. People circled around two or three deep. I pushed in as close as I could. He sang "Stagger Lee," which I knew as the Lloyd Price hit on the Top Ten not long ago over WINS. In this fellow's mouth the song became older, wiser, sadder. When he'd finished, a few people dropped coins in the beret. He smiled and thanked them and introduced his next song.

It was the one about the *Titanic* going down. It was, the singer told us, a happy song, a song with a smile in it. Who could smile at such a tragedy? The singer smiled around at us apologetically. White people, all. The man who wrote the song, the black singer, Leadbelly, had been inspired by the fact that Jack Johnson, the heavyweight champion of the world, had been refused a place on the ship because he was a black. "Ol' Leadbelly," the singer concluded, "couldn't help *gloatin'* a little." Everyone laughed—white people—and the thought hit me, vivid and cleansing as lightning turning night to day, that bigotry was on its way out. The fellow broke into his song. Now the singer turned serious. He looked pained. His face was lifted; his eyes were closed. The city lights played soft and blue on his dark skin. It was a sad song, after all. I thought of all those millionaires decked out in their furs and jewels, refusing to let a black man ride with them. And then they were dumped into a black, icy, mile-deep sea. God's work. God, who held us all in His big hands.

The song ended. The little audience rattled applause, and people leaned over and dropped money into the hat. I wanted to give a dollar, but everyone else was throwing in change, quarters and even dimes, and I didn't want to show them up. I tossed in 75¢. The singer thanked me. I sidled out and stood face to face with Roy Van Arsdale.

Our gazes locked. The peachy radiance died in Roy's cheeks. He stared at me dumbstruck.

"What are you doing here?" I said. He'd told me he was going to Long Island. There'd been a mixup or a change in plans. Not a lie. Not from Roy. But what was he doing here?

Roy didn't speak. His soft blue gaze darted sideways to a thin young man in dungarees and a raspberry-red silk shirt open halfway down his pale chest. The skin of his face was like white eggshell. His eyes were dark smudges. He reminded me of a cat—that sleepy watchfulness.

"Roy?" I said.

He still didn't speak. He looked fat and awkward; revulsion tore through me like a savage wind. I knew what this was and did not want to know. I wasn't ready. The

world had taught me nothing but a few smutty schoolboy jokes. *Little boy blew and his mother caught him.* Ho-
mosexuals lived underground in those days. Roy stared
at me, waiting to see what I'd do. Now, rising slowly in
the wake of that battering wind, came pity—so sharp, so
fierce, it felt like love.

"Have you been listening to this guy?" I said, nod-
ding toward the singer. He'd begun a new song.

Roy didn't seem to hear the question. "Are you
alone?" he said. The large umpire's voice had shrunk to
a quaver.

"Sure," I said.

"Bugs and Bill? . . . "

"They took the train to Philly. Remember?"

Roy's boyfriend watched me with the bland, neutral
curiosity of a cat.

"I just came down here to walk around," I said. "I
was bored. I just wanted . . ."

"Roy, babe," said the friend, "it would be polite to
introduce us."

Roy did. The man's name was John. He gave me his
hand; his gaze brushed mine, flat and disinterested.

"Nice to meet you," I said.

"Likewise."

Roy kept glancing up and down the street, looking
for Bugs and McKnight, who were in Philadelphia.

"I didn't know you were interested in the Village,"
he said.

"I was just curious," I said. "I didn't mean to . . ."
I stopped.

"Didn't mean to what?" John cut in.

"Nothing," I said.

"Didn't mean to barge in on us like this?" he purred,
showing a faint twist of a smile.

"I didn't say that," I told him.

"This is where I live, man. I don't go sneaking around here." He said it as a challenge.

"Fine," I said. "Roy, I'm going."

"Wait a minute," Roy said. "Why don't we all have a drink?"

"Oh, fuck that, Roy," John said.

"I'll see you tomorrow, Roy." I was backing away from them.

"I have to talk to you, Lee."

"Fuck him," John said.

"It'll be okay, Roy. Just don't worry."

He stood there looking crestfallen. I waved to him, turned, and plunged into the crowd weaving toward Sixth Avenue, against the oncoming current of humanity. I found a cab and said good-bye to Greenwich Village.

I couldn't find Roy in Penn Station the next morning, so I rode the train to Philadelphia alone. In Philly I took a taxi to the hotel, where I checked in and left word for Roy and McKnight at the desk that I'd meet them at the ball park that night. Then I went walking.

Philadelphia seemed like a wealthy city to me. That's how I remember it, anyway. I walked the wide, clean sidewalks and looked at the pretty women smart-stepping along in their high heels. I stared in a jeweler's window and saw myself reflected back, standing there alone with my hands shoved down in my pockets, digging under the hem of my jacket. Meeting myself this way was not at all like peering into a mirror to shave or comb my hair. Here I looked different somehow. I noticed the downward slant of my eyes and how narrow they were. They were the Old Man's eyes, I realized—stubborn.

The day inched along. I walked around City Hall, which looked tear-stained from the dirty city air. People were feeding the pigeons in the treeless square. I gave a dollar to a crippled beggar who lay propped against a building with his crutches thrown across his shriveled legs. I ate a wedge of blueberry pie and drank coffee in a luncheonette, and the afternoon was finally gone.

The three of them were there when I walked into the dressing room. Roy, huge and round in his knitted longjohns, was polishing his shoes. His glance did not quite reach my face.

" 'Lo," he said. I saw worry in his face, pale and bright like a fever.

"Hi, Roy. When you get in?"

"Couple hours ago." He buffed his shoe, spat on it, and buffed again.

"You're awful quiet, Roy," Bugs said, unbuttoning his shirt.

"Am I?" Roy paused to inspect his work.

"I said so, didn't I?" said Bugs.

"Who's pitching tonight?" I asked.

"Don't you read the paper?" said Bugs.

"He ain't got time," McKnight said. "Too busy readin' books."

"You ought to try it sometime," I said. "You can read, can't you, Bill?"

"You're never gonna learn, are you, Malcolm?" said Bugs.

"Learn what?" I said.

There was a knock on the door. Bugs was closest, so he opened it. It was the clubhouse boy.

"Letter for Mr. Malcolm," he said. "It came about a week ago. We been holdin' it."

"I'll take it," Bugs said. The kid vanished. Bugs shut

the door. He squinted at the envelope, smiled evilly, and sniffed it. "A young lady," he said. "Name of P. Rogers."

My first thought was that it was a mistake.

Bugs studied the envelope. "P. Rogers," he said again. "From Bryn Mawr. You keepin' someone on the side, Malcolm?"

I only half heard him. He handed me the letter, grinning. The script, flowing and competent, was Pam's. I tore off the end of the envelope and shook out the letter.

I'm in Bryn Mawr for the summer, commuting to work in the city and house-sitting for a former professor who is in Italy. The job is with a summer program to enrich the lives of underprivileged children, if that is possible in this sick country. The children are, of course, black. The house is another world: azaleas, trees, Renaissance prints, a banquet of books and records. I will be here till after Labor Day; then law school.

My father, bless him, has the Covenant *sent to me, which is how I learned that you have become a major-league umpire. How very imposing! When the baseball season began, I discovered that one can, by consulting those hieroglyphics known as box scores, learn who is umpiring. I've known it each time you've been in Philadelphia, and each time I've wanted to get in touch with you. Till now, my nerve has failed me. I am writing instead of phoning because this way it will be easier for you to refuse my invitation to dinner. I have changed a lot, and I'm sure you have, too. But wouldn't it be fun to see your high school sweetheart again? I'm an excellent cook, I promise you.*

My hand fell to my lap, clutching the letter. I stared into space, trying to think.

"A love letter?" Bugs said.

"Looks like it," said McKnight.

"Some guys are just plain greedy," Bugs said. "A nice piece of pork like that Vadnais broad, and the kid wants more."

The talk drifted past me. It had been almost three years since I'd seen Pam. I had not expected to, ever again. I had not even expected to run into her on Main Street or in the post office some Christmastime. She might as well have died, where I was concerned. It had been as if there were no Pam Rogers. I lifted the letter and sniffed it: a faintness of roses. But there was, after all.

I was working first, Roy second, and after the conference at the plate, we walked together to the edge of the outfield grass and stood watching the pitcher warm up, chewing our gum, arms folded on our chests. Spofford, the first baseman, was rolling ground balls to the infielders.

"Well," Roy said, watching the pitcher, "I'm in a hell of a mess, aren't I?"

"No," I said.

"Yes," he said, "they're going to get me sooner or later."

"No, they won't."

"They always do. I didn't resign from that prep school in Virginia. I got sacked."

"How'd they find out about you?"

"Let's just say I did something stupid."

"They won't find out here," I said.

"You did."

"It was one chance in a million."

"Maybe."

"It was."

"I've been so careful."

"Relax," I said. We watched the pitcher twirl and throw, bending his back over the ball. I kept thinking about Pam. Roy's problems flickered distantly.

"Do you hate me?" he said.

"Of course not."

"I know I disgust you."

"You don't."

The PA announced the anthem, and we removed our caps and turned to face the flag. The flag flapped high on the night sky, which was as shiny blue as a new bruise. The anthem commenced.

"Why," Roy said, "did you rush off last night?"

"I felt out of place. Your friend didn't like me."

"John's very proud."

"It wasn't my fault I ran into you."

"No one said it was."

"John acted like it."

"John has suffered," Roy said.

"Not from me."

The anthem surged to its final, rousing notes. "Oh, say does that star-spangled banner yet way . . . hayve . . .'"

"Listen," I said, "we'll have supper tonight, okay?"

"All right."

"Cheer up. We'll get through this fine."

"Think so?"

"Hell, yes."

The last note faded and was swallowed by cheering. The crowd rustled to their seats. Behind the plate Bugs clamped on the mask. *Play buh.* Soon I was deep inside the game.

223

. . .

"It's Lee," I said.

On the other end, an intake of breath and then: "God, I'm glad you called."

"Why wouldn't I?"

"Oh, Lee, it's so wonderful to hear you."

Her voice was the same. No, it sounded bouncier, more confident. I was all in a turmoil.

"Did I call too early?" I said.

"Of course not. My God, I'm just glad you did. How are you?"

"Good. Taking my lumps."

"I'm just dying to see you. Will you come to dinner?"

"When?"

"Tonight?"

"I could take you out, you know. I'm not poor anymore."

"Wouldn't hear of it. You must be sick to death of restaurants."

"I am, come to think of it."

"Six-ish?" she said.

"We've got an afternoon game. I'll come straight out."

The local train at that hour was crammed with fellows coming home from work in the city—men in suits with the scent of money on them, lugging briefcases. They filled the seats and crowded the aisle of the stuffy, lurching train, trying to read newspapers.

The train first click-clacked through tenement neighborhoods. I saw white cracking streets, row buildings, barrooms with no windows. I saw an old black man in gray clothes, wandering woozily—drunk, maybe, or sick. I saw a sharp-faced young fellow, also black, with a paper bag tucked under his arm, standing on an empty street corner, glancing up and down as if he was waiting for someone. There were no trees on that street. I wondered what was in the bag. I wondered who the kid was waiting for. I wondered what his story was and the story of the woozy old man in gray clothes.

Then the city was gone, and I was looking down at big houses and brick apartment buildings. We began stopping, and the fellows with briefcases began getting off the train. The little stations had brick platforms, slate roofs, and cupolas. They looked old-fashioned and sleepy, like the depot in *High Noon*. Just before each stop, the conductor would throw open the door at the end of the car and sing the name of the town. I held my breath each time, waiting for Bryn Mawr, and it seemed like a hundred stops, a hundred sleepy little stations with the businessmen heading home to their wives, before the man said, "Bryn Mawr, *Brynnn* Mawr," and she braked, squealing, and shuddered to a halt.

I'd bought a bottle of wine in a liquor shop in the station, and when I swung down off the train, I was holding the bottle by the neck. I landed on a brick platform in golden sunlight. Sounds—the screech of the train pulling out, voices on the station platform, traffic— whirled around me. The train was gone. I stood with the wine bottle, squinting in the late, sharp light, looking for Pam.

And found her. She was getting out of a car. She smiled, waved, and came running, more beautiful than I wanted her to be. She was a woman now. That was the difference. Time had caressed her, given her one last pat and smoothing. She threw herself at me, hugging me hard; the smell of her perfume blew through me, waking buried feelings. She yanked back, held me at arm's length, and looked at me.

"You look wonderful," she said.

"You do, too," I said.

"God, it's good to see you."

"You, too."

"Come on."

She grabbed my arm, and we headed for the car. There was an energy in her, something nervous, that was new. The car was a shabby Nash Rambler with fins. I sat with the bottle of wine in my lap. Pam wore a skirt. Her legs were summer golden.

"There's the college," she said.

"It's pretty," I said. It reminded me of a castle, with its archways and buildings of gray stone.

"Yes," she said. "Too pretty. Sheltered."

"From what?" I said.

"The real world. Life."

I knew what she meant, but on the other hand I knew fellows who had worked in factories and brawled in barrooms who would not last ten minutes at college. I wasn't so sure where the real world left off.

"Where'd you get the car?" I asked.

"It's Richard's," she said. "I got the house and the car for the summer."

"Richard's the professor?"

"Classics," she said. "His wife teaches American lit at Penn."

"Jesus."

"I've been sort of a protégée. I ended up majoring in classics."

I didn't quite know what "classics" were but didn't say so.

"It's pretty out here," I said.

"Oh, yes," she said. "The Main Line, you know."

"A lot of money, I guess."

"An obscene amount."

"Not the professors?"

"Jesus, no."

"A professor shouldn't be rich," I said. "It would ruin the image."

"No," she agreed. "He should be tweedy and out at the elbow."

The house sat along a narrow hall of a street behind different kinds of high, dense shrubs. Our footsteps echoed on the long wooden porch. Smiling, Pam opened the door, and I was surrounded by the dry, sweet smell of worn wood floors and old books, a dustiness that called frayed rugs to mind, and a magical fragrance of summer roses. I looked around; there were books on all the walls, and a tall, gilt-edged mirror. Silence squeezed the house, and it occurred to me that the only silences I ever knew these days were in my air-conditioned hotel rooms.

"Show you around?" Pam said.

"Do you suppose I could have a drink first?"

Pam looked questioningly at me with those blue, blue eyes. "Is this so painful?" she said.

"I'm kind of nervous," I said. It sounded stupid, and I felt stupid—thick-tongued, ignorant, groping.

"But why?" Pam asked, smiling and gazing deep into me. And before I could answer, she added, "We *are* old friends."

"Yes," I agreed, but I knew that didn't cover the situation, and I guess I knew she knew it, too.

"Come on," she said brightly, "I'll get you that drink."

I followed her through the dining room to the light-splashed kitchen, which smelled of coffee and cloves and fruit. The floor gave underfoot, spongy beneath the linoleum.

"I'm afraid I don't have any beer," Pam said.

"That's okay."

"I've got wine and vodka. It's my turn to be poor."

"Vodka's fine."

She rattled ice out and poured me a huge one, then helped herself to white wine. We went out onto a brick terrace under a grape arbor—a sloping shed roof of leaves. Daylight lingered, striking golden against the distant tops of the old trees. We sat down facing each other on porch chairs. Pam crossed her legs and smiled, and I thought, *Oh God, don't be so beautiful, Pam. Don't be so perfect. Please don't be so beautiful.* I sipped; the vodka bit the roof of my mouth and burned on down. I'd never drunk vodka straight.

"How was your game?" Pam asked.

I sighed. "Oh . . . not so bad. I had a decent game."

"You don't sound enthusiastic."

"We have some problems on the crew. I don't like two of my partners, and they don't like me."

"There are four of you, right?"

"Yeah. I get along fine with the other one. Roy Van Arsdale."

I gulped vodka. She watched me. "Aren't you happy, Lee?"

I took another swig. "It's tough right now. Confusing."

"Why?"

"It just is."

"Come on," she prodded. "If you can't tell me, who can you tell?"

At the moment the notion made perfect sense to me. If I couldn't tell Pam Rogers, who could I tell? The last three years dissolved, falling away like smoke.

"Can you keep a secret?" I said.

"You know I can."

I tugged again at my vodka and started to talk. I told

Pam everything. Bugs, McKnight, Roy, Sunday night in Greenwich Village. I spilled it all, emptying myself. Our drinks were gone when I'd finished, and the sun was touching only the tops of the trees. Pam never took her eyes off me.

"You were always such a dear," she said.

"No. But I'm glad you think so."

"What's going to happen?" she said.

"As long as no one finds out, nothing."

"And if they do?"

"There'll be a scandal. Roy will be through in base-ball."

"That isn't right, is it?"

"I can't worry about that, Pam. I just want to keep Roy in baseball."

"Why would he want to stay?"

"He loves it. He loves umpiring."

"Yes," Pam said, thoughtful. Then she brightened, uncrossed her legs, and came smartly to her feet. "An-other drink?"

"I'm already drunk," I said.

"Good," she said and took my glass.

The screen door banged. I waited, gazing out through the trellis bars to the darkening shrubbery. Shadows spilled across the lawn. It all looked green and mysterious and very beautiful. Pam came back, bumping the door with her hip. She handed me my drink, smiling as if it were her pleasure, her honor, to serve me vodka.

"How's your father?" she asked, settling into her chair.

"Good. Terrific. Your parents?"

"The same."

We both sipped and looked out into the green dusk.

"I would have written you, Pam," I said. "I figured

I'd burned my bridges. I figured you were through with me."

"Things change, Lee. Old bridges come down; new ones go up."

I thought about this.

"What happened to the girl in Florida?" Pam said.

I hesitated.

"You're still seeing her," Pam said.

"Yes."

"Often?"

"She lives in Detroit. I see her when we're there." Which was true, as far as it went. Pam was silent. "What about you?" I said.

"I'm seeing someone."

We sipped our drinks and stared out through the bars of the trellis.

"Why'd you write me?" I asked.

"What a silly question."

Again I felt slow. I wondered if I wasn't quite grasping what was happening here.

Pam said, "I wanted to see you. Why else?"

"But why now?"

She shrugged and smiled. Her ease, her confidence, seemed to flow from a greater wisdom than my own. "I guess my curiosity finally got the better of me," she said.

"Curiosity?" I asked.

Smiling, she got up, then came over and laid a hand lightly on my shoulder. "Don't complicate this," she said. "Don't question it to death."

"I won't," I said, feeling as if I'd reached some dizzying height and could look down only at my peril.

I didn't remember ever eating by candlelight except in restaurants. The house had gone a little downhill, but this professor and his wife lived the good life. The tablecloth was of snowy linen. Two roses, blood red, nodded from a slender silver vase. From the room beyond, classical music played. We'd opened the wine I'd brought—a red—and nearly killed it. Talk had gone this way and that: umpiring, Pam's family, mine, politics. Pam had been growing steadily more disgusted with the way things were going in this country. I agreed with her, more or less. Her work, she said, was next to useless, but at least she was there, learning what poverty was all about.

"What do you do with these kids?" I asked.

"Oh . . . teach them to swim. Take them to museums, the library. Keep them off the streets."

"Are they all colored?"

"Black. Yes."

"Poor?"

"Of course."

"It was awful in Florida," I said.

"It's the same up here," she said.

"No."

"Sure it is. They're just more honest about it down there."

"Maybe so." I didn't know. I had never concentrated on the problem.

"It absolutely is," Pam said.

An idea hit me. "Why don't you bring your kids to a ball game? Sometime when I'm working."

"I don't know," she said.

"Don't they like baseball?"

"I don't know."

"I could get a few of the players to say hi, sign some autographs."

"Are there any black players on the team?"

"Why do they have to be black?"

"God, Lee. Think about it. So the kids can identify."

I shrugged. "All right. Philly's got some Negroes on the roster."

"Blacks," she corrected me.

"Blacks," I said.

She smiled, chasing away the almost fierce impatience that had come over her. "It's a deal. Set it up. We can't pay for it, understand."

"I'll work something out. Maybe the ball club will come across."

"Set it up," she said again. "What the hell."

The record finished, a sudden deep silence, as if the room beyond had gasped and held its breath. Pam put her napkin on the table and popped to her feet.

"I have a surprise for you."

I watched her move out into the lamplight and lift the record from the phonograph. She unsheathed another. The needle bumped down, and there was that rustle before the music began.

It came with the suddenness of a door slamming: a ringing of guitars and the sultry voice, now soft, now snarling, always smooth as butter. Elvis. His very first album. It led off with "Blue Suede Shoes." Pam came in strutting, moving her shoulders. She smiled down at me in a questioning sort of way.

"The professor likes Elvis?" I said.

"His daughters, I expect."

"I haven't heard this in years," I said.

"Can you still dance?" she said.

"I never could dance."

"Oh yes, you could."

She reached; I gave her my hand. The high mirror framed us, showing me how tall and broad I was beside this neat, finely chiseled woman with her treasure of hair splashing her shoulders. We faced each other and paused, shy and self-conscious. Then Pam gave her head, her tawny hair, a shake, and we began to dance—prancing, swiveling, and stomping the dance of our childhood and of the vanished decade of the 1950s.

After "Blue Suede Shoes" we slow-danced to "I'm Counting on You." I closed my eyes and breathed the familiar sharpness of her perfume.

"Just like dancing in the gym," I said. "I couldn't wait for the slow ones."

"No?"

"Of course not. This was the fun part."

"It was a wonderful year, Lee."

"Yeah," I agreed.

"Good old Elvis," she said.

"Too bad he had to go into the army."

"He got out."

"I know. But it's not like it was."

"Things change," she reminded me.

When the song ended, she did not disengage. She arched against me, arms up around my neck. Her smile carried the confidence that had made the evening natural and right from the beginning. Elvis jumped into "I Got a Woman." Pam held on, and I ducked down and kissed her. It was a long, searching kiss. Then, still holding her, I said, "Shall we have dessert?"

"What did you have in mind?" she asked.

"Have in mind?"

"Would you like to go upstairs?" She still held me, still gazed up smiling, unflinching, as if she'd proposed a walk up the block or a drive for ice cream cones.

"Pam . . ."

"What?"

"Just like that?"

"No," she said, "not just like that. We've known each other for years and years and years. My God, all our lives."

"True," I said.

"Don't be old-fashioned."

Love flooded me: I could feel its rush in my bones. I bent down again and kissed her. There was no turning away; I'd let it get too late for that. Gently Pam separated from me. I waited while she blew out the candles on the dining table, then followed her up the wide, creaking staircase, treading lightly, almost sneakily, with Elvis wailing on below.

Pam's bedroom was just at the top of the stairs. A hall light burned dully, shabbily lighting the time-darkened hardwood floor. You could barely make out the pictures on the walls. The bedroom smelled of old perfume, the stale-roses scent of a pillow a woman has slept on. Pam left the door half open, letting in an ooze of dingy light. Elvis came through more thinly now, swirling up the stairway and around the corner. The bed was a double. I sat down on it with my heart racing, half believing, half comprehending. Still on her feet, Pam began confidently to undress—slowly, with each thing done with great attention to detail. It was a ceremony. I could not help thinking of Vicky, who shed her clothes with the naturalness of a tree dropping its autumn leaves. With Pam it became somehow dramatic, each movement heavy with significance.

I watched, scarcely breathing. Her body was as graceful as a figure on a vase. I sat dumbly on the edge of the bed. Pam shucked her panties with a smart flick of her ankle and landed neatly beside me.

She draped her arms around me and dabbed kisses over my face. She unbuttoned my shirt and massaged my chest with a cool, skilled hand. She was in charge. When the moment had come for her, she drew me down beside her. Pam was all movement, all restless, searching energy. She hurried, yet took her time. Each new move was made with great care, with ceremony—and yet recklessly, almost desperately, as if for the last time. I felt like an innocent, as if all my lovemaking till now had been child's play. This was the real thing. The major leagues. Pam finished with a shriek that might have wakened the neighbors.

We lay on our backs a long, long time, gazing at the swirls and meandering cracks of the old plaster ceiling. The music had ended long ago, though I couldn't have said when. Occasionally a car wandered by, poking slowly along as if hunting for something or snooping. My drunkenness had ebbed, leaving depths in me, caverns of wisdom. I was feeling all of life's wonder and poignancy.

"Pam?"

"Hi," she whispered.

"Was that okay for you?" I knew damn well it was.

"Divine," she said.

"Can I ask you something?"

"Sure."

"Who's your boyfriend?"

"You."

"No," I said. "You said you were dating someone."

"His name is Charles."

"Charles what?"

"Brewster."

"What does he do?"

"He teaches English at Bryn Mawr."

"You're kidding."

"No," she said.

"Did he teach you?"

"Yes."

"Jesus."

"He's young. Divorced."

"Jesus," I said.

"Very brilliant and high strung."

"Charles Brewster sounds like a rich snot," I said.

"His family is. Charles has rejected all that."

I pictured him: long and bony. A genuine Communist. McKnight would think so, anyway.

Pam said, "He wants to marry me."

My heart dropped like a stone. "Are you going to?"

"I doubt it."

"Will you . . . keep on seeing him?"

"I don't know."

I wrestled with it, struggling to understand. Pam rolled onto her side. "Don't look so sad," she told me.

I didn't say anything or look at her.

"Hey," she said and smiled. She reached around me, kissing my forehead, my jaw. I wished again that she wasn't so beautiful, so perfect.

"What time is the last train?" I asked.

"Forget trains tonight," she said.

She reached down. I began to forget everything.

"I love you, Pam," I said.

"I love you," she said.

"Can I see you when I'm back in Philly?"

"Of course," she whispered.

We loved more simply this time—and more eagerly, if that could be possible. Pam's cry at the end seemed to come from far off, a ripple that ran wildly about the walls and ceiling. She relaxed with a groan, and I sagged away from her and was hurled into a deep, black sleep.

It was morning when I woke, a warm, blond summer's day with the birds singing busily. Pam was awake. She was propped on two pillows, bare-breasted, reading.

"Good morning," she said.

"I don't believe I'm here," I said.

"You're here."

"Yeah?"

"Take my word," she said.

She didn't have to be at work at any special time. She laid down the book, a novel by Jane Austen, and we made love again, very straightforward. It was like that in all the times afterward: elaborate ritual at first, which would break down in the subsequent lovings, like formalities being thrown aside.

I rode a late-morning train into the city, dazed and happy and feeling as if until yesterday I'd never known excitement.

10

What'll I do, Paulie? Tell me.

Jesus, Lee. I don't know.

I got to tell Vick.

Of course you do.

I'm afraid to, Paul. I'm afraid of what it'll do to her.

You ought to think twice.

What do you mean?

I like Vicky a lot better than I like Pam, you want to know the truth.

You haven't seen Pam in years.

So what?

Paulie, she's gorgeous. I can't even describe how gorgeous she is. And intelligent. You should hear her talk, Paulie. She always has just the right words for things. Metaphors and things.

So what?

So I love her, that's what.

You better tell Vicky.

It'll kill her, Paulie.
Don't be so sure.
Maybe I'll write to her. It might be easier that way.
That's a rotten way to do it.
Okay, okay.

"What about Charles Brewster?"

"What about him?"

"Are you still seeing him?"

"Does it matter?"

"Hell yes, it matters."

"I hardly ever see him. He has no relevance to you, Lee."

"You're phasing him out?"

"Don't try to pin what we have like a butterfly to a card. Enjoy it. Enjoy its beauty."

Metaphors. You ought to hear her, Paulie. She's always right on the money where the English language is concerned.

Pam always sat ramrod straight, impeccably graceful, whereas Vicky slouched. I realized this while watching Vick across the Formica table under the bright overhead light of her parents' kitchen. The family had straggled off to bed. Vick slouched with her arms laid along the edge of the table.

"What's the matter, hon?" she asked.

"Nothing."

"Something," she said.

"Well . . ."

"Come on." She reached across and took my hand. Vick's hands were warm and moist. Pam's were cool and dry.

"It's . . . it's about Roy."

"What about him?"

239

I could look at her now. Talking about Roy, I could receive Vick's quick smile and meet her bold green gaze.

"Can you keep a secret?" I said.

"Sure."

"I mean from your family. From Bobby. Especially from Bobby."

Vick leaned back from the table and traced a cross at her breast. Cross my heart and hope to die.

"He's queer," I said.

Vick hunched lower, closer to me over the table. "You're kidding," she said.

"I'm not."

"You're *kidding.*"

"Lower your voice," I said.

"How do you know?" she asked.

I told her how I'd seen Roy and his boyfriend in Greenwich Village.

"Jesus H.," Vicky breathed.

"Whatever you do," I said, "don't tell Bobby."

"I won't."

"Roy's through in baseball if this gets out."

"It'll get out," Vick said.

"No," I said.

"Want to bet?"

"It won't get out through me," I said.

"Have you told anyone else?"

"No," I lied.

"I'm glad you told me," she said. "You've been acting kind of funny. At least I know why."

"Yeah," I lied.

Vick thought a moment. "Jesus H.," she said again. "I've never heard anything like it."

"Like what?" said a voice behind me.

It was Vick's father. He'd come padding down in his

pajamas. He stood inside the door, squinting against the light. His pajamas were baby blue. His black hair was mussed, his square face puffed from sleeping.

"None of your business," Vick told him.

Mr. Vadnais trudged to the middle of the room. His bare feet were thick and meaty on the gray linoleum. He yawned.

"What the hell'd I come down here for?" he said.

"To take a leak?" Vicky said.

"Don't be fresh," said her father.

"You came down for milk, you goof," Vicky said.

"You're right," Mr. Vadnais said.

We watched him hunt for a glass. He opened the refrigerator.

"Anybody else want milk?" he asked.

"With beer?" Vick said.

Mr. Vadnais replaced the milk bottle and shut the refrigerator. He carried his glass of milk to the door.

" 'Night, you two lovebirds," he said and shuffled into the darkness beyond the kitchen.

Paulie, I hate myself sometimes.

For Christ sake, tell her.

I will.

When?

Soon.

You keep saying that.

I keep thinking about her old man. If only I could protect him from this.

On an off-Monday I lay in a cavern of shade under a giant purple beech, with my head in Pam's lap, listening to her read poems from a book she'd studied at college. She read carefully, firmly, insisting on every word—the way she made love. Her tan hair fell shining past her face.

Beyond the tree's cool shade, the sun burned the sloping green lawns of the campus. Summertime, and the college was deserted. Nearby a freight train lugged through, a mile-long rumble that made the ground ache. Pam read for perhaps thirty minutes, grew tired of it (it had been her idea), and shut the book. I watched her upside-down. She leaned back on her hands and shook her hair away from her face.

"You're upside-down," I said.

"How do I look?"

"Almost as beautiful as right side up."

"Only almost?"

"You're the most beautiful girl I've ever known," I said.

She smiled, and we were quiet a while, listening to the cicadas. Their scratchy whir would rise swiftly, then die away.

"Oh," Pam said, "I forgot to tell you. My kids would love to see a baseball game. It seems they like baseball. I was surprised."

"Fine," I said.

"I told them about meeting the players. The guy they really want to meet is this Ron Chapman."

"Chapman? Chapman doesn't even play for Philly."

"They know that."

"I know they know it. I just . . ."

"What?"

"Nothing."

"Tell me," she said.

"I had a big run-in with him. Didn't you hear about that?"

"Where would I?"

So I told her how Chapman had knocked the home run into the upper deck in Detroit and how I'd nullified

it and what a fuss there'd been. I told her about Opening Day in New York, when Chapman had been picked
off first and how he'd come after me then, too. I kept
going, telling her that he'd been arrested in Alabama for
riding in the front of a city bus and that he was a friend
of Dr. Martin Luther King. I told her of the chip he carried on his shoulder.

"It sounds as if you admire him," Pam said.

"I can't stand him," I said.

"His dislike isn't personal," she said.

"It feels personal."

"He's holding you responsible," she said.

"Which isn't fair."

"It's perfectly fair."

"Did I write the laws in Alabama?"

"Are you doing anything to abolish them?"

"No," I admitted.

"Our forebears were slave owners, Lee."

"Not mine. Frank's parents came over from Scot-
land. And they couldn't have afforded slaves even if
they'd wanted some."

Gently, serenely, Pam said, "There's a collective guilt
we all share. You. Me. All of us."

I remembered my conversation with Vicky the night
I'd nullified Chapman's home run and unloaded him
from the game. Then, I'd almost taken Chapman's side,
the way Pam was now. Vicky had pushed me one way,
and now Pam was pushing me another. I wondered what
I really thought.

Pam said, "At any rate, this Ron Chapman doesn't
sound anything like a baseball player."

"He's a baseball player," I said. "He's another
. . . DiMaggio."

"Well, can my kids meet him?"

"I guess I could ask him."

"I don't want to put you in an uncomfortable position."

I laughed. "It isn't exactly cozy at the moment."

"Make sure he understands that these are black children," Pam said.

"What if they weren't?"

"Just make sure he understands."

I sighed. I didn't want to argue with this woman. I just wanted to love her.

"You're a dear," Pam said.

A week later we worked a series in New York, and the first night I went up in my street clothes, early, to speak to Chapman. The Barons were taking batting practice. I found Chapman by the cage, idly swinging a weighted bat while he waited to go in and hit. It was that quiet hour long before a ball game, when the stands are nearly empty. Only the kids have come, bringing their gloves to chase the balls that are fouled or driven into the seats. The balls *plock*ing on bats and *whap*ping in gloves, the floating, tuneful voices, make a lazy, playground sound.

"Can I speak to you, Ron?" I said.

Chapman gazed down at me, with the weighted bat resting on his shoulder.

"Speak," he said.

"I want to ask you a favor," I said.

"That's funny," he said. "That's *real* funny." The lean, dark face looked as impregnable as a canyon wall.

I plunged on. "It's about some young . . . black kids in Philly."

The tall man studied me. "What about them?"

"I have a friend who's a social worker there. I told her she ought to bring these kids to a game sometime, maybe get some handshakes and an autograph or two. They, um, are all crazy to meet you. Even though you play for New York."

I thought then that I saw the glimmer of a smile, a faint softening. "How many kids?" he asked.

"It could be anywhere from twelve to twenty-five, even thirty."

"Who pays?"

"I'll talk to the ball club."

"No," he said. "I'll buy the tickets. Box seats."

"You sure?"

"They're my people."

I shrugged. "I'll set it up."

"No. I'll set it up. Just tell me where your friend works."

I did. "I'm not sure of the address," I said.

"I'll find it."

"Thanks," I said. I hesitated.

"Anything else?" he asked.

"I guess not."

"I bet," he said, "you want to tell me you're sorry you took a four hundred and fifty-foot home run away from me. I bet you want to tell me you didn't want to do it, but you were just doing your job."

"I guess that's right," I said.

"You disappoint me," he said.

"What did you want me to say?"

"Nothing."

"Nothing?"

"That's right," Chapman said.

"What good would that do?"

"What good is this doing?" he asked.

"None," I admitted.

Then Chapman said a strange thing. He was gazing

away from me to the batting cage, where Huddy Lang, the Barons' shortshop, was hitting. Lang fouled one off his foot and yelled "Fuck" loud enough for the kids behind the screen to catch it. The kids giggled.

Chapman said, "I'm still picking cotton."

I thought, *This is hopeless. This is goddamn hopeless.* And I said, "You're making more than twice as much as I am."

Chapman studied me. He smiled, the smile working slowly up through the blackened-granite face. He didn't speak. The smile was all.

I spun away, powerless and hating the man.

In front of the dugout, Bobby Vadnais was playing catch with George Foske, the Barons' third baseman. Bobby held the ball as I came by.

"I didn't know you and King Kong were friends," Bobby said.

"We aren't," I said. I couldn't knock Chapman in front of Bobby—or any ballplayer. I'd stretched league rules by talking to Chapman.

"How you doing, Bobby?" I said.

"Good," he said. "Been gettin' some playing time."

"So I hear."

Chapman had gone into the cage. In the dugout I turned and watched him. Maxie Lieb was throwing batting practice. Maxie poured one down the middle, and Chapman waltzed into it and pounded it into the seats in left center. The kids chased it. I went into the tunnel. I still saw Chapman's smile.

We went west, and in St. Louis I saw by the newspapers that the Barons were playing a four-game series in Philadelphia. I wondered if Chapman had taken Pam's kids to a game. Probably not. Not after the way our conversation had gone. Pam and I never talked long distance; Pam couldn't afford it, and she insisted it would be unequal if I paid for calls and she didn't. Pam was ahead of her time in all sorts of ways. It didn't matter that I could afford the phone calls. It was the principle.

We hit Detroit for a series with the Barons. I didn't think Chapman would tell me anything, and I was right. He'd reverted to ignoring me. Our first night, a Friday, I worked the plate. Chapman watched a screwball sneak across the outside corner—strike three—and I waved him out of there to a mighty cheer. His striking out didn't help me; I had the crazy feeling he wanted me to call him out. It was as if whatever happened, Chapman had willed it that way.

After the game Vick met me as usual outside the ball park. I kissed her and asked her where she wanted to go, and she said the hotel. She was quiet, I noticed. Shut in. I'd never seen her so still or so distant. Her voice was small and cold. I knew then that she'd found out. I did not guess how, or care. It had happened; there had been a slip, a leak, an eventuality not thought of. There was bound to be.

Vick parked the car and climbed out. She avoided looking at me. We walked to the hotel, silent, and went through the revolving door. The lobby was large and very bright.

"Do you want to eat?" I said.

"Call room service. We have some talking to do."

"About what?" I said stupidly.

She didn't answer. We rode the elevator up without speaking. I reached past her and unlocked the door to my room. The lamp by the bed had been turned on, shedding its wide, low cone of gingery light. The bedcovers had been turned down. I grabbed the phone and ordered some beer and a couple of hamburgers from room service. Vick went to the window, tugged the cord of the venetian blind, and stared out over the wide, black river to the lights of Windsor. I sat down on the edge of the bed.

"What's the matter, Vick?"

She turned from the window and studied me a moment. The heart-shaped face had turned hard and shrewd. *She has never been stupid,* I thought, seeing it perhaps for the first time. *She has never, ever been stupid.* I waited.

"I heard from Bobby," she said, "that Ron Chapman took a bunch of little colored kids to a ball game in Philadelphia."

I wondered how I could have been so dumb. So careless. Bobby and Vicky talked all the time. They talked long distance. It was almost funny the way I'd caught myself, laid my own trap.

"Black kids," I said. I don't know why.

"What?" she said.

"You say 'black,' not 'colored.' "

"I'll say what the hell I want to say."

"They prefer to be called 'black.' "

"Maybe," she said, her voice rising, "I don't prefer to call them what they prefer to be called."

"It's their right."

"Don't preach to me."

"I'm not."

She waved the argument away, swatting it like a mosquito, then leaned against the wall with her arms folded. "I understand," she said, "you had something to do with it."

"With what?"

"With those goddamn kids in Philadelphia, you lying son of a bitch." Tears had sprung to her eyes.

"All right," I said. "So what?"

Her breast rose and fell now under the folded arms, and the tears had broken loose and gone skidding down her cheeks.

"So this," she said, and her voice dropped again. "They came with a girl. The girl is a friend of yours. Now, who the hell is she?"

"Just an old friend."

"What old friend?"

"A friend from high school."

"Who?"

"What's the difference? You don't know her."

"Your high school steady—what was her name?"

"Pam."

"This is Pam, isn't it? *Isn't* it?"

I nodded. "She's in Philadelphia. I ran into her."

"And?"

"She's a social worker in the city, and . . ."

"I know all that. What happened between you?"

I didn't answer. I was staring hard at nothing—at a wall or the carpet or out into the night. Nothing. A shudder rose through me, close to nausea. The chill had entered my bones. I hated myself. No answer came, but that didn't matter. Vick read it in my face, as clearly as if it had been written in lights. I knew she had by the fierce change in her face.

"You bastard," she whispered.

I came up off the bed. "Vick, I want to talk to you."

"You lying bastard."

"Listen to me . . ."

"No," she said. "Not ever again."

Her green eyes were tear-swollen and bright as jewels. I went to her and tried to get my arms around her, but she knocked them away. I reached again; she twisted, ducked, and bobbed clear of me.

"Not ever again," she said and, with her voice climbing and soaring, "Never, never, *never!*"

There was a tap on the door—the fellow from room service. I called to him to come in. He wheeled in the tray, bending over it with his arms splayed out. I saw him glance at Vicky's crimson, tear-slick face. He did not look at either of us again but wore a careful, somber expression. I gave him two dollars, and he squirted through the door and was gone. Vick looked around for her pocketbook. She hoisted it with a proud shrug of her shoulder.

"I gave you everything," she said. She closed her eyes and dipped her head—and fought it. When she looked up again, she was smiling.

"You blew it, buster," she said. "You kicked it."

She turned smartly and yanked open the door. She did not slam it, did not even close it. She didn't bother. She whisked through, vanishing from my life, leaving that door wide open, gaping like a bone-deep wound.

I would have gone after her if I hadn't thought it was useless. All I could do was stumble over and close the door. My knees felt like jelly. I fell over on the bed, feeling as if my guts had been scooped out and knowing that I'd wronged this woman and couldn't ever forget it.

I didn't sleep much. When I did, intermittently, it was to be plunged into emotional dreams of Vick, who gazed serenely at me, wisely, seeing into my soul as I begged her to take me back. I cried in the dreams, confessing all of my sins and throwing myself on her mercy. And she would forgive me. She would stretch out her arms to me but would not smile. Waking, I would groan aloud. In the morning I ate the cold hamburgers and drank a warm beer. The beer was self-pity, tepid and filling. Ordinarily I do not drink in the morning.

I was quiet on the way to the ball park and in the dressing room. Roy kept sending me inquiring looks, but I pretended not to notice. Bugs and McKnight didn't notice my silence until we'd been in the dressing room a half-hour or so. We were sitting around in our long-johns. Bugs was mudding up the baseballs for this afternoon.

"What's the matter, kid?" he said. "What are you so quiet about?"

"Never mind," I said.

"He is awful quiet," McKnight agreed hoarsely.

"He's got girl troubles," said Bugs.

"Girl in Philly, a girl in Detroit," said McKnight.

"He's quite the boy," Bugs said.

I'd been trying to read the newspaper. Hiding behind it. "Better leave it alone, Bugs," I said.

"Sensitive," observed Bugs.

"He's like that," agreed McKnight. "Very precious."

"Why don't you fellows leave him alone?" Roy said. He spoke gently.

"Now, here," said Bugs, "is a fella who never has girl problems."

"He don't seem to," agreed McKnight.

"What's your secret, Fat Man?" said Bugs.

"He don't have girlfriends, period," McKnight rumbled. "That's his secret."

"Well, maybe that's smart," said Bugs. "Look at Malcolm here."

"I don't know," said McKnight. "You can't live with 'em, it's true, but I'd hate like hell to try to live without 'em."

"What's your secret, Roy?" Bugs said. "You got no hormones, or something?"

"At least he can spell the word," I said.

Bugs's head whipped around, and the black eye-

251

brows came crashing together. We were saved by a knock on the door. McKnight, who was closest, answered the knock. It was the clubhouse boy. He'd brought someone to see me. I hurried into my blue trousers and went into the corridor, where Vicky's father waited, his wide, round face pallid and shadowy, as if he hadn't slept. I shut the door quickly. The clubhouse boy disappeared. I was glad to see Mr. Vadnais.

"Lee," he began, "I know I got no business botherin' you before a game. I got no business in the world."

"I'm glad you're here," I said. "How'd you get in?"

"I told 'em I had to see you. I said we were old friends. A personal matter, I said, very pressing."

I couldn't help smiling. The mournful shadows seemed painted on—a comic droopiness.

"It's terrible, Lee," he said. " 'Daddy,' " she says, " 'Daddy, I been betrayed.' She come in last night and made noise in the kitchen—on purpose, you see, so I'd wake up. I come downstairs and find her wild and tearful, as you know." The little man glanced up and down the corridor as though he was afraid someone might happen along who would send him away.

"It's all right," I said. "We can talk."

He passed the back of his wrist over his forehead, though he wasn't sweating. "She picks up a plate from the table, says, 'Do you mind if I bust this plate?' I say, 'You go ahead, kid, if it'll make you feel better,' and she does—she lets it fly against the wall. I don't know why it didn't wake the whole house up, but it didn't. 'Daddy,' she says, 'I'll never trust another man. They're lying bastards, Daddy.' I'm standin' there in my PJs with the light still hurtin' my eyes. I'm slowly gettin' the picture what happened. 'Let's talk,' I say. 'Let's have some beer and talk.' "

He paused, studied the floor a moment, raised his

head, and frowned at the low ceiling. Then he said, "Is it true, Lee? Have you really been cheatin' on her?"

Cheating on her. Cheating. I couldn't answer.

"Yeah," he said wearily but without bitterness. "It's written all over you."

Something I'd heard long ago flashed across my mind: Mr. Maretta in seventh-grade math class telling us how our names are written in lights across our chests, and every time we lie or cheat or steal, some of those lights go out. I looked down at my chest, half expecting to see a feeble scattering of lights, all that was left of my decency. I leaned back against the wall. The cement was cool through the knit of my longjohns.

Mr. Vadnais said, "It's not too late, Lee. She's crazy about you. I never saw a girl so nuts about a fella."

"Not anymore," I said.

"Sure she is."

"She hates me."

"She hates you, and she's crazy about you."

"Not anymore," I said.

"Call her," he said, looking up at me timidly and nervously, clinging to me with his eyes. "Make it up, Lee."

"She wouldn't talk to me."

I was, at this point, tugged two ways. Pam's fierce beauty drew me as completely as ever, yet I'd begun to see I wasn't ever going to stop wanting Vick's forgiveness. I'd begun to see, dimly, that I wasn't going to be whole without it. Not tomorrow, not ever.

Mr. Vadnais said, "She might not talk to you at first, but over time . . ."

"No," I said, "not in a million years." I remembered her pride. I'd loved that about her.

"She'll talk to you if you let her," Mr. Vadnais said. "Can I tell you something man to man?"

"Sure."

"I cheated once."

"You? No."

"Swear to God. I cheated on Mary, swear to God."

The door opened. It was Bugs. "You don't have much time, kid," he said. He only glanced at Mr. Vadnais.

"All right," I said.

Mr. Vadnais said, "Mr. Trovarelli . . ."

"What?" snapped Bugs.

"I just wanted to say hello," said Mr. Vadnais.

"Hello," Bugs said and vanished.

"He seems cranky," Mr. Vadnais said.

"He's a bastard," I said.

"Victoria didn't like him at all."

"She was right," I said.

"Anyway," resumed Mr. Vadnais, "we'd been married six years when I strayed."

"I can't picture you straying."

"Neither could Mary. I was drivin' deliveries for a paper company in those days. This girl worked in the warehouse. She wasn't particularly good-lookin'. I just sort of went along. Intercourse," he finished sadly, "has been performed in some strange places."

"How'd your wife find out?"

"She read me like a book. She threw me out of the house, Lee. I deserved it, too. It took her years to forgive me—I mean *really* forgive me, heart and soul."

"Does Vick know about this?"

"None of my kids do."

Silence now, except for the vague, windy rumble of the crowd building over our heads. I didn't know what to say. I couldn't tell him I would call Vick, and yet I couldn't swear I wouldn't.

"Mr. Vadnais, I got to go."

"I love that kid, Lee. I love her better than I love myself." He swallowed with some difficulty. "Three years you been together. I knew you were shackin' up in Florida. I didn't care, either. I didn't care that you put off marryin' her. She said you were special. Lee . . ." He gripped me just above the wrist, firmly and kindly in his blunt, wide hand. "She might not find anyone else special."

"I'm not special," I said.

"We all make mistakes."

"I'm not special, Mr. Vadnais."

"The Gadinski boy'll be callin' her," he said, still holding me. "He's been waitin' his chance—his old man jokes about it. Tommy Gadinski. Works at the ice plant. Lucky if he's got the brains to change a tire."

"Vick wouldn't go for a dummy," I said.

"In her state who knows?"

"I really have to go," I said.

"Will you call her, Lee?"

I sighed. "All right."

"She's crazy about you."

He had let go of my arm. I stuck out my hand, and we shook.

"I'm sorry," I said.

"Hey, we all make mistakes. Maybe I'll see you, huh?"

"Maybe."

"Think positive," he said.

"So long, Mr. Vadnais. Thank Mrs. Vadnais for all those great meals."

"Think positive."

I watched the little man go shuffling in his baggy trousers down the tunnel. At the corner he turned, sent me a sad smile and a desolate wave, and was gone.

I shot back inside the dressing room. The fellows

255

were ready to go up. Bugs groused at me and had a right to. I hurried into the rest of my clothes, and, cleats *plicking* at the cement, we walked silently up to the light of the ball field.

I had one of my worst games ever. I couldn't concentrate. Between pitches Vicky or Mr. Vadnais would jump to mind. I wondered where Vick was and what she was doing. The sun blazed; the infield dirt held the heat and then returned it, hot as fire. I was hesitant and made some bad calls.

In the seventh the Barons sent Bobby Vadnais to the plate to pinch-hit. The Detroit crowd welcomed him with a bright cheer, in spite of the enemy uniform. Bobby was still theirs. He watched a strike—I was working second, luckily, although maybe if I'd had the plate, it would have forced me to concentrate. Then, guessing fast ball inside—guessing correctly—he swung and hit one off the wall in left, an easy double. Bobby slid unnecessarily. Derwinski, the shortstop, gloved the throw on a hop and walked the ball to the pitcher. Bobby picked himself up and slapped the dust out of his pants. I sauntered over. Bobby did not look at me. The base had been kicked slightly out of line by his slide, and I began nudging it in place with my foot.

"Nice wood, Bobby," I said.

We were a few feet apart. The cheering for the double was feathering down over us. I gave the bag one final nudge with my toe and dared a glance at Bobby. His swarthy face was squint-eyed and rigid. He stood with his hands dropped lightly on his hips. Coolly he looked all around, maybe to see that no one was watching, and then, with a quick birdlike movement, spat his gum in my face.

It bounced stickily off my forehead. I was startled

more than anything, not angry. I glanced once more at Bobby, who was watching the pitcher, still with that hardness in his face. There was nothing to say to him, nothing to say to his sister. Not now, not ever.

We came east. We were going to work a weekend series in Boston, then move down the seaboard to Washington, working each league city in between. We hit Boston on a Friday afternoon. I called the Old Man. I'd been trying to coax him to a game since April, never with any luck, and I'd decided the time had come. June was gone, and we were deep into July. I could go on postponing it forever, I saw. I called him at the hardware store. Mrs. West answered in the little office at the back, which I pictured as I talked. She seemed glad to hear my voice. "We're all so proud of you," she said. I don't know exactly who she meant by "we." Frank was slow as molasses getting to the telephone.

"I got to work tomorrow," was his answer.
"What about Sunday?"
"How'm I gonna get home afterward?"
"With Paulie."
"Paulie's workin'."
"Sunday?"
"All weekend."
"You'll have to take the bus, then."
"I'm not takin' any bus," he said.
"Listen," I said, "come tomorrow. The Wests will give you the day off—don't tell me they won't. Paulie puts you on the bus in the morning; I meet you. After the game I'll drive you home."

Frank hadn't been in a city in at least ten years, and I knew the prospect frightened him a little. The town was enough for him now. More than enough. He fussed

257

and griped but agreed at last to come to the ball game—
the only time, as it turned out, he ever saw me umpire
in the big leagues. Paul never did.

It was a beautiful day, sun-drenched, not a shred of
cloud in the sky. I met the Old Man's bus. He was one
of the last ones out. I'd begun to wonder if he was on it.
He came gingerly down the steep steps, holding on tight,
and stood where he'd landed, blinking and searching the
crowd of faces for mine. He was wearing his wrinkled
old seersucker jacket and an ugly brown necktie. I
shouldered through and nursed him clear of the turmoil where the buses docked.

"Hungry?" I said. There was time to eat if he wanted
to.

"Nah," he said.

"You eat breakfast?"

"Paulie came over and cooked it for me."

"Good. You can get a sandwich at the ball park."

We found a cab and were there in ten minutes. It
was quiet around the ball park at this hour. The vendors
loitered by their stalls, jingling the change in their aprons
and watching the slow trickle of people going by, nobody in any hurry yet. Kids clustered under the high
archways or in the shade of the old trees growing out of
the sidewalk: city kids in sneakers and dungarees, with
their shirts untucked, a city sharpness—something quick
yet careful—in their pale faces.

I remembered coming here with Frank and my
brothers so many years ago. The Old Man was not afraid
of the city then. Joey, long-legged in his tight dungarees
and high-top sneakers, was bouncy and devilish and full
of life. Frank would hold the four tickets splayed like a
hand of cards while he shooed us through the turnstile.
He would give us each a dollar for food and soda to save

himself from being pestered every time a vendor wandered by. A dollar bought you plenty in a ball park in those days. Frank would watch the game silently, hunched over in the hard wooden seat, frowning studiously. Now and then he would stroke his chin thoughtfully, as if puzzled by somebody's strategy or by a fellow's throwing to one base instead of another. Paul and Joey and I would yell and stomp and whistle through our fingers. Joey would holler at the opposing players that they stank and tell the umpires that they needed glasses. Studying the game, Frank seemed oblivious to our racket. The memories swept over me in a flood. Home runs I'd seen by players long retired. A clothesline throw from deep center field, catching the quick Del Best, who had turned too wide around first. On the way home we would eat supper in a roadside restaurant with a giant milk bottle planted out front, bulking up in the distance but looking less and less real the closer you got, till you could see the white paint wrinkling and the time-darkened mustard yellow of the cream at the top. The Old Man would feed us steaks and french fries. They did not sell booze in the restaurant. After a while Joey would commence to act up. He would blow straw wrappers across the room and shoot people the finger when they weren't looking. Then Frank would quiet him with a fierce black look that not even Joey dared ignore. It all came back to me, and I put my arm around my father's thin shoulders and gave him a pat.

"Didn't we used to have fun up here?" I said.

"We did," he agreed.

"We should do this more often," I said.

"I like the ball games," Frank admitted.

We went in through the press gate. The guard gave me a cheery hello and one to the Old Man. We followed the corridors to the umpires' room. The rest of the crew hadn't arrived yet. Our uniforms hung neatly, our trunks thrown open on the floor underneath. There were clean socks and jockstraps on the table. Frank strolled around the little room with his hands in his pockets, inspecting everything. He peered into the shower and the john. He flicked the TV on and off. He opened the refrigerator.

"Can I have a beer?" he asked.

"No."

He took one anyway. The opener hung on a string on the wall.

"Don't get lit," I said.

"I know what I'm doin'," he said. He sat down carefully on one of the folding chairs and set his beer on the table. "This isn't exactly the lap of luxury, is it?" he said, still gazing around.

"Compared to the minors it is."

"When do the others get here?"

"Soon," I said. I'd begun to strip. "Frank? Bugs Trovarelli and Bill McKnight are kind of rough."

"How do you mean?"

"Well, they aren't exactly polite all the time. In fact, sometimes they're rude as hell. I just want you to be prepared."

The Old Man swigged his beer and shrugged.

"They might ignore you," I said.

"I don't care."

"Good." I climbed into my longjohns, then went to the shelf and lifted down the tin of mud. "Want to help me rub up the balls?"

"All right," he said.

"Take your jacket off," I said.

He did, and I hung it up for him. Then we sat together and worked on the baseballs. The Old Man watched me the first couple of times, squinting ear-

nestly, then grabbed a ball. He was slow at first, then began to catch on.

"What's this for, exactly?" he asked, working away.

"Takes the gloss off. A new ball is slippery."

"Baloney," he said.

"It's true. Notice how a pitcher rubs a new ball? He
doesn't rub it to make it smoother; he rubs it to make it
rougher."

"Seems like a lot of trouble," Frank said.

"Here they come," I said.

There were voices outside, and the door was thrown
open. Bugs led them through, grinning about a remark
just made. I'd told them about the Old Man.

"Well, well, well," Bugs said. "This must be Lee's
father."

Frank rose, looking doubtfully at his muddy hands.

"Welcome to our humble abode," said Bugs, offering his knotty hand and grabbing the Old Man's thin,
muddy one. "I'm John Trovarelli, but you might as well
call me 'Bugs.' Everybody else does."

"Frank Malcolm," said the Old Man.

McKnight stepped up, smiling sunnily, taking his cue
from Bugs. "Bill McKnight," he said, shaking Frank's
hand. "And this here bucket a' lard is Mr. Roy Van Arsdale."

Smiling a trifle uneasily, Roy took Frank's hand.

"Delighted to meet you, Mr. Malcolm."

"Same," Frank said and lowered himself into his
chair.

"Where'd all the charm come from, Bugs?" I said.

"I'm always charming," Bugs said.

"Sure," I said.

The three of them began undressing.

"Nice day for a game, Mr. Malcolm," Bugs warbled.

"Real beaut," said McKnight.

"You come up this morning?" Bugs asked.

"Yeah. Rode the bus," the Old Man said.

"I hate buses," Bugs said. "Don't you, Mr. Malcolm?"

"I'm not crazy about 'em," Frank said. "I wish the trains still ran."

"How's your beer?" Bugs said. "You need another?"

"Wouldn't mind."

"Wait a minute," I said.

But Bugs snatched one out of the refrigerator and cracked it open, ignoring me. He slapped the can down in front of Frank.

"I don't think that's a good idea," I said.

"Lighten up, kid," Bugs said. "Kids can be a pain in the ass, huh, Mr. Malcolm?"

"Sometimes," Frank agreed.

"I got two daughters," Bugs said. "Terrific girls, both of 'em, but honest to God, they try to run my life sometimes."

"I know what you mean," Frank said. He looked at his hands. "I'm gettin' tired of this," he said.

"Go wash up," I said.

"Let him do his own dirty work," Bugs said jovially.

The Old Man got up, holding his hands carefully away from his body. He went to the sink, squirted liquid soap in his palms, and turned on the water.

"It isn't comin' off," he said.

"Of course it is," I said. "It's just mud."

"How'd you get roped into that, anyway?" Bugs asked.

"I don't know," Frank said.

"Bill," I said, "I like the new man here. The only thing going against him is he looks like Bugs."

McKnight answered me gravely. "You don't know Bugs," he said. "You don't know Bugs at all."

"I think I'm gonna puke," I said.

"Don't let me stop you," said Bugs.

The three of them had put on their longjohns. Roy sat out of the way by his cubicle. He rustled open a newspaper. McKnight shambled into the john. Bugs joined Frank and me at the table. I'd nearly finished rubbing.

"How many World Series you been in, Mr. Trovarelli?" asked the Old Man. I could see the curse of the beer already—a shucking of the timidity the city had brought on him. My big fear was that he would keep drinking.

"Call me 'Bugs,'" Bugs said, then added, "Jesus— four, five? I can't even remember anymore."

"Seems like you're always in the Series," said Frank.

"Who's pitchin' today?" McKnight growled out from the john.

From behind his newspaper Roy said, "Sanchez and Briggs."

"Good match-up," Bugs said, addressing Frank. "Briggs is a big guy, a hard thrower. Sanchez is a tricky little nigger."

"He isn't a nigger, Bugs," Roy said. "He's Latin. *Sanchez.*"

"Hey, he's chocolate," Bugs said. "Let's not split hairs."

"He's black," I said, "and he's a sweetheart. Never complains, never . . ."

"Sweetheart?" Bugs said. "What, are you in love with him?"

"Your boy's a Communist, Mr. Malcolm," sang McKnight from the john.

"You two guys are gonna bring back vaudeville," I said.

"How 'bout another beer, Mr. Malcolm?" Bugs asked.

"Wouldn't mind," said Frank.

"No," I said. "Positively not."

"Don't pay him any mind," Bugs said, yanking open the refrigerator.

"I won't," Frank said.

"Jesus," I said.

I picked up the last ball, mudded it, and tossed it into the wastebasket. The thing to do was to get Frank the hell out of there. I buckled on the shin guards and put on my shirt and pants.

"What do you say, Frank? You want to go up?"

"I'm sort of enjoyin' it here," Frank said.

"Stick around, Mr. Malcolm," Bugs told him. "Finish your beer."

"Come on," I said. "I want to get you settled before the ushers get too busy." I gave him his jacket.

The Old Man sent me a gloomy look but climbed to his feet.

"We'll see you after the game," Bugs told him.

"Enjoy yourself," said McKnight, still in the john.

The Old Man looked wistfully at his beer. I opened the door. As soon as it closed behind us, Frank said, "What the hell you got against Bugs?"

I sighed. "This way," I said, pointing.

"Tell me," Frank said.

"We don't get along," I said.

"Whose fault is it?"

"I don't know."

"You wise off to him, don't you?"

"No."

"I heard you."

"Let's not talk about it."

"I want to know what's goin' on."

"Nothing."

264

"Like hell."

"Frank . . ." I stopped, and he did, too. We were in the runway just inside the visitors' dugout. The door was open, and we could hear the singsong voices afloat on the ball field, and the steady, rhythmic *plock* of the bat. The Old Man stood with his hands in his trouser pockets. The brown necktie dangled down his skinny chest. "You don't know Bugs," I said. "I'm with him every day."

"He seemed nice to me," the Old Man insisted.

"Please, Frank. Don't spoil this."

"I don't like to see you disrespectful to your elders. What did I always teach you?"

"You're going to, aren't you? You're going to spoil this."

"And another thing—don't be tellin' me not to drink. I'll drink when the hell I want to."

"Suit yourself."

"I intend to."

"It's your funeral. Fuck it."

He pulled out his right hand and swung at me, trying to slap my face. I jerked away, taking the bony cuff on the ear. I skipped backward till a space yawned between us, then stared, wounded and astonished, at my father, who had not hit me since I was ten years old. Frank squinted blackly at me, unregretting.

"Don't you cuss me," he said.

Tears stung my eyes. "Come on," I said huskily.

He followed me. I did not look back. We went out into the dugout, up the concrete steps, and across the field behind the batting cage, the Old Man always several steps behind me. There was a lot of activity—fellows tossing balls back and forth and playing pepper. I knew Frank would love to linger, but I marched straight across to the box seats by the Boston dugout and opened the gate. The Old Man stepped through, hands in his pockets. The usher came scurrying down. He recognized me and grinned.

"Got a customer for you, Mike," I said.

"We'll take care of him," Mike said, still grinning.

"My old man," I said.

"No kidding?" Mike said.

"Can you bring him down afterward?" I said.

"You bet."

"See you, Frank," I said. "Hope you enjoy the game."

"Yeah," the Old Man answered.

"You call a good one, Mr. Malcolm," said the usher. "You got the plate, don't you?"

"Yeah," I said.

"Swell," he said. "I'll take care of your pop here."

I went out through the gate, shut it, and crossed the field. Because he was my father, I'd felt a gut fright when the Old Man had swung at me, but it was giving way now to anger and indignation. There is a moment when you decide that your father no longer has a right to slap your face. I was seething by the time I got back to the umpires' room. Bugs and McKnight were all sunny smiles.

"Hey, I like your dad," Bugs said. "He's a reg'lar guy."

"He is," McKnight agreed.

"He's down to earth," Bugs said.

I ignored them. Roy was hiding behind his newspaper.

"So how come," Bugs said, "he's got this uppity kid?"

"You're smart, Bugs," I said. "I'll say that for you, at least."

"What's he talkin' about?" said Bugs to McKnight.

"Who knows?" McKnight said.

Before the game got underway, the PA announced that the league president was sitting in a box near the visitors' dugout. A short, polite cheer went up, and I turned and saw him, smiling a pasted-on politician's smile and waving to the multitudes. His attending a ball game was nothing very out of the ordinary, though they didn't always boast about it over the PA. Why they did this time I'll never know. It couldn't have been the league president's idea. Naturally I would have preferred to work without my boss watching over my shoulder. It meant that I would have to be especially careful not to let any of the players show me up. When a player embarrasses an umpire, a league official will always want to know why the umpire let him, not why the player tried it in the first place. At least it was so in my day. There was no umpires' union, and we were at the mercy of the league.

Bugs had been right; it was a good pitching match. Briggs, thick and strong, a power thrower, against the petite, tricky Sanchez. Both were sharp. Briggs was often wild, flinging it everywhere but where he wanted it. Not today, though. Today he was in command of that power and speed, and after five innings Baltimore hadn't scratched a hit. As for Sanchez, the little guy was almost always on the plate. He threw the curve, the screwball, and the change-up, and when he had mesmerized the hitter with those erratic scrawls—when the fellow had just about forgotten that there *was* such a thing as a fast ball—Sanchez would let one go hard, snapping his lithe body like a buggy whip. The ball was past before the hitter knew it. He would swing because the pitch was good, but swing late. After five, the Blues had two hits and no runs.

It was an umpire's dream: flawless, swift, rhythmic.

Dimly I was aware of the league president in back of me and maybe, too, of the Old Man, and it wakened me, gave me a motive. My troubles dropped away, forgotten. The game flowed over me. Windup, pitch, *whap* in the big mitt, *stee-rahhhk*. The strike zone, armpits to knees, was as sharp and clear as a window frame. Rising, veering down, floating, shooting, the ball crossed through that oblong or it did not, and I always knew. Windup, pitch, *whap, stee-rahhk.* Windup, pitch, *whap, buh.* The Blues were swinging over Sanchez's pitches, chopping ground balls. The Clippers were late on Briggs. Briggs was fanning at least one an inning. No score after six, no hits for Baltimore, and now I thought of a no-hitter and felt a sharp stirring of excitement. I began pulling for Briggs, but that didn't mean I was going to give him anything. Just the opposite. If I gave him one pitch, one strike, the no-hitter was soiled; it was not entirely his. If I was perfect, he had to be. The crowd saw the no-hitter, too, and began applauding every strike and out. I forgot all about the league president.

In the Baltimore seventh Kirby Kirk rattled a ground ball to third, which took a sudden crazy hop almost over Steigleman's head; Steigleman reacted, snared it, and threw all the way across on the money, nabbing Kirk by one step. I remember McKnight eyeballing the play, glowering and throwing his fist around so hard, you might have thought his arm would fly out of its socket. Lujac tapped a soft fly ball to right. Gray watched a one-two pitch, a curve that fell past his knees, and I whirled and slashed him out of there. Gray's face clouded up, and he fixed me with a mean, sour look, remaining where he was with the bat on his shoulder. I told him to beat it.

The Blues hit again but couldn't score in their half of the seventh, and Briggs trudged out to pitch the eighth. He fanned Smith. Then Whitey Whipple clubbed the fast ball to deepest center field; it soared and hung on the bright blue sky while 30,000 hearts sagged, including my own. The ball peaked and began its slow drop, arcing down toward the bleachers. I thought it was in, a home run, but it fell to the wall below instead, and I watched for the carom. But there was none. Instead, suddenly I saw Wilcox spread against the wall, plastered to it like a spider with his glove hand raised, snaring the ball as he clung there, incredibly high, then falling reluctantly, as if the glue that had held him had slowly let go. His legs buckled when he hit the ground, but he kept the glove aloft, showing it to us—the ball, his catch, the no-hitter. Van Arsdale had danced out to make the call, and he raised his fist as high as it would go, running with it like a torch. The crowd stood, drowning us in noise.

Briggs pitched to Sisler, teasing him outside. Sisler should have waited for Briggs to move the ball in, but he helped Briggs by hacking at the outside pitches and trying to pull them as well—plain bad hitting. Briggs whiffed him. The crowd surged to their feet, roaring. They did not sit down when play began again. Sanchez apparently was a little tired. He walked the first two hitters. Briggs came up, and the crowd smothered him in noise. He tipped his cap nicely, dug in, and dropped a bunt on the grass, sacrifice. Cushman doubled; two runs. Nagle, the Blues' catcher, shot a single up the middle, and it was 3–0. We entered the ninth that way. Three outs, and Briggs had a no-hitter. Three outs, and I had one.

My heart was racing; my mouth felt parched. I walked over to the visitors' dugout for a splash of water. The Clippers were very silent, all watching Briggs intently. I went down the steps and bent to the water cooler. The water wobbled out, slow to fill my mouth. I drank some. The ball boy was saying something to me when I climbed the steps. I did not hear him the first time. I felt a flash of annoyance that I was being spoken to now, which the kid saw. He was very young. A boy. He swallowed and said that the league president wanted to speak to me in his box after the game. I nodded and strode into the sunlight. The league president, I supposed, was going to tell me what a good game I'd worked. *Christ sake,* I thought. *Christ sake. Wait'll it's over.* I looked at the card. Hollings, Zandler, Jackson. Good hitters all. Briggs threw his final warm-up. Hollings dug in. The crowd was cheering already, on and on and on. I'd never heard anything like it—an endless, rolling sea of cheers.

Briggs went to two-two on Hollings. Then he threw the change, fooling Hollings, who lunged, missing by a foot—strike three. Two more outs. Zack Zandler was up. Zack asked for time out, which I had to grant him. Make Briggs wait. Make the crowd wait. Briggs rubbed the ball furiously and stalked around the mound. Zack knocked some dirt out of his cleats with his bat. He stepped into the box and clawed a grip with his back foot. Briggs pulled a deep breath, glared in for the sign, reared, and flung the fast ball, which Zandler looked at. *Stee-rahhk.* I felt like a diver inside the mask, peering out into a sea of noise. Zack backed out of the box.

"Hey, look at that ball, will you?" he said.

Which was his right. The pitcher can demand a new ball any time he wants; the hitter can only request that the ump inspect it for nicks and scratches.

"Jesus Christ, Zack," I said.

"Damn ball looks funny to me," Zack said.

"Sure it does," I said, but I had to do what he asked, so I peeled the mask off and yelled to Briggs to lob me the ball. The crowd booed, moaning and lowing. Briggs swore and tossed me the ball, which I barely glanced at before returning it to him.

"Get in there and hit, Zack," I said.

We could barely hear each other.

"Don't rush me," Zack said.

"I'll rush you," I said.

Zack clawed with his back foot, carefully set down his front, and swished the bat like a cat's tail, all the while eyeing Briggs. Briggs heaved another deep sigh, bent, and peered for the sign. I don't know what Nagle asked for, but Briggs shook his head no. Another sign—Nagle sticking fingers down between his thighs—and Briggs liked it. Windup, pitch.

Curve ball. I would always remember that. The ball dropped away from Zandler—or would have if he hadn't hit it. He was guessing, I think. Good guess. The ball had fallen about waist high when the bat found it with a lightning swing, fat of the bat, crack like a gunshot. There was no need to watch this one, but I did, just to see where the no-hitter went, which was over the wall, over the light towers, probably over the factory across the street. The chanting, cheering, roaring crowd went dumb. Zandler jogged the bases grimly, never looking at Briggs. The crowd stood dumbly.

I tossed Briggs a new ball, which he rubbed hard, then went back to work. Quickly Jackson grounded out. Quickly Whipple lifted a pop fly to first, and the game was history. Still on their feet, the crowd bathed Briggs in a tremendous ovation. Briggs was smiling. I guess it felt good to come that close. Nagle trotted out, his gear swishing and rattling, to shake the pitcher's hand. Briggs accepted the handshake and, instead of going straight in, circled toward me. I'd pulled the mask off. Briggs's wide, square face was ruddy and sweat-soaked.

"Nice game, ump," he said, barking it over the dense noise. "Nice game, Lee."

I shrugged and nodded. The shrug said, I hope so.

I watched him go wearily to the dugout, carrying his glove. His shirt was sweat plastered in the bending expanse between his shoulder blades. The crowd had begun to leave, funneling down the ramps. The excitement was dying, a sweet and sad feeling, like autumn. The grounds crew had scampered out, dwarfish in their baggy work clothes, to rake the dirt of the infield. The bullpen pitchers were taking the long walk in, striding erect with their jackets draped over their arms, like bullfighters. Over the PA, the organ swirled gaily, like froth that would help float away the crowds. The infield looked like flannel where the groundskeepers had smoothed it. The outfield, that taut jewel green, blazed in the gold light of the falling sun. Yes, I thought, a baseball field is beautiful. I remembered that the league president was waiting for me.

The league president had thick silver hair and wore glasses. His gray suit fit him beautifully. He was slender and frail-looking. Beside him sat a young fellow with caramel skin and sugary blue eyes, who smiled a bland smile that was almost shy, almost apologetic, almost cordial, and yet was none of these. I reached across the barrier and shook hands with the league president, who gave me a pasted-on smile.

"Lee, this is my assistant, Tim Drews."

I shook hands with Drews. I was sticky with sweat, and the brown dust clung to me. I wanted to go in. I wanted to sit down and drink a beer. I waited for the league president to tell me what a nice game I'd worked.

"We'd like to talk to you, Lee," he said. The smile had faded away. "Come over and sit down."

The barrier, as you probably know, is just high enough so that no one can reach down and pick up the balls that stray over. I climbed it, and Tim Drews got up and made room between him and his boss. The seats around us had emptied. I settled in between them, my mind careening around, trying to locate what I'd done. It was, I decided, the feud with Bugs. We sat, three in a row, looking out over the beautiful empty ball field. I told myself to be calm.

"You called a whale of a game," said the league president.

"You sure did," said Tim Drews.

"Thanks," I said.

"You're a good umpire," said the league president. "You should have a long career ahead of you."

"I hope so," I said. "What did you want to talk to me about?"

The league president and Tim Drews glanced past me at each other.

"We wanted to ask you about Roy Van Arsdale," said the league president.

My heart fell like a rock. "What about him?" I asked.

"There's a rumor going around."

"I haven't heard any rumors."

"No?"

"I can't think of any," I said.

"We understand," said Tim Drews, "that you and he are close."

I looked at him. He was smiling that bland smile. He couldn't have been much older than I was.

The league president said, "The rumor is that Roy Van Arsdale's a homosexual." He watched me, studying me through the fragile-looking plates of his glasses.

"Baloney," I said.

"Is it?"

"Far as I know."

"As far as you know," repeated the league president.

"Where'd you hear this, anyway?" I said.

"I'm not at liberty to say."

"With all due respect, it isn't something to go spreading around."

"We're not spreading it around. As a matter of fact, that's the last thing we want. Do you know what it would do to baseball if it came out that one of our umpires was queer?"

"It would take years to live it down," said Tim Drews.

"Well," I said, "I wouldn't worry about it. Roy's as normal as apple pie."

"Does he have any girlfriends?" asked Tim Drews.

"None of your business," I said.

"Does he?" said the league president.

"Sir, with all due respect, I can't discuss my friend's personal life with you."

Silence. The grounds crew was unrolling the tarpaulin. The crowd had evaporated, and the abandoned grandstand held a deep silence under its roof. The numbers still danced across the scoreboard. The scores of the other games were posted, with the numbers of the fellows pitching.

"Lee," the league president said finally, "this is very serious. I hope you understand that."

"I understand perfectly well."

"Then you understand how important your cooperation is."

"I am cooperating."

"You have absolutely no knowledge that would indicate that Roy Van Arsdale is a homosexual?"

"No."

"I hope you know what you're doing."

"I do."

"All right, Lee," said the league president. "We won't keep you any longer."

I started to get up, and a thought struck me, dropping me against the wood of the seat. I tried hard to sound only casually concerned. "Are you going to say anything to Bugs about this?"

"Not at present. Why?"

"Well, he and McKnight do a lot of ragging. They could make it pretty rough for Roy."

"Even," said Tim Drews, "if it isn't true?"

"What do you think?" I said.

"The fewer people that know," said the league president, "the better."

"If Bugs had heard this rumor, you'd know it," I said.

"Yes, I think that's true."

"What are you going to do now?" I asked.

"I don't know." The league president summoned his smile. "If Van Arsdale has nothing to hide, he has nothing to worry about."

"He has nothing to hide," I said.

"Good," said the league president brightly. "See you around, Lee. Nice job today."

"Thank you," I said and swung myself over the barrier onto the grass. I could feel their eyes on me as I crossed the deserted ball field. They would be asking each other what they thought. A chilling numbness had come over me. I couldn't think what I ought to do, or if I ought to do anything at all. I went *ka-plick*ing up the empty tunnel and tore open the door to the umpires' room.

Bugs and McKnight were in the shower. Roy sat in his shorts, nursing a beer, his thick, round knees protruding radiantly. The Old Man sat at the table, staring glumly at nothing with tiny, reddened eyes. He was gripping a beer bottle by the neck. On the table were two empties. I will never know how he chugged two beers so fast. I did know he'd had encouragement. I figured, too, that he'd been steadily at it during the game. He was plastered.

" 'Lo, Lee," he said, thick-tongued. "Where ya been?"

I looked at Roy. "Bugs feed him those?" I asked.

Roy nodded. "Where were you?" he said.

"Talking to the league president," I said and whirled and blew past the Old Man to the doorway to the showers. Clouds of steam tumbled over me.

"Hey, kid," Bugs said. "Where the hell ya been?"

"Your dad's been worryin'," said McKnight.

"You slimy bastard," I said, looking at Bugs. "You underhanded, slimy bastard."

Bugs held on to his smile, but beneath it he stiffened. McKnight's face went dark as thunder. The water hissed and spritzed.

"You slimy bastard," I said again.

"Kid," Bugs said, "one of these days you're gonna take it too far, and I'm gonna break you in half."

"And if he don't," McKnight growled, "I will, brother."

"Bugs Trovarelli," I said, "you make me sick. You make me sick to my stomach."

Bugs's smile widened, but it was a startled smile, a smile with no conviction. I spun away. Roy had heard me. He watched me with large, worried eyes, arching his spun-gold eyebrows.

I snatched Frank's half-drunk beer and began emptying it in the sink.

"What the hell you doin'?" he slurred. He hadn't heard me cussing Bugs or hadn't understood. He was in a fog.

"You've had enough," I told him.

I began undressing, ripping off my clothes. I couldn't bring myself to look at the Old Man. All I could think of was Bugs coaxing him to drink. But there were other worries, too, and before I went into the shower I leaned down and whispered to Roy.

"The league president was asking about you. He says he's heard rumors."

Roy's face seemed to inflate, the sea blue eyes flaring wider.

I said, "I told him it was crazy."

Roy swallowed. "The bastards," he said.

"It'll be all right," I said.

"We live in the dark ages," Roy said.

The showers stopped spritzing. I patted Roy's mammoth boneless shoulder and left him, brushing past Bugs and McKnight as if they didn't exist.

11

The Old Man slept all the way home, his head thrown back against the seat. Now and then he would let go a sputtering snore or grumble in his sleep, a gurgling sound that would fade slowly and cease with a last strangled syllable. I was still sore at him for cuffing me. I supposed I'd never thrown the word *fuck* in his face. I couldn't remember it, at least. I had said, "Fuck *it*," not "Fuck *you*," but maybe it was all the same to Frank. Still, that didn't give him the right to swing at me. Not anymore.

He half woke when we arrived. It was dusk—the summer days were shortening—with the cars swishing busily past on the main road beyond the stop sign. I woke Frank and helped him into the house, steering him with my arm around his middle. Zeke, shut in all day, was wild. He barked and yipped and yodeled and flung his shaggy old body this way and that, knocking into things and

smacking them with his tail. I let him out into the backyard and turned on some lights. The Old Man had shuffled to the foot of the stairs.

"I'm goin' to bed," he told me.

"No," I said. "You have to eat, Frank."

"The hell I do. I'm goin' to bed."

I shrugged. You could never make Frank eat when
he didn't want to. "I hope you enjoyed the game," I said.
He hadn't said a word about it.

"Sure," he said blurredly.

"I called a good game, Frank. Did you notice?"

"I noticed."

He took hold of the banister and hauled himself up
the first step. I didn't help him. I watched, wondering if
he'd make it. He was too floppy drunk to hurt himself
falling, I decided. Up he toiled, a step at a time, swaying, teetering. When he reached the top, he paused, as
if resting for another flight of stairs, and then I heard
his slow footsteps in the hallway. I heard him peeing, a
river of beer, an ocean, drilling the back of the toilet until he found his aim. I heard his bed squeak when he lay
down. He would sleep through the night and get up at
five or six without a trace left of the booze.

I got drunk that night. I drank bourbon straight, in
front of the TV, till I seemed to be viewing the flashing
screen through a pane of glass and hearing the voices
and music with ears that were not my own. I would have
loved to talk to Paul, but he'd gone out with Ginny
Crocker. I almost made myself sick, stopping just short
of it, and woke with a savage hangover to the clanking
of pots and pans and the Old Man whistling "In the
Mood."

We didn't make it up that morning. We were both
bundled in a stubborn silence, both nursing wounds. I

had the hangover and was haunted by the league president's suspicion of Roy. The dark ages, Roy had said. I was beginning to think so, too. Dark as night. Ignorant. Bigoted. What had Pam been telling me? Pam was a light in the middle of it. Dazzling, sharp. Everyone else conspired in the dark, conniving to keep bigotry alive. Even Frank, who yesterday had gone over to my enemy, champion bigot Bugs Trovarelli.

I hung around till ten, booze-sickened, drinking coffee and reading the Sunday paper with one eye shut. I said a cool "so long" to the Old Man, who hardly answered, and was on my way.

They always find out. Sooner or later they find out.
    Not this time.
    I want to tell you something, Lee. I didn't quit teaching. I got sacked. You can guess why.
    Click-clack-click-clack through the velvet twilight, darkening fields racing, hurtling, past the big twilight-blotted train window. Click-clack-click-clack toward New York City. Roy's strong, round shoulders filled his jacket like liquid inside a balloon.
    I was careful, understand. I never had a relationship with any of the boys until one of them came to me. He was unhappy, a kind of outcast—like me when I was at boarding school.
    You weren't an outcast, Roy.
    Yeah I was. I was a fat kid, and I wasn't from a good family. Family counts at private schools. Van Arsdale sounds like an aristocratic name, but my father ran a restaurant, totally middle class, which happened to make him wealthy. He was good at it, I guess—or lucky; I don't know. He and my mother would come for Parents' Day and never notice that they didn't fit in. They didn't notice they were being avoided. Or that I was.

I don't think they realized I was fat, Lee. They worshiped me so much, I don't think they noticed I was fat.

So what happened with the kid?

The kid, yeah. Another outcast—no friends, no team sports, no clubs. He had a look about him; you'd call it effeminate. The kids persecuted him. They threw him in the pond; they stole from him. They shaved his head one time. He didn't try to placate them. He called them morons to their faces. The more they persecuted him, the more defiant he was. He was actually very tough inside. He could take as much as they could dish out. I admired that. One day he came to see me about a school assignment. One thing led to another . . .

I'll tell Pam about this. We work two games in New York and then click-clack down to Philadelphia. Pam will baby me, love me, be so proud of me. I will not turn my back on Roy, never never never.

You don't understand, do you, Lee?

Understand what?

Two males. One thing leading to another.

I guess not.

I suppose it doesn't matter.

Finish the story, Roy. How'd they find out about you?

Well, the boy's father was one of these corporate bigshot ex-athlete types who couldn't stand the idea that his son was different. He wanted him to play football, for Christ sake. Football. He thought football was the answer to everything. Anyway, the boy graduated and went home, and we started writing letters back and forth, which was my big mistake. I figured he'd graduated, was gone from the school, and we were safe. I didn't figure on his father. His father began noticing the letters. He got suspicious. One day he opened one of mine. He went through the roof. He and the boy's mother went straight to the airport, jumped on the first plane, and brought my letter to the headmaster. I got canned in record time. See what I mean?

About what?

About people finding out.

You made a mistake, Roy. If you don't make a mistake . . .

Look at your situation. You didn't make any mistakes, but Vicky found out. As Huck Finn says, you can't live a lie.

That's hitting below the belt, Roy. That really is.

What do you mean?

You know what I mean.

You told me you didn't do anything wrong.

I didn't.

Well, then.

If you could meet Pam, you'd understand.

I'd like to meet her.

This time, then. We'll meet for dinner.

Terrific.

But why do I feel so goddamn guilty? I would pay a thousand dollars—yes, I would—for Vick's forgiveness.

Pam's voice over the phone sounded hesitant, careful, but I didn't think anything of it until I alighted on the brick platform by the signs advertising whiskey and Broadway plays. Always when I'd come hustling down out of that little train, a smile had sprung to Pam's face. She would light up to see me, as if in that instant she read the pleasures—of chitchat, liquor, love, and more love—that would flow unending through tonight and part of tomorrow. I got off the train, and this time nothing happened. No smile. Pam only looked at me, squinting a little. I scooped her in my arm anyway and kissed her; her side of the kiss was neutral, and for a moment I had a sense of having come alone up a dead-end alley.

"Well," I said, releasing her.

"Well," she said.

"Here I am."

"Here you are."

"Don't sound so overjoyed to see me."

"I always love seeing you," she said.

"Good," I said.

We got in the car. I slung my suitcase into the back seat.

"So how've you been, Pam?"

"Fine. You?"

"Not so great."

"Oh?"

"Roy Van Arsdale's in big trouble."

"What happened?"

"Nothing yet. The league president had a talk with me. He's heard rumors."

"Honest to Christ," Pam said, voice flaring, impatient. "Why doesn't Roy just tell everybody to fuck off?"

I stared at her. The possibility had never occurred to me.

"Do you know anything about homosexuality?" I said.

"Why do you ask?"

"I don't know."

"I'm not a lesbian, if that's what you're getting at."

"I guess I know you're not a lesbian," I said, but Pam didn't answer, and I knew something had happened. She drove, quiet. Once, she cleared her throat.

"I hear Chapman contacted you," I said.

"Yes, and he invited a whole slew of kids, plus me and two of my co-workers. It was wonderful."

"Yeah?"

"The kids adore him."

"I'm afraid so."

"Don't start," Pam said.

"Start what? Did you hear what happened when I talked to him? He told me he was still picking cotton."

"Well?" Pam said.

"Well what? He keeps trying to humiliate me."

Pam said, "Let's not argue."

"All right."

"It was noble of you to arrange it. I know it wasn't easy."

"It was harder than I thought it would be."

"I know."

"Did he hit?" I asked.

"Three . . . singles, right?"

"One base—that's a single."

"You should have heard us," she said. A smile crept through. "This little cheering section, whistling and hollering for Ron. People started booing us. I don't know whether they were booing us or Ron."

"Probably both."

"I suppose."

"I'm glad it was a success."

We were at the house. Our footsteps thumped hollowly on the long roofed porch. Pam reached around me and opened the door, avoiding looking at me. I put my suitcase down and followed her to the kitchen.

"Drink?" she said.

"You bet."

She chose a glass from the cupboard and broke cubes from an ice tray. I took the vodka bottle from the counter and poured a strong one. Another hangover, coming up.

"I'll be right out," Pam said.

"Can I help you?"

"Nope. Go and relax."

I carried my drink out through the squeaky screen door to the brick terrace beneath the grape arbor. The nights now came promptly: the shadows had overrun the lawn. I drank, then set the glass down by my feet. I could hear Pam fussing in the kitchen—the refrigerator bumping shut, dishes scraping, water spurting. I wondered what had happened. I supposed Charles Brewster, her professor boyfriend, had popped into her life again—bought her a ring and made her an offer she couldn't refuse. Or was she just tired of me? *Why,* I thought, *does she have to be so beautiful?* I drank. A couple of kids went up the street on bicycles, wobbling slowly along under the darkening cover of the trees. One of them said, "When I get my ham radio, I'm gonna burglar-proof the garage." I wondered how you could burglar-proof anything with a ham radio. You probably couldn't. Paul would know. I drank. *She's too beautiful,* I thought. *It isn't fair.* I drank. I was getting looped in record time. The door squeaked and bumped, and Pam came out.

She lowered herself prettily into the chair facing me. Tonight she wore dungarees, tight and faded on her thighs. She looked down at her wine, fingering the stem of the glass.

I said, "I just heard a kid say he was going to get a ham radio and burglar-proof his garage." I laughed. Why this struck me funny, I don't know.

"The Matlock boy," Pam said, smiling faintly. "He loves gadgets. He's got a little airplane that flies on the end of a long wire. It makes a terrific buzzing noise. The Airedales across the street bark and howl."

"I never liked Airedales," I said.

"They're all right," she said.

Silence. I drank. Pam would not look me in the eye; in a way this gave me the upper hand, emboldened me—this and the vodka.

"What the matter?" I asked firmly.

Pam's small, strong shoulders lifted in a sigh. "Maybe it isn't worth talking about," she said.

"Like hell it isn't."

"I suppose you're right."

"Of course I'm right."

"You like me to be honest with you, don't you?"

"Always."

"Lee? Try not to make too big a thing out of what I'm going to tell you. It may not be important at all."

"Just tell me, for Christ sake."

Again her shoulders rose and fell. It was the same deep breath a pitcher takes to calm himself when he gets into a jam, and it seemed to do wonders for Pam. She brightened, looked me full in the face with the calmest, bluest eyes I have ever seen, and said, "I'm having an affair with Ron Chapman."

It was the nearest I have ever come to fainting. The world darkened. It moved. A wind seemed to spring up, beating on my ears. I could see Pam and hear her, but she seemed miles away.

". . . called me the next day . . . happened very quickly . . . don't know if there's any future in it, really . . ."

I was waking. My brain now was filled with a white-blue light—crystal clear, rational, cold as ice. I thought, *He might as well have killed her.*

Pam looked at me and said, "I'm quite sure I'm not in love with him."

Very slowly I said, "Quite sure you're not in love with him?"

"It was so sudden, and then he was gone."

"He'll be back."

"I know."

He did kill her, I thought. *That's just what he did. I would have given my life for Pam Rogers, where I wouldn't give one dime for this woman sitting before me now. Pam's gone. She's dead.*

Slowly I said, "You sick bitch."

She blushed brilliantly, as if I'd slapped her. "It bothers you that he's black, doesn't it?"

"Jesus," I said.

"It does, doesn't it? Ron said it would."

"Jesus H. Christ."

"It just kills you, doesn't it? The age-old white man's phobia."

"You're gonna give morality a bad name, you know that?"

"Think about it. You never complained about Charles."

"I didn't know I had anything to complain about."

She blushed crimson again but did not look away. "It's the nineteen-sixties, Lee. Things have changed."

"What the hell does that mean?"

"Did you think you owned me? Do you think you can own a woman like a piece of property?"

"You sick bitch."

"It kills you, doesn't it?"

"You're right about that," I said. I picked up my glass and drained it with a flick of my wrist, like Bill Mc-Knight. "I'm going," I said. I stood up.

"Don't," she said.

"Don't? *Don't?*"

"Lee . . ."

I yanked the door open and went inside. Pam chased me; the rickety screen door banged twice. She caught up in the dusky hallway, grabbed me, and blocked my way, the way an umpire restrains a ball player who's trying to get at one of his partners—a sort of bearish waltz. Pam's eyes had thickened with tears.

"Please stay," she whispered.

"You must be kidding," I said.

"Please?" The small, shivery voice was begging me.

"What would be the point?" I said.

"I want you to. Isn't that point enough?"

Want, want, want. Get what you want. Get, get, get. And I saw that I didn't have to go. I would lose nothing by staying—no dignity, nothing. I was looking into the uplifted face of a stranger, no more to me than a whore would be. I'd never slept with a stranger. I'd never fucked, I realized, but had always made love. I'd never had the mindless, selfish pleasure of a fuck. *Want. Get.*

"All right," I said. "What the hell?"

I freed myself roughly from her embrace, stalked to the kitchen, and helped myself to more vodka.

I don't remember much about that dinner. It rolled by in a vodka haze. We ate chicken. Pam always cooked chicken. She had become nervous, chatty, eager to please; she wanted to keep me there, God knows why. Just to fuck me, I guess. She'd decided she wanted that. I wanted it, too, but not as badly as she did, and I took advantage of this imbalance, making smart-aleck remarks and generally behaving like an oaf. She only laughed it off.

We went to bed right after dinner. There was no tenderness in it—on my part, at least. It was quick. No ceremony. I didn't wait for her to climax; I paid no attention, but she did anyway. She came with a shudder that sounded hurt and mournful. Sleep drowned me.

I woke with ashes in my mouth and a pounding headache. Early sunlight sprayed the drab, seal-brown wallpaper of the professor's bedroom. Pam lay with the

sheet pulled snug to her chin, staring at the ceiling. No—
not Pam. A stranger. Last night I had fucked this woman,
and it had felt pretty good.

"Hi," she greeted me, cautiously.

"Jesus, does my head ache."

"Can we talk?"

"My second hangover in a week. I must be crazy."

"Please can we talk?"

"And a doubleheader today. I must be crazy."

"Lee. Lee Malcolm."

I looked past her at the bedside clock. Seven-fifteen.
Already I saw myself in the Sunday-morning city with its
deserted streets and sidewalks painted with the straight-
edged shadows of the buildings. I would walk the clean,
empty sidewalks till I found a restaurant and eat eggs
and potatoes and ham and drink coffee out of a silver
pot. I threw off the sheet and heaved myself to my feet.
Blood clubbed my brain.

"What a headache," I said. "I don't know how the
Old Man does it. The Old Man never gets a hangover."

"Lee . . ."

Don't look at her. Tear yourself away. I stepped into my
shorts, nearly tripping.

Pam said, "Will I see you again?"

"Not if I have anything to do with it."

"Don't burn bridges," she said. "Remember?"

"I'm gonna burn this one," I said, "what's left of it."
I was hunting around for my clothes, which had landed
all over the place somehow, as if they'd been spewed
through an electric fan. "I'm gonna blow this bridge up
like *Bridge on the River Kwai.* Johnny Weismuller couldn't
swim across when I get through."

I buckled on my trousers, sat down by the dresser,
and tied my shoes. I didn't know where I'd shave—

somewhere. I stood up and scanned the room for anything I might have left. I'd never brought the suitcase upstairs.

"Will you stay five minutes?"

Don't look at her. Get the hell out of here.

"Five minutes," she said, and I did look, stopping and turning just short of the doorway.

She had sat up. The sheet had fallen from her girlish breasts. Her hair, that tannish color I never could name, fell dancing on her shoulders. She smiled; the smile was as familiar and as old as a song from my childhood. I felt a warming, a melting inside. My conduct last night had been awful.

"Sit down," Pam said, smiling, and I did. "Truce," she said.

The birds sang, moving the new day along. "Why'd you do it, Pam?" I said.

"It had nothing to do with you," she said.

"You don't believe that."

"I *do*. Sexual fidelity is obsolete. It's an ego trip. Why can't I love more than one person?"

"You can sleep with more than one person. You can't love them, though."

"God, you're so old-fashioned. Wake *up*, Lee."

"So, you love me, you love Chapman, and you love Charles Brewster?"

"Why not?" she said.

"Charles doesn't mind?"

"Of course not."

"He will," I said.

My head throbbed distantly. I listened to the birds. I thought of the long afternoon ahead of me in the sweltering ball park.

"Lee?"

"Mmm?"

"Does it really not bother you that Ron's black?"

"Jesus. The son of a bitch seduces my woman, and I'm not allowed to get sore about it."

"I wasn't yours," she said sharply.

"My mistake."

"A big one," she said.

"I was yours," I said.

"No."

"Oh, yes. I was crazy about you. I never wanted to see another woman again."

"No. You were repressing."

"Repressing *what?*"

"Love. Desire. Your own essence."

I saw that we weren't ever going to get anywhere near common ground on this one. It would only get worse the longer we talked.

Pam said, "I'd love to have you stay for breakfast."

I shook my head no.

"Or . . ." she said, arching her eyebrows. Another tussle in the rumpled sheets, she meant. I thought of sweaty early morning sex, always quick somehow, and delicious, with the faded smell of last night's perfume and the dry, stale taste of each other's mouths. *Oh, yes,* I thought. *Oh God Jesus, why not?* I even moved toward her, sliding along the edge of the bed toward this wonderful naked woman with the long, bright hair. Pam's face had turned stark and watchful; it had gone that far. But something intervened—a premonition, maybe—swooping down and grabbing me in the nick of time. I wrenched myself off that bed and away from that woman as if she was fire itself.

"So," she said.

"Never again," I said.

"Your loss."

"Yours, too," I pointed out.

"Both of ours," she agreed. "So where's the point?"

"It's the principle," I said.

She laughed.

I stood in the doorway.

"Will you call me?" she asked.

"I doubt it."

"You'll always be dear to me," she said. "You know that, don't you?" It was an odd smile that she gave me then—wistful and pleased, sorry at the way it had turned out, yet not sorry.

"Good-bye, Pam," I said.

"Good-bye, Lee Malcolm."

Again I thought of staying. I thought of having what I could of her—not just sex but the hundreds of ways she could please a man: the way she talked and the music in her laugh—this morning and other mornings. I knew there could be other mornings. I had to rip myself from that room. I went clomping down the wide old staircase of this house where I'd loved and been happy, this comfortable, kind old house owned by people I would never know. I grabbed my suitcase and pushed through the screen door, beginning to understand what Pam Rogers had cost me.

The first game of the doubleheader stretched twelve innings. The second, a slugfest, lasted nearly as long by the clock. I ached. I poured sweat. At times I thought I would throw up. You deserve this, I kept thinking. You deserve to suffer. The only mercy was that I didn't have to work the plate in either game.

Bugs was at third base in the second game, and after a close play at the bag, the fellows in the Philly dugout began getting on him.

"Get much sleep last night, Bugs?"

"Bear down out there, Trovarelli."

Bugs listened for all of three minutes, then stalked over to the dugout, his black eyebrows shooting down. He told them all to shut up. There was silence in the dugout, but as Bugs was tramping back to his position, Sam Hilliard tossed a towel out onto the grass. The throwing of equipment to express displeasure carried an automatic $100 fine. Bugs arrived at third base, turned, and noticed the towel. He called time again, marched back to the dugout, and threw Al Pardee out of the game. Pardee gaped, unbelieving.

"I didn't *do* it," he said.

"Well," Bugs said over his shoulder, "maybe the jerk who did will pay the fine for you."

Moments like that I almost liked Bugs.

The schedule took us south again, to Washington. We worked a day game in front of a bored crowd of 8,000 or so, and that night after dinner, Roy and I walked into the lobby of our hotel and found Tim Drews, the league president's assistant, waiting for us. Drews was sitting in a soft chair, thumbing through a magazine and eyeing the revolving door.

"Oh Jesus," I whispered.

"What?" Roy said. He'd never seen Drews.

Drews stood up, tall and correct in a gray flannel suit. I remembered the accommodating smile, the blue sugar-water eyes. He stuck out his hand.

"Tim Drews, Lee. I met you in the league president's box up in Boston."

I shook his hand and said nothing.

Drews introduced himself to Roy.

"How do you do?" Roy said.

"You fellas got a minute?" Drews said. He spoke breezily, courteously, like an insurance salesman approaching us about a policy.

"A minute?" I said.

"A *few* minutes," Drews said, smiling.

"Why don't we go have a drink?" I suggested.

"I don't think so," Drews said. "This'll be fine right here." He nodded at the soft chairs in the corner of the lobby. I glanced at Roy. Roy had blanched.

"Shall we sit?" Drews said, still smiling.

"Might as well," I said.

Drews jackknifed gracefully into a chair. He crossed his legs. Roy and I sat facing him. The hotel lobby was empty.

"Roy," Drews began, "did Lee tell you about our conversation up in Boston?" His smile at last was fading.

"Yes, he did," Roy said carefully.

"I told Roy he ought to sue you," I said.

Roy looked at me.

Drews's smile opened out again.

Roy said, "I wish you'd state your business."

"We've been doing some checking," Drews said. "I need to ask you a question, Roy."

"All right," Roy said. He was watching Drews, cagey now, waiting for the blow to come. Waiting to parry it.

"You were fired from the Shipler School," Drews said pleasantly. "The league president would like to know why."

Roy studied Tim Drews. Roy had seen, as I had, that the school had protected him, that Drews had nothing. Zero. Drews's smile had turned eager, prodding. His eyes were blue poison.

"Why I was fired," Roy said, placing his hands on his fat knees, "is my own business."

"Possibly," Drews said.

"Where'd you get this idea about Roy anyway?" I asked.

"Yes," Roy said, "I'd like to know that."

"Tell you what," Drews said. "You tell me why you lost that job; I'll tell you where we heard what we heard."

Roy watched him. "No dice."

Drews let his smile go away, which took some time, then gazed at Roy. Silence. Drews seemed to be weighing it all.

"I hope it's not true, Roy," he said. "Because . . ."

"It isn't," I interrupted. "I ought to know."

"Yes, you ought to," Drews said. "In fact, I'd be very surprised if you didn't."

"Then start believing me," I said.

"I'd like to," Drews said, "because the league president will act decisively in any matter involving the good name of baseball."

"I like his attitude," I said. "Tell him to keep up the good work."

Drew contemplated me. He looked amused.

"One question," Roy said. "Did you come all the way from New York to ask me this?"

"I was in town on business," Drews said.

"Why don't you come out with us?" I said. "Pick up some girls."

"I'm a married man," Drews explained. "Neither of you fellas was ever married, am I right?"

"We're young yet," I said.

"You are," Drews agreed. He stood up. "Sorry to bother you fellas," he said.

"Just doing your job," I said, "right?"

"Just doing my job."

We watched him cross the lobby. His hands were pocketed, his spare shoulders thrown back. The city swallowed him.

"I've had it," Roy said.

"He's got nothing," I said.

"He's got something."

"Listen," I said, "let's go out and have a few. Get our minds off all this."

"Would it be all right with you if I went out alone?" Roy said.

"Why would you want to do that?" I said stupidly.

"I'd like to see some friends of mine."

"Oh," I said. "Sure."

"It's nothing against you," he said.

"You think it's a good idea," I said, "with Drews in town?"

"He's not going to be where I'm going."

I felt rejected. Hurt. "Go ahead," I said, "but I think you're crazy."

"You sound like everybody else."

"I'm talking sense," I said.

"It'll be all right." He smiled.

"Be careful," I said.

I gave him a five-minute start, then rode a taxi up to Capitol Hill. I found a dark, noisy bar where a fellow was whamming out old songs on a piano. The crowd was young and dressy. I found a bar stool and ordered a vodka straight. I swiveled with my drink and inspected the place. I spotted a pretty girl, then another, then another. The world was full of them. I decided I'd wait for one of them to come over to the bar. I devised things to say—witty things, smooth things. I had three drinks, and not one of the girls had moved. They were all in groups, talking vivaciously. I didn't dare try to break in. When the third vodka was gone, I concluded I didn't know the first thing about picking up girls. I doubted I had the courage for it. I tipped the bartender and went back to the hotel.

12

Once, Bobby Vadnais answered and hung right up on me. After that experience I decided never to call when the Barons were playing in Detroit. The younger brother, Steve, answered once, and said sleepily that Vick wasn't home. He didn't sound angry, just sleepy and uninterested. Vick never picked up the phone; she was going to that length not to speak to me. The only person in the house who would talk to me was Mr. Vadnais. He was evasive. He wouldn't tell me what Vick was up to. He was under orders, I guess. He did advise me to keep trying. Think positive, he said. I couldn't think positive, but I did keep calling.

We went west, then came east a week later to Baltimore. Roy usually stayed with his mother while we were working in Baltimore, but we arrived after supper, and that night he opted for the hotel. At about eleven-thirty the two of us got restless and rode the elevator down to the hotel bar. I thought a beer or two might help me sleep.

It was your typical hotel bar, dark and private. A piano squatted in the corner, but no one was playing it. We were already inside when I saw Bugs and McKnight at the bar. Too late to back out, I was thinking; then I noticed that they weren't alone.

They were sitting sideways to the bar, each facing a woman. McKnight's girl was large, with a ropy mound of blond hair piled on top of her head. She had a spreading, shapeless midriff and good legs. Bugs's friend was startlingly young and good-looking. She had red hair and a slender body that draped itself like a scarf over the bar stool and the bar.

Roy and I were caught; we couldn't get by them without saying hello. I assumed it would embarrass them to be discovered in a bar with a couple of floozies, and for a soaring moment I thought we'd stumbled onto a weapon to use against Bugs and McKnight should the time ever come. They were both married men.

Bugs greeted us with a wide grin, displaying the gap between his teeth. I felt a prick of irritation. Bugs was actually glad I'd turned up.

"The Bobbsey Twins," he said, grinning.

The two women eyed us.

"The whale and the midget," said McKnight, furry-voiced. He was pretty loaded.

"He's no midget," said McKnight's friend.

"These are our partners, girls," Bugs said. "Mr. Van Arsdale and Mr. Malcolm. Boys, meet Gretchen and Carol."

Gretchen was McKnight's hefty blonde. She straightened and nodded with a kind of queenly graciousness. Her smile was both haughty and accepting.

Carol looked us over with narrowed eyes and a dry smile, foxlike.

"How do you do," said Roy.

I only nodded.

"They're cute, Bugs," said Gretchen. "Both of 'em."

"Just adorable," Bugs said.

"Why don't you boys join us?" said Gretchen, smiling, and eyeing us glassily. "The more the merrier."

"Sure," McKnight agreed, which surprised me.

Bugs grinned. Bugs was drunk, too, but not sloppily. I doubt Bugs ever was sloppy in anything. All of them were drunk, except maybe the clever redhead.

"Have a drink," urged Gretchen. She motioned grandly to the bartender.

Roy and I stood there stupidly. Roy was smiling, but worry rubbed his face. The bartender had come over. He leaned forward with both hands on the bar, waiting for our order.

"Look," I said, "we're kind of tired. We're just gonna have a quick drink and . . ."

"Ah *Jesus*, Malcolm," Bugs said. "Come on, kid. Loosen up. We're invitin' you to have a drink with us. Izzat such a big imposition?"

Bugs was liquored up, but in his voice at this moment was an invitation to throw the baggage of our dislike out the window, to forget bygones if only briefly and try to make something out of the wisp that was left of the night. And there was Gretchen, beaming at Roy and me, lipsticked smile nestling in her fleshy chin. She was in her glory, men on all sides. I imagined she didn't see much glory anymore.

"We'd be glad to join you," I said. "We just didn't want to intrude."

Roy licked his thin lower lip.

"No intrusion," said McKnight. Fatigue and drunkenness shadowed his face like night on a cliff wall.

"So what'll you fellows have?" interrupted the bartender.

"Wait a minute," said Gretchen. "*Wait* a minute." She lifted her arms and closed her eyes voluptuously, a cat stretching, imagining perhaps the sleek, curving length of her old self or even going so far as to think it was still down there after all. The night had come alive for Gretchen.

"Let's go up to your room, Billy boy," she said. "Let's have a party."

"Guh' idea," said McKnight.

The redhead sat low to the bar, smiling dryly and watching us all.

"What do you say?" Bugs asked Roy and me.

"All right," I said. The idea of getting out of a public place appealed to me. McKnight looked ready to pass out at any moment.

They all slipped down off their bar stools, and the six of us crowded into the elevator. Liquor fumes filled it, sour and not identifiable, though I knew Bugs and McKnight had been drinking Scotch, and the women sweet after-dinner drinks. It was very bright in the elevator. Roy gazed toward the ceiling, still smiling slightly. Gretchen was jammed next to him.

"I didn't get your name," she purred.

"Roy," he said, hesitating as if he wasn't sure.

"I've always liked fat fellas," she said.

McKnight sagged against the elevator wall, eyes half closed.

"Here we are," Bugs said.

In the carpeted hallway Gretchen took off her high heels. She leaned on Roy's shoulder, reaching down and hooking her legs. Her legs were a young woman's. Roy waited while she plucked off first one shoe, then the other. She leaned on him unsteadily. She gripped his shoulder hard.

At the door to Bugs's room we waited while Bugs clumsily inserted the key. He jabbed and missed, jabbed and missed. The late-night stillness had settled into the walls of the long hallway.

"You sure you got the right room, Bugs?" I said.

Bugs leaned back and read the number on the door. "This is it," he said.

"Where's your room, hon?" Gretchen asked me.

"Next one down," I said.

The door sprang open at last. We piled in. The bedside lamp burned softly. The bedcovers were turned down. The room wasn't small, but we cluttered it, expelling the feeling of bedtime and sending the night racing off in a new direction. Bugs grabbed the phone and ordered ice and glasses from room service. Gretchen flicked on the TV. Carol draped herself in a chair and crossed her legs. She hadn't said a word yet. Bugs rummaged in a suitcase and unburied a nearly full bottle of Johnny Walker Red.

"Hope everybody likes Scotch," he said.

McKnight sat leadenly on the edge of the bed. His face looked dark and sick. Gretchen oozed down beside him, lifted her arm around his shoulders, and dabbed a wet smooch on his jaw. Gently, lovingly, it seemed, she began to rub his sagging belly, sliding her hand around and around. I began to wonder how long she'd known him.

"You okay, hon?" she said.

"I'm loaded," he said.

"I know *that*," she said. "I asked were you *okay*."

301

"I guess so," he said.

"Sit down, boys," Bugs told Roy and me.

Roy lowered himself into a chair. I found a perch on the edge of the double bed, opposite Gretchen and McKnight. I was very close to Carol. The two of us were in front of the TV. Carol was wearing white nylons, like a nurse, and heels. An old movie was running—*Holiday*, I realized, with Katharine Hepburn when she was young, and Cary Grant. I had seen *Holiday* on TV with the Old Man the summer Joey was killed.

"What the hell are we doin' watchin' TV?" Bugs said.

"It's a great movie, Bugs," I said.

Gretchen was paying no attention to it. I wondered why the hell she'd turned it on.

"Jesus Christ," Bugs said, "what a dead bunch."

"We need some music," Gretchen said.

I watched Hepburn. She was very young—angular, dark-haired, beautiful. Carol watched, too, bent forward, draped over her own crossed legs. Pretty legs in milky nylon. I felt a twinge of pity for myself and then an ache as deep as love.

"Ever see this movie?" I asked.

"I don't think so," Carol said.

"It's terrific," I said. "Do you like Cary Grant?"

"He's all right."

"That's it? All right?"

She sent me that foxlike smirk.

I said, "Have you known Bugs long?"

"A while," she said, returning her gaze to the TV.

I wondered if she knew that Bugs was married. For some reason I assumed Gretchen knew McKnight was.

"May I ask where you're from?" I said.

Again that smirk. "Cockeysville," she said. "Ever hear of it?"

"I've seen signs for it," I said.

There was a velvety tap at the door. Bugs zipped over and flung it open.

"Where the hell ya been?" he said.

The fellow from room service shrugged. Bugs tipped him, and he was gone.

"Here we go," Bugs said. He began fixing the drinks, no water for anybody. "Billy?" he said.

"You bet," McKnight said.

"You sure, Billy?"

"Shit," McKnight said. "Goddamn."

Gretchen got up and padded in her nylon feet to the dresser, which Bugs was using as a bar. She fetched drinks for herself and McKnight and landed beside him again. Bugs delivered a Scotch to Roy, who sat at the edge of things, solitary. He thanked Bugs and held the glass on his round knee. I got up. The dresser was only a few feet away.

"Carol?" I said.

"Sure," she said.

I handed her a drink. I sat down again. Grant and Hepburn stood together at a mansion window, looking out at New York City. Their gazes locked, their lips brushed, and Hepburn fled the room. He was engaged to her sister.

"It ends happily," I told Carol.

"They always do," she said dryly, as if it irritated her.

"They don't," I said.

She gave a slight, listless shrug and sipped her Scotch.

Bugs, who hadn't sat once, loomed in front of us, blocking the TV. He hoisted a foot onto the bedstead and hunched over his knee. He'd killed half his drink.

"Kid," he said, "I got to tell ya somethin' about dealin' with rookies. I got to give ya a pointer." He watched Carol as he spoke. "Ya got to assert yourself with a rookie. Ya got to put 'em in their place. Yesterday, for instance. You're workin' the plate. Ya got young Billings on the mound. Kid's a punk. He's bitchin' and moanin'. Ya know what you do?"

"Tell him to shut up."

"Take a couple away from him," Bugs said.

"How do you mean?"

"Pitch hits the corner. Call it a ball. He bitches; do it again. Show him who's boss out there."

"I don't know, Bugs."

"Yeah, but I do. First time you get a rookie at the plate—first pitch he takes—it's a strike. It might be six inches outside—strike one, brother. You got to establish yourself."

"I'll keep it in mind." I couldn't say I would do it.

"It's warfare," Bugs said. "They have their tricks; we have ours." He rested his warm brown gaze on Carol. "How ya doin', kid?" he said.

"Good," she said.

Bugs surveyed the room, inspecting the party. His party. "What the hell's Van Arsdale doin', playin' with hisself over there?"

"He's just shy," I said.

Bugs dropped his foot to the floor. "Join the party, Roy," he said. "Come talk to a pretty girl."

"Actually," Roy said from across the room, "I was about to leave."

"Jesus," Bugs said, "don't you like girls, Roy?"

"I like girls," Roy said.

"I'm beginnin' to wonder," Bugs said.

"He likes girls," I said.

Carol, who had been studying Roy, now looked at me.

"I happen to know he loves girls," I said.

"I hope so," Bugs said.

Roy was on his feet. He brought his glass to the dresser. He wore a light-colored summer blazer, I remember—a white shirt opened to a V on his satin-pink chest.

"Thanks for the drink, Bugs," he said.

"Have another," Bugs said.

"No thanks," Roy said. "Really."

There was a breezy, wistful-sounding moan. McKnight's head pitched over, his chin landing on his chest, and he was asleep. Gretchen lifted the glass out of his hand and set it on the floor. McKnight sat there sleeping, corseted upright by old, stiff muscle and hard fat, shoulders hunched like great folded wings.

"Bill," Gretchen said. "Hey. *Bill.*"

"Shit," said Bugs.

McKnight began to snore.

"He drinks too much," Gretchen said.

"Tell me about it," said Bugs.

"Can't you do anything?" Gretchen said.

"I try," Bugs said.

McKnight slowly began to topple sideways.

"Keep him upright," Bugs said.

Gretchen grabbed with both arms. Bugs drained his Scotch and slapped the glass down on the dresser.

"Let's get him to bed," he said.

"Can I help?" Roy said.

"Under the arms," Bugs said. "Alley-*oop.*" They jacked him to his feet, powerfully and without effort, and shouldered him between them.

McKnight half woke. "Guh-damn," he mumbled. "Where's? . . . Shit." His head rolled, dipping to his chest. "What time we leave St. Louis?" he said. They hauled him to the door. Gretchen, on her feet now, hunted for her shoes and pocketbook. The stack of her hair had begun to unravel. She gathered her things and hurried after Bugs and McKnight and Roy, clasping the stuff to her breast and scuttering on tiny bare feet like someone running to catch a bus that was pulling out. The door hung open. I was alone with Carol.

"Well," I said.

"Well, what?" she said.

"I don't know," I said. "It's sad to see that. My old man drinks too much."

The Scotch had deepened the sadness this woman had opened. Oh, to have a pretty girl tonight. Someone kind.

I said, "I remember watching this movie with my father one night on TV. My brother had been killed, and the Old Man and I spent a whole summer watching movies on TV."

Carol looked thoughtfully at me. She was drinking her Scotch in tiny sips. I waited for her to ask how my brother had died, but she said nothing. Down the hall a door opened and shut gently, and Roy stuck his head into the room.

"See you in the morning, Lee," he said. He was smiling. The old peachy light had returned. "Nice to meet you, Carol."

"How's Bill?" I asked.

"They're putting him to bed," Roy said. " 'Night."

" 'Night," I said.

Roy shut the door.

"He's a great guy," I said. "Shy, though. I hope you didn't mind."

"Why would I mind?" she said.

"No reason," I said.

We watched the movie. Cary Grant had swallowed

his doubts for the time being and gone ahead with the engagement to Hepburn's snotty, shallow sister. I drank.

"Do you have a way home?" I said.

"What do you mean?" she said.

"Bugs is kind of lit," I said. "If you need help getting a taxi or anything . . ."

Carol looked me in the eye with a green gaze as dry as stone. "What makes you think I'm going home?" she said.

"I just . . ." I stopped and blushed. I felt like a fool.

Carol said, "Everything's under control, okay?"

"Sure," I said.

She sipped her drink and yawned.

I got up. "I guess I better hit the hay. It was nice meeting you."

"Same here."

Her gaze lingered on me, indifferent, as I put down my glass and stuffed my hands in my pockets.

"So long," I said.

"Yeah," she said.

In the hall I met Bugs.

"Is Bill okay?" I asked.

"He will be."

"Is Gretchen with him?"

"Maybe," Bugs said. "Why?"

"Just wondering."

"You don't like it?"

"I didn't say that."

"She's good for him," Bugs said.

"How long has he known her?"

"A few months."

"How long have you known Carol?"

"Longer." Bugs grinned, showing that gap. "You like her?"

"She's pretty," I admitted.

"See, Malcolm? You're not the only heavy hitter around here."

"I never said I was."

What remained of that night ran most of its fateful course without me. I was asleep, dreaming painless, forgotten dreams. I got most of what happened from Roy. Not all, but most. I've dressed it up a little and flavored it with my own hunches, but I bet I'm close. If it didn't happen just this way, it might as well have.

It had been about an hour since Roy had helped Bugs and Gretchen lay McKnight out on his bed like a cadaver. Then Roy had taken his leave of them, gratefully, and gone to his room. He'd put on pajamas, doused the light, and sped swiftly to sleep. A knock woke him.

Roy guessed it was me. He hadn't been asleep long and supposed I had some new development to report. He rolled out of bed and opened his door. It was Gretchen.

She stood there gazing at Roy with burning, drunken eyes. "It's *you*," she said, slurring the words.

"Who were you looking for?" Roy asked, squinting against the light in the hallway.

"Don't matter," Gretchen murmured.

She might have thought this was my room—she'd asked me earlier which one was mine. Maybe she was looking for Bugs. Who knows? Maybe it didn't matter at this point—Bugs, me, or Roy. Gretchen was plastered. She'd brought a half-full bottle of rye whiskey, which, I learned later, had originated in McKnight's room. She stood shoeless in the hallway, swaying and gripping the bottle by the neck.

"Is something wrong?" Roy asked. He thought she might have had a fight with McKnight.

Without answering Gretchen lurched past Roy into the room. She flicked on the light and plopped down in a soft chair, crossing her legs as if she meant to stay a while. Her stack of hair was collapsing down her neck. Her lipstick had gone stale. The face had turned hard. Alcohol had swamped her with gloom and anger.

"Is something wrong?" Roy asked again.

"None a' your business," Gretchen said.

"Look," Roy said, "I really want to get some sleep tonight."

"Get a glass," Gretchen said. "We'll have a drink."

"I don't *want* a drink," Roy said.

"I do."

"Where's Bill?" Roy asked.

"I don't want to talk about Bill."

"I really wish you'd leave," Roy said.

"I would *like* a drink," Gretchen said.

"Don't you think you've had enough?"

"Do I have to get it myself? Is that the way you treat a woman?"

"Listen . . ."

"Shut up."

Roy sat down on the edge of the bed, wondering what he should do. Gretchen gazed stubbornly around the room, waiting.

Roy said, "Did you have a fight with Bill?"

"Bill isn't in no condition to fight."

"What is it, then?"

"You thick or somethin'?"

"Do you want to go home?" Roy said.

Gretchen sighed.

"You should get some sleep," Roy tried.

"Talk to me," Gretchen said. "Tell me about yourself."

"You wouldn't find me very interesting."

"Got a girlfriend?"

"No."

"Why not?"

Roy shrugged.

"Listen," Gretchen said, "I been goin' with Bill since May. He tell you that?"

"He doesn't confide in me about his private life."

"He's number one," Gretchen said. "Knows how to treat a woman. Knows what to buy her, knows how to act. I'm just crazy about him."

"That's nice," Roy said.

"I know he's married," Gretchen said. "A tragedy. He's Catholic, ya know? Can't get out of it. Marry me in a minute if he could."

"Have you ever been married?" Roy said.

"Nah. Plenty of offers, though."

"I'm sure."

"You ever been married?"

"No," Roy said.

"We're a great pair," Gretchen said. "Aren't we a great pair?"

"I suppose."

"Les have a drink, huh?" Gretchen was perking up.

"I think we both ought to go to bed," Roy said. "I'll walk you down to Bill's room—how about that?"

"Can't," Gretchen said.

"Can't what?"

"I'm locked out."

"How'd you get locked out?"

Gretchen shrugged helplessly. "I dunno."

"We'll have to wake him," Roy said.

"S'impossible. Like tryin' to wake a stone."

"Let's try."

"No use."

Silence. Stalemate.

Roy said, "I really, really, *really* have to go to bed."

Gretchen watched him. Proud, glassy blue eyes. Sad, drunken eyes. She studied Roy, and he could see her face change. He could see a return of hope, a sweetening. Gretchen smiled.

"Hey," she said. "Want some company?"

Cornered. Finished. "If it's all the same to you . . ."

Gretchen heaved herself up out of her chair. She landed bouncily beside Roy, flung her arms around him, and buried his mouth in a wet, skilled kiss. When she leaned back, still holding him, Roy said, "What about Bill? I thought . . ."

"Do I have to spell it out for you? You think that's Prince Charming I got there?"

"Well, no, but . . ."

"Half the time he's too drunk to get it up. I'm lonesome, hon. Do I have to spell it out for you?"

Roy's kind heart opened out to this woman. Maybe, he thought, I can do this. And something else—the thrilling idea that if he could satisfy this woman, it might keep him in baseball. It would create a hell of an uproar; he might even have to fight McKnight. But the noise of it all would be all the more convincing. For Gretchen's sake and for his own, Roy decided to give this his all.

They kissed again, Roy returning it, and went over in a mountainous heap. Gretchen moved hungrily, expertly; Roy could feel his pajamas slipping away. He tried touching her, hoping it would start him. His hands moved, patted, explored. Gretchen touched him back. She kissed, fondled, teased. Roy tried. Oh, he tried. Gretchen helped, using all the sweet tricks love had taught her, but

311

this time they failed. Only Roy's brain worked, nothing else. With his brain he wished, pleaded, prayed. Nothing. And at last Roy quit and sank on his back.

"I'm sorry," he said.

"It happens all the time, hon," Gretchen said, then added, "We aren't beat yet."

"I'm afraid we are."

"Nah."

She got up, shivered out of her dress, and in her slip came back to Roy to try the ultimate remedy, the sweetest trick of all. She shifted around, then leaned, doubled over, her legs tucked underneath her, showing Roy her wide, sloping back in the silver gray of her slip. Roy lay still, trying to enjoy it. He did enjoy it, but nothing happened. Zero. Gretchen tried and tried. Zero.

She gave it up and sat forlorn and bent on the edge of the bed. Her face was scoured of the pride and anger she'd come in here with, which, Roy saw now, had been almost beautiful.

"I used to be thin," Gretchen said.

"I never was," Roy said.

"I was a looker," Gretchen said.

"You still are," Roy said.

"No."

"It wasn't you," Roy said. "It had nothing to do with you."

"Men always say that. You think if Marilyn Monroe was sittin' here you couldn't get it up? You think my Billy'd get drunk and pass out on Marilyn Monroe?"

"You're attractive," Roy insisted. "It's just that . . . I have a different *orientation*."

Gretchen puckered her soft, pale face. "What do you mean?"

Roy could only repeat the sentence. "I have a different orientation."

"Honey, that word is French to Gretchen. You're not tryin' to tell me you like boys, are you?"

Roy, naked as a baby, drew himself up straighter. "Yes," he said. "Yes, I am."

"Jesus," Gretchen whispered.

"I just didn't want you to . . ."

"Jesus, do I know how to pick 'em."

"I'm not a freak," Roy said.

"I know, hon. It's just that you can usually tell a queer."

"You'd be surprised," Roy said.

"Well, I *am* surprised. And you an umpire. What do Bugs and Billy think?"

"They don't . . ."

A fist thudded on the door.

Roy froze. Here he was caught with a woman, same as if he'd been screwing merrily for hours—the appearance of the very thing he'd hoped would keep him in baseball—and all he felt was cold fright. Gretchen snapped noiselessly to her feet. Roy was lost; he could only look at Gretchen for help.

"Ask who it is," she hissed, adding, "Get your PJs on, hon."

"Who is it?" Roy piped up, scrambling into his pajamas.

The answer bored through the door: "It's Bill. You seen Gretchen?"

"I'm in here, hon," Gretchen sang, sounding as easy and natural as if this room was her sister's. As she spoke, she whisked on her dress and zipped it. Roy jumped into bed and pulled the covers up high. McKnight began hammering on the door. Gretchen gave her disheveled hair a couple of pats and yanked open the door.

McKnight stood there, huge in stockinged feet and trousers, his white shirt untucked and opened down his frizzy chest. The big face was scrunched up and groggy. McKnight lumbered into the room. Sleep still clouded his face. He looked at Gretchen. He looked at Roy. He looked at Gretchen.

"Would you mind tellin' me"—the words fell slowly, one by one—"just what in holy hell is goin' on here?"

Gretchen flopped into the soft chair, conveying somehow that she'd been there all along. "I couldn't sleep," she said. "We're talkin'."

"Talkin'?"

"Yeah, talkin'. You weren't exactly lively company, ya know."

"Talkin'?" McKnight said. *"Talkin'?"*

"What else would we be doin'?"

McKnight stabbed a thick finger toward Roy. "He's in his goddamn pajamas, ain't he?"

"Hey, Billy," Gretchen said. "Wake up. Your friend here doesn't like girls, remember?"

McKnight stared darkly and dumbly at Gretchen. "What?"

"Billy, he doesn't . . ." Gretchen stopped. She could see in McKnight's bewildered granite face what she'd done.

Roy just closed his eyes.

"He's tired, is all I'm saying. Too tired."

It was a good try, an honest try, but the cat had slipped out of the bag. McKnight looked at Gretchen's sorrowful face; he looked at Roy's; and he understood.

"The guy's a fairy, Gretch. Jesus, Mary, and Joseph."

"So what?" Gretchen said.

"I been workin' two seasons with a goddamn fairy."

"I'm sorry, hon," Gretchen said to Roy.

"Wait'll Bugs hears this one," McKnight said.

"You got to tell him, don't you?" Gretchen said. "You just *got* to tell him."

"You're goddamn right I do."

Roy barely heard them.

"Come on, Gretch," McKnight said. "Be with a real man. I ain't drunk anymore."

"You're not gonna touch *me* tonight," Gretchen told him.

"Yeah, I am," McKnight said. He turned to Roy. "If I was you," he said, "I'd start packin'."

He jerked the door open and hauled Gretchen out of the room.

McKnight had hauled Gretchen out without retrieving his bottle of rye. Roy was no big drinker; I'd never seen him do more than nurse a couple of vodka gimlets or drink a glass of wine. Now he dumped several inches of whiskey into his bathroom tumbler and downed it in several long swallows. Still in his pajamas, he crept out into the hall. He went to Bugs's door and put his ear close: nothing. Bugs slept. Bugs and Carol. Roy had a few hours, then. He tapped on my door.

The tap repeated itself, urgent. I came bobbing up out of a deep sleep and looked at the bedside clock: three-fifteen.

"Lee. Lee, it's Roy."

I snapped the lamp on, jumped up, and let him in.

Roy's sunshiny face looked drained. It was a haunted man who walked into my room and sat down in the chair by my bed. He set his hands on his thighs. He stared at the floor, at nothing.

"I just lost my job," he said.

"It's three-fifteen in the morning," I said.

"I've been exposed." He managed a half-smile. "In all senses of the word."

I was sitting on the edge of my bed. I didn't say anything. Roy gazed unseeing at the apricot hotel carpet, and finally, in a dull, deliberate voice, he began his story. He spoke slowly. He chose his words with great care, yet spoke with so little feeling, it might have been someone else's story. It took him a while to tell it. He sat with his head bowed, silent again.

"What'll we do?" I said.

"There's nothing," he said.

"There's always something," I said.

"No. There isn't always something."

I knew he was right. He stood up.

"Where you going?" I asked.

He waddled to the door without answering.

"See you in the morning," he said.

"We'll think of something," I said.

He smiled—a bitter smile, not Roy's.

"Get some sleep," I told him.

"Sorry to wake you," he said. "I wanted you to know about tonight. No telling what you'll hear."

"I'm glad you woke me."

"Thanks," he said. "For everything."

Roy went back to his room. He put on a clean shirt and clean trousers. He stuffed some clothes into his suitcase. He grabbed McKnight's bottle of rye.

The desk clerk watched him march through the lobby with his suitcase and the bottle. The clerk didn't like the look of the bottle, not at quarter to four in the morning. Maybe, too, there was cause for worry in Roy's flat stare and energetic trudge. The clerk called Bugs.

Bugs was a married man with a leggy redhead half his age dreaming beside him in a hotel room. Bugs didn't want his night interrupted. The hotel people would look the other way, but Bugs didn't want a visit from the police. He reminded the clerk tartly that Roy's mother lived an hour away and said that Roy was working a ball game tomorrow afternoon and that what he did between now and then was Roy's own business.

Roy kept a car in Baltimore, the way I did in Boston. He did not head for his mother's. When the world sticks a knife up under your ribs, you crawl to family only if there are no arms to hold you. My guess is that Roy was on his way to New York City.

It was still dark when he pulled off the interstate in Delaware. It was raining. He glided down the ramp and stopped beside a cornfield. The car radio was on, an all-night station playing the big bands. You know how radio travels at night. The way I figure it, Roy left the motor running so he could listen to the radio. He'd shut the window because of the rain. He was only going to sit a few minutes, rest his eyes, and take a pull or two at the whiskey. You don't pack a suitcase if you don't expect to see the sun come up. Roy lay back, savoring Benny Goodman and watching the gray dawn seep above the cornfield. He tasted McKnight's whiskey. He slept.

Before a game begins, the decision to postpone because of rain belongs to the home team. Once the game is under way, it is up to the umpires. The teams naturally are reluctant to postpone—ticket holders will cash in their rain checks, reducing future ticket purchases. And no one likes stacking up late-season doubleheaders. So when there is any hope that the rain might stop, the players and umpires will sit around waiting for the home team to make up its mind.

It was like that today, of all days. Bugs, McKnight, and I were waiting in the umpires' room. We all wore our longjohns. Above, several thousand die-hard fans relaxed under the grandstand roof, sipping beer, eating hotdogs, and watching the rain beat down on the green ball field. McKnight had rubbed the baseballs. Now he and Bugs were playing poker. I was stretched out on an old, frayed sofa, staring at the perforated ceiling tiles. An electric fan jiggled, pushing warm air down at us.

Bugs had called me at five o'clock. The police had called Bugs. *He went and killed himself* was Bugs's way of putting it. *Carbon monoxide.*

"Pair a kings."

"Three deuces."

"Shit."

You knew he was queer all along, didn't you, Malcolm? You hadda know.

The poker chips scraped and clacked. Bugs shuffled the cards, a crisp flutter. He dealt.

"Gimme one."

"Don't try to bluff me, Billy. Isn't a bastard in the world can bluff Bugs Trovarelli."

You say nothing to the writers, Malcolm, understand?

The police had told Roy's mother. I thought now how strange it was that I hadn't met her. Roy and I had talked about it. Cook us a terrific meal, Roy had promised. I could still see Roy too clearly to believe he was dead.

You don't tell 'em he bumped himself off, and you don't, so help me, tell 'em he was queer.

I hadn't cried, hadn't wept, hadn't cursed, hadn't yelled. Nothing. A numbness had crept up through me, a nothingness.

"Read 'em and weep."

"You lucky bastard."

Nothingness. I'd ridden the taxi to the ball park with Bugs and McKnight as if in a dream. No Roy in the taxi—it made no sense. The rain slicked the narrow brick fronts of the row houses.

"You ever know anybody who killed hisself, Bugs?"

"Never."

I said, "He didn't kill himself."

Bugs and McKnight stared at me. "No," Bugs said. "He just closed the windows, turned on the engine, and drank whiskey to see what it felt like."

"He didn't kill himself," I said.

"Why," McKnight said, "d'you suppose he did it?"

"People kill themselves," Bugs said, "because they don't have it *here*." He whacked his flat, muscle-strapped belly. "I don't mean to speak ill of the dead, but it's a fact."

"You got to face life," McKnight said. "You got to be a man."

Bugs spread his cards and studied them. "I don't think there's ever been a known queer in baseball," he said.

"If it wasn't for my Gretchen," McKnight said, "we never would have known."

Something stirred in me. An idea. I almost smiled. "Your Gretchen," I said, "was in the sack with Roy. Roy laid her."

McKnight looked at me curiously. His eyes were gray smoke.

Bugs said, "Roy didn't lay Gretchen. He was a flat-out queer."

"Ask her," I said.

McKnight's eyes seemed to grow. His long, shadowy stone face was a mask of both rage and melancholy. Bill McKnight at that moment looked tragic. Monumental and tragic.

But it was Bugs who reacted. The brown face hardened and darkened. The eyebrows plunged. Bugs stood up.

"Take it back, Malcolm."

"What's the big deal, Bugs?" I said.

"I'm sick of your lies, Malcolm. I'm sick of your smart mouth."

I threw my legs over and got up. Bugs stalked me, his shoulders thrown back and jaw stuck out. I back-stepped.

"You're horseshit, Malcolm," Bugs said.

I stood my ground and waited.

"Horseshit," Bugs said and spat in my face. It caught me in the eye, bright and stinging. I squeezed the eye shut and spat at Bugs. I got him. There was a red flash, a splash of fire; Bugs had slapped my face. I spun away from the slap, shoving Bugs, who nearly fell. I backed away. Now I missed Roy with a sharpness that brought tears.

Bugs was coming at me, bent forward. A chair scraped, and McKnight climbed to his feet. He came around the table, the two of them converging on me.

"You guys are too old for this," I said. There was something not quite real about it; it didn't *smell* like a fight.

"We'll show you how old we are," McKnight said.

It hit me then how immense he was. He was as big as Nick Nickinello, and he was big in a different way, pro football big, long-armed, built for crushing.

"You can only push us so far," Bugs said.

"I didn't push *you*, Bugs," I said.

I heard McKnight, a sound of smoke and ground glass: "Nobody bad-talks a woman of mine."

My knees were jelly. "This is ridiculous," I said.

McKnight hit me, a sledgehammer punch that broke my nose and pounded my brain to a billion diamond-bright smithereens. The world swung, a merry-go-round, and I let myself fall. But McKnight wanted more. He'd grabbed a fistful of my longjohns and was lifting me. He hit me again, clubbing my face.

He's gotta work, Billy, he's gotta work.

Gotta work. Thanks, Bugs. McKnight quit and didn't kill me after all. I lay on the floor, half conscious, my throat clogged with blood from my mangled nose.

"Get a towel, Billy." Bugs's voice sounded a mile away.

I heard water running. Now Bugs hoisted me up. The blood was coursing from my nose. Bugs guided me to the sofa. I lay on my back. I accepted the wet towel from McKnight but wouldn't let either of them come near me again.

Twenty minutes later the call came down that the game had been postponed. I'd staunched the bleeding. A broken nose isn't all that painful. The second punch, which left a shiny plum of a bruise under my eye, hurt more—and longer. I managed to shower and dress. Bugs and McKnight had turned quiet. I left ahead of them and rode a taxi to Johns Hopkins Hospital, where a young doctor gave me a five-minute anesthesia and straightened my nose with a silver instrument. I woke from the anesthesia dry retching. I told them to send the bill to McKnight. He must have paid it. I would have heard if he hadn't.

13

The next morning at nine, the league president phoned me in my hotel room. He laid on the phony condolences about Roy, then got down to business.

"How do you feel about resigning, Lee?"

"Resigning?"

"I'd like to fire you, actually."

"On what grounds?"

"You lied to me, Lee. Remember?"

"About what?"

"No more games, Lee."

"Did you hear that McKnight almost killed me last night?"

"It was a clean fight, man to man."

"It was two on one."

"Did you have relations with Van Arsdale?"

"What kind of relations?"

"You know what I'm talking about."

"Two nights ago," I said, "Roy Van Arsdale took McKnight's beloved girlfriend to bed and fucked her up and down."

I could hear the league president's steamy breath on the other end.

"Pardon my French," I said.

"I'd like to fire you, son. You've been more trouble than anyone I ever remember in baseball," he said. "I don't dare, though. I'm afraid if I do that, you'll talk. I think you'll tell stories. There are writers who would print what you told them."

The league president had handed me a weapon. I wasn't going to talk to the writers. Not in a million years. I wasn't going to give strangers the key to Roy's private life. I wasn't going to tell anyone he'd killed himself. I didn't even believe it.

"I might," I said.

"On the other hand, you're not working next year."

I didn't say anything.

The league president said, "It can be neat or messy. It's up to you. If you go quietly after the season ends—if you resign—I'll put out a release regretting your departure. If you fight us, we'll fire you for incompetence."

"Incompetence?"

"It'll do," the league president said.

"Well," I said, "I don't think I want to work next year, if you want to know the truth."

You could almost hear his lips peel back in a smile. "It's best for us and probably best for you," he said.

"For the good of the game, right?"

"Yes. For the good of the game."

Those were his last words to me. We said good-bye, glad to be rid of each other.

The writers never did ask me about Roy. The papers described his death as an auto accident, which was fine with me. The police must have lied. The league put out a release saying that Roy's car veered off the interstate in the rain. The writers grabbed it and repeated it. The stories weren't long. The public isn't much interested in the death of an umpire—especially a second-year man.

The rain had come back, and at noon Bugs rang me in my hotel room to tell me tonight's game had been called off. The outfield was under water, and the storm wasn't budging. Tomorrow was an off-day; then we were flying to St. Louis. Bugs recited the information in a businesslike way, then said, "How ya feelin', kid?"

I was lying on the bed, looking out at the narrow brown and gray buildings shooting up in the rain.

"The cheek hurts more than the nose," I said.

"It don't surprise me."

"He beat the shit out of me, Bugs. Two punches."

"He's a tough customer, kid. I wish you'd have thought of that."

"Busted my nose."

"I figured."

I looked at the rain-darkened spikes of the buildings. "Bugs," I said, "I think I'll fly home today. Meet you out in St. Louis day after tomorrow."

"Not a chance," Bugs said.

"I want to see my father," I said.

"What if you get hung up somewhere? I can't risk that. We got a new man comin', never worked a big-league game. I don't want to work three men in that kind of situation."

"I'll get there."

"The league won't pay your fare."

"I don't care. I just want to see my father."

There was a pause. "All right. Go see your father, kid."

It was the last real conversation I ever had with the great Bugs Trovarelli. He and McKnight hardly spoke to me the rest of the season.

I called the Old Man to say I was coming home. I hadn't spoken to him since we'd quarreled. That had been the day the league president and Tim Drews had first asked me about Roy. I'd worked the plate; Briggs had nearly thrown a no-hitter. It seemed like a couple of years ago. I reached Frank at the hardware store. He didn't sound surprised or sore. He sounded busy. I could hear Mr. West in the background, chitchatting with a customer. I told the Old Man not to wait up for me.

It was dark when the plane bounced down in Boston. There was no rain. I caught the last bus to the Cape. It was after ten-thirty when she groaned to a stop at the old white brick railroad depot, now the bus station, at the end of a dead-end street with the woods rising dark beyond the railroad tracks. Only a few trains came through anymore. On the other side of the street stood the newspaper office, a one-story white clapboard building with a pair of elms standing sentry out front. A light burned in the corner, and I knew it was John Hillman, the editor, who had written kind stories about my career. I wondered what he'd write now. Five people, besides me, spilled down out of the bus. They all jumped in cars. The cars muttered away into the night. The bus growled, wheezed, and grumbled back the way it had come. Now I could hear the crickets and the soft whispers of the trees. If you've grown up in a small town, you know how far away it can seem from the troubles of the world. I picked up my suitcase. Home was a short mile away. Through the corner window of the newspaper office, I glimpsed John Hillman. His sleeves were rolled up, and he was sitting with his big arms folded over his chest, frowning at his typewriter. I set out, chasing and catching my shadow under the street lamps.

The Old Man was asleep. Zeke didn't bark. I drank in the familiar smell of dog and mildew. Frank had made up my bed. I lay awake a long time, listening to the crickets and the stirring of the trees. Frank woke me early, clanking pans and whistling "Stardust." I washed and dressed. The Old Man was frying eggs when I got down there.

"Hey, buddy," I greeted him.

He inspected my bruises with his morning-reddened eyes. "Who slugged you?" he demanded.

"It isn't anything," I said.

"A ballplayer do that?"

"No. You hear about Roy Van Arsdale?"

Frank nodded. "Paul said I should call you."

"You didn't need to call me," I said.

"How'd you get the shiner?"

"It's a long story. We friends again?"

"I dunno."

"I was outta line," I said.

"I guess I was, too."

"Shake," I said.

He put down the spatula and we did.

"You're gonna burn those eggs," I said.

Frank stared at the eggs and said, "Zeke died."

My heart fell a mile. "When?" I asked.

"A week ago."

"Why didn't you call me, Frank?"

326

"Oh . . ."

"Because of the fight we had?"

"Yeah, I guess."

"Stubborn," I said.

"Yeah," he agreed.

"No more of that," I said.

"No," he said.

"Buddies?"

"Buddies."

He scraped out the eggs. "These are for you."

"What did he do?" I said. "Just go to sleep?" My throat had tightened up.

"He was outside. He'd been drinkin' out of the big mud puddle in the driveway. I guess he just fell over."

"He loved to drink out of mud puddles," I said. Tears blurred my vision. I hadn't cried for Roy until Bugs had slapped me, and yet I was weeping hot, shiny tears for an old, dumb dog. I wondered what was wrong with me.

"He loved mud puddles," Frank said. "Mud puddles and garbage."

I ripped off a paper towel and blew my nose. "He ate apple cores," I said.

"He ate onions."

"Frank, I'm going outside for a minute."

"Eat your eggs first."

"I can't."

"What the hell'd I cook them for?"

"I'll eat them, Frank. Just give me a minute."

I pushed through the screen door and sat on the wooden steps. The honeysuckle was in bloom again, sweet in the cool morning air. Zeke had been old; his hind legs had hurt; he'd lost most of his interest in food. It would have gotten worse and worse. He should have died, really. I knew he was only a dog and that in a little while, perhaps even a matter of hours, the cutting edge of the loss would begin to smooth over, and Zeke would soon be a pleasant, painless memory, the kind that brings smiles. I remembered now that Vicky had loved Zeke. I wished I could tell her that he'd died.

I picked myself up. Frank had made me some toast. I sat a .d ate while the Old Man stood with his hands deep in his pockets, gazing out through the tall, light-plastered windows.

"Frank," I said, "let's get a new dog. Let's go to the pound this morning."

"Nah."

"We have to. We've always had a dog."

"Yeah, but I'm old now. What happens if I kick the bucket?"

"You're not gonna kick the bucket."

"Yeah?"

"If you kick the bucket, I'll take the dog."

"You can't have a dog in your line of work."

I finished the burned eggs. I slopped jam on the toast. "I got something to tell you, Frank."

He looked in from the window. His hands were still in his pockets. "You been fired," he said.

"I'm resigning after the season ends."

"Resigning, my ass. You been canned."

"How'd you know?"

"When I come to the ball game, I saw somethin' was up. I saw you weren't gettin' along with Trovarelli. There was just somethin' wrong."

"It wasn't Trovarelli. I could have survived Trovarelli."

The Old Man eyed me. He was not happy, but in the glum look he gave me, I saw acceptance. What was done was done.

"I had to do what I did, Frank."

"Yeah?"

"I made a lot of mistakes this year, but this wasn't one of them."

"You gonna tell me about it?"

"On the way to the dog pound."

"The dog pound isn't open yet, and we're not goin' there anyhow."

"Yeah, we are. Maybe Paulie wants to come along."

"Forget it. I'm too old for a new dog."

That night Paul came to dinner, bringing Ginny Crocker to see the puppy and help name him. The animal shelter people had told us he was about two months old. The cops had found him, abandoned, by the roadside. He was part hound, part yellow lab, I would say—brown and blond, with hanging triangle ears. His paws were still enormous for the rest of him; his eyes were squinchy; his skin still hung in folds. He was curious about everything, bouncing around on those soft, slippery paws to inspect everything and to sniff it, nudge it, and spring clumsily backward, slipping down, if it happened to move. He peed on the floor, of course. "Come here, you little bastard," Frank would say, a grin sneaking through, and he would scoop the puppy, hooking him with one hand, and plop him on the newspaper we'd put down.

It was strange seeing Ginny, who had been a year behind me in school, now the lover of my older brother. I guess it was strange, too, for Ginny; she was very shy with me. Of course, she'd always been that. I shook hands with her and with Paul. The puppy stared at them—new people, new smells. Ginny dropped to her knees, and the puppy charged her, threw his paws up on her chest, and washed her face. Laughing, Ginny hoisted him up, holding him under his front legs, as if she were lifting a baby under his arms. I decided right there that Ginny was fine. I told Paulie so in the kitchen. He smiled. He was mixing whiskey sours for himself and Ginny. She liked that sort of drink, in moderation—whiskey sour, daiquiri, vodka gimlet—and so Paul had learned to make them and drink them. Which told me something. I knew Paul was going to marry Ginny before he did.

In the kitchen, too, I told Paul quickly how I'd lost my job. I'd told the Old Man in detail; he had said nothing, only listened broodingly, weighing it all up in his mind. For now, Paulie glanced at me to make sure I was all right and, deciding I was, gave me a strengthening brother's pat on the back. That was all for now. We took the drinks out, straight bourbon for me and Frank.

"Now, then," Paul said, "what are we gonna name this pup?"

The puppy was floppily asleep on the Old Man's lap.

"How'd you name Zeke?" I asked.

"It was Joey's idea," Frank said.

"There was a kid in his class named Zeke," Paul said.

"Who?" I asked.

"Zeke Saunders."

"That's right," I said.

"Joey said the dog reminded him of Zeke Saunders."

"Zeke Saunders is still in town," I said.

"Drives a bulldozer," the Old Man said.

An idea hit me in the face. A brilliant idea. "How about Nick?"

"Someone you know?" Paul asked.

"Sure. Nick Nickinello. Runs the umpire school in Florida, remember?"

"Nick," said the Old Man, holding it on his tongue. "I don't know if I like it."

"I do," said Paulie.

"It's a good calling name," offered Ginny.

"I vote for it," Paul said.

The Old Man looked down at the thing in his lap, now blissfully asleep, softer than velvet. The puppy smelled of warm milk and sweet crackers. Later I would find out that a baby has the same smell.

"All right," Frank said, "Nick it is."

I raised my glass. "To Nick. Both Nicks."

Everybody drank. Ginny gazed sideways past the rim of her glass, eyes brightly seeking Paul.

"To the future," Paul said.

"Whose future?" asked the Old Man gloomily.

"All of ours," Paul said.

"Hear what your genius brother did?" Frank asked him.

"Yeah, and I'm goddamn proud of him."

"Jesus," Frank said, as if he was surrounded by crazies.

I got up and went and sat on the arm of the sofa, close to the Old Man. The arm sagged under me. It was going to break someday and drop me on my ass.

"I'll do fine, Frank," I said. "Promise."

"All those years down the drain," he said. "Where do you go from here?"

"I'll look around. Talk to some people."

I thought of John Hillman, the newspaper editor. I thought of the light in the corner window of the newspaper office when I'd gotten off the bus last night—the long, lone spear shining out across the railroad tracks and dying in the blackness of the woods. I saw Mr. Hillman there with his necktie loosened and his big arms clamped to his chest, thinking and thinking before he moved those thick, gentle hands to strike the keys of his typewriter.

Year in and year out he sat there, and so had his father—sitting faithfully into the night while the clock ticked and the townspeople went to bed, made love, died, and gave birth. Faithfully, faithfully.

"I might talk to John Hillman," I said. "He might have some ideas."

"I want you to do somethin' worthwhile," Frank said.

"I'll talk to Mr. Hillman."

"He always asks after you," Frank said.

On his lap the puppy woke and stretched, as elastic as a cat. The sleepy, hooded eyes measured the distance to the floor, and Nick slopped down, legs giving as he landed. He began nervously to sniff here and there.

"He has to go out," I said.

The Old Man pulled himself to his feet. "Come on, you little bastard. Come on, Nick."

"Better hurry, Frank," said Paulie.

Frank scooped up the puppy and rushed him like a hot potato through the dining area and around the corner into the kitchen. We heard the screen door bang.

"When do you go back?" Paul asked.

"Tomorrow. I got to fly to St. Louis."

"Why don't you come out with us tonight? Drink some beer. We'll put Frank to bed and go out on the town."

"I don't want to crowd you two," I said. "Three's a crowd."

"Not when it's family," Paul said.

14

Roy's replacement was a burly, sour-faced fellow named George DelBello, who had been laboring in Triple A ball for eight or so years and who, by the look on his face, seemed to have given up hope of ever making the bigs before this lightning bolt of good luck had hit him. He was in his early forties, I would guess. In his dim way he quickly read the situation and naturally cast his lot with Bugs and McKnight. I don't blame him. Imitating Bugs, he would nod me curt hellos and curt good-byes and avoid me like a leper in the hotels. George DelBello. He lasted about nine years, and then the league nudged him out early to pasture.

The season dwindled—a month, three weeks, two. The days shortened. About the seventh inning of a day game, the shadows would creep out over the plate and inch toward the pitcher's mound. The sunlight grew richer and oranger, but it no longer baked us. I began to take pleasure in the game itself, rediscovering the beauty of it all. Once, after Sammy Lewis sailed through the air to snatch a ball above the center field fence in Baltimore, I was so moved, I forgot to ring the out. I smiled when I saw Earl Smith, the Chicago catcher, gather a long throw one-handed in the bowl of his mitt, whirling as he took it, sweeping the mitt over the sliding runner and lifting it again in a single fluid motion, like a bullfighter one-handing a cape. I smiled, too, when Philadelphia intentionally walked Burns to pitch to Jackie George, loading the bases, and Jackie promptly cleared them with a home run. The colors seemed brighter to me that last month, the sky and grass, the freshly laundered flannels of the uniforms, and the browns of the different infields—reddish in some cities, grayish in others, and in still others, brown sugar, like the sea bluffs at home.

I didn't see Ron Chapman until the second week in September. We were in Chicago. I worked third base the first game, and our paths never crossed. The next night, I was at second. He struck out his first time up, but in the fourth inning he dropped a single into right field. There were two out; the game was scoreless; and Chapman had stolen thirty-some bases: everyone in the ball park knew he'd be running.

He did, on the second pitch. Smith's throw was perfect, on the corner of the bag; Whitman snared it and swiped with his glove as Chapman slid, plowing in head first on his belly. Whitman swept the tag over him and elegantly raised the glove. He looked at me questioningly, expectantly. He thought he had the out. He didn't. I threw my arms out, palms down, *safe*.

"Oh, *man*," Whitman said.

"He was in there," I said.

"*Man*," Whitman moaned, shaking his head.

"Can I have time?" Chapman asked.

I gave it to him. Whitman walked the ball to the pitcher. Chapman strolled off the base and began slapping the dust from his pants. I gave the bag a kick, straightening it, and said, "How's Pam?"

Chapman stopped brushing and glanced at me.

"Fine," he said.

"She say anything to you about Roy Van Arsdale?" I'd wondered about this. It didn't matter a whole lot now, but I'd wondered.

"She told me," Chapman said. He eyed me, suspicious.

"You know what, Ron?" I said. "He was picking cotton. He was *really* picking cotton."

Chapman scowled, an unpleasant stirring in his hard, beautiful face. "That's what you think," he said.

"It doesn't mean you aren't," I said.

I looked; Chapman's face swam with emotion, a rich brew of bitterness, pain, anger, pride, hope, and love. What was missing was laughter. It was nice not hating this man, not feeling that powerlessness.

Whitman was jogging back to his position. I walked away from Chapman.

"If you're upset about the woman . . ."

I spun, so abruptly that Chapman broke off in midsentence.

"I'm not," I said. "Not a bit."

It was true, and Chapman knew it. He stood with his hands on his hips, tall and powerful, and gazed at me with an odd and sudden thoughtfulness. I turned my back on him, and we never spoke again.

The season ended in Philadelphia on a cold gray afternoon in front of a small, bored crowd that lapsed into silence when Boston jumped way ahead in a game that didn't matter to either team. The pennant race had been over since mid-September, when New York had bounded away and clinched. Boston was stuck in fourth place, Philly next to last. By the seventh inning, the kids had begun lobbing crumpled Dixie cups onto the outfield, banging the wooden fold-up seats, and chasing each other around the empty sections. The game ebbed away, and the crowd melted. Ninth inning. Morgan loped under a fly ball and gloved it nonchalantly. Deschamps struck out, waving at the ball like a blind man, his mind now on other things. Newhouse flagged a ground ball backhanded, straightened, braced, threw in time, and the season, as well as my career, was finished.

I drifted in, looking at everything for the last time. The bullpen pitchers strode in, pitching arms sheathed in their windbreakers. Kids clustered at the rail by the dugouts, begging autographs. The grounds crew scampered out, unfurling the tarp. I watched it all unfeelingly, as in a listless dream.

In the umpires' room I sipped at a beer, watching my three partners eat and drink and listening to them talk. They were in fine moods, ebullient with their winter's rest ahead of them. They wolfed their beer and sandwiches, then lumbered into the shower. I listened to the rush of the water. I thought now of the end of my baseball seasons in high school, how the locker room would be littered with scraps of tape, dirty socks, towels, and jockstraps, which nobody would bother to pick up. I remembered how I did not want to surrender my uniform to the bin of damp, stinking clothes that would be washed and tumble-dried and not come back to me. I hated to see it end. Every year.

My partners emerged from the shower—my last look at Bugs's knotty calves and the scarred, dangerous body of Bill McKnight. I watched them dress. They talked of golf. The winter baseball banquets. The warmth of Florida. I wondered if they would manage to see their girlfriends, Carol and Gretchen, in the off-season. I didn't know where DelBello lived and didn't care. They took turns primping in front of the small mirror. McKnight parted his wet black and gray hair. Bugs snugged up his necktie. DelBello brushed his lapels. I watched the rugged, sun-browned faces in the mirror.

"Well, kid," said Bugs, "it looks like *sayonara.*"

"Yes sir," said McKnight.

I got up. I had taken off only my cap. I hadn't worked the plate and wasn't wearing the pads.

"So long," I said.

They shook my hand, not warmly: Bugs, McKnight, DelBello.

"You made it interestin'," Bugs said. "I'll say that much."

"The measles are interestin', too," said McKnight.

DelBello smirked appreciatively.

"You could have been a good umpire, kid," Bugs said.

"Too bad," I said.

"It sure is," Bugs said.

"So long," I said again.

"So long, it's been good to know ya," McKnight said breezily, like the song.

They walked out of my life: Bugs in a red plaid blazer, strutting like a bulldog; McKnight in a mouse-brown suit, shambling; DelBello in a raincoat. Gone. Their trunks lay in a row by the door, waiting for the clubhouse boy to ship them home. A neat row, like coffins.

Now it was silent. I could hear water dripping from one of the shower heads. *Plip, plip, plip.* The silence of the deserted grandstand crept down through the steel and concrete, nestling like the cold of winter. Socks, jock-straps, and towels littered the concrete floor. Shower steam dampened the room. This was the way it ended. One day, it ended like this for every ballplayer, every umpire. Ruth. DiMaggio. Bill Klem. I went to the refrigerator and plucked another beer. I sat.

I'd finished most of the second beer and begun contemplating the seemingly immense task of showering and packing, which my partners had sailed through gaily and without ceremony, when someone knocked on the door. I assumed it was the clubhouse kid. I called to him to come in. The door swung open in the solemn way doors creep open in ghost stories, and in walked the last person I expected to see—here or anywhere.

Her face seemed paler. The peppercorn freckles danced on either side of her nose. She carried a coat over her arm. She was dressed smartly, as always: white shirt with a button-down collar, like a man's, and a red skirt. Her pocketbook rode on her hip. She slid over against the wall by the door. She looked at me warily. I could feel my heart knocking.

"You look surprised," she said.

"Well, yeah," I said.

You don't forget a voice. A face can blur in the memory, but a voice stays as clear as yesterday.

Vick said, "I took a train down from New York. We're there for the World Series. To see Bobby."

"How'd you get in here?"

"Trovarelli spoke to the guard. They were leaving just as I arrived."

"That was nice of Bugs," I said. I felt furiously hot and cold, like having the chills with a fever.

Vick said, "I'm sorry about Roy."

"It was awful," I said.

"What really happened?" she asked. "What was he doing on the road at that hour?"

"Can I trust you?"

"You're a great one to talk about trust," she said. "You're a real authority on the subject." She looked away, smoldering.

"I tried to call you," I said.

"I know."

"You could have talked to me at least."

Vicky closed her green eyes and opened them. "What happened to Roy?"

"They found out he was queer. McKnight had this floozy in the hotel who tried to rape poor old Roy. McKnight walks in and finds the two of them. The woman spills the beans. Roy got drunk and took off in his car at four in the morning. They think he committed suicide."

Vick brought up a slow sigh. "I'm sorry," she said softly. She unstuck herself from the wall and began to prowl. On the table were the sandwiches that had gone uneaten, and the empty beer cans.

"Want a beer?" I asked.

"No."

"Sandwich?"

"No."

"Want me to kill myself?"

"It isn't funny," she said.

"No," I agreed. "It hasn't been funny since you left."

"What happened to your girlfriend?"

I started to say, "What girlfriend?" but caught myself. "Does it matter?"

"I suppose not." She picked up a sandwich, contemplated it, and tossed it back on the tray. She began pacing again.

"I wish you'd sit down," I said.

She kept moving.

"How's your old man?" I said.

"He still likes you, the dope."

"Bobby spat in my face," I said.

"You deserved it," Vick said. A smile flickered.

"All *right*," I said. "I got fired; I suppose I deserved that, too."

Vick stopped pacing. "What for?"

"Covering up for Roy. Being a smart-ass. Lots of things."

"Poor kid," Vick said.

I began unbuttoning my blue shirt. "It doesn't matter," I said. "It isn't the life for me."

"What'll you do?"

I shrugged. "Go home. The town won't be such a bad place to live."

Vick prowled over to the refrigerator. She took out a beer. Then she sat down on one of the metal chairs. She arched her back and crossed her legs, and as I watched, I knew I loved her.

"There's a lot to be said for a small town," I said.

"Take your shower," Vick said, "and let's get out of here."